By Edward Cox from Gollancz:

The Relic Guild
The Relic Guild
The Cathedral of Known Things
The Watcher of Dead Time

The Song of the Sycamore

THE SONG OF THE SYCAMORE

Edward Cox

This paperback first published in Great Britain in 2020 by Gollancz

First published in Great Britain in 2019 by Gollancz
an imprint of The Orion Publishing Group Ltd
Carmelite House, 50 Victoria Embankment
London EC4Y 0DZ

An Hachette UK Company

1 3 5 7 9 10 8 6 4 2

Copyright © Edward Cox 2019

A CIP catalogue record for this book
is available from the British Library.

ISBN (Mass Market Paperback) 978 1 473 22683 8
ISBN (eBook) 978 1 473 22684 5

Typeset by Deltatype Ltd, Birkenhead, Merseyside

Printed in Great Britain by Clays Ltd, Elcograf S.p.A.

MIX
Paper from
responsible sources
FSC® C104740

www.gollancz.co.uk

For Jack & Marney
I love you more than anything

I

The Song of Always

Chapter One

The city of Old Castle rose from the wasteland like an abscess swelling on the festering skin of a diseased world. Across its neighbourhoods and districts a siren called, lifting and falling with an ominous wail that sent citizens scurrying for their homes. Hiding like monsters in burrows, they prayed that this latest threat from the wastes would pass the city by, while fearing that this time, judgement had come to demand penance for their crimes. The people of Old Castle were rank with guilt. The city was populated by murderers.

And it was my home.

Through the chill of evening shadows, I made my way to the outskirts of Old Castle. No breeze disturbed the air, no sound accompanied the siren's wail; light from a setting red sun did little to warm a tense ambience. Beyond the last of the buildings, I began crossing a stretch of open ground, heading towards the city wall. But it wasn't me walking, not really, not any more. I could see through my eyes, hear through my ears, smell the stench of the city, but I had no control over my direction. My footsteps weren't made of my own volition.

I neared the city wall, a sturdy construction, thick and high, unbreakable, but at that moment it seemed merely a thin veil constructed for the illusion of safety. The huge turrets rising atop it housed the mighty ether-cannons which protected the citizens from the horrors of the wastes. But not from me.

'He's close.'

These words gurgled from an oily mass slithering over cracked, stony ground ahead of me: a ghoul, wheezing wet breaths, hissing with anger. This thing had been a woman in life, a simple soul; but in death, an oozing puddle fuelled by injustice, out for revenge. Caring nothing for the danger approaching Old Castle, the ghoul sang her Song, a Song of obsession and need, and I couldn't deny her plea for vengeance.

Whirring.

Rattling machinery.

Up on the wall, the turrets were turning, sweeping the aim of their long, fat cannons left and right. A low, familiar drone came next, baritone beneath the undulating siren, rumbling through the empty streets behind me. From the centre of Old Castle, a great beam of energy shot towards the cloudless pink sky like a waterspout. The city had activated its ether shield. High above the buildings, the energy gathered into a monumental ball of clear, wavering magic before dispersing, smearing, spreading across the length and breadth of Old Castle, forming a barrier between the city and the sky.

Above me, the edge of the shield curved downwards, creating an umbrella that descended liquidly to the ruined ground outside the wall. In a matter of moments, this hive of guilt-ridden souls was secured within a dome of ether power like a city in a snow globe. Sunlight refracted, the siren changed its pitch, the breeze dropped and the air became stifled. The bitter taste of ether dried the inside of my mouth. But it wasn't really my mouth now.

'Closer,' the ghoul hissed.

Cannons tracked the movements of whatever monstrosity

4

was coming from the wastes as I followed the ghoul along the line of the wall. With no choice in the matter, I was led to a set of stone stairs rising to a pot-bellied watch post nestled between two turrets. The ghoul slithered up the stairs and I climbed after her like the dutiful puppet I had become.

No sign of movement came from beyond the watch post's darkened doorway, but I knew a man hid there, a murderer who had nowhere left to run. He had taken sanctuary in the watch post in a vain attempt to hide from death. His subconscious understood what was coming for him, and why. The dead deserved vengeance.

Reeking of sewage, the ghoul hissed in anticipation, gurgled with longing. Like a snake, her darkness oozed up around the doorway to form an oily frame. I stared into the gloom beyond.

'*Your sins have returned to you.*' My Mouth, using my voice, but it wasn't me speaking. '*Won't you come out and atone with dignity?*'

No reply.

The man in the watch post was by no means the first murderer I had tracked that day, and he wouldn't be the last. I'd been leaving a trail of blood behind me for two days now, and there was an endless river's worth waiting to be spilled yet.

Whatever will remained to me, I tried to force it into my legs, to make myself turn around and walk away, but I no longer had the strength or presence to make a difference to my actions. I stepped through the ghoul's stench, entered the watch post, and the man attacked immediately.

He came out of the gloom, big and strong, a blur of motion in the dim light shining through the viewing slit in the back wall. With one arm, he pulled me into a tight embrace, spitting a curse into my ear as his free hand thrust a knife into my side. The blade couldn't penetrate my ribs and sliced over bone before its tip ripped out of the skin beneath my chest. I was too far gone to feel the damage inflicted upon my body and pushed the man away with force enough to send him sprawling.

'Kill him,' the ghoul hissed from the doorway.

The murderer sat on the floor, staring up at me. He was no Magician; he couldn't see the ghoul of his victim. His expression became stunned when I pulled the knife from my body and showed no distress at the hot blood soaking my shirt and trousers. Panic filled the man's eyes when I used the blade to point at him.

'*The dead call me Sycamore. I am their Shepherd.*'

With another curse, he jumped to his feet, fists clenched and ready to fight. I stepped close to him, dodged a clumsy punch and drove the knife into the side of his neck, down to the hilt. Such a simple and fluid act. I wished I could have turned away and covered my ears as the man dropped to his knees, choking, clawing at the knife's handle with fingers slicked in arterial blood. Desperate, struggling to breathe, his eyes pleaded with me. He looked to be approaching twenty, the prime of life but not yet old enough to have seen the horrors of war.

When he toppled, falling face down and dead, the ghoul gave a peaceful sigh and slithered across the floor. The oily darkness mingled with the pool of blood spreading around the corpse of her murderer. As though in a show of gratitude, a single tendril reached out to touch my boot before the ghoul faded and disappeared. Finding peace through vengeance, she journeyed on to the other side.

The city siren continued to wail. I continued to drown inside myself.

Stepping over the corpse, I peered through the watch post's viewing slit to gaze upon the desolation outside Old Castle. The sun was about to kiss the horizon, a sinking red orb quivering through the watery magic of the city shield, shedding the last of its rays upon a broken landscape. Shadows stretched and pointed at the city; the glassy summits of hillocks reflected light with majestic starbursts of rainbow colours. Millennia of humanity's bad choices had been trampled down into a plain of scorched rock and rusty metal. This was the wasteland. This was the world now called Urdezha, ruined beyond recognition, just like its people.

It looked as though a dust storm was blowing in. A bank of debris rolled across the plain like fog on the sea, hued red by the sun's backdrop. But this was no act of nature. The storm had been kicked into the air by the hundreds of feet galloping towards Old Castle. A herd of beasts. A stampede of monsters. They were too far away to see in great detail, but these creatures were as big as houses, thundering along on four legs, too many to bother counting. With stocky bodies covered in bony spikes and long horns protruding from great heads, the herd's charge looked unstoppable. Was this an act of war? Had the herd been driven this way by Old Castle's enemies? It didn't matter. The creatures of the wasteland were never a match for the might of a city.

Along the city wall, ether-cannons took aim and fired with oddly subdued *whumps*. Ether knew ether, they said, and the shield allowed the lethal bursts of magic to pass through its energy and race across the wasteland trailing streamers of displaced air. The first wave of shots smashed into the herd's front line, punching the life from the monsters. The cannons fired again – and again – and the charge faltered under their fury.

Through the sound of the siren, the drone of the shield and the *whumps* of ether, distant roars reached my ears. The cannons spat so many bursts of magic that the enemy was soon obscured by dust and debris. Whether or not the remaining monsters had turned tail and fled, leaving their fallen as carrion on the wastes, not one of them emerged from the storm. The abscess of Old Castle wouldn't be lanced today, but ... '*Soon,*' said a voice inside me.

I placed a hand on the wall to steady a sudden flush of fatigue weakening my legs. The knife wound in my side wasn't critical, but it was bleeding freely. I needed medical attention, food, sleep, but none of them would be given to me. As long as I could draw breath, my body would continue this rampage, while my spirit, my essence, *me*, slowly spiralled down into the oblivion of Nothing.

The moment of weakness passed, and a voice gurgled from behind me.

'Sycamore.'

Another ghoul had materialised. It stood in the watch post's doorway, formed into the rough approximation of a human shape. It held no discernible features and oily shadows dripped from its outstretched arms. The ghoul's presence came as no surprise; it was simply the next victim of murder to find me. And in this city, on this world, there would always be a next victim.

Chapter Two

Every person carried with them into death the final moments of their life like memorials grieving for the last spark of corporeal existence. The Song of the Dead, it was called, a lament that was not designed to endure. It faded from memory until a spirit learned to let go and achieve true freedom. Most moved on to the unknown of the other side; others chose to remain as peaceful ghosts to haunt the places where they had lived. And then there were ghouls, those who refused to stop singing the Song of the Dead because they could not accept the manner in which they died.

'Help me, Sycamore,' said the ghoul in the doorway.

Sycamore, Shepherd of the Dead, spirit of vengeance. I struggled to remember who I was within his possession. *Wendal Finn*, I told myself. *I am Wendal Finn*. My mantra, my last rock of salvation, surrounded by the endless depths of an unforgiving sea.

'*Little ghoul*,' Sycamore said, and he made me step over the corpse on the watch post floor. '*Can you tell me your name?*'

He asked this because if a ghoul couldn't remember its name then its murderer was unobtainable, perhaps already dead. In such cases, there was nothing to be done and Sycamore would banish the ghoul from his sight. But, to my dismay, this one remembered.

'Clay Hysan.' The name was spoken with an urgent hiss, and with its uttering changed an *it* into a *he*.

'*Sing me your Song, Clay Hysan. Show me how you died.*'

I knew what happened next. Without words or melody, Hysan's Song came as a drab monochrome vision, a preter-natural glimpse into the recent past which broke down the walls of the watch post and superimposed itself over the environment. The vision muted the voice of the city and delivered me to a sparse room somewhere in any one of Old Castle's many hidden corners; a room without windows and steeped in the flickering shadows of candlelight. Wax dripped onto bare floorboards. Dirty smoke drifted.

Hysan appeared in his Song as he would have in life. A wretch of a human, his grey beard and hair long and greasy. His naked body, brittle and grubby, had been strapped on its back to a wooden table into which words of magic had been carved. It was easy to assume that Hysan had been stolen off the streets where he lived, chosen to be a subject in the rites of the woman standing over him.

Of indeterminate age, the woman was dressed in a dusky gown that covered her from neck to foot. Sweat beaded on a head shaved smooth. With the look of a predator, face masked by concentration, she used a medical scalpel with the thinnest of blades to slice a symbol into the skin of Hysan's stomach. This woman was a Magician. Her touch was so delicate that she drew no blood. An adept, then, casting a spell. She was saying something, either talking to her captive or reciting an incantation – it was impossible to tell for her lips moved without sound. It was always the same in these visions: the Song of the Dead came in near-total silence.

Clay Hysan was looking at me, and his voice I *could* hear, speaking to Sycamore.

'I never learned her name.' A dry and close rustle, whispered in a vacuum, narrating his moment of death, his Song. Hysan expressed dispassion, detached from the cruelties being inflicted upon him. 'She never explained why she did this to me.'

And why would she? The Magicians of Old Castle were like fleas riding on the backs of the vermin who ruled the cities of Urdezha. Some would call them the bane of the Scientists; others, a necessary counterpart. They were secretive, hidden, keeping their purpose and reasons close to their chests. Magicians answered to their own kind only, but this woman would be answering to Sycamore.

'She promised a hot meal and a contract of employment,' Hysan explained as the woman completed the spell on his stomach and stepped back to admire her handiwork. 'Said the Magicians had need of someone like me.'

'*Indeed*,' said Sycamore.

The homeless made excellent spies. They understood how to manoeuvre through the city's every shadow and unseen space, and the Magicians paid them well for their services, especially when they needed to spy on the Scientists. Of course Clay Hysan would have jumped at this Magician's offer. Unfortunately for him, her intent had clearly not lived up to her promise.

'I never got my meal,' Hysan said as though reading my thoughts. 'And no, the contract wasn't what I thought it'd be.'

The woman's breath misted as she spoke into her hand and then released the words onto Hysan's stomach with a flourish. They settled on him like wisps of smoke. Blood rose from the thin cuts, just enough to detail the spell in lines and swirls of red. A barren tree, I thought the symbol resembled. The Magician blew upon the blood and it congealed, hardened, turned to scabs.

'*The spell's purpose?*' Sycamore thought to me. I didn't know. Perhaps an experiment to further magical prowess, or maybe part of a clandestine plan – it didn't matter. Whatever the purpose, its casting had resulted in murder.

Hysan said, 'It didn't hurt. I just felt more and more tired, and then I wasn't alive any more.'

With further words of magic and a deft hand, the Magician sliced a circle around the scabs before gently cutting under them. With care and infinite patience, she worked the scalpel until the complete spell separated from Hysan's body and floated up several inches, carried on a gossamer leaf of skin. Crimson steam began to rise from it. The magical script carved into the tabletop beneath Hysan glowed with a dim radiance. The Magician dropped the scalpel and raised her arms, chanting the crescendo of her incantation silently to my ears.

'Find her, Sycamore.' Hysan's monochrome eyes darkened with fury. 'I want my vengeance.'

And in the Song, he died. His body shrank, dried, withered, and his spirit left him. Black with the anger of injustice, it oozed over the table, stretching before slapping to the floor in oily drops. The vision faded. The final image was of the Magician staring at her spell, a red symbol on a leaf of skin thinner than a sheet of paper now resting on her open hands.

The wail of the siren returned to me; candlelight died, replaced by the gloom inside the watch post at the city wall. The ether-cannons had stopped firing. Hysan's ghoul loitered in the doorway, once again in the dark and featureless shape of a human. His stink offended my nostrils. The Song of the Dead had been sung. It was now mine to avenge.

'*Come, then, Clay Hysan,*' Sycamore said, retrieving the knife. It made a sucking sound as it slid free of the corpse's neck. I thrust it into my jacket pocket without cleaning the blade. '*Lead me to your murderer.*'

Chapter Three

Falling, dwindling inside my own body, but still dregs of happiness remained to me, lingering memories of laughter, of a love and hope that once held back fear of an uncertain future. There was belief, too; an innocent confidence that the walls of Old Castle would always stand between the citizens and the wars and monsters of the wasteland. But details, specifics, who I had shared these dregs with, were fading fast. I was desperately clinging to the dying ideals of the man I once was, the man who could no longer recall what events had led him to this point.

Sycamore cared nothing for what I had been through or what it had lost me – and I had lost ... more than I could remember, something important.

For two days straight, he had been running my body into the ground, I recalled that much. The faces of every victim who had died on this killing spree remained as clear fragments in my shattered memory, along with every desperate word that had begged me to *stop*. Two days, and now with a fresh knife wound in my side – that I was still walking at all impressed Sycamore; he saw it as a kind of strength not to be wasted. So here I was, a host for a monster, traipsing after a vengeful ghoul, heading towards my next victim.

By the time Clay Hysan had led me to edge of Old Castle's

western region, the siren had stopped and the shield had been deactivated. Night was falling and the air was fresh again with the chill of winter. Now the danger from the wastes had gone, a few citizens were braving the outdoors. Dressed in shirts and trousers and dresses of inexpensive fashion, they couldn't see the ghoul leading me, couldn't meet the eye of the bedraggled and blood-spattered vision of Wendal Finn, but they feared what I hosted.

Driven by instinct, they gave me a wide berth on the street, recognising deep down that an animal higher than them in the food chain was on the hunt. As I passed them, downcast expressions and defensive body language revealed the way Sycamore's presence affected their thoughts; perhaps, after all, it would be safer to return home for the night and wait for the sanctuary of morning.

Hysan's ghoul led me down a main street which ran alongside a high wall, signifying the beginning of a district known as the Fusion. Sycamore was slowly devouring my being, my essence, but he was also absorbing my generic knowledge of Urdezha, of this city, and his curiosity was piqued by the wall. He wanted to know what lay on the other side.

He was fascinated to learn that the Fusion was a small and forbidden inner district, where only the highest-ranking Scientists were allowed to go. It was home to the city's main reactor, a feat of magical engineering which tapped into the ether-growth far beneath Old Castle. The reactor drew up power for the shield generators and ether-cannons; it provided the energy by which the populace survived. Without ether, this city would crumble and blow away into the wasteland, meaning that security in the Fusion was permanently high.

Sycamore pondered this.

As Hysan's oily ghoul led me away from the Fusion's wall

and into a narrow side lane flanked by dirty lodging houses, my feet felt less sure on the stone paving. Strength was draining from my legs. I could hear Sycamore's thoughts, *feel* what he was thinking. Perhaps it was time to possess a new host. I would have to die before he could free himself from my body; a simple enough task, but he worried because I had shown him how some humans were harder to possess than others. How long had we been together? Sycamore decided that he had neither the time nor the patience to disrupt his work unnecessarily. Better to use his current host until the very end – an end which *had* to come.

By now, the city watch were likely discovering the bodies I'd been leaving behind. It was only a matter of time before they followed the trail and caught up with me. Sycamore would select a new host then, someone from the Scientists' hierarchy with access to the Fusion. There, he could meddle with the ether reactor, disable the shield and cannons, allow the monsters of the wasteland to wreak carnage on Old Castle's streets. With access to the Fusion, he could cause a citywide catastrophe that dealt with every murderer at once instead of one at a time.

The citizens had no idea what I had brought to their world.

Venturing deeper into the west, we skirted the Tinman District, not a particularly nice part of Old Castle. The Scientists ruled, but the north and south were their main territories, so that was where the bulk of the wealth went. East and west were home to the larger population, the drones of society's hive, and the streets were not so clean there, the houses not so luxurious. I was vaguely aware that I had lodgings in the Tinman District, but did I live there alone? Was anyone missing me? What had I lost?

Something important ... something I had once sworn I'd never forget.

The banality of life in this region was advantageous to the

Magicians; it helped them avoid the unwanted attentions of the ruling caste. So when the ghoul led me down a stinking alley, where darkness stalked and even the filth kept old secrets, to the back door of a decrepit building, I assumed that we had arrived at one of the many Magicians' dens in the area. But the words burned into the chipped and worn wood of the door told a different story.

Dark as charcoal, the words were a simplified form of an ancient alphabet, not unlike magical script. Salabese, the language of the Gardeners. Loosely translated, the words read: *Cleanse your spirit*. But to Sycamore, they might as well have said: *Purchase empty promises*.

Clay Hysan gave a gurgle of encouragement and his ghoul collapsed to a black puddle which oozed through the gap under the door. Sycamore had me draw the knife from my pocket and push the door open. It swung closed behind me.

Chapter Four

A Vestibule of Aktuaht, a place of spiritual well-being. It was a smallish room, square, no more than twenty feet in length and width, the ceiling low and dirty. The alley door was the only way in or out, and the Vestibule was empty.

'*Strange*,' thought Sycamore.

Wall-mounted candles flickered light onto a floor of hard-packed earth, grey and dusty. The staleness of old smoke hung in the air, along with the kind of stillness that suggested only spiders and insects were watching me. No citizens sat on the single rickety pew, which was positioned before a worn stretch of floor flanked by two rows of four wooden pillars and which led to a large brazier atop a stone pedestal. The ghoul of Clay Hysan was nowhere to be seen, but I could feel he was close, detect his stench.

Intrigued, Sycamore steered me between the pillars towards the brazier. Salabese script had been carved into each one, no doubt telling the fables of the afterlife which my possessor found so ludicrous. The black metal dish of the brazier held a layer of ash. Behind it, a faded and flaking picture had been painted on the wall. It depicted a golden sun in a blue sky, shining down onto a thick and lush forest: a representation of the peace and spiritual harmony that supposedly waited on the other side.

On the floor beside the brazier, a wicker basket had been filled with the little brown wings of sycamore seeds. I dug into them with the knife's blade, unable to prevent Sycamore's scoff escaping my mouth. Uncertainty was a key factor in faith, and many believed that these seeds provided nourishment for the dead, food for a spirit when it entered the afterlife and journeyed to Aktuaht.

This offended Sycamore.

Aktuaht: a Salabese word which meant *judicature* or *trial*. It was the name of the spiritual realm that lay between the land of the living and the other side. A court, of a kind, where the dead received final judgement from three eternal Gardeners: Truth, Mercy and Wrath, the last knights from the Order of Glass and Words, an ancient sect whose calling was to protect the weak and defend justice.

The three Judges of Aktuaht decided whether a spirit deserved condemnation to Nothing or passage to a paradise they called the Garden in the Sky. I prayed now to the Order of Glass and Words, whispered apologies for my atrocities, begged Truth, Mercy and Wrath to put me on trial. If they could save the last of my spirit from Sycamore, then I'd take my chances that Aktuaht would witness a good soul worthy of heaven, where the sky was blue, the sun golden and the land was not a ruined waste.

'*Aktuaht is a lie,*' Sycamore thought to me. '*Death is death, the other side is freedom, and there is no judgement in between. As for the Knights of Glass and Words, the truth about their Order is better left unsaid.*'

I tried not to listen, but his discourse came through feelings that bled into my drowning consciousness, demanding that I comprehend a stark reality of human existence before my death: false faith was easier than no faith, and the Magicians were very good at providing the lies that made life easier to live. They ran the Vestibules of Aktuaht, where, for a single coin, citizens could buy a blessing, burn a handful of seeds and earn the kind of favour that offered peaceful nights of sleep and promises of the Garden in the Sky.

The ash in the brazier was dead and cold. No seeds had been burned for at least a day or more. The candles were lit, but the light shone for no one but me. Why was the Vestibule empty?

Hissing, Clay Hysan materialised between the wooden pillars. His darkness rose from the floor to form a human shape, oozing and dripping shadows. Something about the stance of his featureless ghoul relayed mournfulness rather than vengeful anger.

'Well?' Sycamore said, joining him between the pillars. He shrugged my shoulders. '*You led me here?*'

'Help me,' Hysan gurgled. 'I don't know what I want.'

An odd thing for him to say, given that if there was anything a ghoul knew, then it was definitely what it wanted.

'*Where is your murderer, Clay Hysan?*'

'This isn't fair!' The ghoul made a sound like a man screaming underwater. 'I deserve my peace!'

To Sycamore's surprise, Hysan's darkness split, shredded into oily curls that burst and dissipated like puffs of smoke until all that remained where he had stood was a circular leaf of skin upon which thin lines of scabs formed a magical symbol resembling a barren tree.

'*What is this?*'

The leaf burned to dust with a blaze of quick fire. The symbol became wisps of crimson mist and flew at me with such speed that Sycamore had no time to dodge them. Each wisp hit me in the chest, one after the other, but there was no sensation of impact as the crimson magic sank through my clothes and pricked at my skin. Sycamore ripped my shirt open, popping buttons, and discovered that the symbol had re-formed on my bloodied and scarred chest, smoking, reeking, searing my flesh as though I had been branded. And that was when I saw it: the thing I had lost and forgotten.

From a chain around my neck hung two wedding bands. One was mine. The other was my wife's. I had lost *her*. She was dead.

The door to the Vestibule opened and Clay Hysan's murderer entered.

Head bald and dressed in a Magician's gown, the woman from the vision took a few steps before stopping to consider me with the calculating eyes of a hunter. A beast of a man entered after her. Broad, shaggy-haired, almost seven feet tall, he closed the door and stood guard, his cold expression alive with the threat of violence in the candlelight.

Sycamore considered this an interesting turn of events. I tried in vain to recall my wife's name.

The woman stepped further into the Vestibule. '*They say a messenger has come to Old Castle from Aktuaht.*' She spoke in Salabese, her voice smooth with confidence. '*The dead are calling him Sycamore.*' She stopped where the pillars began and gave me a triumphant smile. Her pupils were dilated; there was magic ready at her fingertips. '*They say you are eternal, inexorable, but* I *say you are as weak as the blood and bones you wear.*'

A Magician's trap, and Sycamore had blindly walked into it. A situation that was easily remedied, he decided. I lifted the knife, intending to cut my own throat so the spirit of vengeance could release himself from his host, but the Magician said, '*No you don't,*' and cast the spell she was holding.

On the pillars, hiding amidst the Salabese script, small words of magic glowed with rose-coloured radiance. The light scratched at the symbol on my chest and fatigue beset every inch of my body. My fingers opened and the knife thudded to the earthy floor. Sycamore dared not let me take a single step lest I fall over, and had me glare at the Magician instead.

'*Oh.*' She pouted mockingly. '*Have your sins returned to you?*'

Behind her, the beast of a man snorted his amusement.

I swayed on my feet. Sycamore wondered if he had under-estimated the humans of this city.

Offended, he said, '*Who are you to dare cast your spells on me?*'

The Magician shook her bald head. '*I'm led to believe that a name in your hands will result in dire consequences.*'

'*That depends on who introduces me to you. What have you done with the ghoul of Clay Hysan?*'

'*He is … safely hidden from you.*'

My lip curled into a snarl. '*You are a child playing a dangerous game, Magician.*'

'*Ah, but it's a game that I'm winning nonetheless.*'

The words of magic on the pillars flared brightly. The spell on my chest grew, the red lines searing out to cover my stomach and snaking around to my back. There was sensation then, a deep, dull ache that didn't just belong to me but also to my possessor. I felt stronger, my being more intact. And Sycamore … I felt his incredulity as his control faltered. His consciousness began sinking. Mine rose, piecing its shattered parts back together. Sycamore could do nothing as the spell overcame his possession and I reclaimed my body.

The sudden release from subjugation forced a bellow from my mouth, aimed at the Magician in rage and confusion and heart-ache. She stepped back from me as though wary of a wild animal.

Instinctively, my hand gripped the wedding bands hanging from my neck and I remembered the name of my wife. 'Eden!' I shouted; and then, 'Fuck!' as pain from my wounds hit me, mixed with my fatigue, and drove me to my knees.

Hot tears ran down my cheeks. Sycamore despaired as he sank deeper inside me, clutching uselessly for a hold that might allow him to clamber back up and into control. But he couldn't prevent the Magician's spell from pushing him down and down until we had switched places and he became the helpless observer, trapped in a flesh prison.

The Magician was breathing heavily, both anxious and excited, surprised that her trap had worked.

'Let's get him to the old monster,' she said to her henchman. 'Quickly.'

Without a word, the man came for me. He grabbed my collar and yanked me up. I barely had the strength to keep my feet on the floor and hung limp and hopeless ... until he prised my hand away from the wedding bands. Until he tried to pull the chain from my neck. Then I closed my eyes and summoned a primal fury. Thrashing, screeching, my teeth clamped on the first thing they could find and bit down, hard. A roar of pain preceded the taste of blood in my mouth and I chewed on something tough and difficult to swallow.

The Magician shouted, 'Tamara, no!' but couldn't prevent me from being punched so hard that nothing mattered any more.

Chapter Five

Wendal Finn ... my name is Wendal Finn.

I died young, though I wasn't truly dead. I fought in the war, and it was the war that broke me. The army discharged my service before my tour of duty had officially ended. They couldn't understand the ailment that had fucked me up beyond reason – I still didn't understand it now. Eventually, the army had decided the surest way to wash their hands of a useless shell of a soldier was to send him back to Old Castle, where I discovered my wife was dead. *That* was what finished me off.

No one warned me that I'd find an official notice at home, a cold scrap of paper informing me that Eden had committed suicide mere days before my return. It said her body had been welcomed to a reduction house. *Welcomed*, as though that meant she had been peacefully laid to rest. I was invited to pay my respects at any one of the city's Gardens – a euphemism confirming that nothing physical remained of the woman I loved.

It was the final stroke, the emotional breakdown which ensured my condemnation. It was the day I lost the battle for my spirit and became a possessed killer who had now attracted the attention of the Magicians.

Darkness receded into candlelight. Air, cool and damp, kissed my skin. There was no pain, no chaos; I had been brought back from the brink of Nothing, but I couldn't feel my arms and legs.

Immobilised, I lay on the floor of a room I didn't recognise. The Magician whose trap I had sprung stood over me in the flickering light of naked flames, staring at something ahead. Above her, magical script decorated the ceiling, written in substances I didn't want to guess at. The atmosphere felt heavy, oppressive. I tried to speak, but no words passed my lips. My tongue was as useless as my limbs.

'Dyonne Obor,' said a voice – muffled, oddly threatening in its neutrality. 'You have brought ghouls to my house. I am not pleased.'

The Magician drew herself up. 'With respect, Mr Sebastian, precautions have been taken. I allowed no ghoul to follow this man into this room.'

'You might as well have. This *thing* attracts the dead from all places.'

I lifted my head and looked down the length of my body. I was naked. My knife wound had been stitched and the red lines of a spell criss-crossed my already scarred chest and stomach. I gazed beyond my feet, focusing on the far end of the room. A bloated mass was kept suspended two feet off the floor by a host of ceiling chains. Each chain disappeared into a dark, thick robe the size of a two-soldier tent. The mass was so large and misshapen that it couldn't possibly belong to a human; and yet it was crowned with the triangle of a hood which some inner instinct told me hid intelligent, human eyes.

A man stood beside the mass. He was caked from head to foot in a pale grey chalky substance, dry and flaking upon his skin. A cloth bearing glyphs covered his eyes; a transparent mask covered his mouth. A line of what appeared to be viscous, snaking water flowed from the mask and joined the chains inside the tent-sized robe.

A distant memory reminded me that no one ever saw or heard the highest-ranking Magicians, the Grand Adepts of the Salem. Their every word and mood were channelled through a proxy. Eden had told me that.

The proxy pointed at me. '*It* is an animal. *It* ate your bodyguard's thumb.'

My head thumped down to the floor. The taste of blood lingered in my mouth.

The Magician called Dyonne Obor said, 'Tamara was a fool, Mr Sebastian. He should not have tried to steal from this man and learned his lesson the hard way.'

A derisive hiss came from behind the mask. 'Why did you bring *it* to me?'

'Because *he* has high value. I had good reason to bring his consciousness back from the brink.'

'Explain. Quickly.'

'Three days ago, this man returned from the wasteland carrying a great asset. His name is Wendal Finn, but the dead call him by another name, and it is the same name that we Magicians have all heard whispered in recent times.'

In my head, I begged them not to say it, to preserve the first state of peace I'd known since the war, but the naked proxy drew a shuddery breath and said it anyway.

'Sycamore.'

That word … how many times had a ghoul wept it to me as though driving nails into my ears? People had died because of it.

'So, this is him,' the mass, the proxy – Mr Sebastian – said. 'The killer who has been stalking Old Castle's streets – I am not much impressed.'

'*As the Gardeners are my witness, his wrath is mighty,*' Dyonne said in Salabese. 'Look beyond the host, sense for yourself how many ghouls are seeking retribution from what is inside him.'

'Yes.' A silent, contemplative pause. When the proxy spoke again, Mr Sebastian had changed his tone, now accepting yet still suspicious. 'The host is young. Most war survivors return home filled with patriotism for the Scientists. We cannot be sure where this Wendal Finn's loyalties lie, what kind of man he is.'

If they had asked me, I would've told them that my loyalty was all theirs if they could remove this *thing* that possessed me. I could feel Sycamore, somewhere deep in my being, slithering like a snake, searching for a weakness in the magic that was keeping him locked down inside me, searching for a way to rise again. Too true his fucking wrath was mighty. Given the chance, he'd have me kill every person in this room.

'The wasteland changed Wendal Finn in wild ways,' Dyonne said sternly. 'The death of his wife has shattered his heart. He has nothing left but his skin and bones and an empty life. Wendal Finn is the perfect host, and we cannot allow him to walk the streets of Old Castle as a freeman.'

'True, but I am not so convinced of his suitability.'

'With respect, he would already be dead without my intervention, and I beg the Grand Adept of the Salem to remember the faith he has shown in my judgement in the past. Have I not delivered where others have failed?' A sly lilt crept into Dyonne's tone. 'Unless, of course, you would prefer to let the Scientists discover Sycamore and convert him into a *good* citizen?'

'Or I might *prefer* to throw the host to the wasteland and end the quandary here and now! Be mindful of who you are talking to, Dyonne Obor.'

Dyonne averted her gaze, suitably admonished. 'Mr Sebastian, please. My intervention has trapped Sycamore but my spells will not last. They need bolstering with magic more adept than mine. I beg that you cast the Song of Always upon the host before it is too late.'

'Oh, is that so?'

I wasn't sure what they were talking about. The Song of Always – it rang a distant bell. Had Eden told me about it in the past? One thing was for sure, Sycamore didn't like it, squirming somewhere inside me at its mention.

'There is sense to endorsing such an adept spell,' Dyonne pleaded. 'Sycamore is ours, for now, but we can only use him in our feuds with the Scientists if he is kept tame and protected. If we do nothing, he will escape to claim a new host or disappear altogether.'

Shit. Feuds? I tried to speak again, but my tongue remained a dead slug in my mouth.

'This is a dangerous entity that you believe we can tame.'

'But it is infinitely more dangerous to let him loose. My judgement is sound, and is this not what the Salem desire?'

Mr Sebastian contemplated for a moment. 'The risk of losing Sycamore to the Scientists is our greatest threat. The Gardeners only know how *they* might use him. I cannot deny that there is sense in casting the Song of Always to preserve Sycamore and keep him for ourselves, but Wendal Finn is disturbed, delicate. The host is in need of taming himself.'

'Indeed.'

'Then would you act as his custodian, Dyonne Obor?'

'Me?'

'You have an objection?'

'No!' Dyonne used the perfect measure of surprise and pride. 'You … you honour me, Mr Sebastian.'

'Keep your trickster's tongue still! Custody of the host is what you came here to claim, and now I entrust it to you. The Salem's favour has been well earned, it seems, and you damn well know it.'

Dyonne bowed her head humbly.

EDWARD COX

'Be warned,' the proxy continued. 'No living or *un*living thing can gain access to this man unless you are given directive by me. Watch him closely, shield him at all times. If Wendal Finn cannot be controlled, he must die, and the spells cast that will banish Sycamore for good lest he come for us all.'

'Of course.'

'You have proved yourself worthy countless times, Dyonne Obor, but you will attend this responsibility with renewed and impeccable vigour. Do not disappoint the Salem.'

Dyonne looked down at me, a smirk on her lips, cold triumph in her eyes. 'Understood, Mr Sebastian.'

If they said any more, I didn't hear it. The bitter taste of magic scratched the back of my throat and once again darkness rushed in.

Chapter Six

'Sycamore. How strange that name must sound from the lips of the living.'

I hadn't realised my eyes were open until Dyonne came into sharp relief. She had moved me to my home, a sad single room on the third floor of a five-storey lodging house which still held the fading atmosphere of a happier life. Dyonne sat on my bed, and I on a chair within a ring of magical script written in chalk on the floorboards. I had been dressed in a simple shirt and trousers. Beneath the shirt, the spell branded onto my body itched. The stitches in my wounds felt tight. The whole right side of me ached.

There was something out of place in my lodgings, a threatening presence that wouldn't quite come into view, as if it were shrouded in shadow, but thankfully Dyonne was alone.

'Wendal, if you're worrying about Tamara, he is elsewhere having his wound dressed, pining for the time when he had two thumbs, no doubt. I don't think he and you will be friends.'

My hand was clenched into a tight fist. Fingers unfurled stiffly to reveal a chain sitting on my palm. It was threaded through mine and Eden's wedding bands. The rings were real metal and the only things of worth that I owned, materially and emotionally. I looped the chain over my head, disturbed that someone else had touched the rings but comforted by their presence as I tucked them under my shirt.

I glared at Dyonne. 'What do you want from me?'

'Acceptance.' Amused, Dyonne tapped the books lying on the bed beside her. Eden's journals, piled up beside the letters I'd written her from the wasteland. 'It seems your wife had an interest in magic. But she was a dabbler, not even yet a novice.'

My gaze lingered on the letters and journals. 'Those aren't for your eyes.'

'Oops. Too late.'

Dyonne's voice was fine and smooth as smoke drifting in the air. I felt calm but strange. It was as though the two of us sat safe inside a bubble of stark clarity, beyond which the rest of my lodgings were obscured by a smeared darkness. Ghouls, I quickly realised, pressed against Dyonne's magic, trying to get to Sycamore but held back in silent turmoil.

'I can make this a permanent arrangement for you,' Dyonne said. 'Keep the ghouls at bay for good. Mostly.'

With thoughts clearer than they had been in a long time, I accepted that I was in the shit up to my neck whichever way I looked at the situation. 'What do you *want*?'

'The bigger question is what do *you* want?' She gestured to the letters and journals. 'These belong to a life that is over now, Wendal. I can replace them with whatever you desire. Women? Men? Intoxication? You could live a life of impunity and hedonism. Within reason.'

Within reason ... Sycamore remained an ache inside me, like bad food poisoning my gut. But he was still, as though he slept. How long would that last? I was no fool and neither was this woman. Secrets, double-edged pacts and dangerous games – that was what the Magicians were about. Dyonne Obor was searching for whatever would encourage me into subservience, and that was the one thing I thought I'd leave behind in the war.

'Well?' Dyonne said softly. 'What is it to be?'

I was hardly in a position to say *no thanks* then walk away and rebuild my life as a normal citizen. The Magicians wanted Sycamore and they had used me to trap him. They weren't letting him or me go now. I supposed Dyonne was offering to help me make the best of a bad situation. She had pulled me back from the brink of Sycamore's oblivion, given me a second chance at life, but only by dumping me into a no-win scenario. Could I feel grateful for that? I didn't want to die, but what *did* I want?

My gaze drifted up to the ghouls smeared blackly across Dyonne's magic. The wasteland had opened my eyes to many things, most especially the horde of spirits roaming Urdezha. The dead didn't always journey on to the other side, more often than most realised.

'I want to talk to my wife.' The words came unbidden, in a rush, as though thinking about them too long might steal the chance away. I pointed at the dead pressing down on us. 'She must be among them.'

'It is possible,' Dyonne said dubiously.

'Can you find her?'

'What makes you think she wants to be found?'

From among the letters, Dyonne plucked out Eden's official notice of death and sent it fluttering into the air with a sound like crackling flames. People who killed themselves were never happy in the world they had left behind. What had made my wife so unhappy that she had ended her own life?

I stared at the notice on the floor. 'I need to know.'

'To what end, Wendal? You can't change what has happened. Or is Eden supposed to haunt you, her spirit bound to you in ... what? Everlasting love?'

'I don't know, I ...' I didn't like this calm; it was unnaturally induced and alien. An effect, no doubt, of the spell seared into my skin. I dug beneath it, discovering ever more of the real me that Sycamore had repressed. 'I just want to talk to her.'

'Hmm.' Dyonne looked unconvinced. 'The dead occasionally have their uses – they led us to your location in Old Castle, for example. But to seek their help in finding one lost spirit among the infinite horde and chaos?' She gestured to the ghouls filling my lodgings, her face awed. 'Look at them all. I won't deal with the dead so intimately, for every Magician knows madness lies that way.'

Funny how I believed her while wondering if she was telling the truth. My jaw set and my resolve hardened. If any warmth in my heart had been saved from Sycamore, any memory of the good life I had once led, it was because of Eden.

'You asked me what I want, and I want my wife.'

Dyonne pondered. 'I suppose I could steer you in the right direction. But this kind of help comes at a price, Wendal.'

The conversation between Dyonne and Mr Sebastian rattled around my brain and I placed a hand over the wedding bands beneath my shirt. 'What price?'

'Oh, I think you already know the answer to that.' The predator returned to Dyonne's eyes. 'Sycamore belongs to the Salem, the Magicians. The only question left is how willingly his host will allow us to use the gift he has been given.'

Yes, I knew it, but I recoiled all the same. She was talking about the reason I'd spent the last month wanting to bore a hole in my head and pull out my brain. 'Fuck you!'

Dyonne clucked her tongue. 'Do try to retain a little dignity, Wendal. It will make this negotiation far simpler for all concerned.'

'What negotiation?' I tensed on the chair and pain flared from my wounds. 'Cooperate or die – that's the choice you're giving me.'

'Yes, we would kill you, *if* you left us with no option.' Dyonne's smile lacked kindness. 'It is also possible that we would lock you up in a room which never sees the sun and take what we want anyway. You heard what Mr Sebastian had to say, Wendal – if you insist on acting out like a fucking idiot, then this won't end well for you.'

I chewed on my words for a moment. A game was nearly always won because a player understood the rules better than her opponent. Eden had told me that. I'd been losing this game since the day Sycamore had possessed me out on the wasteland.

'You have become a unique creature, Wendal Finn, and what I'm offering is not your best but your *only* way forward. I will save you, if you'll let me.'

'This isn't fair.' Tears suddenly sprang to my eyes. I did *not* want to die, but – 'I never wanted this.'

'Yet it is yours nonetheless, bright and terrible, and we Magicians are so thankful that we found you. We have need of Sycamore's wrath, but we cannot allow him to roam free.' Dyonne stood up, approached me, face sympathetic. 'The war has filled the wasteland with the spirits of the dead, but this city has its own ghouls. They are imprisoned by the rage of their murders. Sycamore would give vengeance to them all if left unchecked. The Salem wishes to be more selective with his ... *clientele*. In the meantime, you and I are to be his tamers.'

I wasn't blind. Dyonne was offering me my sanity, control of my body – for the most part. The spells on my skin, the magic which had been forced upon me – they would keep Sycamore locked down, dormant inside his host, until such a time that the Magicians had need to let him out of his cage. To spill blood with my hands.

'Think of Eden.' Dyonne pursed her lips. 'I will help you find her spirit, and all I ask in return is your obeisance. Is that really so bad?'

Fuck it all. Without this Magician there was nothing for me but darkness and a lonely death. No pleading, no bargaining would get me out of this, and Dyonne knew the name of the only woman who could hook my cooperation.

'So, what do you say, Wendal? Have we reached an accord?'

I nodded and wept into my hands.

Slowly, tenderly, Dyonne pulled them away and stroked my hair. 'You're a lucky man.' I half-laughed, half-cried at the absurdity. 'It's true. You are a romantic fool but lucky. I have never loved anyone as deeply as you love Eden. However ...'

She stepped away and considered the ghouls with her back to me. '*I* trust you, but Mr Sebastian is concerned that the host for his asset is so damaged that he will prove to be a liability. Therefore, he has prepared a rare spell that will alter your perception of mortality.'

Dyonne opened her hand. On her palm, a crystal had appeared. It was uncut, jagged like a miniature mountain range, and gave off a faint rose-tinted silver hue. It was ether. A crystal of that size was worth more than everything anyone owned in this lodging house combined.

'A safeguard for our deal, Wendal.' Dyonne crushed the ether as though it was no tougher than dry sand and released the spell it held.

I knew what magic felt like; I'd experienced the vibrations and pressure on my skin and the dryness in my mouth in the past when I had been around Eden's experiments. But the magic Dyonne summoned in that moment damn near ripped the air from my lungs. So powerful and elemental. Sound and vision became painfully sharp with an abruptness that made me groan.

The ghouls fled, retreating to the corners of the room.

Unnatural light glared off Dyonne's bald head. Her pupils were so wide that her irises were thin hazel rings. For the first time, I noticed the scars on her hands, words of magic cut into her skin; and in one of those hands a weapon had materialised.

Short and silver, embossed with dark lines in a design that looked like foliage growing along its barrel – this was no ether-cannon, no kind of projectile weapon that I'd seen before. It looked ancient even by ancient's standards. Dyonne aimed it at me. Fearful, confused, I stared into the black hole at the end of the barrel.

'The Song of Always,' Dyonne announced before pulling the trigger.

The weapon's hammer fell upon a dirty, powdery combustible that ignited with a roar of thunder. I raised my hands but nothing hit me, and time slowed. Fire ballooned from the weapon with fluid grace; smoke rolled like waves on a grey sea. A shower of red sparks poured from the barrel, and through the smoke and fire came a spinning ball of metal.

Inexorable, it hovered a few inches from my face, droning like a bee, but coming no closer.

'I claim your life and give you the moment of your death,' Dyonne growled. 'You cannot escape it, Wendal Finn. This bullet will always be there, following you, just out of sight, but ready to strike.'

I could feel the bullet's heat, its willingness to crack open my skull and puncture my brain.

'For now, I reserve this moment.' There was something furious, wild about Dyonne then. Beads of sweat glistened on her head and her teeth were clenched, as though strained by the effort of holding magic too powerful for her. 'I will keep you safe from all harm, but should you ever cross me, ever try to deny the

Magicians their right to the entity you host' – I flinched back as the bullet zipped an inch closer to my face – 'your moment of death will find you wherever you stand.'

With a sucking sound, the projectile disappeared, along with the reek of smoke and the ancient weapon. Dyonne appeared to grow. The bubble of protective magic changed, becoming like a scoop or vacuum that gathered up the ghouls, dragging them screaming into a sphere of watery darkness that hung in the air above us. I wanted to both shy away and reach out and touch the sphere. It was like staring into a window of unknowable things.

'Your Song is sung.' Dyonne drew herself up regally, wiped sweat from her head. 'And so, Wendal Finn, it is time to show you just how unique you are.'

II

The Shepherd & the Sycamore

(Three Months Later ...)

Chapter Seven

The dead called me Sycamore. I was their Shepherd.

The crossbow was kept atop a crockery cabinet in a pantry, a forgotten trophy stored in what looked to be a simple case. But upon bringing it down, I discovered the case was in fact made from real wood. Rare and expensive to humans; a bonus for Wendal Finn – but that was for him to worry about later. I blew a layer of dust from its dark lacquered top and opened it.

A plain, unremarkable weapon, the crossbow sat on a soft, padded interior. A single bolt lay beside it, a decorative projectile designed as a commemorative piece but no less lethal because of it. The polished head was engraved with words that celebrated the long service of the recently retired army officer who used to own this house. The crossbow was heavy but its action smooth as I pulled the string back, locked it and notched the bolt.

A ghoul stirred in the pantry's doorway. Like a patch of oily darkness, it slithered impatiently, stinking of sewage, gurgling with the usual sound of a drowning man. Its image, sound and smell heated my blood with a pounding need for vengeance. The ghoul beckoned to me, urged me to follow it, begging for justice.

With loaded crossbow in hand, I was led out of the pantry and into the kitchen. Silver light from the night sky spilled through a window, illuminating the gloom, shining on the pots and pans hanging above a stove still warm from the day's cooking. The aroma of fried fish lingered on the air. Only households in the southern parts of the city, where the wealthiest Scientists lived, could afford real fish. Wendal Finn had always found the aroma greasy and unappetising.

The ghoul led me down a hallway into a dining room where a large centre table played host to empty padded chairs and a bureau with decanters of better-quality alcohol than most in the city could afford. The ghoul paused beneath a family portrait on the wall. It lingered long enough for me to notice that this family had never had more than two members – one man, one woman; a husband and wife – before slithering off into the lounge. Its darkness oozed over comfy-looking couches and racks filled with books, finally heading to the corner where a skeletal staircase spiralled up to the next floor.

The ghoul ascended. I followed.

Follow. That was all I had been doing for the past three months. Before the Magicians claimed control of me, *I* decided which host to inhabit, *I* decided which ghoul to avenge. But now my decisions were made for me. I couldn't escape the prison of Wendal Finn. The Magicians occasionally let me out to do their bidding. During these brief moments of freedom, there was always a victim of unavenged murder waiting for me, whose passion for justice had become a sweet addiction which I eagerly fed – but I couldn't escape the Magicians' leash which always dragged me back into my cell. I had become a puppet, a servant, as weak as the body I wore, forced to experience the slow drip of time as humans did, to *feel* life as they lived it.

But my patience would outwait them all.

The ghoul was nowhere to be seen by the time I reached the top of the stairs and found a large, rectangular landing. Five bedroom doors surrounded me, all of them closed. A soft voice came from behind one, speaking with a low tone – too low to understand, but I knew who it belonged to. The door didn't creak when I pushed it open.

Light glowed through drawn curtains. The bedroom smelled of flowers, though none were on display. The owner of the house lay asleep in a four-poster bed. An older woman, pinched face, mouth open, snoring lightly. She wore a sleep mask and the covers were pulled up to her chin.

'*Waste is not an end. Waste is survival.*'

The voice came from a glass pyramid that rested on a bedside table. Mostly clear but frosted in places, a dull light pulsed along its base.

'*Waste is a way of life.*'

The pyramid was transmitting Dreamtime Theory, a philosophy that played across the city at all times. It ran on a subliminal frequency, drilling straight into the unconscious minds of humans. But I could hear it audibly. The voice spoke for the Scientists, the controllers, the ones who had raised the human race to its greatest height before crashing them down into a wasteland; and the transmission was designed to grease the wheels of their governmental machine. It worked, for the most part, on *good* citizens who followed the Scientists' way. The Magicians used spells to block it out.

'*Every* good *citizen understands their responsibility to Old Castle.*'

The woman in the bed mumbled agreement in her sleep. I bared my teeth at her. She went by the name Agtha Martal.

Not long ago, Agtha had murdered her husband and made it look like an accident. He had never treated her badly, and her motives were boredom and greed. Boredom because with her husband retired and home for good, she'd had to give up a secret life of social engagements and lovers; greed because as reward for his years of service to the army, he had been given a slice of a lucrative fishing business on the coast just outside the city. Agtha wanted that business, the wealth and social standing it would bring, all for herself. So she had poisoned her husband and *almost* got away with murder.

I knew this because her husband had sung the Song of the Dead to me.

Byon Martal's ghoul materialised in the corner of the room. It gurgled with an insistent noise, hungrily seeking justice for his murder, egging me on. Gladly, I obliged, aiming the crossbow at his widow's face, judging the position of her right eye beneath the sleep mask.

An odd feeling rose inside me, as though Wendal had turned his back on what was to come.

'When life ends,' the pyramid said, 'the reduction houses will welcome your loved ones. We will ensure that they provide new Dust for your fellow citizens.'

These people! They would be laughable if they weren't so dangerous. They would be glorious if they weren't so corrupt. Any benefit that would come from this woman's death belonged to the Magicians.

I pulled the trigger. With a *snap*, the bolt shot into Agtha's eye and pierced her brain. Her snoring stopped.

A wave of putrid air filled the room, the stench of war and the wasteland. Byon Martal's gurgling became satisfied, appreciative, and his ghoul melted to a puddle that stretched across the floor until it touched my boot and became the likeness of my shadow. Then the ghoul evaporated, an avenged spirit at peace, travelling on to who knew where?

The smell of flowers returned to the room. I felt the first stirrings of Wendal climbing up to regain control of his body and mind, signalling that it was time for me to crawl back into my cage. The Song of Always ensured that I couldn't claim true freedom. Not yet.

And the voice of the Scientists said, '*Nothing is forgotten.*'

Chapter Eight

Life's conspiracy had made friends difficult to come by, and I only had one – Janelle Memphis. But even she wasn't too keen on me at that moment.

'This isn't going to end well,' she whispered.

'Why ever do you say that?'

Her big blue eyes narrowed at me in a trademark glare of, *Fuck you, Wendal.*

In the gloom of a basement, the tangles of Nel's hair danced in the flickering light of a single candle flame. Her face usually held an unconcerned and welcoming expression but was now creased into something more anxious.

'It'll be fine,' I promised, with absolutely no foundation for my convictions. 'Trust me.'

Around us, words of magic had been written in chalk on the walls, ceiling and floor; over empty wine racks, old beer barrels and support pillars. They even decorated the open stairs leading to the upper floor. The script appeared random and chaotic yet somehow formed a beginning, middle and end like a narrative that spiralled around the basement, ending at the man sitting in the centre of the floor.

'I asked for you to come, and you came,' the man said. 'For this, I will make you grateful.'

He didn't say much that was coherent. He didn't sound stable when he did.

The growl in Nel's throat was almost inaudible. She was always asking, 'Why do I let you drag me into shit like this, Wendal?' I never had a good answer, but she had stood by me all the same for nearly three months.

The man in the basement was Jon Johnny, though I doubted anyone knew his real name. He was cleanly shaved, his hair short – almost neat. He wore a simple moth-eaten robe and would've appeared healthy enough if not for the waxy sheen on his face and the look in his eye that said his perception of the world was somewhat askew and damaged.

'I don't like this, Wendal.' Nel's hand was thrust deep into the cloth satchel hanging from her shoulder. You never knew what she was keeping in her satchel.

Jon Johnny was a fallen Magician, an addict who didn't know when to stop. He had probably been suffering the torment of magic poisoning for years. Between the words that Nel and I could understand, he hummed an incantation, preparing a spell.

'It is written that only the Gardeners held the keys to heaven's gateway,' Johnny said. 'But I know where the dead sing for the last time, where their Songs are judged by the Order of Glass and Words. I have created a gateway to Aktuaht.'

The *gateway* he was referring to was no more than a hole in the basement floor, which he sat in front of. The area around its rim was stained by what looked to be old blood and vomit.

'We should leave,' Nel stated.

Johnny had resumed humming his spell. A collection of small jars sat on the floor around him, some containing oils, others powders of various colours, which he occasionally sprinkled into the hole.

'I can help you find her,' Johnny told me.

Nel rolled her eyes. This was by no means the first time she had heard somebody say that they could help me find Eden's spirit, but would it be the last? The legend of Aktuaht was a crock of shit, according to Sycamore. But then Sycamore had never cared if I believed him or not. He always claimed that the truth was beyond my comprehension. He wasn't one for straight talking.

The problem with Jon Johnny was that he *was* a problem. For someone else. We were beneath a gambling house in Reaper Town, a particularly unsavoury area in the east of Old Castle. The Sharpened Card – the gambling house – had recently been taken over by a hoodlum called Mutley, who, if she had bothered to check why the place was being sold so cheaply, might've noticed the mad Magician living in her new basement.

Only Johnny knew where he had come from, and his magical antics had scared away the Sharpened Card's clientele. His influence was palpable; nothing that could be put into words, he just gave the place a bad edge, like a tick burrowed into the flesh of the building, slowly spreading disease. Mutley, devoid of gamblers for her establishment, didn't know how to get rid of Johnny, and so she had sought the help of the Magicians. Her plight had reached the ears of Dyonne Obor, and that was where I came in.

'I will open the gateway if you wish it.' Johnny was rubbing pungent oil into his hands, readying, I suspected, to cast his spell whether I wished him to or not.

'Wendal—'

I stayed Nel with a raised hand and stepped closer to Johnny. 'What have you been told about my wife?'

'Her name is Eden Finn.' Johnny sprinkled a powdered catalyst into the hole. With a *whump* of combustion, orange flames began to glow. He leaned over them. Sweat glistened on his face. 'She's waiting for you on the other side.'

Nel stepped in front of me, her whispers hoarse and angry. 'This fucker is well past the point of crazy. I haven't seen anyone this bad since the war. *We. Should. Leave.*' She punctuated each word by jabbing a finger at me. '*Right. Now.*'

There was a conflict of interests going on here. Dyonne had sent me to the Sharpened Card because she thought Johnny might be useful in my search for Eden. Mutley, however, was waiting upstairs with her cronies for news that I had got rid of Jon Johnny for her. *Find out what you need and then solve the problem*, Dyonne's letter had said. I had no idea what happened next, but experience told me that the situation would find a painful resolution one way or another.

'When I open the gateway,' Johnny said, 'call for Truth, Mercy and Wrath. Ask the Judges to summon your wife.'

'Don't listen to him,' Nel implored. 'He's talking shit.'

I knew she was right, but I couldn't – *wouldn't?* – take her advice. All my roads led to Dyonne Obor. She had spun her web over the city, and I could barely move without dancing along one of her threads. She fed off the fact that I'd leave no stone unturned in my search. Undoubtedly, by sending me here, she was now owed a handy debt by the crook who owned this place.

'This is wild magic, like wastelander magic.' Nel's face was pained. 'There's no telling what his spell will do. He's lost control and needs better help than ours.'

And Johnny said, 'Aktuaht awaits.'

Nel saw my resolute expression and clenched her teeth. 'Listen to me, Wendal. I'm sorry, but you won't find Eden today.'

Then when? Tomorrow? Next week? Next year? Dyonne had told me so many times that only the mad genuinely dealt with the dead. I always thought she said it to mock me, but what if there was some truth to it? What if Jon Johnny's madness was the key to finding Eden?

'No stone unturned, Nel.'

She held my gaze for a moment then stepped aside, muttering, 'Don't say I didn't warn you,' before moving behind me to stand by the stairs.

I nodded at Johnny.

'Aktuaht is here,' he said.

Eagerly grabbing a vial from the floor, Johnny popped the cork and poured a white substance, thick like gruel, into his mouth and swallowed. He closed his eyes and a moment passed before he groaned in pain. Leaning over the hole, his gateway to Aktuaht, he retched and gagged until he brought up a pallid mass, a fleshy sac that slid from his mouth like a giant maggot, containing something that glowed.

'Shit,' Nel hissed.

The sac split, spilling a wispy fluid into the hole. It crackled when it hit the fire, turning the colour of its flames from orange to vibrant blue. Coughing and gagging, Johnny pulled the remnants of the sac from his mouth and throat, letting it slap to the floor. And that was when his spell backfired on him.

Johnny shrieked as the blue fire shot from the hole and gripped his face with claws of flame.

'I fucking warned you, Wendal!'

Nel had spoken the truth; I wouldn't find Eden today.

Johnny scattered vials and jars as he fell back, thrashing, struggling for breath, dragging the fire clear of the hole. It slithered over his body, covering him completely, and he writhed as it devoured his robe and smothered his screams to silence.

This *was* wild. The only spirit Johnny had summoned was his own.

As Nel spat out a line of curses and rummaged in her satchel, panicking, I watched with fear and fascination, recalling the war, recalling the clansfolk who I'd seen use this spell on the wasteland. Berserkers, they were called, and they summoned their own spirits to turn themselves into human bombs. They exploded with jellified spirit-matter which burned with a heat that even water struggled to douse. I had seen city soldiers incinerated when berserkers summoned their own spirits. I remembered with despair being caught in one of their explosions myself.

'Get away from him!' Nel shouted.

I didn't need telling twice. Rushing to the stairs, I started to climb, but stopped when Nel didn't follow.

Johnny was on his feet, staggering from side to side. He wore the blue fire like a vaporous suit, a superimposed version of himself, inside which he drowned, screaming silently. I felt a wave of heat coming off him. This was the most tortuous state of existence: a spirit ripped from a living body, both locked in agony. If the spell reached a crescendo, spirit-matter would burn down the basement and probably eat through the gambling house above.

Nel stepped forwards, a metallic sphere in her hands. She twisted it like she was trying to wrench it into two halves. It clicked, whined, and red lines appeared on its surface.

'You can't be serious?' I said.

'Yeah, *I'm* the one making stupid decisions.'

'A grenade, Nel? In this space?'

'Hold on to your balls.'

Johnny, tortured but silent in the cocoon of his own spirit, was beginning to break apart, expand, explode. Nel rolled the sphere across the basement floor and it stopped at his feet. She pushed me up the stairs, chasing after me, and then we fell entangled on the steps when the grenade detonated.

The concussion was dull, releasing a spiteful buzz in the basement, causing a pressure that made my ears pop painfully.

A vacuum stole the air from my lungs. The blast shook dust down from the ceiling and the stairs rattled precariously. For a moment, I couldn't catch my breath and felt sure the building would collapse on us. But Nel's home-made device was more controlled than that.

Jon Johnny and his spirit were entwined in barbed lengths of red magic that squeezed and crushed as they buzzed, liquefying him to harmless bloody jelly that dripped to the floor with big, heavy splashes. By the time Nel's grenade had exhausted itself, Johnny and his spirit were no more than a steaming gelatinous mound that filled the basement with a gag-inducing stench.

Nel pushed me off her and got to her feet. She brushed away dust and cobwebs from her coat and hair, while giving me a bitter look. '*Now* can we go?'

Chapter Nine

Hope – that was what drove me; that was all I had left. Hope for a stagnant existence on a broken world. I never envisioned my life turning out this way.

'Here's to good business,' Mutley said, 'and a job well done.'

I hadn't intended to hang around at the Sharpened Card, but Mutley insisted that we join her for a drink when we emerged from the basement – to celebrate Jon Johnny's demise, she said, which Nel thought an excellent idea, claiming that she deserved a drink after what I'd just put her through.

'Good business,' Nel toasted, clinking her glass against our host's.

We sat in an alcove at one end of the public gambling room, in the light of ceiling lanterns and a table candle. A few of Mutley's cronies stood at the bar, talking quietly; a few others had already begun the process of cleaning up Jon Johnny's remains. Otherwise, the place was empty. There was something eerie about the sea of dust-laden games tables, devoid of gamblers. The Sharpened Card felt unnervingly still.

'Bottoms up,' Nel said and drained her glass in one go.

Mutley refilled it from the bottle on the table. I sipped mine, politely declining a top-up. I'd never liked the sour taste of wine.

Mutley didn't seem to care; she wasn't exactly trying to hide that she preferred Nel's company to mine.

Mutley was a tall woman, broad, strong-looking – pushing thirty, at a guess. Her hair was short, as dark and smartly cut as the suit and shirt she wore. There was a hardness to her face, cynicism in her eyes, no nonsense in her body language – tough yet calculating – and it was easy to see that she had the charm and guile to be a criminal of Reaper Town. And the shine she had taken to Nel was reciprocated, apparently. During the brief time we had all been sitting together, my friend had gradually edged closer to our host.

'Finally, I can open for business,' Mutley said, sipping her wine. 'Thanks to you.'

She said it to Nel alone, which was fair even though she hadn't been told it was Nel's grenade that saved everyone's skin.

'As reward,' Mutley continued, 'I'd like to give you membership to the private tables upstairs. If you'd like that.'

'Deal,' Nel said brightly. 'I bloody love the dice tables.'

Not that she had money to gamble with.

'What about you, Wendal?' Mutley didn't take her eyes off Nel. 'Are you a gambling man?'

I shook my head. 'I don't have the luck for it.'

'No, I don't suppose you do.' Mutley considered me, looked unimpressed. 'A good fixer never places much faith in luck, am I right? That *is* what you do for the Magicians, yes? Fix problems?'

'Oh, don't bother asking,' Nel said, leaning into Mutley. 'He won't talk about what he does for the Magicians. Not even to me.'

'Well, that seems a little uncharitable.' Mutley pulled a pack of cheroots from her inside pocket, took one out and lit it. 'But then Magicians do enjoy their secrets.' Her eyes didn't leave mine as she blew smoke into my face. 'Are you going to finish your wine, Wendal?'

The underlying hint was heavy and unmistakable, though Nel didn't seem to notice. My business at the Sharpened Card was concluded. Which was fine by me. I didn't know what I was still doing there, anyway. Sickened in the aftermath of another miserable incident – another death, another dead end – I just wanted to walk away as usual, go home and get shit-faced to forget. And I had a lot to forget. If Jon Johnny wasn't enough, the murder of Agtha Martal was fresh on my mind from yesterday. There was nothing worth celebrating here.

'I should be going,' I said, pushing the glass away. 'Are you coming, Nel?'

'No, I'd like to stay for another drink.' She smiled at her host. 'Or maybe two.'

'Then that's settled.' Mutley's glare left no uncertainty as to whether or not I should leave the table now. 'Thank you for your time, Wendal. My people will show you out.'

Nel winked and gave me a little wave before I walked away.

Chapter Ten

They came, hundreds of them, charging down the valley beneath an ash-filled sky that glowed blood-red with the light of a hidden sun. A swarm of wastelanders, bearing weapons and armour cobbled together from aeons of detritus crushed into the hostile landscape. Their cries rose as a united ululation, the fearsome call of clansfolk that was heard so often across the spaces between the cities – battle cries and curses and promises of death, bellowed in the language of the Gardeners.

And they were coming for me.

An advance cavalry of berserkers rode upon the backs of bears – huge, shaggy beasts, savage and powerful enough to bite and rip foes limb from limb. But the bears wouldn't get the chance to sink their teeth into me because, like their riders, they were sacrifices; the berserkers were already screaming the incantations that would summon their own spirits, preparing to erupt with burning spirit-matter. The valley rumbled with the thunder of a thousand pounding feet. The ground's crust broke and churned into a storm of debris.

This was how my dreams remembered the wasteland. Remembered the war.

More warriors lined the tops of the valley walls, jeering, lofting their weapons. Naked and unarmed, I had been trapped between the charging army and the valley's end, where a gigantic, dense graveforest began. Behemoth corpse-trees, as wide as houses, growing so tall that their highest branches disappeared into clouds of ash, cast a shadow over me with the cold promise of death should I enter the forest. The clansfolk promised me the same if I remained where I was. I trembled, terrified.

But Eden wasn't afraid. She stood staring into the graveforest's darkness. Her clothes were the simple gown of a Magician; her hair was long and straight, red as the unseen sun. I asked her to help me. Her shoulders shook, whether from crying or laughing I couldn't tell, but she wouldn't turn to me. Sometimes, in my intoxicated dreams, my wife refused to show me her face.

'Eden, please—' Something moved stealthily among the shadows of the graveforest. An instant later, the glint of a blade announced an attacker springing into the light. 'No!' I shouted, but Eden did nothing to prevent the spear piercing her chest and emerging covered in blood as it ripped through the back of her gown.

I watched, too terrified to move. It happened so fast that I saw little of the attacker's identity. A flash of armour beneath a hooded robe – armour made from amber glass and decorated with magical script – was all my eyes detected before my wife was hoisted onto broad shoulders and carried into the darkness of gigantic corpse-trees.

Left to the mercy of the clansfolk, I looked up at the smeared light of the sky and begged the Gardeners for salvation—

'Sycamore, someone's crying.'

But it wasn't me.

'Can't you hear it?'

The voice did not belong to the dream, though it made the visions crumble and fade away before the clansfolk could reach me. My consciousness poked its head above the effects of the jenkem.

'I can't stand it, Sycamore.'

Heart racing, tangled in sweat-stained sheets, I focused on the pasty cracked ceiling of my lodgings. In a flurry of motion, I leaned over the side of the bed and retched bile onto bare floorboards. Slowly, my breathing calmed and my mind gained a stronger grip on reality.

'Make him stop.'

The only evidence of the speaker to be seen was nestled in a high corner of the room, above the words of a spell which had been seared into the wall. A ghoul bubbled as a patch of oily darkness there.

'Go back to sleep,' I croaked.

The spells glowed briefly. The ghoul burst into vapour, leaving nothing behind.

Kicking away the sheets, rising through the stink of my un-washed body and my vomit, I moved to the basin in the corner of the room and turned on the tap. The water was tepid, tasting of old pipes as I splashed my face and rinsed out my mouth. The last fog of intoxication parted to reveal a headache, and I realised that someone *was* crying. An edge to the sound took it beyond the generally accepted definition of *upset*. Tears of desperation, wailed with an innate fear that cut to my bones with the blade of empathy. It came from outside.

Crossing the room, I opened the only window in my lodgings. For the first time in more than two days, fresh air blew in, cool and clean to chase away the guilt.

'Get up,' a woman ordered.

'No!' was the tearful reply.

Down in the filthy lane that ran between my lodging house and another, a man lay on his back, eyes pinched closed, rubbing his thigh. He wasn't much younger than me but his crying sounded younger than us both, as primal as a child's. He had obviously just been knocked to the ground; two city watch officers stood over him, an older man and woman. He wore a plain constable's uniform and held cuffs. She wore the uniform of a sergeant and carried a baton, looking very ready to use it again.

'Don't make me go,' begged the man on the ground.

'You'll defend the city as is your duty!'

'I-I don't want to die.'

A runner. His time to fight in the war had come and he was too terrified to accept it. I couldn't blame him.

'Coward!' This came from further along the alley, on the opposite side, from a woman leaning out of her window. 'I lost two sons to the wasteland, and they didn't die so you could run and hide.'

'That's right,' said a man, his furious face appearing from behind the woman. 'Serve your fucking city, coward!'

The sergeant pointed a finger at them. 'Go inside!' she commanded, and they did, slamming the window behind them. She then gestured to her constable, who pulled the runner to his feet roughly.

The sergeant gazed up at my window. I ducked back quickly, but not before catching her eye. When I looked again, the runner had been placed in cuffs and was being led along the alley on unsteady legs, head bowed. The sergeant looked back at me a couple of times, and then was gone from sight.

'Poor bastard.'

I looked up to see Nel leaning out of her window, smiling down at me. 'Hello, Wendal. I was beginning to think you were dead.'

I blinked at her a few times, deciding that I felt as though she wasn't too far wrong. 'I've been busy,' I said.

'Yeah, I could tell by the interesting aroma coming up from your room.' Nel gave me a knowing glare. 'When was the last time you ate?' I took too long thinking of an answer and she rolled her eyes. 'I'm heading into work,' she said. 'I'm on my own today, if you fancy a free meal.'

The idea of food set hunger pains rumbling in my gut. 'That'd be good. I'll meet you there.'

'Have a wash first, Wendal. I can smell you from here.'

After a visit to the latrine, I made my way down to the communal bath beneath my lodging house. The water was hot and clean, cloudy with floral soap. It made me feel a little more human, but I didn't linger to relax in the warmth. A couple of my neighbours were already in the bath when I arrived. One was an overweight man with far too much body hair, submerged to his shoulders and apparently asleep. The other was a fragile-looking woman with sunken cheeks and hollow eyes, who stared at me whenever I wasn't looking directly at her. I didn't know their names but I'd seen them both around the place before. I didn't speak and got on with washing myself.

People came and went from my lodging house, and no one seemed to live there for long – besides Nel and me. My neighbours hardly noticed my presence, which was fine as far as I was concerned. They weren't the sorts I wanted to know anyway, not after seeing the things some of them had left behind in the latrines on my floor. Sordid books and blood-stained clothes and devices for purposes I couldn't even begin to guess. It made me shudder. This place had changed for the worse since I became the property of the Magicians, as if the building had died with Eden. No families lived here any more, no laughter to be heard, though sometimes I could swear there were children crying in the night. It was difficult to tell if the sound was real through the amount of jenkem I used.

When I'd finished washing the stink of a two-day torpor off my body, I wrapped myself in a towel and made my way back up to my lodgings, where I discovered a note had been slid under the door in my absence. It was from Dyonne – a summons. She wanted to see me at noon.

Chapter Eleven

Nel worked in a dingy tavern called Piper's situated close to where we lived in the Tinman District. It was a clear day as I made my way to it, but while I walked down Pharaoh Street, a chilly shadow suddenly fell over Old Castle and made me shiver. At first, I didn't think much of it; it wasn't unusual for the sun to disappear behind the thick smoke belted into the air by the various reduction houses around the city. But the forge chimneys weren't belting out smoke today. Instead, there was an immense formation of black clouds in the sky. The citizens around me looked unfazed by its presence, but it disturbed me.

The clouds were many leagues off, not only high in the sky but also stretching down low, perhaps all the way to the wasteland. Even from such a great distance away, I could still see that they were roiling, billowing. Yet they appeared fixed, shot through with streaks of orange like fire, but otherwise entirely too dark, sooty. Storms had a habit of coming fast and angry out of the wastes, but this was no ordinary storm. It reminded me of the explosions I'd seen in the war but on a monumental scale. Like a *wall* of storm.

Since the citizens were going about their daily routines, hurrying along the street, bustling in and out of stores and conveniences, entirely unconcerned by the strange sight and the shadow it had cast, I reasoned that its presence was old news to the city, and I asked Nel about it when I reached Piper's.

'Well,' she said, 'if you didn't spend so much time indulging your habit, you'd know what it is.'

Nel was the only server on duty. I sat at the bar, while a few other customers ate and drank at tables and Piper's enjoyed a lull between breakfast and lunch. The rich smell of cooking came from the kitchen out back.

'That storm was started by an explosion,' Nel continued. 'It's hanging over Alexria.'

'*Alexria?*' The next city you'd come to if you travelled north-west from Old Castle. It was over a hundred leagues away, yet the storm was big enough to see from here? 'What happened?'

'The Scientists aren't saying much, but I hear all kinds of shit in this place. The most popular rumour is that Alexria's defences failed during an attack. Clansfolk or monsters – I don't know, maybe both – but something from the wasteland got inside, and you've seen the results for yourself.'

'Fuck … that can't be true, can it?' Because as far as anyone could trace back, the clansfolk had never been strong enough to take down a city. 'The explosion came from *inside* Alexria?'

'That's what the Scientists are saying,' Nel said. 'I don't think anyone really knows what caused it.'

'What about the citizens? Are they all right?'

Nel shrugged.

I swore again. 'Why is nobody panicking?'

'You slept through the show. There was plenty of panic a couple of days ago. You should have been there. The roar of the explosion woke me up. The city sirens went off. I nearly shit myself. Came down to see you but you wouldn't open your bloody door.'

'I was busy.'

Nel rolled her eyes. 'The Scientists were quick to transmit

a statement telling us that we were safe. What happened to Alexria wouldn't happen to Old Castle, they said – which, of course, means they know more than they're saying.'

The Scientists always did.

'Anyway, it's old news now, Wendal.'

I pondered Alexria's fate while Nel went off to get me a bowl of stew, some bread and a jug of water. She laid them out on the bar, and then stared at me until my silence confirmed that she wasn't getting a thank you.

'You're welcome,' she muttered before attending to her chores.

I tucked into the stew. It was good, hot and salty; the bread freshly baked, steaming when I ripped it open.

'I keep thinking about that poor runner,' Nel said with her back to me, stacking clean glasses and tankards behind the bar. 'I considered running on the day I went to war. I suppose everybody does.'

I mumbled something non-committal through a mouthful of food. My thoughts remained on Alexria.

'Still, at least you got to see your girlfriend in action.'

I froze, a piece of bread in my hand poised over the stew. Nel was talking about the city watch sergeant who had accosted the runner.

'I hope you remembered to blow her a kiss.'

'She's not my girlfriend,' I said, jabbing the bread into the stew and stuffing it into my mouth.

'Could've fooled me. I *do* live above you, Wendal. I hear what you get up to with her. You know, it's that creepy man who lives below you who I feel sorry for. You must break the bed every time she—'

'She's *not* my girlfriend.'

'She was in here yesterday,' Nel continued happily. 'I think she was looking for you.'

'Drop it.'

'She doesn't seem to like me much.'

'Nel, shut up.' It was too complicated an issue to address in my current state of mind. 'Tell me more about Alexria.'

'I don't know why you're so uptight about her.' I could see Nel's smile through the back of her head. 'I'd never be like that about *my* girlfriend.'

I froze again. 'Pardon me?'

'I have a new girlfriend.'

It struck me then that the last time I'd seen Nel was after the incident with Jon Johnny in the Sharpened Card's basement. I'd left her drinking sour wine with the establishment's new owner.

'Oh, please tell me your girlfriend isn't Mutley.'

'What if she is?'

'She's a criminal, Nel. From Reaper Town.'

Nel raised a finger. 'That's a little judgemental, Wendal. Mutley owns a respectable business, and we've become quite close.'

'Close, eh?' I stabbed at the stew with a spoon. 'What's her real name?'

Nel shrugged. 'She likes to be called Mutley.' She smiled over her shoulder at me. 'I tell you, Wendal, I've got a good feeling about this one.'

Two customers came to the bar and saved Nel from my angry retort. With a grumble, I continued shovelling food into my mouth.

Imagine Nel as a baited hook dangling from a line in the middle of the sea, hoping to catch a big fish. There was no skilled fisherman on the other end of the line, no preparation or plan – just Nel trying to hook a life that was better than the one she had. Her problem was that she had decided long ago that her happiness was the responsibility of someone else. Someone rich, someone with standing, someone who could improve her existence.

I'd given up trying to decide why Nel kept on running away from herself. She was intelligent, skilled, could've chosen any number of professions after the war. Yet here she was, serving food in a rundown tavern, hanging out with the likes of me, while waiting for something better to come along. Nel had fought in the war seven or eight years before me, and she would tell you that she survived the wasteland unscathed. But something was missing in Nel's eyes, something unnameable that I recognised, shared, and that was probably why we were friends. But unlike me, she had choices, options for the direction of her life which she never took, and that was what I found most frustrating about her. Stepping out with someone from Reaper Town was exactly the sort of trouble she would get herself into.

Having finished serving drinks, Nel leaned over the bar and looked at the sack on the floor beside my stool.

'What's that?'

'Merchandise.'

'For who?'

I didn't reply and she huffed.

'One day, Wendal, you'll have to tell me who your boss is.'

I shrugged and drank some water.

Nel knew a lot about me, though certainly not everything. She knew that I could see the dead; she was glad that she couldn't. She believed that the Magicians contracted me for work from time to time, but the nature of the work itself had to remain secret. Which wasn't far from the truth, but I spared her the details for good reason. As for who it was among the Magicians that I called *boss*, I kept that from her, too. Dyonne Obor wasn't exactly someone you were quick to associate yourself or anyone else with. Not if you were smart.

Nel didn't need to know what I truly was. She had been my constant companion pretty much since my search for Eden began. Along the way, her discovering that I was sometimes called Sycamore had been unavoidable. I never explained what the name meant, but if she harboured any suspicions, I was grateful that she kept them to herself – and that she respected me enough to accept my warning that she should never mention the name Sycamore to anyone at any time.

'It's always the same with you,' Nel complained as she wiped down the counter. 'I don't see you for days on end, and then you turn up looking for a free meal, carrying *merchandise*.'

'You invited me,' I said. 'And I'll pay for my food when you give me the money you owe me.'

'Fuck you, smart arse. My point is, we're as thick as thieves one moment, and the next you won't open your door to me, even when I damn well know you're home. I worry about you, Wendal.'

She did, it was true. She also worried that I might mingle with the kind of people she'd like to know. Always a hook in the sea.

'You want to share? Fine.' I finished the last mouthful of stew and threw the spoon into the bowl. 'I last saw you, when? Over two days ago, now. And between then and now you've met the love of your life. Again.'

'I never said I was in love. I said I had a good feeling.'

'Mutley must be rich.'

'Possibly.' Nel's grin was as wide as it was infectious. 'She *could* be the one, right?'

'Nel, she's from Reaper Town.'

'I don't need to hear it, Wendal. If you want me to respect your private life, then you respect mine. And try being happy for me, once in a while.' She threw the cleaning cloth over her shoulder and turned to straighten the bottles of liquor behind the bar. 'We're all searching for our Eden, you know.'

Nel winced and met my level glare with an apologetic face. 'Sorry. I didn't mean anything by it, I—'

'It's all right.' I smiled.

'Any new leads?'

'Nope.' I finished my water and slid off the stool. 'But I'm hoping for one this afternoon.'

She narrowed her eyes at me. 'Let me know if I can lend a hand.'

I nodded and grabbed the sack. 'Thanks for the stew.'

Chapter Twelve

Old Castle had its wealthy quarters, its poor quarters and the places in between inhabited by the larger population. At one time, I would've said that I belonged to the lower-middle, but now I didn't know which subset could claim me. Perhaps I really was unique, straddling the blurred line that weaved between social structures, where I often frequented the secretive pockets in the west of the city where the Magicians dwelt.

One such place was a tavern in Tinman Market that stood on the corner of Levee Street, where gangs marked their territories and pickpockets were sharp. It was an unassuming sort of place, nameless, easy to miss and very unlike Piper's. Its tinted windows prevented passers-by from seeing in but allowed customers to see out. Yet entrance to this tavern was reserved for a select type of clientele.

I sat at one of its tables drinking strong coffee and smoking a dark brown cigarette. Candles burned and dripped wax on table-tops and from wall-mounted holders. Naked flames crackled in musky air that smelled of age. No one manned the small bar. Dyonne sat opposite me, wearing her usual plain, dusky gown and an unimpressed expression as she stared into the open case lying on the table between us. The crossbow inside didn't look so threatening now.

'Do you know what happened at Alexria?' I asked.

'No,' Dyonne said, not looking up from the weapon. 'Wendal, is this really all you could find?'

I stared out of the window at the busy market.

Eden once told me that an object couldn't define its existence no matter the purpose for its creation. She said a fork, for example, could no more choose to put food in a mouth than it could choose to stab a throat. Only humans made those decisions. *We* defined an object's essence. *We* were culpable for its every action. My wife used to say lots of things like that.

Dyonne huffed.

At the centre of my head, a dull ache pulsed. My stomach hadn't settled after eating my first meal in more than two days. Guilt and anger lingered like a bad memory. This was the hangover from reaching yet another dead end: my paltry reward for being Sycamore's *object*. I longed to feel nothing for what he made me do.

'Wendal, you've brought some shit to me in your time, but *this*?' Dyonne shook her head.

An amused snort came from behind her. At a separate table, Dyonne's bodyguard Tamara sat glaring at me. As big and ugly as ever, he was covered in old scars, his hair unruly and streaked with grey. His meaty hands were clasped before him and one of his thumbs was missing, a scarred stump where it used to be. Tamara never spoke, never acted unless Dyonne issued an order, but he'd never had trouble conveying that he wouldn't forget that I'd bitten off one of his digits for trying to steal the rings hanging from a chain around my neck.

Dyonne looked up from the crossbow. 'Honestly, this is all you're bringing me today?'

I stubbed out the cigarette and gave her a withering look. 'Just make me an offer.'

'All right. I'll give you thirty bits for it.'

'The case alone is worth five times that.'

'You think so?' Dyonne pulled a dubious face. 'Sure, it's real wood but not so rare. As for the crossbow, it's made from plain old Dust. Nothing special about it.'

I sipped my coffee. 'What about the bolt?'

'A worthless retirement gift – it has the owner's name engraved on the head. I could bring a lot of trouble to my doorstep by trying to sell the stolen property of a recently deceased war veteran.' She grimaced into the case. 'Did you use it to kill Mr Martal's wife?'

I rolled another cigarette, lit it from the table candle and blew out a long, slow line of smoke. She didn't need me to answer the question. The bolt still had Agtha Martal's dried blood on it.

Dyonne rocked her head from side to side. 'I *suppose* I could stretch to forty. As a favour. From me to you.'

Dyonne loved to haggle. I didn't. 'I'll take a hundred for the lot.'

'*By the ether in the sky!*' she said in Salabese. 'You offend me, Wendal. That's not even close to a friend price.'

Her voice sounded like sunshine, her words scented like flowers in summer. Dyonne mostly kept herself mysterious and unknowable, but after three months of working for her, I'd learned a thing or two about this Magician. Along with the scars on her hands, glyphs and spells had been cut into the inside of her mouth and on her tongue; every word she spoke, every breath she took was laced with magic. She could coerce most people into seeing her way of thinking, most especially me.

'I tell you what,' Dyonne said sweetly. 'For you, I'll split the difference. Let's say seventy bits.'

'Fine,' I muttered, flicking ash.

'I knew you'd see sense!' Dyonne clapped her hands in delight. 'Tamara, my purse please.'

The big bodyguard rose and placed a cloth purse on the table with a *chink*. He smirked at me, clearly satisfied that his master had ripped me off yet again. Dyonne opened the purse and counted out seventy bits in a short stack of black glassy disks, each stamped with a white number one, five or ten. As Dyonne cinched the purse closed, I scooped up my payment and put it in my jacket pocket.

'Get rid of the crossbow and bolt,' Dyonne told Tamara as she closed and locked the lid. 'Be careful with the case – it's real wood, don't you know. Easily worth five times what I paid for it.' She gave me a wink. 'Take it down to the old monster.'

Tamara did as he was told, carrying the case to the back of the tavern and disappearing through a door.

The old monster, Dyonne's name for Mr Sebastian, her boss – the boss of most Magicians, in fact. There were five Grand Adepts in Old Castle, collectively known as the Salem. There was no higher rank to which a Magician could ascend, and the members of the Salem were older than anyone else in the city, but unnatural long life and years of magic poisoning had rendered them barely human.

I'd not laid eyes on Mr Sebastian since the day I met Dyonne. He dwelt somewhere beneath the tavern, a place I'd not been summoned to again, where Magicians gathered and did whatever it was Magicians liked to do. He remained the only Grand Adept I'd ever been allowed to meet, which suited me just fine. I wondered if the old monster cared that I, the host for his *asset*, still existed.

Dyonne grinned at me. 'You are perilously close to becoming a *good* citizen, Wendal.'

I finished my coffee and took a drag of the cigarette. 'How do you figure that?'

'Mrs Martal has no next of kin. Everything she and her husband owned now passes to Old Castle. Today, my friend, you have made the Scientists a little bit richer.'

'And you.' Because Dyonne never used Sycamore unless it benefitted the Magicians in some way. Mr and Mrs Martal's fishing business was most likely being passed to someone more sympathetic to the Salem's needs even as we spoke ... or her death simply meant that the Scientists had lost an influential ally. Only the Grand Adepts could answer that for sure.

'What can I say?' Dyonne opened her arms in a helpless gesture. 'I take what opportunities the Gardeners leave before me.'

The Scientists would tell you that kind of sentiment was a whole lot of shit. So would Sycamore.

Crushing the cigarette into the ashtray, I offered a wan smile. 'Do you have anything new for me?'

'Actually, yes.' Dyonne regarded me. 'Do you know the Garden near Public Square?'

She knew damn well that I did. I had been there often enough in the last few months. 'What about it?'

'Go there this afternoon. Someone would like to meet you.'

'Someone?'

'She says she has information.'

'That's what you said about Jon Johnny.'

'Ah, yes – an unfortunate outcome,' Dyonne said as if there was nothing unfortunate about it. 'But there's always a silver lining, Wendal. You have helped to provide the Magicians with a solid contact in Reaper Town, which is not to be sniffed at. As for this new lead, I sincerely hope it works out better for you.'

I stared into those hazel eyes so packed full of secrets, holding them until Dyonne groaned.

'You're always so cynical, Wendal, but …' Dyonne gave an exaggerated shrug. 'I am no more than a messenger in this quest of yours. Do only charlatans and the insane boast of communing with the dead? The Garden near Public Square – go there this afternoon and find out for yourself.'

I grabbed my tobacco pouch and stuffed it into my pocket. 'Then I suppose I'll get going.'

'Good luck, Wendal.' Dyonne rose and made her way to the door at the back of the tavern. 'Take care of Sycamore. We will be needing him again soon.'

Chapter Thirteen

Three months ago, I was a dead man. Sycamore had dragged my existence down to the lowest place possible where he had all but ground everything I was into the oblivion of Nothing. Dyonne pulled me back. I supposed I should have been grateful, but how could I be? My choices had been submerged in the waters of my grief like an ancient baptism until I had clung to the last hope, shining as a single star in an empty sky: Eden.

My wife had always injected sense into my world; she helped me consider what I couldn't see, and had done so since our youth. I recalled one occasion, when we were crossing the line between childhood and adulthood together – five, maybe six years away from going to war – she had asked me what I wanted for the future. Where did I see myself heading?

She had started this conversation because of her fears that we had reached a crossroads in our relationship: could I be considering a life as a *good* citizen? Even back then, and years before, Eden had known that her heart belonged to the Magicians' way; and as soon as she could escape the strict disciplines of her mother – a *good* citizen to the core – she intended to practise the art of magic. Did I oppose this? Was it time for us to head in different directions at that crossroads?

I had realised then that I depended on her personality, her

love, her very presence, and wanted to be with her for ever. But I would never lie to her, and she knew me so well that she could tell if I tried. The Scientists' way didn't appeal to me, I'd told her, but I didn't lean towards the Magicians, either. In truth, I didn't know what I was or what I believed, but I wanted to travel through life with her; wanted her by my side when I passed into Aktuaht and beyond into heaven.

This answer had pleased Eden, but in that thoughtful, internalised way with which she considered everything. A Scientist, a *good* citizen, didn't believe in Aktuaht and the Garden in the Sky, but a Magician *knew* that the paradise of the Gardeners waited on the other side. I might've been undecided, confused, and perhaps I would be for always, but at least Eden recognised that our relationship was built on the foundations of a shared faith. A few years later, I had become her husband.

Life without Eden felt inconceivable to me, both then and now. So here I was, still searching for her to inject sense into my world, even after her death. I needed to find Eden to give meaning to the things I had seen and done.

From the nameless tavern and the meeting with Dyonne, it was less than half an hour on foot to Public Square, so I decided to walk to the Garden instead of taking the under-rail. Far to the north, the sun continued to hide behind the ominous storm hanging over Alexria. It looked to me as if it had changed since I first saw it that morning. It wasn't dissipating, but was it spreading? Heading this way? Absurdly, I felt as though it was looking at Old Castle.

I passed through Public Square, where a platoon of young soldiers stood to attention before their commander. Evenly spaced in six neat rows of five, they each had short swords sheathed at their waists and helmets tucked under their arms, and they were dressed in dark green uniforms armoured with plates of reinforced Dust. Pensive was a good word to describe their faces; oddly still a good way to describe their audience.

New recruits, fresh out of basic training, about to begin their City Service: a year-long tour of duty fighting in the war against the clans of the wasteland. A distant memory came back to me of how they were feeling – turmoil, panic, uncertainty in the face of the unknown. They were me a year or so ago, and they had good reason to fear.

Around the square, pedestrians and shop-owners held a silent, respectful vigil. Loved ones and relatives observed with a mixture of pride and sadness. The only sound was a low hum coming from the large glass transmission pyramid glowing faintly behind the platoon's commander, whose own face was coldly neutral. She looked old enough to have been through this routine a hundred times, to have long ago learned that it was better not to grow attached to the soldiers she trained.

Every citizen served a tour of duty when they reached the age of twenty.

My eyes were drawn to one solider whose face was streaked by tears. The runner, the young man I'd seen outside my window. Armed and in uniform now, his eyes were turned to the sky. His hands visibly shook. On the other side of the square stood a detachment of city watch, ten officers in all. In their midst was the sergeant who had caught the runner, who Nel referred to as my *girlfriend*. She stared at me. Her name was Lana Khem, and our relationship was a little … unusual.

She gave me a discreet nod. I looked at the runner again.

Eden once said that survival was the only true commonality shared by every citizen over the age of twenty-one. Statistics showed that a quarter of this platoon wouldn't return from the war. And most of those who did would come back as *good* citizens, adhering to Old Castle's laws exactly as the Scientists wanted them to, like children clinging to their parents, searching for order and security. The wasteland would do that to a soldier. However, a few returned damaged beyond repair.

I was eighteen when I married Eden. She was nineteen. After only a year of married life, her tour of duty came up, and I saw her off in this very square, wondering how I'd cope without her, praying that she'd come back. But when she did return, our paths merely crossed as City Service came calling for me. Eden and I never knew each other as survivors. Her husband had been an undecided statistic when she last saw him.

In a clear, harsh voice, the commander barked an order and the platoon about-turned crisply to face the city watch with a crunch of boots. As well trained as they could be. The transmission pyramid projected the image of a huge face above it. Grainy and green-tinged, it was the kindly face of an elderly, bearded man. The official face of the Scientists.

'These proud soldiers wish to defend Old Castle.' The image's voice – a gentle, deep tone – reached every ear in the square, but it was addressing the city watch. 'Will you lead them to their duty?'

Sergeant Lana Khem stepped forwards. 'It would be an honour,' she declared.

'Then go with the blessing of the Scientists.' Light pulsed inside the pyramid with every word. 'And may victory bring our heroes home.'

The face was an age-old recording, speaking empty words for the ears of tradition.

The city watch surrounded the platoon and began marching it out of the square. The soldiers would be escorted to Old Castle's west gates, where they would then face the savage plains of the wasteland beyond. Some onlookers wept as they left; most applauded. Lana Khem led the parade. I'd see her again soon.

She had a habit of being where I was.

The platoon marched out of view. The face of the Scientists faded to nothing and the crowd went about life as normal. A wind picked up and I looked at the storm in the distance.

I didn't die in the war, but I would never call myself a survivor.

Chapter Fourteen

As I made my way to the Garden near Public Square, the sun finally cleared the fire-streaked clouds over Alexria and the great shadow lifted. The sun burned large and red in a pink sky, but its warmth did little to deter the afternoon chill that swept through the streets and encouraged me to pull my jacket tight around my body. It was late Mars, the first month of spring, though the season was clinging to winter's last breath.

Old Castle was one of many cities built on the wasteland over the millennia, though it was the only city I'd ever known. The smell of cooking food hung in the air and the chatter of voices formed a wash of nonsense. I felt like a wisp weaving between the living; unseen, unheard, faceless in a faceless crowd. I wanted them to see me, I wanted to be a part of their everyday lives, but Dyonne Obor and the Magicians had made sure that wouldn't happen. Sycamore was my spirit.

The hubbub of the city became a background hum, dampened by tranquillity, as I stepped through the tall gates of the Garden. The air became heady with sweet scents, and colours were varied. Flowers were one of the few natural commodities produced in Old Castle, and the first spring blooms decorated the Garden, growing from beds of Dust made into rich brown soil. Hedges, too, and one or two old trees.

The Gardens could be found throughout Old Castle, and citizens used them to remember lost loved ones. Thankfully, there were few mourners in attendance – a father with his two young children, and a middle-aged woman, alone and tearful. I walked down a path flanked by bushes of pale roses, finding an empty bench in a secluded area. I sat down to wait and remember.

In front of me, a pedestal – one of many in the Garden – rose from a square of grass. A glass pyramid, much smaller than the one in Public Square, sat atop it, inside which small mirrors were set at varying heights and angles. I fished an information node from my trouser pocket – a clear resin bead, as small as a pebble. When I slotted it into the hole at the base of the pyramid, a pinprick of light shone, bouncing from mirror to mirror, directed up and out of the glass.

An image began to form in the air.

The Scientists would tell you that only they really understood ether, how it could be broken, how its power could be distributed – though the Magicians would say that the Scientists had only learned how to pervert its magic. Ether had been gifted to us by the Salahbeem – the Gardeners themselves – ten thousand years ago, before they left Urdezha. They had sown its seeds into our world, and it was hard to imagine what Urdezha had been like without it.

There were places on the wasteland, rare and deep beneath the ground, where huge crystalline growths of ether formed in subterranean caverns. There was no bigger concentration of magic to be found in the world, and every city had been built upon one. Everything that required energy was plugged into an ether-growth, from the largest forges of the reduction houses to the small and simple appliances like these transmission pyramids. The magic of ether was everlasting, it was said, and it could record and store thoughts, information, imagery.

Though the ether crystal in my node was smaller than a grain of sand, once the magic of the ether-growth below Old Castle connected to it, the pyramid projected the grainy green image of a double sycamore seed slowly spinning, forever falling. This was the image I'd chosen to represent the daily hurdle I had to clamber over in the search for my wife.

I came to this Garden to ponder questions – so many questions. Why did she kill herself? That would be the first thing I'd ask Eden when I found her spirit. I'd often wondered if she had done it out of grief; among her possessions had been an army notice informing her that I was missing in action, and when a soldier went missing on the wasteland, they didn't return. But I didn't *know* if that was the reason, couldn't believe it. Magicians respected life because the Salahbeem, the Gardeners, had taught them to do so, and the Judges of Aktuaht would condemn any spirit who had taken her own. It didn't make sense that Eden would do what she did, even in grief.

So much I didn't understand. So much I didn't *feel* without her. What would Eden think of what I had become?

'Terrible news about Alexria.'

I practically jumped out of my skin when the woman spoke. I hadn't noticed her approaching.

'I heard it was a clansfolk attack and they didn't leave much of the city standing,' she continued, joining me on the bench. 'Must've been bad if it made that storm. And if you ask me, it's getting ready to blow our way.'

I stared at her.

She wore a thick shawl, which had attracted a few twigs and leaves, as had her wild hair, suggesting that she might live in the bushes of the Garden. Elderly – mid-fifties at least. She reached out with gnarled fingers and slipped an information node into the pyramid next to mine. The miniature image of a sturdy tree, boughs full of leaves, appeared above it.

She sighed, explaining, 'It's the tree in Under Park.'

I knew the one she was talking about and eyed her suspiciously. Old Castle couldn't boast many healthy trees. The one in Under Park, I remembered sourly, was a sycamore. The image hovered in the air like an accompaniment to the seeds spinning next to it.

'My husband proposed to me while we stood under that tree, sheltering from the rain. This city could do with more romantics like him, don't you think?' Her old eyes were glassy with the threat of tears. 'I lost him years before you lost Eden.'

My instinct was to shout at this stranger, to tell her that she had no right to say my wife's name. But then, Eden was the reason she was here. Supposedly. I looked out over the Garden, saying, 'What do you know?'

Her demeanour changed, a greedy sheen replacing tears. 'What's it worth?'

'Depends how good it is.'

She chuckled and sat back. 'Lots of people come to me for comfort and wisdom. They like to hear messages from the dead, or wish to know the future. Which do you want?'

She fancied herself a spiritualist or oracle of some kind. Dyonne had put me in touch with a lot of these types over the last three months. Few of them were genuine, and none had been helpful to my search so far.

Suspecting another waste of my time, I said, 'And I suppose these people pay you well, do they?'

'Some are more generous than others. Depends how desperate they are.'

I swore under my breath, fishing two one-bit coins from my pocket. 'This had better be worth it.'

She plucked the coins from my hand and they disappeared beneath her shawl. 'I've been hearing your name a lot lately. Not your birth name, mind, but' – she gestured to the image of the sycamore seeds – 'you don't need me to say it aloud.'

'You'll have to do better than that.'

'A friend of mine would like to talk to you. He's very keen, in fact, but, uh, isn't exactly alive, if you follow me.'

'A ghoul? Tell him to get in line.'

'No, no – not a ghoul. There's nothing unavenged about him.'

'A ghost, then.'

'He decided to stay in Old Castle instead of moving on to the Garden in the Sky. I would've brought him with me, but he doesn't like to stray too far from home.'

'Home?'

'I'll get to that that later. My friend knows who you are, Wendal – and what you do. He told me about your search for Eden.'

I was already losing patience. She wasn't saying anything she couldn't have got from Dyonne. 'You need to work harder for your money.'

'My friend says he knew your wife. Back when he was alive.'

I scoffed. 'Did he also tell you that he's not the first person to lie about that?'

'You wear your wedding bands on a necklace.'

True, the rings were hidden from view beneath my shirt, but again this was nothing Dyonne couldn't have told her. I was about to say, 'Give me my money back,' when she said something that made me take notice.

'Yours used to be on your finger, but your wife always wore hers on a chain.'

I tried very hard to think of a way she could know that, but I came up blank, unless ... unless it had come from me or Eden.

'You're suspicious, and I don't blame you,' the woman said. 'This city and every other on Urdezha is full of charlatans, probably more than you realise. Maybe if you see my friend, it'll prove to you that I'm not one of them.'

'Who is he?'

'Name's Abdon Klyne. He was a veteran of the wasteland in life. Became an archaeologist before he died. Taught survivalism at Temple University.'

That surprised me. Archaeologists, survivalists – dangerous people and certainly no friends of the Magicians. 'He worked for the Scientists?'

'He would tell you that he worked for himself, but I suppose you're right.' She considered for a moment. 'Klyne knows more about the Scientists than anyone outside their inner circle, and he reckons they're up to something nasty. Experiments ... with the dead.'

'The dead?'

'That's what he said, and I'm inclined to believe him.'

I wasn't. 'The Scientists have no purpose for spirits. They don't get involved with that kind of thing.'

She levelled a look. 'Don't they?'

'Even most Magicians don't like dealing with the dead.'

'No, they let *you* deal with them instead.' She flashed a grin, revealing chipped and stained teeth. 'Funny thing about being in your position – in the world of the living you're barely noticed, but on the other side you're quite famous. Or maybe that's just your alter ego.'

'Stick to the point.'

She chuckled. 'I warned Klyne that you wouldn't be sweet on me. "You'll have to give me something firm to tell him because he won't take my word for it," I said. No joy, though – he wouldn't tell me what the Scientists are doing. But he wants you

83

to know that if you love Eden and you're serious about finding her, then you need to understand that you might be looking for her in the wrong places.'

'What's that supposed to mean?'

'Buggered if I know. Klyne wants to tell *you*, not *me*. I'm just a messenger.'

Now, where had I heard *that* before?

I didn't like this woman's tone, didn't like her expression, didn't like the way she obviously knew I could be manipulated by Eden's name.

'So that's it,' she said. 'Personally, I can't see the harm in paying Klyne a visit, but that's up to you. See him, don't see him, whatever you want. I've got my money.'

She gave me a moment to ponder her proposal.

'And where might I find him?' I asked.

Her grin returned. 'Temple University – where he used to work. Know it?' I did. 'He likes to haunt the library in the west tower. But he's none too keen on the living, so it's best to visit him after dark when it's closed and empty – if you've no objection to picking a lock or two.'

I reached out and removed my node from the pyramid. The sycamore seeds disappeared and I got up to leave.

'I have to admit that I'm curious about what Klyne knows, too,' the old woman said. 'Think I'll do some digging myself.'

She switched her attention to the image of the sycamore tree in Under Park. I walked away.

'Maybe we'll talk again, Wendal,' she called after me. 'Once the storm's blown in.'

Chapter Fifteen

The violence of unavenged murder could anchor spirits to the world of the living as embodiments of anger, ghouls seeking justice, and some of them found vengeance through Sycamore. Through *me*. I had never been blind to this. My eyes had always been open. Eden was no ghoul. There was nothing unavenged about her spirit. She had killed herself. Her decision. Her choice. No revenge to be had. But could suicide bring peace? I hoped not.

I used to believe in Aktuaht, but I didn't any more. Sycamore's continual derision of what he called childish myths and desperate need had seen to that.

He once said to me, '*It's a matter of finding clarity of perspective within fear of the unknown, Wendal. Aktuaht can only be real if the Salahbeem were indeed the Gardeners, gods – which is what the Magicians believe. The Scientists, however, believe that while the Salahbeem were so highly evolved that they might have appeared godlike, they were, in actuality, as mortal as humans, and therefore unlikely to be controlling any aspect of the afterlife. But whether Aktuaht is a human concept or real, one undeniable constant remains – it is a handy myth by which a hierarchy can perpetuate the conditions it wishes to place on life. Aktuaht enforces obedience.*'

And when I asked him what *he* believed, what he knew about

the other side and the Salahbeem, he replied with his usual evasion: '*I don't believe in anything, Wendal. I simply know the truth.*'

Sycamore might have succeeded in crushing my belief in Aktuaht, but I refused to give up on the Garden in the Sky. I *had* to believe that heaven was real; that the Gardeners had created a place better than the wasteland, where the best of us could rest in peace. And Eden *was* the best of us.

She and I once made a romantic pact to enter the Garden in the Sky together: whichever of us died first would remain in Old Castle to haunt the other, waiting for the day when we could journey on to the other side hand in hand. But her ghost had never come to me. Surely that meant her spirit had journeyed on without me, whether or not the afterlife conformed to the ideals of heaven, whether I was right or wrong about Aktuaht. And that was why I feared death. Sycamore had ensured that the Garden in the Sky was the one place where I couldn't search for my wife.

There was no afterlife for me now. Sycamore had devoured my spirit in order to possess me, chewed it out of existence and replaced it with himself. Without him, I was a flesh-and-blood shell, empty on the inside. Without him, I was a dead man, destined to crumble into the condemnation of Nothing. Everything I was, every memory I had, would cease to exist. I had my mind but no spirit. And so my search to find Eden had to remain on *this* plane, which perhaps meant finding a way to steal her back from heaven. I didn't care whether I had the right to do this or not; she had left me when I needed her most, and I deserved to know why.

I spent the rest of the afternoon riding the under-rail. For two bits, you could buy a ticket that permitted travel for the entire day. There were twenty stations in Old Castle. Alighting at any of them would usually place you within ten minutes' walk of where you needed to be. But I didn't get off. I rode around beneath the city, the sound of wheels *tick-tacking* over tracks and the sway of the carriage like a metronomic rhythm keeping my concentration in time with the scratches of my pencil on the pages of my journal.

Barely noticing the comings and goings of other passengers, even when they crowded me at busy stations, I stayed in my seat, writing word after word.

I had filled several journals over the past few months, each recording the leads and dead ends I had encountered so far. The trouble was, every person I'd met along the way – living or dead – had been filtered through Dyonne, and I'd had no choice but to accept that Dyonne was in no rush to help me find Eden, even if she denied it.

Why did Dyonne Obor do anything? She was selective with her information, her reasons clandestine, utterly devoted to the Grand Adepts of the Salem. It was impossible to tell when her words could be trusted or not. The only thing I had worked out for certain was that a ghoul had to meet certain criteria before it gained access to Sycamore, and the specifics were known only to the Salem, or so Dyonne said. While the jobs she gave me benefitted the Magicians in some way, she had no impetus to fulfil her side of our bargain. I sometimes wondered if she had ever intended to, back when it was first struck. She had put me on a leash, and on the one occasion we'd clashed over it, things hadn't ended well for me.

About six weeks, maybe two months ago, no closer to finding Eden, sick of the self-loathing I felt each time Sycamore used my hands to destroy life, I had confronted Dyonne at the name-less tavern where we always met.

'I've done everything you've asked me to do,' I said bitterly. 'It's about time you did something for me.'

'Time?' Dyonne sounded genuinely perplexed. 'I wasn't aware that the clock was ticking on our arrangement.'

She had already paid me for the bounty from the latest kill, and we had been discussing the newest dead end she had led me to in my search: a blind beggar from the shanties who had been more skilled at filling his wooden bowl with bits than telling the truth.

'You owe me, Dyonne.'

She regarded me with an expression of curiosity. 'Have I lied to you in some way? Have I not been fulfilling my promise?'

'You could have done more.'

'Wendal, it is not my fault—'

'Yes, it is!' I snapped. 'You keep me running in circles that only ever bring me back to *you*!'

And it was true. I had tried to make my own contacts, find my own way in the search, but through a mixture of magic and a fierce reputation, Dyonne had rendered me off-limits to a network of people who might've been able to help unless *she* allowed them to gain access to me.

'You're a cheat and a liar, Dyonne.'

Her curiosity became a hard glare. 'Careful, Wendal.'

'You told me you'd find Eden.'

'No, I said that I would help *you* find Eden for *yourself*.'

I banged a fist on the table. 'Where is she?'

Behind Dyonne, the ever-present Tamara stiffened, coiled, ready for the order that would at long last give him the chance to exact revenge for his thumb.

Dyonne raised a hand, staying her bodyguard. 'You're upset, so I will let your disrespect pass unadmonished. But please remember – Eden is not my responsibility. You and Sycamore, however, *are*. To forget that it is *you* who works for *me* is a dangerous thing to do.'

Perhaps I had started believing in the power of Sycamore, his brutal efficiency in the art of murder, or maybe I was just that fucking tired of what I was seeing as a fool's quest; either way, I asked, 'Do you think I'm no threat to you?'

'I think you should watch your mouth and leave while you still can.' Dyonne's pupils dilated, on the cusp of channelling magic. 'You can't comprehend what serves as a threat to me.'

'You're scared. You need me as much as I need you.' The bitterness in my voice had been matched by my confidence. I honestly thought that some part of Dyonne *had* to be frightened of me. Perhaps I was right, because when I added, 'Maybe I'll ask the Scientists for a better deal,' Dyonne said, 'Tamara, hold him,' before casting her magic.

I had intended to defend myself, but Tamara was quick for a big man and frighteningly strong. He took no risks with his digits this time, holding me down in my chair, gripping me painfully under the chin so my teeth could get nowhere near him.

Heat pressed on my face. A drone filled the air like a bee buzzing.

The bullet from the ancient weapon hadn't materialised since the day Dyonne fired it. I had come to suspect that it wasn't real; that it was an illusion to control me, as baseless as the leads Dyonne kept giving me. I was wrong. She summoned the bullet then, spinning, no more than two inches from my forehead, and Tamara forced me to face it.

My stalker, my reaper, my moment of death.

Beyond it, Dyonne's predatory eyes bored into mine.

'Let me remind you,' she growled. '*I* decide how you live. *I* decide how you die. If you doubt this, perhaps we should end our relationship now. What do you say, Wendal Finn?'

Of course I had relented, and I never doubted the bullet's

existence again. The Song of Always, a powerful spell usually reserved for the Grand Adepts of the Salem. Only they were skilled enough to cast it, and they used it to preserve their moments of death and attain perversely long lives. The Salem had conjured the Song of Always to protect Sycamore, and they had given it to Dyonne and allowed her to cast it upon me. Harsh experience had since taught me that this spell truly was my moment of death. It seemed that I could die by no other method. Should Sycamore ever escape, the Song of Always would keep me upright and alive, staving off Nothing, but only for as long as Dyonne and the Salem allowed it.

So what chance did I stand without Dyonne Obor? She was my custodian and had been permitted the use of magic greater than her own to control me. If I acted against the Salem, her cherished masters, she would summon the bullet, and everything I had ever been would blow away like dust on the wasteland. This life was all I got. I needed Eden to come back, remember me, answer my questions, just ... talk to me like she used to. And then I could face Nothing without regret.

I was a Magician's fool, the Salem's perfect assassin, with no choice but to accept my place in their games, while praying all the while that Dyonne would one day give me something genuine to go on. I wondered, with my pencil poised over the page, if Dyonne had finally deigned to show me the right direction by sending me to the elderly woman in the Garden.

I looked up, thinking, as the train stopped at Under Park Station to let a sizeable cluster of citizens disembark and leave the carriage mostly empty. After a brief tattoo of doors slamming shut, an unseen conductor blew a whistle and we trundled off again.

The old woman knowing about the wedding bands was a small detail but enough to hook me. Eden had indeed worn her ring on a chain around her neck because she said wearing it on her finger hindered the casting of magic. The metal heated up, had even burned her once. The night before I'd gone to war, Eden had taken my ring from me and put it on the chain next to hers – for safekeeping, she'd said, to keep me close.

Was it possible that the old woman could know about the rings without information garnered from the spirit world? For all I knew, it might've been common practice among Magicians. I'd certainly never noticed Dyonne wearing rings on her fingers, or any other kind of jewellery, but then it wasn't as if I was allowed access to other Magicians who I could ask.

I thought long and hard but couldn't remember ever telling anyone about Eden's ring – not Nel, not Dyonne, nor any other acquaintance. The old woman claimed she had come by the information from her *friend*, this ghost called Abdon Klyne, and if that was true then was it likely that Eden had told him herself?

My thoughts remained on Klyne as I disembarked at Tinman Station and made my way home. The sun was low in the sky and night was falling. In the distance, the fiery storm continued to brood over Alexria. It was definitely moving, spreading. Watching Old Castle?

I kept my head down, flicking back through the pages of my journal as I walked. Not one of the charlatans, dabblers and deluded idiots I'd encountered so far had ever mentioned the Scientists before. Most had been dedicated to showing me how bad they were at using magic or just plain lying. The old woman in the Garden was an anomaly.

The Scientists and the Magicians were always at odds – that much had never been a secret in Old Castle, or any city on Urdezha, I would've thought – and the jobs that Dyonne had given Sycamore had been related to this ongoing feud, some more obviously than others. But this was the first time anyone had brought the Scientists up in specific relation to Eden. Considering how unfavourably she'd viewed them, I found it doubtful that she would make friends with someone who had spent his life working for them.

The Scientists were up to something with the dead, and I was looking for Eden in the wrong places. According to a deceased archaeologist. According to a stranger in a Garden. According to Dyonne's latest lead.

I decided to go through my other journals when I got home, check for any references to the Scientists that I might've forgotten. I already knew, however, that I would be going to Temple University to see if the ghost of Abdon Klyne was real. There was too much here to ignore. No stone unturned.

However, when I arrived home, I discovered a visitor waiting for me.

Chapter Sixteen

A bitter smell laced the air. A cake of jenkem smouldered in a burner beneath the closed window. A thin line of smoke ghosted up and dispersed in dreamy puffs as it hit the ceiling. I breathed in a lungful and felt its intoxicating effects tingle upon the periphery of my perception.

A pair of boots had been placed on the only chair in my lodgings. On the small table next to it, a city watch uniform had been neatly folded – a sergeant's uniform.

Lana Khem lay in my bed, a single sheet clinging to her naked body. Her usually neat and tied-up hair hung in loose curls. Her brown eyes were glazed, looking in my general direction but struggling to find me. Her face searched for an expression. She smiled lazily and whispered a single word through the jenkem smoke.

'Wendal.'

I wondered what else Lana could see besides me. Jenkem first relaxed the body and calmed the mind before anaesthetising all cares and inhibitions and inducing rich, vivid dreams. Just for a while. I remained by the door, breathing in more smoke in the hope of hurrying its effect.

'How was your day?'

I shrugged.

'Have you eaten?'

I didn't say anything.

'What do you feel like doing tonight?'

It was like listening to bad acting in an amateur stage production of a relationship. I hated hearing it.

'You must be tired.' Lana stretched beneath the sheet, content and drowsy.

I should have told her to return the key to my lodgings, to leave and never come back. I should've told her that weeks ago.

Slipping off my jacket and hanging it on the back of the door, I said, 'How are you, Lana?' Saying anything felt better than staying mute.

'Some old, same old,' she said, sighing. 'I've missed you.'

'I've missed you, too.' Hollow, perfunctory words, spoken limply.

'Come to bed.'

Lana watched me undress. She took in my naked body, seemed pleased by what she saw. She never mentioned how thin I looked, never mentioned the words of magic on my stomach and back, the red stains of the spells which kept a spirit of vengeance trapped inside me. Nor was she put off by the old scars beneath them, the remnants of burn wounds suffered during my last days of fighting in the war. Lana pulled back the sheet, as though to reveal a secret. She had scars of her own.

When I lay down beside her, she wrapped the sheet around us and I fell into her embrace. Her muscles were toned and her skin was rough. Her dusty hair smelled of Old Castle's streets.

It was hard enough dealing with my own afflictions, let alone Lana Khem's. Perhaps she was addicted to me, or was it obsession born from a quirked sense of guilt?

Lana had been the city watch officer who had dealt with Eden's suicide, who had found her dead body in this very room.

My wife had pressed a hand-held ether-cannon to her chest, over her heart. At point-blank range, the blast had torn a hole right through her. Lana hadn't wanted to tell me that, but I had made her.

Not long after I became the Salem's pet, Lana began visiting me. At first, it was to return the last of Eden's effects. I'd already reclaimed our wedding rings – I sometimes think it was the shock and emotion of seeing them that finally weakened my defences enough for Sycamore to take control of me and set us off on our murderous spree. Lana had brought the last remnants of Eden's life, including the notice announcing my status as missing in action – apparently my wife had carried it around with her. But afterwards, Lana kept on visiting me. To see how I was coping, she said, to give me any help I needed, and somehow we ended up like this.

Lana pressed her mouth to mine, eyes closed as if she was thinking of someone else. Her fingers trailed over my scars.

I should have told her to stop. But I never did.

Back then, I'd thought it was only a matter of time before Lana arrested me; that she *had* to find out about my deal with Dyonne and what I was doing for the Salem. In retrospect, I think she had been, and still was, looking for forgiveness. She considered Eden's suicide as her failing somehow. In a way that I didn't understand, Lana blamed herself and felt the need to make up for her misplaced guilt, and she did so by filling a void in my life, replacing some of what I'd lost. So she could help me feel normal? Not so abandoned?

Lana straddled me and I groaned – as much from intoxication as from how good she felt. She bit my earlobe, whispering, 'I love you,' but it was the jenkem talking.

We never met in mundane circumstances. There were never any meals, no theatre trips – nothing approaching a normal relationship. I could count the proper conversations we'd had on one hand. We enjoyed each other while intoxicated. Because jenkem eradicated the need for reason. It was the unspoken agreement between us, the barrier that spared us from ever getting to know each other at all.

Lana ground against me and I held her tight, close. Her lips parted mine and our tongues met. Reality started to blur, and when I closed my eyes it was Eden's face I saw, her body pressed against mine, slick now with sweat.

I'd never told Lana that I didn't blame her. I'd never said that it wasn't her fault. Perhaps I thought that if she knew, she wouldn't come back, and these strange moments where she played surrogate wife to a widower would end. She helped me to remember how Eden had felt, tasted.

I rolled on top of her, keeping my eyes closed to savour the image of a different face. The bed complained and Lana moaned as she built to orgasm. Passion rose, our teeth clashed, and Lana spat curses as she climaxed. I quickly followed, with her finger-nails adding marks to my back.

After, we lay embraced, breathing heavily into each other's ears. By the time I rolled away, Lana was already asleep, slipping peacefully into whatever visions jenkem had brought her.

On the cusp of slipping away myself, my tenuous link to reality was preserved by something stirring in the corner of the room. My gaze drifted to the words of magic seared into the wall next to the door. Above them, a ghoul bubbled like boiling pitch.

'I've been dreaming again, Sycamore.' A female voice, always sad. 'Did you know the dead could dream?'

'Go away, Itch.' This ghoul, my *Itch* – even Sycamore could not sate her cravings. She was a thorn in my side, the one haunting that couldn't be stopped. 'Just … go away.'

'I travel the wasteland.' Itch shifted her form, but I couldn't focus enough to see what shape she had taken. 'I live wild with the clansfolk, seeing things that you wouldn't dare to imagine, sparkling and pure.'

'You're full of shit,' I mumbled. 'Go back to sleep.'

'But I don't want to dream. I don't want to go back.' She wept with a sound that hurt my ears. 'I want to be free.'

'Fuck off, Itch.' I started laughing.

'Sycamore! Give me justice!'

And I was still laughing when the jenkem finally snatched me away. Behind my eyelids, Eden was waiting …

A lake filled the width of the valley floor, flanked by high, sheer walls of rusty rock. Its surface was smooth and glassy, glistening beneath the sun, clear all the way down to its bottom. The water looked pure enough to drink, inviting enough for a cool swim. But the lake was toxic, capable of melting flesh from bones in minutes; and hiding down below in underwater caves, monsters waited for their meals.

This was the wasteland.

'Urdezha is covered in scabs,' Eden said.

She stood on the lake's shore, staring out at a bed that floated like a raft, carrying the sleeping form of Lana Khem. I stood next to Eden, smiling.

'If the Scientists aren't careful,' she continued, 'they'll drill so deep into the wasteland that they'll reach Urdezha's skin. And that will be the day when they find so many festering wounds that they'll have to admit how they ruined the world.'

I loved the sound of her voice, the confidence it carried. 'Tell me how they ruined it, Eden.'

'The wasteland is a brittle veneer of existence, Wendal, created by every single mistake the Scientists ever made. If it crumbled to dust and Urdezha was allowed to heal, the world's natural state would be alien, hostile to humans. Over the millennia, the Scientists have ensured that we're no longer the natives. Urdezha has had enough of us.'

'Are you really so sure?' I recalled us having this conversation before. 'Seems to me we're pretty good at surviving.'

'Only by perverse will and ingenuity. Not by any right of natural selection.' She snorted. 'The Scientists are fucking barbarians.'

'They're not the only ones to blame. Magicians must fit into your argument somewhere.'

Eden turned to me and her admonishing chuckle made my heart skip. Red hair long and straight, eyes like green jewels, face without blemish, sculpted. Beautiful. 'Oh, Wendal. I'm not arguing. I've thought my opinion through, as you damn well know.'

The lake in the valley had never been part of this debate; this location had come much later for me. The words belonged to the dusky hours before dawn in Old Castle, while Eden and I lay in bed in our lodgings. I would've had this conversation a thousand times over, in any location, if it meant Eden stayed with me. Sadly, these snippets of happiness were not meant to last.

From behind us came the boom of an explosion. Eden cocked her ear to the sound as it echoed down the valley. She faced the lake, looking beyond the water to the opposite end of the valley where, in the near distance, the giant corpse-trees of a graveforest rose above sheer walls of rock.

'One day,' she said, 'someone's going to find something on the wasteland, something old and forgotten, and it'll be too powerful for the Scientists to handle. They'll try, of course, but this artefact will bite back and bring every single city to its knees. That's how the war will end.'

I remembered my line. 'You're avoiding my question.'

'I'm *trying* to answer it, but it's not as simple as you'd like, Wendal. Ask yourself – what would the Salahbeem think if they returned and discovered that we had survived?'

'They already know we survived.' I grinned. 'They can see us from the Garden in the Sky.'

Eden made a disgruntled noise. 'I meant hypothetically. Look at it with a Scientists' eye. Would the Salahbeem be amazed that we'd managed to survive? Disgusted by how we did it? Respect our ingenuity or wonder why they didn't just destroy us before leaving Urdezha?'

I shook my head. She was talking about ancient history, after the Salahbeem disappeared and the human race brought itself to its knees in the Ether Wars. 'Who knows what really happened ten thousand years ago?'

'The Salahbeem expected the worst of us to die out, that's what.' Eden's eyes drifted up to the sun, so large and red in the sky. 'Yes, Magicians have to take a share of the blame for the wars that turned Urdezha into *this*. But here's the difference – without the cities and their technologies, the Scientists would be lost and pointless. The Magicians, however, would accept the natural order. Let the world itself control its ether and decide who gets to live. Because *we*, the Magicians, respect that one way or another, all life has to meet its end, otherwise what worth does it have?'

'Yet the Salem get to use the Song of Always and live longer than anyone? And here's another contradiction for your argument, Eden. You call the Scientists barbarians, but what about the Magicians' Lore of Ascension?'

'You don't know what you're talking about, Wendal.'

'I know enough! The only way one of the people you're defending can ascend to the rank of Grand Adept is to kill a current member of the Salem. Tell me that's not barbaric. The Scientists don't fuck each other over for the sake of rank. They work together.'

'As I said, you don't know what you're talking about. Besides, no one has ascended to the position of Grand Adept for centuries.'

'You can only say that's true for Old Castle. There are a lot of cities—'

Another explosion was followed by the *whumping* of ether-cannons. From somewhere unseen, the battle cries of the clans-folk rose as a united howl.

'*Longevity for the pursuit of elevated knowledge,*' Eden said, but not in her own tones. I sighed; the private moment had ended and she now spoke in Salabese using my voice. '*That is why the Grand Adepts use the Song of Always.*' Eden looked at me. The green of her pupils had changed to the shape of sycamore seeds. '*And no Magician has ascended to their rank in centuries because the current Salem members are far too clever at hiding their moments of death. They are all but immortal.*'

The debate forgotten, memories of a cosy, pre-dawn moment receding into more recent matters, Sycamore stared at me.

In the conscious world, he and I couldn't communicate; the Salem had made sure of that. But somehow, in the depths of jenkem dreams, the restraints loosened and we met in the subconscious. He always spoke in Salabese and I in Babel, the language of the cities. I'd never told Dyonne that this occurred; I liked that it was the one secret I could keep from her, though I just wished that Sycamore wouldn't use Eden's image when he came to me.

'*You spend too much time feeling sorry for yourself, Wendal. Here and now, you cling to this romantic notion that you will be reunited with your wife, while never considering who else you could be searching for. Typical of you humans. You see only hope when the truth would spare you a futile existence.'*

'Love will do that to a *human*, not that you could ever understand it.'

'I have been trapped long enough to gain a broader insight into your concepts and emotional limitations. I feel them as you do.' Sycamore looked out over the lake. *'You need to clear your mind, Wendal, straighten your perspective. For example, do you remember Clay Hysan?'*

How could I forget him? He was the reason I was stuck with Sycamore. Or was it the other way around?

'Don't you ever wonder where Dyonne Obor hid Hysan's ghoul?' Eden's image narrowed its sycamore-seed eyes. *'He cannot be her only victim. Magicians might be good at covering their tracks, but they are a cut-throat bunch and not one of them achieves a high rank without facing obstacles that require …* removing. *Dyonne must keep a secret closet somewhere, in which she hides the ghouls of her victims. If you could find but one of them, Wendal, I would exact revenge for what Obor has done to us.'*

We must have had this conversation a hundred times before and I didn't have the energy to go through it again. In the beginning, it was a more heated argument, but had dwindled to a somewhat passionless ritual over the weeks and months. He wasn't trying to exact revenge for anything. The Song of Always meant he couldn't kill me and that really pissed him off. What he wanted was for me to go poking my nose where Dyonne didn't want it so I'd become the liability that forced her to release my moment of death and give my possessor freedom.

'Forget it,' I said tiredly. 'It's not going to happen.'

Sycamore smiled. *'Give it time.'*

I flinched. The cries of the clansfolk were growing louder in the valley.

'*Do you trust the old woman in the Garden?*' Eden said with my voice.

'No,' I stated.

'*Hmm.*' Sycamore watched the bed drifting on the still water. '*You're wondering why Eden would befriend someone who worked for the Scientists. Doesn't sound like her, does it?*'

'I ... I'm not sure any more.'

'*This is certainly a strange lead for Dyonne Obor to give you. Suspiciously helpful, at first glance.*' Sycamore pushed a hand under the collar of Eden's gown, pulling out a chain and showing me the solitary ring hanging from it. '*Whoever you do or do not trust, you are going to see if the old woman was right about this Abdon Klyne, aren't you?*'

I nodded. The clansfolk were getting closer. I could hear the sound of their charging feet, but I didn't dare look to see if they were in sight yet. 'What choice do I have?'

'*None that you're willing to see. You gave away your choices three months ago.*' He directed my attention to Lana Khem. '*You made your bed, Wendal, no matter how much you like to blame me.*'

'Yeah, you're entirely blameless.'

'*I do wish you would exceed your limitations.*'

The clansfolk's charge shook the valley floor. Rumbles sent debris rattling down the walls and set ripples to spreading across the surface of the lake. But it was movement on the far shore that grabbed my attention now.

An anomaly had distorted the air. A straight thin line of silver light rose eight feet at least from the ground like a crack in reality. The line widened to become a ragged hole, filled with starless space. I'd seen this kind of distortion before, what felt like a thousand times in these jenkem dreams, but its presence was never my doing. The silver-lined hole in reality was a gateway, an ancient and powerful transport device the likes of which hadn't been seen on Urdezha since the days of the Salahbeem, and it had been conjured by Sycamore, taunting me with one of *his* memories.

'*Your problem, Wendal, is that you refuse to accept that your existence was never continued for the purpose of finding Eden.*' Unconcerned by the army of wastelanders charging towards us, Sycamore pursed Eden's lips. '*Try considering something bigger than yourself for a change.*'

The gateway's darkness bulged outwards and an ethereal woman stepped from it. The gulf of the lake lay between us and she was too far away to see in great detail, but I knew what she looked like. As with the gateway, Sycamore had brought her to my jenkem dreams many times before.

She had no hair and her skin was such a pale blue that it was almost translucent. Her ears were small and pointed, pressed flat against her head; her nose was two slits on a smooth face and her mouth a small pursed circle; but her eyes were large, clear ovals, entirely devoid of colour. She wasn't human. She was so much more than that. According to Sycamore.

Dressed in the splendour of shimmering amber armour decorated with ancient script, she was a Gardener, one of the Salahbeem. She had come to these dreams so many times that I'd long ago stopped feeling awed to be in the presence of such a legendary being, whose legacy had seeded all that the human race had become. If she was truly a Gardener at all; Sycamore's word was hardly trustworthy.

'*What do you think, Wendal?*' Sycamore's pity cut through the roars of bears and the screams of berserkers that had now risen above the war cries of the clansfolk. '*Is she a god or a mortal?*'

No matter how many times this Gardener appeared, Sycamore wouldn't allow her to come close or speak. He never explained why she haunted his memories or revealed her name; he would only say that she had lived sometime during Urdezha's distant past. The script riddling her amber armour sparkled with the rose tint of ether, and the suit denoted that she had held a special position among her kind. This mysterious Salahbeem woman had been a knight from the Order of Glass and Words.

Truth? Lies? What did it matter?

The Gardener held some kind of device in her cupped hands. It glinted glassily in the sunlight, hued the same as her armour. Unhurried and calm, she blew upon the device and it emitted a high-pitched whine barbed with bursts of static. With eerie grace, the knight cast it into the lake before turning to step back through the gateway. The ragged hole closed to a crack of silver and blinked out of existence behind her.

Sycamore said, '*The true frustration of being trapped inside a human is that I view life as one of you while knowing of things that you could not comprehend. I am not supposed to be here, Wendal, but I suspect that you and all your kind will have to learn that the hard way.*'

The device exploded with a dull boom beneath the toxic water. The lake's surface became agitated, frothing and boiling, rocking the bed upon which Lana Khem remained asleep. The explosion roused something in the depths. A geyser shot into the air. A monster rose with it. It was difficult to see in all the confusion and froth, but in a brief moment of violence, of scales and claws and teeth, the monster smothered the bed, dragging it down into the lake, taking Lana with it.

The clansfolk were almost upon me, their united voice deafening. But I wouldn't turn to face them and kept my eyes firmly fixed ahead. I started trembling. No matter how many times these fucking wastelanders came for me in these dreams, I couldn't master the fear they brought.

Sycamore patted my shoulder. '*Expand your awareness, Wendal. Good luck with Abdon Klyne.*'

Eden stepped into the water and dived beneath the surface.

I closed my eyes.

Chapter Seventeen

I was rudely awoken by a knock at the door.

Sitting bolt upright, cursing as morning light lanced through the window and into my brain, scorching my eyes along the way, I was irritated by a second knock. Urgent. I climbed from the bed, hopping to the door as I pulled on my trousers.

The jenkem dream rattled around my brain like the pieces of a shattered mirror. I'd put them together later. Lana had already left my lodgings without waking me, as was her way, as we both preferred it. We didn't like facing our dysfunctional relationship with sobriety.

I reached the door and yanked it open, interrupting a third bout of frantic knocking. '*What?*'

Nel rushed into my lodgings, bringing with her a waft of bad air from the corridor. She slammed the door shut and pushed her back flat against it, pressing a finger to her lips, wide-eyed and panicked. Moments passed, and I gave her a look that hinted I wasn't in the mood for a lack of explanation.

'I just got home from Mutley's,' she said quietly. 'But when I got upstairs—'

She cut herself short as footsteps approached. Nel flinched as something hard rapped on the door behind her, and a voice that carried a sneer shouted, '*Rent!*'

'Stadham,' Nel whispered fearfully. 'I don't have any money, Wendal.'

'For fuck's sake, Nel.' I grabbed my shirt from the floor and put it on before shoving Nel out of the way and opening the door so it hid her presence.

Mr Stadham, our small and venal landlord, greeted me with a leering yellow smile. 'Morning, sunshine.'

The tone of his voice set my teeth on edge. I caught another waft of bad air out in the corridor. It was coming from the communal latrine on this floor.

'Can you smell that?' I said.

Stadham sniffed the air and expressed disgust. 'Yeah, something's off.'

'It's the stink pipe. It's blocked again.'

Another smile full of stained teeth. 'Ooh, someone really should fix that.'

Stadham was a brittle man with a pinched face and squinty eyes like a carrion monster on the wasteland, always on the hunt for easy pickings. He wore a thick coat that practically drowned a body that couldn't have comprised more than thin skin stretched over fragile bones like a bag of rattlesticks. His hair was silver and slicked back. His arthritic fingers were curled around the head of his walking stick, which I had always assumed was made from bone.

He looked me up and down impatiently. He wasn't alone. Flanking him were his two bodyguards. He referred to them as his *nieces*. I could see the family resemblance to each other, but not to the scrawny old bastard standing between them. They looked mean, though; hard faces carrying the trophies of many fights. Their clothes were dark and loose, plain but roomy enough for easy manoeuvring. Their jackets could easily conceal weapons. Knuckles calloused, hair shaved short, expressions dispassionate, they never spoke. Always ready for orders, the nieces were Stadham's Tamara.

'Why am I still waiting?' Even the most genial person would find it easy to grab Stadham by the back of his head and ram his smug face into the wall. 'Chop-chop!'

I made to go and fetch my rent money, but Stadham laid the end of his walking stick on my shoulder and cast a suspicious gaze into the room behind me.

'Seen that bitch from upstairs?' he said. 'I think *you* call her Nel.'

I resisted the urge to snatch the walking stick and break it over his head. 'No.'

'Funny how she's always so aloof on rent day, don't you think?'

'She's probably trying to get away from the smell of the latrine.'

Stadham chuckled. 'I'm beginning to take her absences personally, and ... well, it'd break my heart if I had to evict her.'

The nieces bristled, and I could almost feel Nel holding her breath behind the door.

'Yeah, that'd be a damn shame,' I said sourly.

Stadham's yellow smile became thin. 'Seeing as you two are such great mates, maybe you could cover her. Like you did last week. Up to you, of course.' He removed the walking stick from my shoulder. 'Off you go.'

Grinding my teeth, I pushed the door to so I could get to my jacket hanging on the hook on the other side. I fished forty bits from its pocket and gave Nel a glare while I was hidden by the door. She wrung her hands together, mouthing, 'I'm sorry,' and, 'Thank you, thank you, thank you.'

Stadham looked disappointed when I paid up for us both, like he had been hoping for a reason to give his nieces some exercise. 'Well, I suppose I'll see you next week, then.'

'Fix the stink pipe.'

'Yeah, yeah. Come on, girls.'

They left, I closed the door, and Nel tackled me with a hug, saying, 'I promise I'll pay you back,' before I had chance to utter anything scathing.

From out in the hallway came the muffled sound of Mr Stadham rattling his walking stick against someone else's door. I had a bastard of a headache.

Nel watched as I moved to the basin and splashed water on my face. She smiled sweetly. 'It's funny if you think about it.'

'Hilarious.'

'I'll make it up to you, Wendal.'

'Like you did last time?' I huffed – more from resignation than any genuine anger – and dried my face while giving my mind a moment to catch up with itself. 'Actually, there is something you can do for me. Are you busy tonight?'

Nel's appreciation evaporated into a more defensive stance. 'I'm seeing Mutley.'

'Can you spare me a couple of hours first?'

A frown came next. 'Why?'

'You know Temple University?'

'Maybe.'

I rolled my eyes. 'Big building with towers in Scholars Gate. You'd have to be blind to miss it, or stupid—'

'*Fine!* I know it.'

'Good. Meet me there tonight, first dark.'

'Why?'

'I need you to break into it for me.'

'I hate you, Wendal.'

Chapter Eighteen

That night, hiding from view in a deep recess in the wall surrounding Temple University, I smoked a cigarette while waiting for Nel to show. Leaning against the locked side gate to the university grounds, I marvelled at the sky.

Since I could first remember, the night had filled me with awe. The twin moons were small and beaten, but their passage was fleeting and barely noticed because they were not Urdezha's brightest celestial bodies. In high summer, the night could be almost as bright as the day, and so much more beautiful. In a terrible way.

A mighty swarm of ether orbited the world. Millions of crystals, some indistinguishable from the pinprick stars, others larger and closer than the moons, but each reflecting the light from the hidden sun with majestic glares of rose-tinted silver. Magical, invisible during the day, they were synchronised in their orbits and wondrous to behold; yet most would tell you that the swarm of ether crystals was Urdezha's curse. A barricade. There was good reason, Eden had said, why our moons were called Fear and Panic.

So long ago now that nobody could be sure of exactly when any more, the Salahbeem had come. All over Urdezha, gateways had opened like rips in reality and these preternatural beings had stepped from their world into ours. The Gardeners, the bringers of magic – they came in peace and offered friendship. They wanted us to be travellers like them, and many of us had thought them gods. They gave us ether. They gave us technologies and secrets. The Salahbeem changed the face of Urdezha and showed us just how little we understood about the star-dotted void between the worlds. We welcomed them and their guidance at first, for a century, it was written. Then we threw it all back in their faces.

Ancient history was dogged by myths and legends, and the views of the Magicians and the Scientists differed on the truth behind our visitors; but it was said that Urdezha had been a lush and vibrant world when the Gardeners came – a paradise compared to what we had now – and on this beautiful world, the human race was ripe to reach the pinnacle of its growth. But we used everything the Salahbeem taught us to advance ourselves into ignorance. Not content with the gifts and wisdom our visitors freely offered, we tried to steal the secrets they hadn't yet told us, not questioning whether or not we were ready for them but believing we had attained a state of rapid evolution that made us equal to our teachers. For many, the goal became to prove that the Salahbeem were not gods but as mortal as humans, and we succeeded in driving them away.

The Scientists would tell you that the Gardeners filled the sky with ether crystals because they feared our greatness and the retribution we would exact upon them if we could leave Urdezha. The Magicians would say that the barricade was to prevent any poor, unsuspecting traveller ever again discovering the inherent ignobility that matched anything good in our race. Sycamore would tell you that humans and the Salahbeem were as bad as each other.

The truth was lost to time and myth, but one thing was

certain: when the Salahbeem fled Urdezha, their legacy proved how little we ever truly learned from them. Who would control the ether-growths that the Gardeners had abandoned and left behind beneath the world's skin? The human race divided into opposing opinions. The Magicians believed that no one should control ether; let magic be wild and free for all, they said, let the world flourish and grow from its power. The Scientists had more selfish ideas. And so the Ether Wars began. Within just a handful of decades, it was written, we reduced Urdezha to the wasteland.

My cigarette died under my boot when I saw Nel approaching. Hands deep in her coat pockets, satchel hanging from her shoulder, she walked along the path that cut through the park outside Temple University. Stepping out of the recess, I waved, and she hurried towards me, eyes nervously scanning the area for anyone watching. Attired more for going out than breaking in, Nel's hair was tied into a neat bun, and her make-up failed to hide the disdain on her face.

'You look nice,' I said.

'Don't be a smart arse, Wendal.' She pulled from her satchel a small case containing her lock picks. 'I'd really like to be somewhere else, so what do you need?'

I pointed at the side gate.

With a grumble, Nel shoved past me and inspected the gate's lock. She wore a musky scent.

'I take it you're still planning to see Mutley tonight?'

'Uh-huh. And I don't want to be late, so let me concentrate.'

I kept watch while she worked.

In the army, Nel had been an engineer. She could fix almost anything, arm or disarm the most complicated of traps, and her understanding of magic was sufficient enough to concoct the nasty devices which had got us both out of one or two scrapes since we'd met each other, after I came back from the wasteland. Plus, she had a talent for getting into places that people didn't want her getting into. After the war, Nel could've worked in a technology division for the Scientists, but that would have meant applying herself to something. It amused me to see her picking a lock while dressed so smartly.

'Got it,' Nel said. The lock clicked and the gate opened a crack with a small groan of unoiled hinges. 'Be lucky, Wendal. I'll see you later.'

'You're not finished yet.'

She glared at me.

'Just two more locks, Nel. Promise. I think.'

'If I end up spending the night in a cell, I'll never forgive you, Wendal.'

'Oh, I'm sorry. Am I putting you out?'

'Just show me the fucking locks.'

I led the way, creeping through the darkness of the gardens beyond the gate, heading towards the main entrance.

I'd visited the university earlier in the day, to get the lay of the land. The library in the west tower was open to the public and had been filled by all those *living* people with whom Abdon Klyne supposedly didn't like to mingle. At the end of the day, the university's main entrance and the door to the library inside were locked for the night.

The main doors opened as we approached and we ducked into the cover of a statue's huge square plinth. A night guard stepped out carrying a lantern in one hand and a baton in the other. He put the lantern down and locked the door. We waited for him to head off on a patrol of the grounds, and when his light disappeared around the side of the impressive university building, Nel released a breath and said, 'I swear you're doing this just to piss me off.'

'Come on.'

Leaving cover, we approached the building. I checked through the window to ensure the security desk inside wasn't manned by a second guard. 'I reckon we have less than an hour before he comes back.'

Nel once again applied her skill and made short work of the lock, relocking the door once we were inside.

The reception area smelled dusty and old, dimly lit by a few candles burning in wall-mounted sconces behind the desk. Enough light for someone to read by, but not enough to lift the surrounding gloom.

Nel stuck close to me. 'I don't like the dark, Wendal.'

I took a candle from one of the sconces and, protecting its flame with my hand, led the way further into the university.

The hallways were flanked by closed doors to lecture rooms, the staircases wide and solid underfoot. Nel held on to the back of my jacket, and the shielded flame cut through the darkness with weak, sputtering light as we made our way to the west tower library.

The university was, of course, funded by the Scientists. I supposed that made it dangerous territory for me, and not just because I had broken in. Dyonne had set me off down this path, so I had no choice but to walk it, even if she and the old woman had sent me into the lair of the Magicians' age-old enemy.

'What was that?' Nel whispered sharply.

She was jumping at every creak and groan the old building made. It was no laughing matter; Nel was terrified of the dark. That was how we met.

Not long after I'd started working for Dyonne, Nel moved into the lodgings above mine. She'd knocked on my door one night, asking if I had any spare candles. The clouds had been thick and black over Old Castle, blocking the light of the ether-filled sky, and the city was unnervingly dark. There weren't many ether lamps on the streets or in buildings, and certainly not in the old western part of the city where we lived. Nel obviously needed company, was scared of facing the darkness beyond the flame of a candle by herself.

I wasn't particularly sociable now, but I was even less so back then; I had been struggling to adapt in a strange and dangerous new life and just wanted Nel to go away, ignore me like the rest of my neighbours. Then she did something amazing. She made me laugh. As nervous and frightened of the dark as she was, she relaxed enough to joke, and I realised that *I* had made her feel safe. Which made me feel good about myself for the first time since returning from the war, and so I started talking. I opened up to Nel and told her about Eden, about my search for her spirit. And she *listened*. We talked and talked until the clouds cleared and the sun rose.

Nel had never known my wife, but she understood, without judgement, my drive and desire to find her. She helped me reconnect with the living, and from that dark night onwards we had been firm friends.

'You're such an arsehole, Wendal. Why do I let you drag me into shit like this?'

'Because you'd be homeless without me.' Conversation, I decided, was the best way to calm her nerves. 'So tell me, has the Sharpened Card reopened yet?'

'Yep – the day after you were there. The place is heaving. Packed every night so far.'

'With criminals?'

'Citizens, too, you judgemental bastard. Even seen a few Magicians there.'

I came to a halt and faced her. 'No one good comes from Reaper Town, Nel.'

'No? You should meet the strange fucker who lives below me.' She stopped looking for monsters in the shadows. 'What's your problem, Wendal?'

'You do remember how you met Mutley, right? We killed someone for her.'

Nel looked ready to punch me. 'I don't need another lecture. Let it go or I'm leaving.'

Irritation was better than fear, I supposed.

It wasn't long before we reached the stairs that spiralled up around the inside of the west tower's fat body, and we began the arduous climb to the library. We passed closed doors. Nel complained about the number of steps, and complained a lot. At the top, we came to the double doors of the library itself.

'Give me some light,' Nel said.

I moved the candle closer to the door as she inspected the lock.

I frowned as something Nel had said sank in. 'Did you say you've seen Magicians at the Sharpened Card?'

'I did.'

Gambling, openly visiting the establishments of criminals – the Magicians were far too clandestine for that kind of thing. Nel must have been talking about novices and apprentices, lackeys, but when I asked her, she said:

'No, these seem to be full adepts. Only a couple of them, and they don't gamble, as far as I can tell. There's some shady business going on, but then' – she flashed me a sharp look – 'you probably know all about it already.'

I didn't reply. Even if I did know of anything going on between the Magicians and Reaper Town, Nel knew I wouldn't say. As it was, there was nothing I *could* say. The Magicians owned Sycamore, but his host wasn't trusted enough to be counted as one of them.

'Listen,' Nel said as she fiddled with the lock, 'I know you don't approve, but I get on well with Mutley. She makes me happy and she has the most *amazing* chemicals.'

I didn't like the sound of that. 'Chemicals?'

'Those Magicians – they're working for Mutley as apothecaries or something, and what they cook up is so much better than jenkem. *Far* too expensive for the likes of us.' She looked up with a grin. 'But my girlfriend likes to share with me. She's good like that.'

Nel returned to the lock. My brain raised a question: *Nel's girlfriend is from Reaper Town, owns a gambling house, and she's employing Magicians to manufacture chemicals?* I searched the question but could find nothing in it that had a good answer.

I didn't air my concerns, however, as the lock clicked and the doors opened. Nel moved aside and I took a peek into the library.

Books. Lots of books, crammed into shelves and cases that rose from floor to ceiling on every wall, where ladders led up to three tiers of balconies. The glow of the night sky spilled in through a huge skylight, pale and eerie, shining down onto a host of reading tables. At one table, a man sat by himself.

I ducked out and turned to Nel. 'Can you see anyone in there?'

She gave me a troubled frown before peeking for herself. 'No. Can you?'

I looked again. Ghosts only appeared if they wanted me to see them. With a curt gesture, the man at the reading table ordered me into the library.

'What can you see, Wendal?' Nel staved off my answer by waving a hand in the air. 'Actually, after last time, I don't want to know. Just … go and do your thing. I'm off.'

'One more favour before you leave.'

She stared at me.

'Please, Nel. I can't get out without you, and I don't know how long this will take. I need you to keep watch for the guard.' She snatched the candle from me, spilling wax. 'Wait here. I'll be as quick as I can.'

Chapter Nineteen

'What's your name?'

I made my way to the reading desk at a cautious pace, my question echoing around the library. The man watched me shrewdly.

'Do I look like a ghoul to you?' he said.

He didn't. Anyone who saw him would swear he was alive – not that many people *could* see him. But if the dead didn't remember their names, trouble followed, and I'd been caught out before.

I stopped ten feet from him. 'Tell me your name.'

'Abdon Klyne. Good enough?' The ghost jabbed a meaty finger at the chair on the opposite side of the desk to him. 'Stick your arse on that seat.'

I looked back at the open library door. The glow from the candle shone through it, but Nel remained outside, keeping watch. A familiar feeling rose in me and I did my best to push it down. How many times had I been in a situation like this, hoping that someone – *anyone* – would lead me to Eden?

'You're still standing, Sycamore.' Klyne's voice had no echo.

'My name is Wendal,' I said, sitting down.

He chuckled. 'Yeah, I know.'

Klyne had the appearance of someone who had seen far too

much of the wasteland. His skin was tanned, weather-beaten, leathery from years of exposure. The haunted and scarred look in his eyes carried a lifetime of hardship. With short hair, silver and thinning, Klyne had reached a ripe old age when he died, somewhere close to sixty, yet he was thickset and strong, carrying a challenging, no-nonsense manner. And he was sizing me up.

'What did you do in the war, Wendal?'

I shrugged. 'Does it matter?'

'Does to me. I can tell a lot about a person by their look, and you have the look of someone who was more than your average grunt, even if you do need some meat on your bones. What did you do?'

'I was a tank-rider.'

'Knew it!' Klyne grinned broadly. 'There's strength in your step, good coordination – and you must have a quick mind if you wore a tank-suit. They don't hand you an ether-weapon if you're stupid. You must've had specialist training before the draft, am I right?'

Actually, I hadn't. I'd worked in the factory of a reduction house before the war, making building materials from Dust. Eden had worked at a baker's. In basic training, they told me I had *natural aptitude*. But I wasn't here to recount my time as a tank-rider, or think about my life as a reduction-house worker, though it seemed far simpler and preferable now.

'I met a friend of yours,' I told Klyne. 'She said you have something to tell me.'

'If you're talking about Ing Meredith, she's not my friend,' Klyne growled. 'She's a sneaky fucker who can't decide which side of the fence she's on. Still, I shouldn't be ungrateful. Meredith's been a help to me, in her own way. She agreed to pass on a message to you, and here you are.'

The old woman – Ing Meredith, apparently – had said that

Klyne was an archaeologist in life. It was easy to see that was true, and it meant he was as tough as fuck and more than a little deranged. Certain war survivors became addicted to the wasteland. Some became career soldiers and spent their lives fighting the clansfolk. Others joined the Scientists' most select and rare band of servants: the survivalists.

They roamed the wasteland like scavengers, hunting for treasure from the past: the technologies of our ancient ancestors, secrets the Salahbeem might have left behind – any age-old marvel trampled down and buried by the aeons was priceless to the Scientists. A survivalist undertook the harshest, most isolated profession a soldier could. And the very, *very* few who lived through it returned to cities to become archaeologists, who then taught a new generation of tough and deranged soldiers the art of survivalism. They became Abdon Klyne.

'Meredith helped me to adjust to the afterlife,' Klyne said. 'She introduced me to some of my fellow ghosts. Boring lot, to be honest, but they have some interesting things to say about you.' He took stock of me again. 'They reckon you went mad after the war, and it wasn't because your wife killed herself, was it?' His eyes drifted up and away. 'Funny, though – Eden never struck me as the type for suicide.'

I glared at him across the table. 'Knew my wife, did you?'

'I did.' Klyne's eyes focused. 'We were lovers.'

It was a simple statement, and he didn't care about my re-action to it. I gave a disbelieving scoff.

In ordinary circumstances, I wouldn't have liked what I was hearing but would have found nothing surprising about it. Eden thought that her husband had died on the wasteland, and I'd already reasoned that she might have begun a new life without me, found other lovers, as much as I hated the idea. But these weren't ordinary circumstances, and in making his claim, Klyne's ghost seemed to be forgetting that I knew my wife well. There was no way she'd take a lover who was so closely affiliated to the Scientists.

'We were only together a short time,' Klyne said. 'Before I died, of course.'

'And when did you die?'

'I reckon a couple of months ago. Hard to be sure. Time doesn't really mean much now.' Klyne gave an ironic snort. 'All those years I survived on the wasteland, and then my heart decides to give out, just like *that*!' He clicked dead fingers. 'I don't believe in Aktuaht. I don't care if the Garden in the Sky has a place for me. I like Old Castle and I'm not ready to move on. Glad I met Eden before I went, though.'

'I think you're full of shit,' I said.

He fixed me with a stern look. 'And *I* think what you really want to know is when Eden and me were together. It was around four months ago, maybe, while you were away on your City Service. She came to me, here at the university. Said she wanted to learn from me.'

'*Learn* from you?' This was getting harder to believe, and I felt the presence of another dead end approaching. 'So now you're telling me she enrolled at the university to study survivalism?'

'No, there was nothing official about our arrangement. She needed access to the restricted areas of the library.' Again, the ironic snort. 'It was obvious she was up to something on the sly, but I didn't mind. It's not every day a good-looking woman like Eden is willing to screw an ugly old bastard like me. Didn't take much to sweeten me up. But I think she was lonely, Wendal. She talked about you sometimes. She thought you'd died in the war—'

'I don't need to know.'

'Oh, but you do.' Klyne clenched his teeth. 'I can tell that you don't want to believe me, and I'm getting tired of it. If the wedding rings story wasn't enough to convince you, then ask me something – anything I could only know if I'd been close to Eden, and then maybe we can stop fucking about.'

I stared, tight-lipped.

'All right,' said Klyne. 'What about the birthmark on the inside of her thigh? Who knows about that besides you? Certainly not her father – she never even met the man. As for her mother, she didn't want Eden marrying you in the first place—'

'Stop!' My tone was harsh, jealous.

'I'll stop when you start listening.'

With a calming breath, I told myself to accept what I was being told. Because that was the thing about the dead: they didn't talk to the living unless they wanted to, and they didn't share the same perspective as us. All sin and guilt and heartache left them – unless they came back as a ghoul, full of rage and out for vengeance. Ghosts, on the other hand, were free and had no use for lying. Only the truth remained to them, and the purity of their honesty could cut to the bone. If Klyne said that he and Eden had been lovers, then it was true.

'Are you ready now, Wendal?' There was no mockery or un-kindness on Klyne's face. 'Because my patience is thin at best.'

I had to be careful. I'd experienced first hand the intolerance of the type of person who chose the life of a survivalist. I'd met one, during my last days in the war. August Jakob had been her name. Cruelly pragmatic, she had given me no reason to remember her fondly. With Klyne, there was nothing his ghost could do to me physically, but he could disappear if I pissed him off too much. I reminded myself that this situation was a good thing. For the first time since all this started, I was apparently talking to someone who genuinely knew the Eden I had hardly known: the woman who had survived the war and ended her own life. It was a reason to hope, but still …

'Eden hated the Scientists and anyone who worked for them,' I said with a sigh. 'Why would she come here?'

'For one, I don't consider myself a Scientist. Or a Magician. I'm not interested in their games. Two, there's a bit of story here, Wendal.'

Klyne's expression changed, not so much softening but more with satisfaction that I would no longer fence with his words. 'Your wife was curious about the treasures of the wasteland. She was particularly interested in any recent discoveries the survivalists might have made – asked if I'd heard of anything big being found.'

The library creaked and I looked at the doorway. Candlelight filled it, but Nel didn't appear with any warnings. 'What did you tell her?'

'That there are hundreds of cities on Urdezha. Only the Scientists know what's been found on the other side of the world. But nothing in Old Castle, not to my knowledge. Didn't stop Eden trying to find out, though.'

'Why?' I said, confused, quickly adding, 'I mean – why was she interested in this stuff?'

'I assumed she was working for the Magicians. Spying on the Scientists.' Klyne shrugged. 'I never asked. I didn't care.'

I did. Had Eden become a Magician's spy?

'She came here at night,' Klyne continued. 'She read through the most recent survivalists' reports, listened to information nodes, watched recorded transmissions – anything concerning discoveries – and I explained whatever she didn't understand.' He winked at me. 'She could even persuade me to give her access to the most classified records in the university.'

I waved the comment away. 'Did she find what she was looking for?'

'I think so. Maybe. She never said, but ...' Klyne looked uncertain. 'I met her here every night for two weeks, more or less. Then one day she didn't show up, and I never saw her again. I didn't even know she had killed herself until recently, when I started talking to the ghosts Meredith introduced to me. They told me about this man they're all frightened of, you see – a man who gives justice to ghouls.' He paused at that, intrigue flaring in his old, dead eyes. 'What did you see on the wasteland, Wendal? What does *Sycamore* mean? We ghosts don't know, and no one wants to talk to ghouls. Except you.'

'Let's stick with why I'm here,' I said. 'What else could your *friends* tell you?'

'They said you struck some kind of bargain with the Magicians. You'd be their assassin if they helped you find a way to bring your dead wife back from heaven. And when they told me the wife's name was Eden Finn – well, alarm bells went off. I'm not a big believer in coincidence, Wendal. I hadn't given much thought to what Eden had been looking for, but when I heard that she hadn't come back because she'd killed herself, something didn't add up and I got interested.

'It was pointless trying to go through all the reports and nodes that Eden did – she accessed so many of the bloody things, I didn't know where to begin – so I kept my ear to ground, listened in on lectures and the students in the library, eavesdropped on private meetings between professors and visiting Scientists. You'd be surprised by what people talk about behind closed doors, when they think no one's listening. I heard a rumour, Wendal. Something *was* found on the wasteland, and it's in Old Castle.'

I leaned in. 'What?'

'No one seems to know. The people I heard talking about it are as curious as you and me. They know the artefact exists, that it has been here for a while, but not what it is.'

The library, for all its spaciousness, suddenly felt cramped and confined. 'But you think it's the same thing Eden was looking for?'

'All I have are suspicions, but my gut tells me it fits. And listening to my gut kept me alive longer than most citizens. This discovery – I can tell you that it hasn't been made known to some pretty high-ranking Scientists, and that means the Directors of the Quantum are keeping it under wraps. If that's true, you can bet your life that it's something important and dangerous.'

The Directors of the Quantum, the inner circle of the Scientists and the Salem's counterpart.

'When Eden didn't come back, I put her from my mind,' Klyne continued. 'But when I heard about this mystery and reckoned it had to be the thing she was looking for, I knew I was right about her. She was spying on the Scientists, and that means ...'

He paused to let me put the pieces together.

'The Magicians know about the artefact, too?'

'If that's the case, then there's a war going on between the Quantum and the Salem over it. A war in the shadows, hidden from the rest of us.' Klyne aimed a finger at me. 'And you might be standing in the middle of it.'

Again, I wondered how little I knew the Eden who had survived the war. In my jacket pocket, my journal itched to be updated. 'The old woman,' I said. 'Meredith – she told me the Scientists are experimenting with the dead. Is that what they use this thing for?'

'Not directly, I don't think.' Klyne leaned forwards, tapping the desk with a finger. 'See all those ghouls who come looking for you? Are you *really* so sure you're giving them the peace that you think you are?'

'Pardon me?'

Klyne leaned back. 'My friends don't know what the Quantum has got its hands on, either, but they tell me that the dead are in real trouble. Not me and them – we don't want to leave, anyway – but for those seeking the other side?' Klyne gazed around the library, as if contemplating all the wisdom and knowledge that we, as a race, refused to learn from. 'The Scientists are playing with their new toy, Wendal, and it's stopping the dead leaving Old Castle. You could say their experiments have closed the door to heaven.'

My mind froze. 'What?'

'I don't know how, and I don't care why, but this is important to you because the dead don't lie. My friends have no idea how long the Scientists have had this artefact. So, what if it *is* the thing Eden was looking for? What if these experiments have been going on since before she killed herself? Maybe Eden can't leave, either? You might need to narrow your search to the streets of Old Castle.'

My mind unfroze and raced.

Klyne's eyes narrowed and he leaned to one side to better see something behind me. 'Is she with you?'

Nel had entered the library. Swearing under her breath, she closed the doors behind her quickly but quietly.

'The guard's back,' she said, using her tools to lock the doors. 'He's coming up the stairs.'

Amused by Nel's panic as she hurried towards me with the candle, eyes searching the library for hiding places, Klyne looked particularly interested by the way her free hand was thrust into her satchel, like he knew she was rummaging for a device or weapon.

'Let me guess,' Klyne said to me. 'She's an engineer. Crazy fuckers. Excellent survivalists, though. Not as good as tank-riders, mind, but—'

'Wendal,' Nel hissed, oblivious to the ghost with me, unnerved that I was still sitting in the chair. 'We need to find another way out.'

I looked to Klyne.

'Come on.' The ghost chuckled. 'I'll take you out the back way before she does some damage.' He rose and beckoned me to follow him. 'You'll have to visit again one day, Wendal. I'd love to know what you saw on the wasteland.'

Chapter Twenty

Eden and I had been friends long before we became lovers. We met at school, and it was our shared tragedy that drew us together. We had both lost our fathers to the wasteland. Eden's parents married young, as we did, and her father hadn't survived his City Service. He died in the war before she was born. My father had been a career soldier. To my memory, I only saw him a handful of times before he stopped coming home.

My mother had been older than my father, and she birthed a child late. She died of old age just before I left school. Eden's mother was still around, somewhere in Old Castle, but she had never liked me. For some reason, she got it into her head that I was to blame for her daughter walking away from the life of a *good* citizen and following the Magicians' way. She never forgave Eden for marrying me. The night before our wedding, she had tried one last time to talk 'sense' into Eden. It hadn't gone well, and as far as I knew, that was the last time mother and daughter had seen each other.

But *I* had caught a glimpse of her, weeks ago now, sitting in the carriage of an under-rail train. Our eyes met through the window, but she hadn't recognised me and looked away as the train pulled out of the station. I wondered how much regret had surfaced within her grief upon hearing of her daughter's suicide.

Up until today, I had believed that no one on Urdezha knew Eden as well as I did. I used to tell myself that I was the only person who could've stopped her doing what she did. But now I wondered, if I had returned from the war undamaged, if Eden hadn't killed herself, would I have known my wife at all? Would she have even wanted me to come home? The time period that Klyne was talking about ... it must've meant that he had been Eden's lover just after she found out I was missing in action. So soon? It wasn't easy to admit, but I couldn't shrug off a nagging feeling that on the day I went to war, Eden had let me go for good and begun a new life which had led her to a bad place.

The image of my wife and Abdon Klyne sharing intimate moments wouldn't leave my head, and I didn't talk after we sneaked out of Temple University. The meeting with the ghost had left me distracted with thoughts aflame and refusing to keep still. I walked with Nel, heading for Scholar Station, but halfway there, she stopped, concerned by my brooding introspection.

'What's going on, Wendal?' She laid a hand on my arm. 'What happened in there?'

'I ... I'm not sure.' I rubbed my forehead. 'You should go. I need to think.'

'All right.' Nel smiled. She knew when it was better to leave me alone. 'Come and see me if you want to talk.'

I nodded, thanked her for her help and left her to catch the under-rail to Reaper Town.

I decided to walk the rest of the way home. The wind had picked up, carrying an icy chill, blowing dust into my eyes. There was a faint metallic taste to the air. From the north, dark clouds were moving in, slowly swallowing up the light of the ether crystals in the sky. They illuminated the distance with streaks of orange lightning. I didn't want to think about whether this storm was coming from Alexria.

Reasoning that it would probably alter course before it reached Old Castle, anyway, I continued on, head down, oblivious to any citizens out as late as me. Klyne's story ran over and over in my mind. *The dead don't lie* ... I wished that wasn't true. My thoughts refused to slow down. What had Eden been looking for?

There were a lot of schools in Old Castle, and all citizens received a free education before their City Service came up. But only a select few of those who returned from the war were given a university education – funded by the Scientists, of course, who cherry-picked the most patriotic candidates from the survivors. I didn't suppose they would have ever picked me, but Eden was everything they looked for – intelligent, curious, practical, academic – but she had chosen the Magicians' way not the Scientists': two philosophies that opposed each other fundamentally, especially on the application of magic.

For the Scientists, magic was a source of energy that fuelled wondrous inventions, machines and technologies. It powered the reduction houses, magical forges that reduced all waste matter to Dust. Dust was the miracle creation without which we couldn't survive. It could become anything: food, medicine, building materials, cloth – whatever we needed. The Scientists ruled the cities of Urdezha with the power of magic and the promise of life.

The Magicians, however, celebrated magic purely for its existence. It was Urdezha's blood, a gift, and it wasn't meant to be broken and enslaved to fuel perverted creations. Natural, free and wild – magic was a force to be accepted, thanked, and only the most adept could beg its favour. The irony of this belief was that Magicians held to it while dwelling under the protection of the Scientists. Without the cities, they would stand as little chance as anyone else on the wasteland, where monsters roamed and the clansfolk reviled cities as evil hives spawning demons who rose against them time and time again. But these ironies and differences had been born aeons ago, diluted over millennia, becoming vague traditions for today.

The stigma of the Salahbeem had laid the seeds of discontent between them. While the Magicians worshipped this mythical race as gods, the Scientists considered them a power-hungry enemy who had underestimated the human race. The Gardeners had arrived under the pretence of teaching and guiding and befriending us, but their real reason for coming to Urdezha so long ago was far different: subjugation, to make us their slaves, to rule our world – that was their true goal.

The Scientists hypothesised that the Salahbeem had probably invaded many realms and worlds under the guise of kindness and wisdom throughout their history. As for their reasons, conjectures ranged from stealing resources to the continued growth of an ever-expanding empire. No one knew the truth because it was lost to the distant past. But the Scientists claimed that, in coming to Urdezha, the Salahbeem had finally bitten off more than they could chew. We rose against them, drove them away, sent them fleeing before a superior might. The barricade of ether in the sky would seem to invalidate claims of this *might*, as would the fables and myths that were so important to the Magicians.

Friend or foe, Gardener gods or highly evolved mortals, the reality of the Salahbeem had been watered down and smeared across ten thousand years of history. Their remnants and legacies had shaped opinions of life and interpretations of death. Whether the Salahbeem remained on the periphery of our reality, controlling the other side and selecting only the worthy for their paradise, or whether they had gone for good, trapping us on Urdezha, while the other side remained as mysterious as the Scientists would have it; the most powerful legacy that the

Salahbeem's enigma had created would always be magic. In their wake, the Scientists and the Magicians had gone to war over it.

Ether was the source of all magic, all energy. In an ancient time, the Scientists had won the Ether Wars, but in defeat their enemy couldn't be crushed entirely. As long as there was ether, there would always be Magicians, no matter how many the Scientists might've liked to expel from the city. I wouldn't go as far as to say there was peace between them – perhaps more a begrudging acceptance of an equilibrium, a tradition born millennia ago. If either side retained a specific agenda against opposing philosophies, I didn't know, but it was commonly accepted that the Quantum and the Salem manoeuvred against each other in the dark. And not just in Old Castle.

Had these secret manoeuvres led my wife to Abdon Klyne?

I stopped to roll a cigarette. Not many people were out to-night. Lightning speared the distance and the wind picked up. My hands were shaking, but not from the night's chill. Why wouldn't Klyne's information sit right in my head?

Eden used to talk about her aspirations for moving up the ranks of the Magicians. Dyonne had once called her a novice, a dabbler, and that was true – but only to a point. Eden had been serious, training herself, trying to prove her worthiness to the Magicians so that they might accept her as one of them. Klyne was trying to convince me that she had achieved the first step of her aspirations.

The Scientists had made a new discovery, some secret dug up from the wasteland. Somehow it was trapping the spirits of the dead in Old Castle. If Eden had been trying to find this thing, as Klyne believed, then in all likelihood she had been doing so for the Magicians. It would mean she had been accepted, become an apprentice. It would mean that Eden had a Magician master.

I struck a match and shielded the flame from the wind as I

set it to the cigarette, resuming my walk through the cold city under ether-light. But I was no longer heading straight home. Klyne's story whirred in my mind.

I needed to talk to Dyonne; she held a high rank and could find out who Eden's master had been, or if she even had one. But the trouble with Dyonne was that she summoned me, not the other way around. There was no point trying to find her at the nameless tavern until she was ready to see me again. So, I returned to the Garden near Public Square instead. The old woman called Ing Meredith had said she was going to investigate further, and I hoped to find her in the Garden with fresh information. But all that greeted me was hollow wind in the empty night-time. Somewhat desperate to find out more, I went home to pursue the last and most tenuous source currently available to me.

Chapter Twenty-One

The first signs of dawn were tinting the gloom outside my window when I arrived at my lodgings after nearly two hours of walking. I sat at my table, drumming my fingers upon its hard surface – wood created from Dust – and stared at the words of magic on the wall beside the door.

The Scientists had found something important and dangerous, Klyne had said. Could this thing be bad enough to convince Eden to kill herself? Her spirit couldn't be among those trapped in Old Castle. She would have come to me by now. Wouldn't she?

My eyes drifted up to the corner of the room. 'Wake up,' I said. 'I want to talk to you.'

The magical words glowed briefly. Above them, a ghoul materialised like a dark cobweb, with oily, wet movements. It coalesced into the shape of a person: an adult female but the size of an infant. Her knees were drawn to her chest, arms wrapped around her shins like the mummified corpses that were some-times found on the wasteland. Lastly, her gaunt, haunted face appeared, chin resting on her knees. She looked very pleased to see me.

'Is it here?' Her voice oozed like slime. 'Has the day come?'

'No,' I said.

Her face crinkled like paper. 'Then when, Sycamore?'

'Soon,' I lied softly, quickly, heading off a bout of weeping. When ghouls cried, the sound could shatter your eardrums and their tears were thick and popped with the reek of the wasteland's foulest quagmires. 'I need to ask you something—'

I stopped, sighing, as the ghoul's grey gaze drifted up and into some faraway place, unfocused, unhinged, no longer in the moment. 'I dreamed of the wasteland again. I saw such majesty.'

'I need your help.'

'I need yours.'

'Concentrate, Itch.'

'No. Give me peace.'

I began to regret waking her up.

Itch – *Itch You Can't Scratch* – my unaffectionate moniker for the ghoul I couldn't get rid of. She had appeared in my life near the beginning of all this, but she was no client given to me by Dyonne. Somehow, Itch had slipped through the Salem's filter and found me on her own. Dyonne couldn't explain how she had managed to reach me, but Itch wasn't going anywhere until she had claimed justice through Sycamore. And therein lay the problem.

Itch couldn't remember how or why she had been murdered, or who her murderer was. She couldn't recall her moment of death, had no Song to sing, and this was *very* bad for me because it meant she couldn't tell me her name. A name was the key to invoking Sycamore. Only upon hearing it would the spirit of vengeance rise to take me over. No name, no Sycamore, but that didn't matter to Itch. She was haunting me nonetheless, and she wasn't likely to stop any time soon.

Sycamore had explained in a jenkem dream that Itch's lack of memory meant one of two things: her murderer was either already dead or in a place even he couldn't reach – maybe the maximum-security gaol in the north, or out serving a tour of duty on the wasteland – and there was nothing he could do until they were roaming free in the city again.

Dyonne could do little about Itch, either. She said that the ghoul was a force of un-nature that she didn't understand, an anomaly. If Dyonne tried to get rid of her, her ghoul would simply pop up again, wild and desperate and angry, always returning to me, but never remembering her name. We were stuck with each other. So Dyonne did the only thing she could: cast the spells which confined Itch to my lodgings and kept her mostly quiet. There she would remain, haunting me, until her murderer was found and she remembered who she was and how she died. *That* was the day we were both waiting for. I hated how I'd grown so used to her in my life.

'You'll find peace soon enough,' I said, praying that it was true. 'Will you answer some questions for me?'

'I wish my dreams remembered,' Itch said, further musing, 'I would really like to know *why*.'

She drifted off again. The almost pleasurable look on her face made me feel miserable. It wasn't really me she saw sitting there, wasn't me she was talking to. It was Sycamore.

'Itch!' I shouted. Her eyes gained focus with an angry shade of orange. 'Was the injustice of your death the only reason you didn't go the other side?'

'What other reason do I need?' Itch growled. 'Some fucker killed me and I want my justice!'

'And you'll get it.' I raised my hands in placation. 'But tell me – could you leave if you wanted to?'

'You're not making sense, Sycamore.' Itch liquefied into a wet swirl of rage before re-forming into a mummified corpse. 'Why would I leave without vengeance?'

I would never wish Sycamore upon myself, but this ghoul's

fury had a whole lot of insanity poured on top of it, and I dearly longed to give her what she needed. Dyonne's spells stopped Itch following me around and incessantly whispering and crying into my ear. They couldn't, however, stop her thoughts swinging between confused ramblings and obsessively focusing on her murder. Such was the way of ghouls.

I leaned forwards, hoping to encourage a moment of co-herence from her. 'Let me change the question – when the time comes, do you know *how* to leave? Do you know the way to the other side?'

Itch nodded, dislodging thick, filthy tears. 'Through you, of course.'

'No, that's not what I mean.'

'Doesn't make it less true.'

'Itch, I've heard a rumour that the door to heaven is closed. Do you know anything about it?'

'Fuck heaven!' Fiery orange returned to the ghoul's eyes. 'You'll do right by me, won't you, Sycamore?'

I pinched the bridge of my nose. 'Listen to me—'

'Promise you'll make my killer hurt and squeal and beg for life.'

'Go back to sleep.'

'Sycamore—'

I slammed my hand on the table. 'Sleep!'

The spells flared. Creaking like old, dry rope pulling taut, Itch collapsed into herself and disappeared, leaving behind a vague smell of the wasteland that no soldier could ever forget.

I groaned, rubbing my face. It had been worth a try.

I knew that sleep wouldn't come. I considered lighting some jenkem but remembered that Lana Khem had used my last cake, so I remained at the table and updated my journal with the details of this strange night. By the time I'd finished, hand aching from writing furiously, eyes bleary from tiredness, I was left with questions, the answers to which my mind burned to know. Could my wife's spirit really be trapped in Old Castle? What had the Scientists found? Had Eden become a Magician's apprentice?

Collecting all of Eden's journals from the bookshelf, I lay on the bed, reading through them, trying to find clues, anything I might have missed, but there was nothing of use. Maddeningly, Eden's entries stopped a few weeks before her suicide, at the point when her life had apparently changed. I lay there and thought and thought and thought, until ...

I hadn't meant to fall asleep, but a knock at the door startled me awake. At first, I thought it must be Nel, home by dawn from her night with Mutley; but when it came again, the three hard thumps gave me a cold feeling.

I opened the door, already knowing that I'd see Tamara's huge frame filling the doorway.

'What do you want?' I demanded.

Glowering, without a word, Tamara held out a folded piece of paper between the index and middle fingers of the hand missing a thumb. He strode away the moment I snatched it from him.

I stared at the piece of paper, not wanting to unfold it, but I did, eventually, reading a note from Dyonne. She had written down a set of directions. To Sycamore's next client.

Chapter Twenty-Two

The day was going to end in guilt and misery, so my first stop was to acquire a salve to ease the pain.

Near my lodging house, down a side lane called Fox Way, there was a humble tobacconist's, a small shop run by a simple man whose amiability hid a shifty side to his business. I was the only customer when I entered, a bell jingling to announce my arrival. The shopkeeper stood behind the counter. The shelves behind him were stacked with jars of cut leaf, paper packets of cheroots and boxes of cigars. Tobacco was the cheapest natural produce in Old Castle, affordable to all, but I wasn't there just to refill my pouch.

The shopkeeper frowned towards the door as though struggling to see who had entered. Which he was; Dyonne had seen to that. Outside of a very small circle of friends, I practically had to wave my hands in front of people's faces before they noticed me. Such was the nature of my position.

'Good morning,' I said loudly, approaching the counter. The shopkeeper's frown turned into an easy smile as his eyes were finally able to focus on me. 'A quarter of rum leaf, please.'

'Certainly.' The shopkeeper pulled down a jar from the shelf and began filling the leather pouch I gave him with dark tobacco using a set of silver tongs. 'That'll be one bit, sir.'

As he put the jar back on the shelf, I placed a single bit next to the filled pouch, followed by a ten-bit coin. 'I'm also looking for something a little more medicinal.'

'Medicinal, sir?' The shopkeeper looked at the money before giving my face a long study. 'Have you tried the apothecary's?'

'They couldn't help.' I came to this shop at least once a week but the shopkeeper struggled to remember me, so we had to go through this routine time and time again. 'They don't prescribe anything for bad dreams.'

'Ah, having trouble sleeping, are you, sir?'

'The war does that to survivors.'

'Indeed it does.'

'I was told that you can suggest an alternative remedy.'

'Told by who, sir?'

'Someone who knows I'm discreet.'

'Hmm, let's see.' Some part of him must have remembered me because his smile returned as he decided that I had a trustworthy face, like he always did. 'Maybe you could try my method, sir. Sends me right to sleep, it does.' His eyes dropped to the ten-bit coin. 'Two cakes, is it?'

I nodded. He scooped up the money and disappeared out back, returning a few moments later with a small package wrapped up in brown waxed paper. The manufacture of jenkem was technically illegal, but I'd never known anyone who had been arrested for using or selling it. As long as you could keep your mouth shut, a lot of blind eyes were turned in Old Castle.

Thanking the shopkeeper, I slipped the jenkem cakes into my jacket pocket along with my pouch of tobacco, left the shop and caught the under-rail at Tinman Station.

The instructions on Dyonne's note were sending me to Keep Town, which was situated on the central edge of the city's south side, not far away from the Fusion. The carriage was warm and smelled of hot bodies, but it wasn't too packed. Unnoticed by other passengers, I staggered down the carriage and managed to find an empty two-seat bench between a woman dozing with her head against the window and a married couple with a young son sitting on his father's lap.

The journey from Tinman District to Keep Town was less than ten minutes but it felt like an eternity lay ahead of me. I tried not to think about the immediate future, but a familiar nausea churned my gut all the same. Ing Meredith and Abdon Klyne would have to wait. Very soon, I wouldn't be in control of my own body. On the window next to me, superimposed like a ghost over the rushing darkness of the rail tunnel outside, someone had scratched the words *Fuck the Scientists* into the glass. Personally, I'd have swapped the last word for *Magicians*, but each to his own.

I'd never describe myself as privileged, but very few people ever got to meet a Grand Adept of the Salem, not even the bulk of Magicians following their edicts. I didn't suppose I'd get the chance to meet with Mr Sebastian again, and certainly not with the other four Grand Adepts in Old Castle, or learn their names. And if I did, it wouldn't be for any good reason. But however secretive the Salem were, the Directors of the Quantum were more so. The chief Scientists – their names, identities and number were known only to a select few of their highest-ranking lackeys, and if I had ever seen a Director on the street, I certainly didn't know it.

Magicians, with their simple gowns and shifty mannerisms, were easy enough to spot. Scientists, on the other hand, looked like regular citizens, surrounded by the bulk of Old Castle's population which went about life accepting the Scientists' rule. Were the Directors of the Quantum the same? Did they look like me, *us*? There was a rumour that, like the Grand Adepts of the Salem, the Directors had found a way to give themselves unnaturally long life. So maybe they had grotesquely mutated over centuries and pulled the city's strings while hiding in dark and secret places, barely human now. The truth was known to but a few, and all citizens accepted that the Quantum knew everything that went on in their city; that they saw all.

But was that true?

Sycamore often wondered why the Quantum of Old Castle hadn't come looking for him. Once, he said, '*They must know I am in their city and who is my host.*' Perhaps they couldn't see everything. Perhaps they could and didn't care. As long as they left me alone, I chose not to think about it. Dyonne Obor already gave me enough to deal with.

As the train approached Keep Town Station, it came to a standstill and the lights in the carriage blinked before switching off. The moment of darkness lasted long enough for worried murmurs to arise from the other passengers. The child in front of me whimpered and his mother soothed him. When the lights flickered back on, many in the carriage shared suspicious glances, but no one said anything as the train trundled into the station.

A portly platform supervisor opened the carriage door and announced, 'Last stop! Everybody out.' He was flustered, eyes full of concern. He dampened the few groans of complaint by explaining, 'By order of the Scientists,' which meant that this disruption wasn't due to train malfunction or a problem on the line. Ether power to the under-rail was being cut, reserved for the city's defences. It meant something bad was coming from the wasteland.

Feeling detached from my fellow travellers, I followed the horde off the train and up the wide stone steps that led out of the station. There was some consternation on the streets. Cold rain was falling. The wind had picked up and the rusty taste in the air was more pronounced. Citizens walked hurriedly to be out of the rain, while others clustered beneath shop awnings, pointing at the darkening sky.

The storm which had apparently resulted from the explosion at Alexria hadn't altered course or dissipated, and it was much closer to Old Castle than when I left the Tinman District. A roiling black, streaked by orange lightning, was coming fast out of the wasteland, blocking the sun and shading the late morning with twilight, swirling towards the city.

I reassured myself that if the storm really was that big a threat, then the city shield would have activated by now and the siren would be blaring. The Scientists had reserved Old Castle's ether power as a precaution, nothing more. Had to be. Still, it was hard to ignore the doomsayer talk coming from the groups of people I passed as I followed Dyonne's directions through the rain. I was sopping wet and miserable by the time I reached a deserted back alley.

Shaking water from my hands, I approached the rear door of a bathhouse at a cautious pace. The door didn't lead to a typical kind of bathhouse and it wasn't a public amenity; it also provided masseurs and steam rooms and a private lounge, all for the price of an expensive membership fee. Sycamore's client was waiting for me outside.

I could smell the ghoul – that unmistakable stink of the wasteland – before I saw its darkness slithering under the doorstep, and I kept my distance. You never rushed into these situations – Itch You Can't Scratch had taught me that much. I steeled myself.

'I can see you.' My throat was dry in the rain. 'Tell me your name?'

The darkness oozed from under the step as an oily puddle before rising up to form its shape in the alley. I could never guess how a ghoul would appear to me. Sometimes they remained as puddles; other times they took on monstrous forms. This one appeared as she must have in life. A woman wearing drab ragtag clothes, her colours washed out to dreary monochrome. She was younger than me, too young to have seen the war. The sadness on her face was matched by the anger in her glistening eyes.

'I've been looking for you.' Her voice rustled and crunched like sun-baked dirt under army boots. Sycamore stirred inside me, preparing. 'My name is Miranda Nhils.'

The ritual of invocation immediately overpowered me with a harsh fatigue that dragged my consciousness down into my being. It felt like drowning only to discover that you could breathe underwater. A sensation of slow falling, drifting into a place where my eyes couldn't see the light any more, where Old Castle faded away and there was no air with which I could speak a single word. But I could hear *him*, sighing as he rose to take control of my body. And with my voice, Sycamore said, '*Sing me your Song, Miranda Nhils. Show me how you died.*'

Chapter Twenty-Three

The dead called me Sycamore. If I ever went by another name, it was now lost to an ancient time.

The human race existed in the shadow of a glory that might have been, clinging to a stilted era in which none of them lived for very long. Unless they were *altered*. Unless they were a Grand Adept of the Salem. There was no higher rank among the Magicians, but it could only be attained by achieving the improbable, the seemingly impossible. If a Magician were ambitious, cunning, *lucky* enough to kill a Grand Adept, then his reward would be a position in the Salem itself, a rite of passage that would not, *could* not, be denied by tradition. This was the Lore of Ascension, but the current crop of Grand Adepts were too wise, too aware and paranoid ever to let it come to pass.

The Song of Always – by creating their moments of death, claiming them, hiding them, the monsters of the Salem had ensured themselves unnatural long life and no other method by which they could die. Who knew what form these *moments* took? Perhaps, like Wendal Finn's, a bullet from a long-forgotten weapon was the tradition. Whatever. A Magician seeking to invoke the Lore of Ascension would have to find the one and only thing that could kill a particular Grand Adept, and this was why invokers were rare; if caught, what I could only imagine would be excruciating death awaited, and the Salem were very good at smelling rats.

This was why no one had ascended to the Salem in centuries, not in Old Castle or probably any city on Urdezha. Was a similar rite endorsed by the Directors of the Quantum? I believed so. They and their counterparts were the keepers of stagnation and almost impossible to depose. But I could do it ...

One day, I would be free of the damned flesh prison of Wendal Finn, and I would bring the ruling castes of this city to their knees. The road to leadership was paved with blood and murder, and the dead were no allies to those who ruled. With freedom, I would again hear the Songs sung by the ghouls of so many victims. I would find them, and they would lead me to the places where these moments of death had been hidden. The Salem believed they had protected themselves, prepared rites and spells that would banish me from Urdezha should I escape, but they were playing a dangerous game by holding me prisoner. Given my way, the Grand Adepts, Dyonne Obor, the Magicians, the Quantum and the Scientists, every rotting soul in this city ... I'd kill them all.

For now, I would keep my patience and make do with one human at a time.

The ghoul of Miranda Nhils stood beside me in the bathhouse, a bedraggled young woman straddling the grey line between the land of the living and ... somewhere else. Shrouded in humid mist, the chill of vengeance kept me cool. Humans bathed communally in a large bath of steaming water, cloudy with soap and glowing faintly with the magical energy drawing heat up from the ether-growth far below Old Castle. The privileged were always the last to be inconvenienced, and power had not yet been cut to this exclusive club. The misty air smelled of flowers and cleanliness; the atmosphere trembled with impending death.

Was it Sycamore's presence people reacted to, or that of a ghoul? Perhaps it was both. Whichever the case, men and women stopped enjoying their communal bathing the moment Miranda and I entered the room. They didn't so much see us as listened to the subconscious whispers that blew upon the flames of a lower animal's instinct for flight. Conversations ceased mid-sentence, smiles died on faces, moods soured, and one by one, not quite understanding why, they left, downcast and wrapped in towels.

They hurried out, wordless and unseeing, and the ghoul beside me lusted after vengeance. Miranda and I walked on to the next bathroom.

This world! The wasteland *was* Urdezha, spattered with the last dregs of civilisation. Between the cities, across the oceans, there was nothing but desolation and monsters; and through this damnation, humans threaded a network of communication. Scientists with their arrays and transmissions, Magicians with their spells and rites – each city spread its knowledge to the next, and the next, moulding a race into a dual entity. When speaking of the Quantum or the Salem, humans spoke not of any particular chapter in any one city; they spoke of a collective. They were a hive mind of information, shared stupidity, plots and plans. The Scientists and the Magicians had risen through the silt of Urdezha like a nest of insects ruled by two queens.

The Quantum might claim to have won the Ether Wars, but in reality, they and the Salem had drawn themselves to an impasse, where the human race's extinction could only be avoided by a coalition for survival. And how miserable their drones and workers looked when my presence cleared them from the next bathroom. Miranda Nhils sighed as a man hurried through her apparition, shuddering without knowing why as he left. A woman and another man stepped around me but didn't truly see me in their hurry to escape the crawling, ominous air I had brought to this place. I pitied these people as much as I loathed them.

Most citizens plodded along without giving much thought to the fact that they were following the Scientists' way. Employment and security, clothes on their backs and food in their mouths: a day-to-day existence of maddening banality which never questioned or asked for more. The Scientists had their control, for the most part, the majority rule. What it was the Magicians wanted, I didn't think even they knew any more. Opposition because someone had to do it? Because it was important to the hive structure and social harmony? The Ether Wars had been contained but never concluded, and the only people who truly understood this were those who denied the two-queen hierarchy of the cities: the homeless.

In life, Miranda Nhils had been a dormouse. An abandoned subset of Old Castle's society which slotted into a place the Scientists didn't look and the Magicians struggled to see. Dormice dwelt beneath the noses of citizens, making homes in their homes, in the gaps between terraced buildings, in the attic space house owners didn't realise they had, in secret hollows beneath their floors – any warm place large enough to sleep in. When they weren't begging on the streets, dormice were always close to someone, hidden and silent, listening for sounds of detection with keen ears. They were perfectly placed should anyone require an informant in the ongoing feuds between the Quantum and the Salem; but trafficking information came at a price. And that was why Miranda had brought me to this bathhouse.

The ghoul and I cleared two more rooms of bathers. In each, a small transmission pyramid was fixed to one wall like a glass stud, glowing faintly through the steam. From each pyramid came the subliminal prattle of the Scientists, Dreamtime Theory drumming its lessons into the minds of *good* citizens.

'*Life is a gift to be cherished,*' the sonorous voice said. 'We *will preserve it for you.*'

With Miranda at my side, I reached the changing room at the end of the bathhouse. There I found a man, alone and hurriedly pulling clothes from a locker, trying to dress while still wet. He had heard the subconscious whispers like the other bathers, disrupting the lessons of Dreamtime Theory with innate fear; but unlike his fellow bathers, this man could see me. Because he had to.

His name was Brandon Quinn.

I knew this because Miranda Nhils had shown me what he did to her.

'*Feel proud to serve your city on the wasteland,*' the Scientists said. '*Fight with honour. Protect your lives and homes from the clansfolk.*'

Before entering the bathhouse, Miranda had sung the Song of the Dead to me and the vision of her murder had been violent and lurid. Brandon Quinn was a Scientist, much closer to the inner circle than the average lackey, working in the Fusion and living in the south of Old Castle where the houses were big and full of secret spaces. Miranda had been spying on him for the Magicians. Quinn had access to special projects that the Quantum would rather keep secret.

Quinn had discovered the Magician's spy in his house shortly after a sensitive discussion with a trusted colleague. It was supposed to have been a private conversation, in confidence, but the ears of a dormouse had been listening from her hiding place. She would had got away with it had a weak floorboard not snapped under her weight and brought Quinn to investigate before she could escape.

'*The clansfolk would take everything from us.*'

Brandon Quinn stood frozen, shirt in hand. He and I stared at each other.

'The worst part is, I'd been in his house two days and hadn't found much out.' As always happened, the ghoul had narrated the moment of her death while participating stoically in its re-enactment. The vision had come to me in the alley at the back of the bathhouse where Wendal had first found Miranda. 'The Magicians wanted to know what he was working on, but he never worked at home, left no notes, nothing. I thought I'd struck rich when that meeting came about.'

The Song had surrounded me like the memory of an alternate reality superimposed onto the alley. I had stood amidst the storage boxes and cobwebs of Quinn's attic, watching as he reached behind the water tank and pulled Miranda out by her hair.

'I didn't really understand the conversation he had with his friend,' Miranda had told me while she tussled with Quinn. 'He mentioned some kind of stone. Said it was like nothing the Scientists had found before.' She had twisted free of Quinn, backed away from him, pulling a makeshift blade from her sleeve. '*Black stone*, he called it. He and his friend were trying to figure out how to control it.'

Miranda had lunged at her attacker, slicing his arm. Quinn shouted a silent curse, slapping Miranda to the attic floor. He produced a small ether-cannon and aimed it at her.

'The Scientists are struggling to understand this stone,' Miranda had told me, staring up at me from the floor, prone before her attacker, already knowing what happened next. 'Quinn was terrified of it, and he knew I'd heard too much. This was the big secret the Magicians wanted to know more about.'

She had sprung to her feet and leapt at Quinn, smothering

the ether-cannon in his hand. One shot, one point-blank blast of magical energy, and the weapon punched a hole through Miranda's midriff, sticky and dripping. The vision of her death had culminated with Brandon Quinn realising what he had done. He had dropped to his knees, vomiting before sobbing, and the ether-cannon had rolled away from him across the attic floor ... the same ether-cannon that Quinn pulled from the locker in the changing room now.

'Stay away,' he said, bare from the waist up. He wasn't choosing fight over flight. The only way out was through me. Quinn was an animal backed into a corner.

'Give me peace, Sycamore.' Miranda, bedraggled, stinking of the wasteland, had a smile on her face. 'I want to watch him die.'

'I'm warning you.' Quinn's hand trembled as he aimed the ether-cannon at me.

And the Scientists said, *'The clansfolk are soulless savages. There is no afterlife for them. The other side reserves peace and eternity only for* good *citizens.'*

What an unfathomable race these people were. They had proof that death was not the end, that the spirit endured in an afterlife, but did they take solace from this? No. They had once achieved greatness, living for three times as long as they did now, on a paradise of a world. Yet they ruined Urdezha and themselves because they would rather be the pestilence that turned a paradise into a wasteland than accept that some secrets were not for the living to know. The heralds of their own decline, ignorance remained prevalent in their every action to this day, especially in the graceless manner with which they shied from death.

'I mean it!' Quinn shouted, but the lack of confidence in his voice ensured his words were far from intimidating.

He couldn't see Miranda but he knew she was there, deep

down in that subhuman part of his brain where the teachings of Dreamtime Theory festered. And he understood that I had come because of what he had done to her.

'*Your sins have returned to you, Brandon Quinn,*' I said. He translated my Salabese and the murderous intent in my gait as I walked towards him. '*The dead call me Sycamore. I am their Shepherd.*'

Quinn pulled the ether-cannon's trigger with a cry of despair. The slim metal tube bucked in his hand. The air displaced with a *whump* and the force of magic hit me in the chest, taking my breath away, knocking me down onto my back. My head cracked against the wet tiles. Wendal's frailty threatened to tip him into unconsciousness, but I kept him awake.

Panicked, Quinn forgot the rest of his possessions and tried to make his escape. He skidded to a halt when I sat up and shook my head at him. The ether-cannon had burned a hole in my shirt, big and circular and smouldering. The blast would hurt Wendal like mad when he regained control, but his skin and muscle and bone were unharmed.

'How?' Mouth working wordlessly, Quinn backed away as I got to my feet. 'I hit you ...'

'*This body sings the Song of Always,*' I told him. '*If only its death was yours to give, Brandon Quinn.*'

The blast had jolted Wendal into stirring inside me, not with pain but with intrigue in this story of black stone. Had it come from the wasteland? he wondered. When was it found? Was it affecting the dead? His questions came with a curiosity that managed to cut through the addiction that Miranda Nhils's lust for violence was feeding.

'*Tell me more about the black stone,*' I found myself asking Quinn. '*What is it?*'

Tears in his eyes, Quinn tried to fire the ether-cannon again, and then again, but only produced impotent clicks from the trigger. It was a small weapon, and the ether crystal inside must have been no bigger than a grain of Dust, so it would take a while to regenerate enough magic for a second shot that wouldn't stop me anyway. His attempts fuelled my anger and banished the power of Wendal's influence.

I reached Quinn and slapped the weapon from his hand while kicking his legs from under him. His cries were silenced when I pinned him to the floor with my hands wrapped around his throat.

He gave up, weeping silently as I choked him into uncon- sciousness. Wendal urged me to keep Quinn alive, question him some more on his work, but it was too late for that now. I was lost to Miranda's lust, and she laughed while I squeezed Quinn's neck until the final beat of his heart gave the ghoul the vengeance she deserved.

'Peace,' Miranda sighed.

Her ghoul had already lost its form: a monochrome woman ruined in the prime of her life melted into a puddle of darkness. It slithered towards me, stretching as it reached my feet to form my shadow, then faded to nothing. Miranda journeyed on, whether to heaven or the Scientists' plots and plans, I no longer knew.

With the voice of Dreamtime Theory droning on and on, I stepped over Quinn's corpse, picked up the ether-cannon and left the bathhouse. I heard the howl of wind before reaching the city street.

The weather had worsened, whipping up into a gale. Grit and rain swirled and flew, stinging and biting. It was somewhere around midday, but the sky was as black as starless night. Wendal Finn rose, climbing up inside me, and in that moment we shared a body, shielding our eyes, struggling to stand against the wind's ferocity. The few citizens around us were quickly deserting the streets, shouting warnings to each other and pointing at the sky. The city shield activated with a rumbling drone and the siren began to wail.

The storm from Alexria had come to Old Castle.

Chapter Twenty-Four

Old Castle's shield pushed back against the storm, but the immense pressure of this unnatural weather front squeezed moisture through the magical energy and the rain fell hard and fast. Each drop was slick, filled with ash, drenching the city in dirty slime and releasing an airborne metallic taste that burned the back of my throat. There was no thunder to accompany the flashes of orange lightning that danced and crackled over the shield. To fill the void of the sky's eerily silent voice, the siren rose and fell. Its wail commanded citizens to clear the streets and remain indoors; a discordant song that gave the few caught out in the storm extra reason to scurry for their homes.

But not me. I staggered through the streets, using the walls of buildings for support, one arm wrapped around my ribs. The aftermath of Quinn's attack felt as though a bear of the wasteland had stamped on my chest. I couldn't have hurried to be out of the storm if my life depended on it. The under-rail wasn't running, either. I had no choice but to brave the weather and make a lumbering way home.

The wind howled and whipped around me; most of our ether power must have been diverted to the shield directly above, leaving the sides of the city under the protection of the ether-cannons alone. Filthy rain saturated me, icy-cold but doing little to cool the rage of Sycamore lingering inside me, failing to drown my guilt and misery. My emotional capacity was full; I couldn't worry about the storm, what had caused it, what it might do to Old Castle. Each bright flash of silent orange only served to remind me of Brandon Quinn, how his neck had felt in my hands, how his expression had relaxed when his heart beat its last. This memory was mine, for always, collected and stored along with all the other murders Sycamore had used my body to commit.

I was guilty and innocent and helpless.

With the siren singing alongside the wind, the stinging rain and the foul-smelling filth blowing into my face, I battled my way from the south of Old Castle to my home in the west, desperately wanting to crawl into the release of jenkem-induced sleep.

The siren was still singing by the time I reached my lodgings a couple of hours later. Nel had let herself in and was waiting for me, sitting on my bed, clutching her satchel to her chest, surrounded by flickering light. Relief replaced some of the fear on her face when I entered and shut the door behind me. She had lit every candle I owned.

Nel wrinkled her nose as I shrugged off my dripping coat and hung it up. 'You stink, Wendal.'

'The whole city stinks.'

She frowned at the ragged burn hole in the front of my shirt. 'What happened?'

'Bad night,' I said, taking the shirt off and throwing it on the floor.

Nel's eyes flitted to the window, shaking in its frame from the wind. 'How bad is it?'

I shrugged. My head throbbed, my body ached, my mind needed to shut down and I didn't want company. 'Now's not a good time—'

'Wendal, I'm scared.'

'I know.'

'I was too scared to use the latrine. Sorry, I pissed in your basin.'

I couldn't help but smile despite feeling like shit, or deny the frightened child's expression on Nel's face.

She almost smiled back. 'I heard today that Alexria was destroyed completely, *all* its citizens dead. They're saying it's the clansfolk. They've found a weapon or some magic on the wasteland, and it can destroy ether-growths. What if it's true? What if they've brought it here?'

'The clansfolk didn't do this,' I promised her. 'And you shouldn't listen so much to what *they* say. No one knows what happened to Alexria.'

Nel shivered. 'Want to get shit-faced?'

'Definitely.'

I fetched the cakes of jenkem I'd bought earlier that day from my jacket pocket. Sodden, despite the wax paper wrapping. They'd take too long to dry out to be of use now. Nel saw my disappointment and told me to forget the jenkem. She opened her satchel and took out a dark brown bottle of beer. A poor substitute.

'I don't want to get drunk, Nel.'

'Wait a moment.' Following the beer, she produced a small ampoule from the satchel. After uncorking the bottle, she snapped it open and dripped the clear liquid contents into the beer. 'Mutley's chemicals,' she explained. She swirled the beer and then took a swig. 'Here, try some.'

I sat beside her on the bed and took the bottle, staring at it. 'Does Mutley know you've got this?'

'Just try it, Wendal.'

Even though the ampoule hadn't held much of the chemical,

it gave the beer a distinct sour edge that dried the inside of my mouth, tingling in my throat when I swallowed.

'I like to dilute it,' Nel said as I handed her the bottle. 'Neat, it'll take your breath away. Better than jenkem, but much more expensive. Mutley calls it Liquid Ether, and she reckons it'll stop your heart if you take too much. Magic is used to ferment it.'

'Sounds dangerous,' I said, taking a second, longer swallow.

We passed the bottle back and forth without speaking. The rising and falling of the siren's song became a distant drone. With each swallow of the chemical, I cared less and less about the storm, and I was content to be sitting with my friend. If Dyonne had ever done anything right by me, it was allowing Nel into my life. Dyonne kept me invisible to most of the city, but obviously she thought that having companionship was good for me. And she was right. The same went for Lana Khem, I supposed. A shame Dyonne had extended the courtesy to my landlord, too.

Nel, afraid, nervous, glanced at the window each time lightning illuminated the rivulets of dirty water running down the pane, but after a while, she made a contented noise and closed her eyes.

'Can you feel it?'

I could. Not only had the chemical mellowed my mood but also tinged the room with rainbow colours, and I felt detached.

Nel drank the last mouthful of beer then lay down on her side on the bed. I did the same, lying behind her, my hair and skin wet and stinking, and put my arm around her. She held my hand.

'I hate the sound of that siren.' Nel slurred her words. 'It makes me think about the wasteland.'

'All soldiers do,' I replied, drowsy. 'We're the sum of our war memories.' Eden had told me that. 'It proves we survived.'

EDWARD COX

'But others died in our place.' Nel gripped my hand tightly. 'You believe me, don't you, Wendal? I mean … I never saw the monster, but … but *it* killed my friends. It wasn't me.'

I pulled her in close. 'I believe you.'

I knew what came next: a story Nel had told me before, but never while sober. She had been trying to deny her nightmares of the war for as long as I'd known her, but intoxication sometimes made her vulnerable enough to let them bubble to the surface.

During her City Service, Nel had been part of a detachment sent to clear out one of the clansfolk's underground burrows. It had been a trap. Wastelanders were good at laying traps. They had already evacuated the burrow, leaving behind a beast of the wasteland, some savage monster Nel claimed she never saw because she and her platoon had been plunged into total darkness.

'They were screaming, Wendal.' Nel's fingernails dug into my hand. 'I didn't know what was in there with us, but I was fucked if I was going to let it get me. I panicked, went mad, I … I …'

She had used every weapon at her disposal, every device she had constructed, and blindly wrought havoc in that burrow. In the end, she had blown a hole in the burrow ceiling. When the light flooded in, she saw she was the only one left standing in a scene of carnage.

'I still remember how the sunlight hurt my eyes,' Nel slurred. 'Everyone was dead, Wendal. They were … *smeared* over the floor and walls. So much blood. I couldn't tell what was soldier or monster.' Her breath hitching, she pushed her face into the pillow. 'But that thing ripped them apart. It wasn't my fault.'

It was a wonder she hadn't killed herself in the process. 'You did what you had to,' I whispered softly. 'You survived.'

'I hear them screaming in the dark.' Nel's grip on my hand relaxed. 'I'm safe in the light.'

'You're safe *here*,' I lied. 'We'll protect each other.'

'You never told me, Wendal.' Nel sighed. 'What happened to you on the wasteland? What did you see?'

'Too much.'

Nel fell asleep. I felt her slow breaths against my aching chest, and she didn't hear the new sound that accompanied the siren – or perhaps she did in whichever faraway place intoxication had taken her.

Dull booms shook the window like thunder arriving late to the storm. These distant concussions came from the city's mighty ether-cannons. It meant that some hostile force had followed the storm to Old Castle. The wasteland had arrived.

My thoughts lingered on Alexria. *Could* the clansfolk be responsible for this?

To make matters worse, Itch woke up and appeared high in the corner of the room. Her mummified face was blurred by colours as Liquid Ether threatened to pull me down after Nel.

'Someone's crying, Sycamore.'

It was me. Strange, I hadn't realised I was crying, but I was, heavy sobs that shook my body and squeezed gentle moans from my mouth.

A *boom* shook the window. I buried my face in Nel's hair.

'Can you hear the city?' Itch said. As though conducting the siren, her skeletal hand weaved a figure of eight in the air, trailing many colours. 'The wasteland never forgets us, and one day it will swallow us whole.'

'Shut up, Itch. Just ... *shut up!*'

Nel murmured in her sleep, and Itch said, 'I don't want to be here, Sycamore. When will you give me peace?'

I didn't reply. The rainbow colours had finally opened a door to Eden and my mind rushed to meet her ...

*

Upon an icy crust on the wasteland, platoons were mobilising: at least four hundred soldiers preparing to march across desolation and fight clansfolk wherever they found them. Milling, working as quickly and efficiently as any good city soldier should, they were striking the temporary camp which had been set up near the mouth of a valley, loading it into a long train of ether-wagons.

The night was cold. Frost bejewelled the ground, sparkling beneath a bright night sky, brilliant with drifting ether crystals, shedding rose-tinted silver light and casting long shadows in the valley. In the distance, the silhouette of a city sat on the horizon. A storm hung over it, clouds so dark they blocked the radiance of the sky, yet alive with the orange glow of internal fire, barking spears of lightning.

The soldiers worked hard to be away from the area as soon as possible. It was too dangerous for such a large company to linger in one place for long. Who knew what was watching from the wastes?

'Those wagons,' Eden said. She and I observed from up on the ridge, standing close to a steep path that led down to the valley floor. 'They can travel huge distances in a single day, bringing supplies and correspondences. They take letters and the wounded back to the cities, and it's rumoured that the Directors of the Quantum use them to meet face to face with other chapters of the Scientists. But we never use the wagons to fight.'

My brain was adapting and regurgitating one of the last conversations Eden and I ever had, during the brief time we spent together between her coming home from the war and me going off to serve my city.

'See the cannons mounted on them?' Eden continued. I could – long, fat tubes housing head-sized crystals of ether, with a cannoneer sitting behind them, ready to fire lethal bursts of magic. 'They're there to protect the train, but imagine a fleet of them, the destruction they could cause, especially from the air – if the Scientists could figure out how to get them to fly, that is.'

But they couldn't. We used to fly, according to the myths of an ancient time. Some of us even made it to other worlds, it was said. But the Salahbeem took our gift of flight with them; and the Scientists, no matter what they tried, simply could not get a magically powered vehicle to lift any more than five feet off the ground. The wagons floated, sure, but they didn't really *fly*. I remembered Eden telling me that, and what she said next:

'The Quantum limits military technology because they don't want to give these poor bastards too big an advantage.' She watched the soldiers down below, shaking her head sadly. 'No Scientist on Urdezha is fighting for glory or victory. If they were, they'd throw everything they have at the clansfolk and clear the wasteland within a few years. But what would that achieve?'

'Overpopulation in the cities?'

'Exactly.'

Commanders barked orders, urging their troops to dismantle the camp faster.

'This isn't a war, Wendal. It's a cull. The Scientists are ensuring we don't exceed our means, but one day—'

'I know. Someone will find something on the wasteland that changes everything.'

Eden closed her eyes as a cold night breeze blew on her face and ruffled her red hair, and with this breeze, her demeanour changed to something less savoury. '*And maybe that day has come.*' She opened her eyes to reveal green pupils in the shape of sycamore seeds.

I groaned and stepped away from her. 'Can't you ever just leave me alone?'

'*Unfortunately not*,' said Sycamore.

The camp had been loaded into the wagons by this time, and

commanders were ordering their troops to form ranks before the backdrop of a city under a storm. At the other end of the valley, in the near distance, the shapes of giant corpse-trees in a grave-forest could be seen, rising high, taller than the biggest towers, huge leaves tinted by the sky's light. All the usual scenery that accompanied these dreams.

Using Eden's image and my voice, Sycamore said, *'Your wife never thought of coincidence as a thing to be believed in or not. It either happens or it doesn't. What do you think, Wendal?'*

'Depends on the facts at hand.'

'Which was her point, I imagine. Do you have any facts?'

Did I? Dyonne had led me to an old woman in a Garden, who in turn sent me to see the ghost of an archaeologist. Past experience had taught me never to place much faith in discovering *facts*, yet …

'The dead don't lie,' said Sycamore. *'Abdon Klyne was Eden's lover, and you're wondering if he wasn't the only one.'*

'Shut up. You don't understand what this feels like.'

'I understand that you believe what Klyne told you, and now you've heard what Miranda Nhils had to say. You believe their stories are related.'

Reluctantly, I turned my thoughts to Brandon Quinn. If I hadn't spoken with Abdon Klyne, I would've thought nothing of Quinn working on a special, secret project for the Scientists. That they had made a discovery was nothing out of the ordinary; the wasteland was always being searched for treasures. But Quinn had been so frightened of this thing called black stone that he was willing to kill over it. Was black stone the same discovery that Klyne had said the Scientists were experimenting with? Coincidence?

I said, 'What are the chances of the Scientists discovering two different but important treasures at the same time, in the same city? They have to be the same thing, don't they?'

Sycamore looked at me as though he knew what I was really saying: that black stone could be the same thing Eden had been searching for.

'*Aren't you suspicious, Wendal? Since you returned from the wasteland, Dyonne Obor has been dangling your wife before you, using her name to ensure that you are subservient to the Salem. But now she decides to give you a lead which provides, on a plate, more information about Eden than you've so far managed to gather in three months of searching.*'

I could find nothing to say. Aside from the eyes and the cruel twist to the lips, Sycamore was a perfect representation of Eden. He even carried her smell. Dusty. Real.

'*You need to let your inner cynic help you accept that a fairy-tale ending is not heading your way, Wendal.*'

Down in the camp, the soldiers – armed, armoured, bearing heavy packs on their backs – lined up before their commanders, faceless beneath their helmets.

'I'll talk to Dyonne.'

'*You think she will be helpful?*'

I had to try; Dyonne had led me down this road to begin with, after all.

'*All our roads lead back to her, too,*' Sycamore said.

'Dyonne holds a high rank, she's close to the Salem. If she doesn't already know what the Scientists are up to, then she can probably find out.'

Sycamore sighed. '*What you're really hoping for is confirmation that Eden was apprenticed to a Magician.*'

'It's worth a try.'

'*Wendal, please* think*! The Salem controls everything their Magicians do. If one of them was your wife's master, then the Grand*

Adepts would likely know it already. Abdon Klyne and Miranda Nhils are dead, but the woman in the Garden, Ing Meredith, is very much alive, and the living are all too good at lying and deception. Something is very wrong here.'

He sounded as though he was making a reasonable point, but I didn't want to listen. 'We'll see.'

Down below, commanders shouted marching orders. The platoons evacuated the area, each heading in a different direction, off into the night and a war-that-wasn't-war. I found it hard to remember the names and faces of the soldiers I had served with, who had died before my eyes. In the end, all soldiers had only themselves to rely on. Such was the way of the wasteland, of the cull.

'Your obstinacy has made you blind to the dangers you are hosting, Wendal. Free me, let the Song of Always end, let me hear the dead singing again. More depends on it than you realise.'

'I'm not going over this again.'

'You comprehend so little. How much time do you think you have? How long do you think this game can last?'

The platoons had disappeared from view and the train of ether-wagons were preparing to leave for the storm-beleaguered city. Sycamore pointed at it, roiling and flashing on the horizon.

'Rumour is that this storm was created when the ether-growth beneath Alexria exploded. What if it is now seeking to do the same at Old Castle?'

'It's just a storm,' I said, shivering. 'It'll blow away.'

'Ether knows ether, Wendal. The Salem used it to cast their spells on you. On us. If Old Castle's growth detonates, the Song of Always will not protect you from an explosion of such concentrated magic. For you, time is always running out, the game has always been ending.'

And if Sycamore could claim freedom by sacrificing a hundred thousand humans, it was a price he was willing to pay.

His lack of compassion, his alien, unknowable existence sickened me. Always. I'd given up asking him to explain exactly what he was, where he had come from, to enlighten me on his history and reasons. Sometimes he said he was the spirit of vengeance, other times an embodiment of ridiculous human myths. His favourite was to say, *'You are me, Wendal, but I am not you.'*

He never gave a straight answer because he said I wouldn't understand the truth. This bizarre relationship was heavily stacked in Sycamore's favour. He absorbed every piece of knowledge I possessed, while giving nothing in return and never caring to understand the man I was.

A flesh-and-bone prison – that was how he saw me, a *thing* to escape.

'Old Castle is going nowhere, and neither are you,' I told him flatly. 'You'll still be with me when I find Eden.'

'Blind hope cannot save you, Wendal. I should not be on this world.' Sycamore set off down the path to the valley floor. He stopped, my wife's face thoughtful as he turned to call back, *'Dyonne Obor is a devious Magician who undoubtedly knows something about black stone, but she will tell you nothing.'*

I watched until he had reached the train and jumped up on the rear wagon. The train began its journey towards the city beneath the storm, drifting into shadowy distance illuminated by flashes of violent lightning. Then I noticed the lone figure the wagons had left behind: a tank-rider concealed within the shell of a tank-suit.

Humanoid in shape but taller, broader than any man or woman, the tank was formed from armoured plates held in place by the magic of ether. Its glass helmet glinted beneath the night sky. The short cannon on its shoulder scanned the area. With heavy footsteps crumbling the ground, the tank-rider strode into the valley.

Movement on the opposite ridgeline caught my eye. A crack of silver light split open into a dark gateway. The mysterious Salahbeem woman appeared, once again stepping into the intoxicated world of my dreams. Her Glass-and-Words armour sparkled like the ether crystals above. She held some kind of ether-cannon, longer and narrower than those we used. An assassin, a knight from an ancient order, she dropped to one knee and aimed the weapon at the tank-rider below.

I turned away. I didn't want to be there any longer.

Chapter Twenty-Five

It was a relief to wake up the next morning and find Old Castle still standing. But the storm hadn't blown away as I'd hoped. Apparently fixed over the city for now, it hung as a silent and brooding presence of roiling darkness shot through with orange fire and lightning. The ether shield was coping well, keeping it up in the sky, but the storm showed no sign of burning out, and I couldn't shrug off a creeping anxiety that it was searching for the weak spot which would allow it to give Old Castle the same fate as Alexria.

Time is always running out. Sycamore's jibes plagued me. Had a countdown begun for the city's existence?

The good news was that a note from Dyonne had been slid under my door during the night. She wanted to see me that morning. So, leaving Nel asleep in my bed, I went to meet her at the unnamed tavern on the corner of Levee Street.

'Now *this* is nice,' Dyonne said, admiring the ether-cannon that had once belonged to Brandon Quinn. She pursed her lips. 'Though, in truth, I already own more impressive pieces.'

Typical. Give with one hand, take with the other.

If Dyonne was at all concerned about the storm, she showed no sign, focused for now on pretending to deliberate over how much she was willing to pay for the cannon while, behind her,

Tamara sat staring at me. I'd asked Dyonne about the menace hanging over the city when I first arrived, but she shrugged and said, 'It's just a storm, Wendal,' so I told myself that if she and the Salem weren't worrying about it, then neither would I. It almost worked.

'Hmm,' the Magician said, turning the small metal tube over in her hands.

Dyonne wouldn't be rushed, though I willed her to speed through the irritating barter routine that she enjoyed so much. I was desperate to talk about my search for Eden.

I rolled a cigarette and lit it from the table candle. Outside, refuse crews were shovelling ashy sludge into waxed sacks and loading them onto wagons. The sludge covered Tinman Market and the rest of the city. All over, the dirty fallout from the storm was being gathered for the reduction houses. It made the air smell of rust. At least the filthy rain had stopped. More power must have been added to the shield overnight to stop it squeezing through.

'It's home-made, not particularly decorative,' Dyonne said, holding the cannon up to the light. 'The ether inside is probably stolen.'

'It works – trust me on that – and it's better than the usual crap I bring you.' I flicked ash, trying to quieten my uneasy impatience. 'Someone will pay well for its protection, especially after last night.'

Dyonne aimed a dry glare at me. 'Thank you for your input, Wendal. Now do shut up and drink your coffee.'

I did. It was hot and strong and exactly what I needed after the fun and games of Nel's chemical the previous night. Liquid Ether had left a strange taste in my mouth and I felt a little groggy, but that was nothing compared to the hangover jenkem usually gave me. I felt fresher, alert. Even so, Sycamore's warning lingered like a bad memory.

The glass pyramids on the streets had been transmitting a statement from the Quantum all morning. The floating face of the Scientists had calmly assured all citizens that the storm was not an attack. An accident had occurred at Alexria. Specifics were unclear, but the Scientists confirmed that this accident had indeed caused the city's ether-growth to detonate. The result of such a monumental explosion had been the violent weather front hanging above us now. But what happened to Alexria wouldn't happen here, we were promised. The shield could handle the storm, but so much of our ether power had been diverted to it that the city would have to function at quarter capacity for the time being.

The under-rail wasn't running at all. Only half of the reduction houses were operating. Power to non-vital appliances and amenities had been cut off. For today, businesses were closed, and citizens were advised to stay off the streets while the refuse crews cleaned up. This state of emergency would remain until the threat ended. There wasn't much else to do, the Scientists had said, except sit tight and wait for the menace to burn itself out. However, the storm wasn't the only danger that had come out of the wasteland last night.

The hostile weather had driven a swarm of skarabs towards the city. Evil creatures, big, like hybrids of insects and humans that swarmed in their hundreds and reproduced faster than rats. They would have covered Urdezha if they weren't so fond of eating their young; they would've unleashed carnage in the streets had the ether-cannons not blown them away. Though, as it was, the cannons still missed a couple that managed to scale the city wall. This kind of thing happened rarely, but thankfully the city watch had been on hand to take care of them.

During my tour of duty, I had helped to clear a skarab nest.

I shuddered to remember the mutilated bodies of the soldiers who had been used as hosts for their eggs.

'All right, Wendal,' said Dyonne. 'I'll give you a hundred and fifty for it.'

I accepted immediately. I could've got more for the ether inside the cannon, but today wasn't about money and haggling.

Tamara gave Dyonne her purse. She counted out my payment, clearly suspicious at my lack of argument, before sending her brutish bodyguard downstairs with the weapon.

As soon as Tamara had gone, I took a final drag off my cigarette and leaned across the table. 'Listen, Dyonne, I need to talk to you about the last lead you passed on to me.'

'Actually, I want to talk to you about that, too.' She gave me an appraising look. 'Wendal, have you abandoned your search for Eden?'

I paused halfway through stubbing out my cigarette. 'What?'

'There must be a reason why you didn't meet with Pearl.'

'Who?'

'The contact I'd arranged for you when last we spoke. She said you never showed.'

'I ...' I sat back, flummoxed. 'I *did* make that meeting, but it wasn't with anyone called Pearl.'

Dyonne raised an eyebrow. 'Excuse me?'

'I went to the Garden like you said. A woman called Ing Meredith met me there.'

'Meredith?'

'Well, she didn't introduce herself at the time. Abdon Klyne told me her name when—'

'Wait!' Dyonne sat forwards, her manner brusque. 'Abdon Klyne, the archaeologist?'

'You know him?'

'*Of* him, yes. He's a lackey for the Scientists, and he is dead.'

'I know, Dyonne. Meredith sent me to his ghost.'

'Is this some kind of joke, Wendal?'

'No.'

'So you're fraternising with the fucking Scientists now?'

'What? No!' I shrank under the dark and dangerous look that came to Dyonne's eyes. *Something is very wrong here*, Sycamore had said. 'I was following the lead *you* gave me. Meredith and Klyne knew so much about me and Eden that I ... You didn't arrange this?'

'Do I look happy?'

This wasn't how I'd imagined today's meeting playing out. 'I don't know what to tell you, Dyonne.'

Her voice low and menacing, Dyonne cursed in Salabese while aiming a quick glance at the door leading to the tavern's lower levels. She produced a small curved knife from the sleeve of her gown, which disappeared again after she used it to prick the end of her finger. Whispering incoherently, she squeezed out a drop of blood, dabbed it on the table and cast a spell, a quick pulse of magic that caused the air around us to waver and block out the room's ambience. I'd seen Dyonne use this spell before, when she needed to create a private bubble in which to have a sensitive conversation.

'Tell me everything.' Her words sounded close and dry inside the bubble. Her tone was calmer, but her demeanour hadn't relaxed. 'Leave nothing out.'

I didn't dare do anything but tell Dyonne the whole truth. I started at the beginning, with meeting Ing Meredith in the Garden, which had led to meeting Klyne's ghost at Temple University. I gave as much detail as I could remember, explaining that Eden had, apparently, been using Klyne as a source of information, and that he suspected she had been spying on the Scientists. Dyonne's attention became finely tuned when I told her that Klyne believed Eden had been trying to find out about a new treasure, an important discovery that was affecting the dead.

'The thing is,' I said, 'it might tie in with the last client you gave Sycamore. It can't be a coincidence, Dyonne. The ghoul was a dormouse, and she was murdered by a Scientist named Quinn. She'd been spying on him because he was working on a secret project, something from the wasteland that's like nothing the Scientists have seen before. He called it black stone. Does that mean anything to you?'

'No.' Dyonne stared into the middle distance with concerned contemplation. 'Why should it?'

'Klyne said that it's stopping the dead leaving Old Castle. If that's the case, then I thought ...'

Dyonne focused on me as I trailed off. 'You thought what, Wendal?'

I licked my lips. 'If the Scientists have had this thing long enough, then maybe Eden's spirit—'

She stopped me with a disgruntled growl. 'I can see where you are going with this, but you have to understand—'

'Please listen to me, Dyonne. Miranda Nhils was spying on the Scientists for the Magicians, so her ghoul must have been questioned before she was allowed to reach Sycamore.'

'Therefore, you believe that her interrogators must have told me what she told them?'

'If you don't know, you could find out, right?' I spoke quickly, urgently, trying to dispel a growing feeling that Dyonne was about to cause the headway I'd made in the last couple of days run through my fingers like sand. *She will tell you nothing*, Sycamore had said. 'And ... and if Eden was spying, then she must have been working as an apprentice. She had a master.'

Dyonne drummed her fingers on the table, either from irritation or consideration, I couldn't tell which.

'Wendal, there are five people in this city who control all plots and plans of the Magicians. They are the Grand Adepts of the Salem, and I am not so worthy as to have ascended into their ranks. However, if the Scientists have indeed made a startling new discovery, then rumours of it would have certainly reached my ears by now, whatever Miranda Nhils said. Yet I have heard nothing. You have been hoodwinked.'

Truth or lies? I went with the latter because the alternative was too hard to bear. 'No. Abdon Klyne, Miranda Nhils – the dead don't lie.'

'Oh, Wendal, I wish you'd learn to heed my experience.' Dyonne sighed. 'Do you know why Magicians are reluctant to deal with spirits? Why Scientists have no interest in them at all? Because they can be trapped, questioned, but not controlled. They can be threatened but not harmed. They have no reason to be loyal to anyone but themselves, useless at keeping secrets. Ask yourself – how stupid does a ghost need to be to prefer remaining *here* instead of escaping to the Garden in the Sky? The mind boggles! No, the dead do not lie, but they are foolish, and they can be deceived, and this Meredith, it seems, is a master deceiver.'

I shut my ears to what I was hearing. 'She knew who I was, Dyonne. She knew about Sycamore.'

'I've no idea how she got to you or who she is, but I intend to find out. Be sure of that.'

'Then what about Eden?'

'I've no doubt that Abdon Klyne genuinely met your wife. His other claims might sound rational to you, might seem to connect with this Quinn and black stone, but only in retrospect. Ing Meredith – who knows what deceptions her meddling has conjured? But I think she has led you into forcing details to match your desires. Perhaps her intent was to make you paranoid.'

Dyonne held up a hand to stop me jumping in. 'There are

many Magicians who take on apprentices. Permission is required from the Salem first, and although the identities of candidates are not made common knowledge, I do believe, in this instance, that my masters would have found it prudent to inform me if they knew of your wife.'

'But would they? For certain?'

A hiss of exasperation came from Dyonne's mouth. 'What are you looking for, Wendal? Do you want me to question the Salem? To satisfy your desires by admitting that it is *possible* I was kept in the dark and someone in Old Castle took Eden on as an apprentice?'

'I ... I just want to know if it's true.'

Dyonne thought for a moment, her eyes never leaving mine. 'Please see this scenario for what it looks like to my experience.' Her frustration was as much for me as for the situation. She should have tried sitting in my seat. 'I cast spells – *daily* – to keep you hidden from our enemies, yet this Meredith found a way through my veil. *That* in itself should disturb you enough. She knew how easily you could be manipulated by the mere mention of your wife's name, and she used it to lead you into the sphere of the Scientists. I very much doubt that Meredith is working for herself. What if the Scientists are on to Sycamore? I don't think you need reminding of what will happen should the Quantum get their hands on you.'

They would rip me apart just for the chance to study what was inside me. *If* there was anything left to study after Dyonne had unleashed my moment of death.

'I understand how you are feeling,' Dyonne continued, sympathetic but stern. 'We have *both* been duped, and it does not sit well with me. I promise to ask around about Eden's apprenticeship, but please don't hold to hope. You must be strong, now, calculated, and do as I tell you.'

I could sense what was coming next, and the disappointment didn't so much crush me as make me feel as though I was withering before the woman who held my leash.

'You will stay out of the way and leave this matter to me,' Dyonne said. 'I need guidance from the Salem, and I can't imagine that Mr Sebastian will be pleased. When I have spoken to him, I will tell you all that I am *allowed* to tell you.'

Which meant Sycamore was right. She'd tell me nothing. My expression and body language relayed that belief.

'We cannot risk exposing Sycamore to the Quantum.' Dyonne reached over and patted my hand. 'I'm sorry, Wendal, but this is just how it has to be.'

Miserable and angry, I glared as Dyonne dispelled her magic and rose from her chair. She made to walk away then stopped, frowning thoughtfully.

After a moment, she said, 'Do you know the shanties near the cliffs?' I affirmed with brooding silence. 'Go there, tomorrow morning. Your mind clearly needs distraction, and I see no reason why your search for Eden can't continue along *normal* avenues.' She nodded decisively. 'I will arrange for Pearl to meet you at her home there. And Wendal, make sure you're talking to the right person this time.'

Chapter Twenty-Six

Eden used to talk about how the Scientists feared inaction. It bred statistics they didn't like, bad numbers both in and out of the cities. Ether enabled us to sustain the equilibrium of existence, but its use needed limiting otherwise its magic couldn't regenerate fast enough and the energy it provided would run perilously low. Inaction would overpopulate a city, exceed an ether-growth's extraordinary capabilities and lead to ruin.

But in my lodgings, inaction was driving me crazy. Angry, confused, fearing the sky, I wondered if the storm would keep on hammering at the city shield until Old Castle's ether-growth was drained of the power to sustain it.

I needed to occupy my mind and battle against a feeling that time was indeed running out and an urge to ignore Dyonne's orders. So I reread every journal I'd filled so far, wrote furiously in my current journal, pushing aside my feelings while I went over and over the last couple of days, searching for reasons, facts, conclusions that would prove why Dyonne was wrong. But feelings were all I had in the end, swirling around the proclamation of a sly Magician that conflicted with the words of an old woman and a ghost.

So what if Meredith had duped Dyonne? It didn't mean that she had duped me, or Abdon Klyne. If she really was working alongside the Scientists to capture me, then she could have led me directly to them. I had followed her instructions willingly, was led easily, so why toy around with me? Why would the Scientists need to use her at all?

Sycamore's suspicions made sense to me now. Something *was* very wrong here. If Eden really had been a Magician's apprentice, then in all likelihood the Salem had information about her, and of course they would keep that from me. The mystery of what had happened to my wife, where her spirit had gone, was the hook they used to ensure my obedience. I was convinced that Dyonne was troubled by what had occurred because someone, finally, was going to lead me to the truth, and the Salem wouldn't like it if they lost access to Sycamore. After I had found Eden, I would no longer play the part of their pet assassin. Dyonne knew it and so did her masters.

Somewhere inside me, I sensed Sycamore encouraging my current line of thinking. Ing Meredith could be the key to his freedom and the answers to my questions. Or was Dyonne right to say that I just *needed* it to be that way? Did it matter that I couldn't think of a single reason why Meredith might want to help me? Why had she got involved in this? Was I paranoid?

Refusing to switch my brain off with jenkem, I spent a sleepless night tossing and turning, thinking and overthinking, until dawn arrived, and I went upstairs to knock on Nel's door. She was home with a mood as shitty as mine. She looked tired, hungover and like she had been in a fight. I didn't ask how she got a split lip and a bruise under her eye, just said, 'Let's go,' without giving an explanation. She didn't ask for one, either, and headed out with me for the shanties on the eastern edge of the city.

With the under-rail not running, we had a couple of hours' walk ahead of us. The storm had blocked out the sun and the city was darker than it was on most nights. The citizens were trying to continue life as normal, but the chirp of their voices came with a forced lightness that was unwilling to acknowledge the danger above, as though to do so would bring the sky crashing down on them. Their expressions were tight and their body language cowered beneath the roiling black and the fiery lightning that stabbed at the shield without a sound. Nel, too, was doing her best to ignore the ominous situation, but the whole city was scared.

'The shield is giving me a headache,' Nel mumbled.

I nodded in agreement.

It was the drone it made. It rumbled through the city, almost too low to hear, but at a frequency that pressed against my temples. Ordinarily, this wasn't a problem. There was rarely cause to keep the shield activated for long; as fast as dangers came out of the wasteland, they were just as quickly dealt with. But this storm was in no hurry to leave, and the shield's drone was fast becoming a constant headache for all citizens. I found a strange solace in the discomfort, though; as long as it was there, it meant our ether-growth still had enough power to protect the city.

I couldn't take my eyes off the storm. It appeared to be fuelled by an inner fire that kept it raging, almost healthy-looking. So much power and violence kept at bay by a thin sheath of ether magic. If the shield deactivated, even for just a moment, I dared not imagine how much ruin the storm would cause to the city. It was too alive, like it was growing in strength instead of raging towards dissipation. I couldn't shake an absurd notion that it somehow knew what it was doing. Was it hungering for our ether-growth?

Nel flinched and ducked as a fat streak of lightning struck and clawed at the shield with a blinding flash. 'Fuck's sake,' she spat.

She and I hardly said a word to each other as we crossed

the width of Old Castle, and then only begrudgingly when we arrived at our destination sometime around late morning.

'Who are you supposed to be meeting?' Nel grunted.

'Someone called Pearl,' I grunted back.

The refuse crews hadn't bothered visiting this area. The shanties formed a small but tight-knit community, and its people had cleared away the storm's fallout themselves. Drying to sodden grey ash, the sludge had been shovelled and swept into mounds on the outskirts of a settlement comprised of waste that had avoided recycling at the reduction houses: boxes and crates, waxed cloth and leather, metal, wood, stone, glass – any discarded Dust product had been used to build substandard hovels for the displaced.

'Have you been in a fight?' I asked Nel.

'Yeah,' she said gloomily. 'With Mutley.'

'What happened?'

'She found out I'd been helping myself to Liquid Ether.'

'I thought she liked to share with you.'

'Well, her generosity ran dry last night.' She looked at the sky and shuddered. 'This fucking storm is turning everyone crazy.'

But not in the shanties. Adults, gaunt and dishevelled, sat around cook fires, talking as their lunch bubbled over crackling flames in cauldrons. They hid their concerns about the storm so the children playing around them could do so unhindered by fear. There was something content about this place.

'It didn't last long,' Nel said. 'I mean, I gave as good as I got, but you've seen Mutley. She's twice my size and *fuck me* she can fight! I got out, quick.' She touched a finger to her split lip and winced. 'Turns out that Mutley's temper and my smart mouth aren't a good mix.'

I faced Nel, feeling guilty now that I hadn't shown her much concern. 'Are you all right?'

'I really don't want to talk about it, Wendal.' She frowned. 'What's up with you?'

'I don't want to talk about it, either.'

'Let's get on with it, then.'

A few of the children ran around us as we made our way further into the settlement. Ash had added an extra layer of dirt to the grime of the lifestyle given to them by their parents, who aimed a few suspicious looks our way. The children found nothing unusual about our presence. They were happy, carefree, shouting and laughing, but no one was ever given the option of agreeing to the social pact they were born into. Eden had told me that. She and I never discussed having children.

The shanties were close enough to the coast to be technically outside the city. Less than a quarter of a league beyond the collection of hovels, I could see the tall ether-cannon turrets that lined the eastern clifftops, looking out to sea, protecting Nephuin Town – the fishing settlement down below them. I could hear the sound of waves crashing on rocks and the cry of gulls. I could smell salt in the air, despite the lingering aroma of rusty metal. The shield was focused on the storm above Old Castle. The city walls and the ether-cannons were all that stood between us and the wasteland.

Not really fancying my chances with questioning any of the adults, I caught the eye of a child and beckoned her over. She came, cocksure and smirking, a gaggle of friends trailing behind her.

'I'm looking for Pearl,' I said. 'Do you know her?'

The girl stuck out her chin. 'Maybe I do, maybe I don't.' Her friends giggled.

'Is that a yes or a no?'

'Depends.'

'On what?'

She lost a little of her confidence. 'Well ... *you* know?'

I managed a smile. 'Sorry, you've lost me.'

Nel slapped my arm with a backhand. 'Just give her a coin, you tight-fisted bastard.'

The gaggle laughed. I fished a single bit from my pocket, jerking it back when the girl tried to snatch it from my hand. 'Pearl?'

Wide-eyed and hopeful now, she pointed over the way to a woman sitting outside her hovel, whittling a piece of wood. The girl ran off excitedly with her gang, clutching the coin like a prized possession.

The woman didn't look up when Nel and I stood over her. 'Something I can do for you?' she said in an unwelcoming tone.

'Are you Pearl?'

'That's what they call me.'

'I've been told you have information.'

She looked up. A dirty face full of distrust. 'Wendal, is it? Thought you'd take me seriously this time, did you?'

'We'll see.'

Her eyes drifted to Nel and then back to me. 'You'd better come in, I suppose.'

Placing the wood and whittling knife aside, she rose and disappeared through a leather flap into her hovel.

'Friendly sort,' Nel said. 'Do you want me to wait out here?'

I looked at the satchel hanging from her shoulder and shook my head.

Pearl's home was untidy with bric-a-brac and rubbish, reeking with a damp, unwashed smell. Pearl sat on a sackcloth pillow behind a low table which had obviously once been part of a crate. She told us to sit on the pillows on the opposite side of the table, then produced a tatty pouch and rattled its contents.

'These are the bones of my grandfather's left hand,' she said.

'He was a powerful Magician. The rest of him is buried on these very grounds. From beyond life, he protects the shanties. He—'

'Let's not fuck around,' I said, throwing five bits onto the table. 'You've been told who I am and why I'm here, so just get on with telling me what you think you know.'

Pearl scooped up the money and then stared at me. I could feel Nel staring at me, too. I didn't care how offensive I was being; I wasn't there to make friends. In fact, I didn't know why I was there at all other than to satisfy Dyonne's orders. I just wanted Pearl to say enough to confirm she was another charlatan, and then I could get on with a decision I only then realised I had made.

I was going to track down Ing Meredith for myself. Fuck Dyonne's orders. There was more to this than the Magicians would ever let me know. Sycamore had been telling me that for months.

Pearl said, 'My grandfather sang his Song to me when he died, passed his gifts to me. Now I can commune with the other side.'

She upturned the pouch, scattering finger bones on the table. Nel rolled her eyes at me. This was all too familiar, part of a routine we'd witnessed countless times. Nel's reaction said it all; it told me, yet again, that I wouldn't find my wife today. Only this time I had no argument.

'Hmm.' Pearl was leaning over the bones, apparently reading their formation. 'I see a woman here.'

I sighed. 'Let me guess – her name's Eden.'

'No.' Pearl looked as surprised as me that she'd said that. 'Strange ... she's not the one you're looking for.'

'Sorry to interrupt,' Nel said, sitting forwards, 'but I think you'll find that she is.'

'Shut it!' Pearl snapped. 'Unless you want me to talk to the spirits following *you* around?'

Nel clamped her mouth and drew her lips into a line.

'Eden,' Pearl said to me. 'She's behind … no, she's *not* the first …' With a finger, she pushed a few of the bones into a different configuration. 'She's gone. This isn't right.'

'What are you talking about?' I said.

'You're … you're not looking for Eden.' Pearl loosened the rag which served as her neckerchief, an expression of concern on her face. 'Who are you looking for?'

For a moment, I feared she had some genuine talent and was picking up on my decision to ignore Dyonne's orders. But this had to be part of the act. *Had* to be. Gaining confidence through uncertainty, leading me to piece together what I wanted to hear – it had been done to me a hundred times before.

'The bones.' Pearl became panicked. 'They're not speaking to me.' She began scratching at her neck as though insects were crawling over her skin. 'They're speaking to *you!*'

She scrambled backwards, staring fearfully at the remnants of her grandfather's hand. This didn't feel like the act of a charlatan; Pearl looked genuinely scared. 'You have to leave.' Her voice came through hot gravel and she began coughing and gagging, gripping at her throat.

'Oh no.' Nel jumped to her feet, dipping her hand into her satchel. 'Not again.'

But rather than unleashing anything as wild and untamed as Jon Johnny had, Pearl relaxed, falling limp to her side on the waste-covered floor. Her eyes closed and a tense expression spread across her face.

'Wendal? Wendal, are you there?'

It wasn't Pearl's voice. It belonged to someone I'd met before, someone I'd just been thinking about.

'Meredith?'

'I haven't much time, so you have to listen quick. Did you go to see Klyne?'

'Shit!'

I rose and backed away, looking at Nel who mouthed the words, 'What the fuck is going on?'

'Wendal!' Meredith snapped through Pearl. 'Did you speak to Klyne?'

'Yes. Yes, I spoke to him.'

'Then he must have told you about the treasure Eden was looking for.'

'Black stone.'

'Yes! That's what the Scientists are calling it. It's something old, Wendal, and the Magicians definitely know about it, too. The Salem are trying to stop the Quantum using black stone, and Eden ...'

Meredith fell silent and my every muscle tensed.

'Eden what?'

Pearl stirred, and for a moment her voice overlapped with Meredith's. 'The Magicians had her looking for it. Eden had a master.'

I stepped forwards. 'Tell me who.'

'I ... I have to leave. She's too close.'

'Wait!'

'Don't give up on me, Wendal, no matter what you hear. I'm going to help you.'

'No,' I shouted. 'Don't go.'

Pearl let out a groan and opened her eyes. 'What did you do to me?'

'Bring her back,' I demanded.

It was clear by her expression that Pearl had no memory of what had occurred. Shivering, she wrapped her arms around her. 'Leave,' she whimpered. 'Now.'

Nel took my arm, but I didn't let her lead me out. I wanted to grab the woman on the floor, shake her until Meredith came back. Only when Pearl screamed, 'Get out!' was I compelled to move.

Outside the hovel, Nel rounded on me, disturbed. 'What just happened, Wendal? Who the fuck is Meredith?'

But I was only half-listening, more concerned that the shanties now appeared deserted. Not one adult or child in sight. Food boiled in cauldrons over unattended fires. Gulls cried from the distance. The storm raged silently.

'Where did everyone go?' Nel narrowed her eyes at something behind me. 'Who's that?'

On the other side of the fires, Tamara stood glaring at me, his thick arms folded across his wide chest.

'You'd better leave,' I told Nel, feeling cold.

'Why? Who is he?'

'I'll explain later. Trust me, Nel, you have to go.'

She nodded and walked away, giving the imposing form of Tamara a wide berth.

Chapter Twenty-Seven

Tamara ushered me into another ramshackle hovel. He waited outside, leaving me to face Dyonne Obor alone. The Magician sat at the same kind of low, makeshift table that Pearl had used, a triumphant look in her eyes.

'You didn't honestly believe that I'd let you go running off without supervision, did you?'

No, now she mentioned it, it didn't sound like the sort of thing she'd do. 'You set me up.'

'There was a good chance that Ing Meredith would try to contact you again, so I thought I'd lay a trap.'

Evidence of the spells Dyonne had cast laced the air with the tingling, bitter residue of magic. Both women, it seemed, had used Pearl as a proxy.

'Did you catch her?'

Dyonne shook her head. 'Not this time. Meredith is a slippery customer, but she'll soon run out of hiding places. Sit down, Wendal.'

I declined, not only because I felt like being defiant, but also because this hovel was as damp and stinking as Pearl's, and the backs of my trousers were already wet and cold from sitting there.

'I want to know what Meredith told you,' Dyonne said.

'She didn't get the chance to say much at all. I think she felt you there and fled.'

'I suppose that was wise of her. She told you nothing about your search? Didn't try to arrange another meeting?'

I weighed the odds, deciding that Dyonne wasn't testing my loyalties; that she genuinely didn't know what Meredith had said. I wasn't in the mood to be as forthcoming with the truth as I had been last time and shook my head. 'Who is she?'

'An irritation who has dived into waters far too deep for her.' Bitterness laced Dyonne's tone. 'Meredith is a dormouse. She has some skill in magic, I can't deny her that, though I sorely doubt she is anything like the oracle she thinks she is. I admit to feeling a little embarrassed, Wendal. How I was ever hoodwinked by such a buffoon is a mystery.'

Buffoon or not, Meredith had revealed that Dyonne had a blind spot. I liked that. 'Is she working for the Scientists?'

'Actually, no. I was wrong about that one. Meredith works for herself. She is the self-proclaimed *Queen* of the dormice.' Dyonne scoffed at the title. 'But I was right in saying that she isn't helping you, Wendal. She is trying to get to *me*, to the Magicians.

'Meredith does not like us using dormice as spies. As you recently witnessed, some of them die in service to us. In retaliation, she has been meddling in the affairs of the Salem and threatens that she will continue to do so until we stop coercing *her people* into harm's way. But now, in gaining access to you, Meredith has overstepped a dangerous line, and the Salem has ordered her death.'

Could it be that Meredith had revealed information that Dyonne didn't know? Or had she revealed secrets that Dyonne was keeping from me? *The Magicians definitely know about black stone . . .*

'I won't lie to you, Wendal. Meredith has embarrassed me before my masters. Mr Sebastian has ordered me to exact her execution personally.'

I rubbed my face. Tiredness had sunk into my bones. 'So what now?'

'You lie low and stay out of everybody's way until this matter is resolved.' There was no room for argument in Dyonne's tone or expression, but she wasn't saying anything unexpected. 'I've been warned that Meredith's interference could exacerbate the current feud between the Salem and the Quantum. I haven't been told how.'

I perked up. The current feud? 'Black stone?'

'I *do not know*, or weren't you listening? If black stone is real, then knowledge of it is above my rank and I will not question the decisions and wisdom of my masters.'

Truth or lies? 'But—'

'No buts, Wendal. Whatever else Meredith claims to be, she has a network of dormice at her disposal, and she is unhinged enough to deal with the dead. That means she could uncover *many* secrets. She might be a buffoon, but she is dangerous. Until the Salem is satisfied that her threat is gone, your search for Eden will have to wait.'

The familiar anger, the frustration, burned. I opened my mouth, but Dyonne raised a hand to stop another word passing my lips.

'And before you ask – yes, I looked into whether or not your wife had a master. All I have discovered so far is that Eden Finn was never apprenticed to any Magician I know, and I do not believe that she was to any of those I don't.'

Teeth clenched, I looked at my feet.

'It might be hard to swallow, Wendal, but please remember that I have to follow orders, too, and I trust in them. You will go nowhere unusual, and you won't speak to any more strangers.'

I looked up and Dyonne held my hard stare until I relented with a nod.

'Go home and stay there,' she ordered. 'Get some food on the way because you have a wait coming. It shouldn't be long, but ... stay low until you hear from me.'

Chapter Twenty-Eight

'You think it's something bad?' Nel said. 'Bad enough that Eden would ... you know.'

'Kill herself over it?' My spoon worried at the bowl of stew Nel had given me. 'I just don't know.'

'What are you going to do?'

Good question. The only answer I had was a shrug.

Piper's was filling up with hungry citizens ready for their evening meals. The tavern was hot and smoky, busy with voices. My conversation with Nel had been frustratingly disjointed so far as she and the other two workers had to serve a horde of customers, most of them talking about the storm and arguing over the rumours they'd heard in a wash of nonsense that prickled against my senses.

In fleeting moments, I'd been filling Nel in on the brick wall that had been earlier placed before me. I explained what she had witnessed at the shanties, told her about Meredith, and when I related what I'd found out on the night we broke into Temple University, she had said, 'So, Eden had a lover, huh? You all right?' I'd been lying when I'd told her I didn't care about that, and got on with explaining how my 'boss' was now forbidding me from following up on any of the information I had gathered.

I wasn't sure that this was what Dyonne meant when she told

me to get some food on the way home, but ... fuck her. I needed company.

'Meredith *could* be clever enough to deceive Klyne,' I said miserably. 'But why bother? He *really* believed what he told me, Nel. Unless I'm allowed to dig deeper, I can't prove any of this is true. I only have what my gut's telling me.'

Was it my gut, or was it Sycamore's encouragement?

Nel was summoned by yet another customer demanding service. I pushed the bowl of stew away and rolled a cigarette.

If Eden were here now, she'd probably remind me that none of the food served at Piper's contained real meat. Nothing in the city was real beyond plants and *us*; and even we would one day be welcomed to a reduction house along with the other rubbish to be recycled back into society as Dust. *Ever wonder who you're eating?* Eden once asked me.

I lit the cigarette, took a long drag and stared at the stew. Not since the days of the Salahbeem had we buried our dead.

'Here's the thing,' Nel said, rushing back. 'Meredith can't be too clever if she's deliberately pissing off the Salem, but let's say Klyne's right. Let's say the Scientists really have discovered this stone and Eden was looking for it. Do you need to know what it is?'

'I don't follow.'

'What difference would it make?'

'A lot, actually.' I blew out a line of smoke, glaring at Nel as though she was stupid. 'If black stone is preventing spirits leaving Old Castle, then Eden could be closer than I realised.'

'Which is my point,' Nel stressed. 'The Scientists are always up to something with whatever they've got their hands on from the wasteland. Who cares what it is this time? Black stone might've made your search a whole lot easier, and that's the only thing you need to know about it, right?'

'No, because …' I flicked ash, my thoughts bright with angry clarity. 'Because I suspect everything begins and ends with this black stone, Nel. If Eden was looking for it, then she was working for the Magicians, spying on the Scientists. It means that Eden had a master.'

'Which your boss reckons she didn't, and Meredith might be full of shit.'

'Don't you get it, Nel?' I felt like I was vibrating, gathering energy from the storm above. 'If it's true, then someone in this fucking city can tell me why my wife killed herself.'

'Oh.' Nel chewed her bottom lip. A fresh clutch of customers approached the bar. 'Hold that thought, Wendal.'

Piper's was getting ever more crowded and I felt closed in by the customers, alienated by their debates as I sat on the barstool, smoking and brooding.

Leave no stone unturned, I had decided a long time ago. I had grown accustomed to running in circles for Dyonne, to a half-life which allowed to me to care about no one save myself, Nel and the spirit of Eden. But this? This was different. This felt like confirmation of something that the monster I hosted had been telling me all along. I didn't live with limited choices; I had no choices at all. I would never find peace while the Salem wanted Sycamore.

But what could I do? The Grand Adepts themselves were involved now. Meredith might have found Dyonne's blind spot, but Mr Sebastian and his ilk were a different matter. I had neither the guile nor the resources to investigate behind their backs. What could I do?

'Your girlfriend's here,' Nel muttered to me as she fetched a bottle of wine.

Glancing back over my shoulder, I saw Lana Khem had entered Piper's with two other city watch officers. While her colleagues took one of the two empty tables left, Lana came to the bar beside me. At first, I thought she might talk to me, but she didn't even look in my direction and gave Nel her order.

'Three stews,' she said curtly. 'And a jug of water.'

Nel smiled perfunctorily. 'Anything else?'

'Some bread. Bring it to our table.'

Without a word of thanks, Lana strode away to join her officers. The city watch ate for free anywhere in Old Castle as long as they were on duty, but it was customary for them to tip the servers. Lana hadn't bothered doing that, either.

'Fuck off, you chilly bitch,' Nel said under her breath before shouting Lana's order through the serving hatch behind the bar. 'Sorry, Wendal.' She held up the bottle of wine she was still holding. 'I'll get back to you in a minute.'

'Don't bother,' I said, glancing at Lana. 'I need to go.' But I didn't want to be on my own. I wanted to talk to someone who actually cared about me, who made me feel not so small in this shitty world. 'Come to my room after work.'

'Can't do it,' she said, dampening my hopes. 'I'm seeing Mutley tonight.' She winced at my look of displeasure and gestured to the bruise on her face. 'She wants to talk.'

'Don't go back,' I said. 'Just … let her go.'

'For what it's worth, you were right, Wendal. Mutley's not good people, and I don't fit in at Reaper Town. I'm going to end things tonight. Don't worry. I know what I'm doing.'

Which, given Nel's track record, was probably the most worrying thing she could have said. I didn't argue, however, thanking her for the food before making my way through the crowd to the door. I could feel Lana's eyes on my back as I left.

Chapter Twenty-Nine

Jenkem couldn't tempt me. Sleep wouldn't come. I paced my lodgings, alone and in bad company. I couldn't stop thinking about a timeline that ended at the big, ugly void into which Eden had fallen.

There were forts dotted around the wasteland, between the cities; small army facilities, each heavily fortified and capable of housing around two hundred soldiers. They were important supply depots and medical resources in the war, and no one stayed at them long – unless they were too injured to fight, which had been me, around four months ago. With two months of my City Service remaining, I had been interned into the infirmary at Fort Icus, severely wounded from what I had experienced on the wasteland during the days prior.

I couldn't recall much about my stay or how I got there, but I remembered the nurses and doctors being afraid of me. Sycamore was already inside me, but I was still fighting him as he slowly devoured my spirit, and he hadn't yet possessed full control of my body. Both myself and not, I blacked out regularly, sometimes for a day or more, and would wake up strapped to a hospital bed, beset by ghouls that no one else could see. But my awareness had been such that I knew I'd been admitted to the facility at the end of Noveb last year, and that I spent roughly a month there before a train of ether-wagons bound for Old Castle took me home at the very end of Deccem. Janus and a new year had arrived on the day I met Dyonne.

When I was first admitted to Icus, Eden was still writing her journals, filling them with her usual philosophical musings and magical experiments. The trouble was, she always wrote in Salabese. I knew enough for conversation, but deciphering her handwriting had been hard. As far as I could tell, she had recorded little about where she had been or who she had been there with, but that was nothing unusual and life had seemed normal for her. However, she had written nothing of her concerns for me, either, or her hopes that I would return from the war. And she had also stopped replying to the letters I had written her from the wasteland. I remembered intending to write to her from Icus, but obviously I never did. If I had, she would have known that I was still alive.

Eden's last journal entry was dated early Deccem last year, maybe a week after I had been admitted to the fort's infirmary. Sometime between then and the days prior to my return to Old Castle, my wife had become embroiled in something that led her to take an aging archaeologist for a lover and then to hold an ether-cannon to her heart and pull the trigger. And there lay the darkness of my void.

I had discovered not one shred of information concerning the last weeks of Eden's life. It was as though her very existence had been swept under the carpet. Even if Dyonne wasn't keeping me on a short leash, I didn't know anyone I could ask about that time. Eden's circle of friends were never mine – not that I'd ever really had many – and outside our marriage we had practically led separate lives. We always came home to each other at the end of the day, just ... rarely talked about the day itself. But now I had met Abdon Klyne. Now the game had changed.

Magicians liked to keep their secrets, and I was convinced that Eden had stopped writing her journals because she had been accepted, and her master had ordered her not to catalogue any of the secrets she would be exposed to in her new life as a Magician's apprentice. Meredith was right. Dyonne was wrong.

How did I search for Eden's master when Dyonne and the Salem had cut off all my roads? *Don't give up on me*, Meredith had said. However much she had hoodwinked the Magicians, I didn't believe she was a liar. She wanted to help me, her reasons a mystery, but help all the same. She remained my best hope, though with Dyonne on her trail, she had more chance of killing a Grand Adept and joining the Salem herself than surviving the next day or two. By the fucking Gardeners, I felt helpless!

With a growl of frustration, I kicked my jenkem burner, sending it clattering across the floor. Itch stirred at the noise, bubbling in the corner of the room.

'Go back to sleep,' I shouted. 'Right fucking now!'

The ghoul obeyed, and I flopped onto the bed, burying my face in the pillow.

What did I really know about any of this, anyway? I drifted on the periphery of the city's machinations, barely a citizen, occasionally being dragged into the feudal games played by the Salem and the Quantum. I understood nothing while clinging to … what? A romanticised fiction? Something that would never happen? Did Eden even want me to find her?

Mind alive with thoughts of my wife, I sank into a restless half-sleep, seeing her face, how she pursed her lips while she wrote, how she looked at me when she thought I was being stupid; I remembered the colour of her hair, her eyes, the smell of her skin. Over and over, memories and hopes, all crashing to debris at the feet of Dyonne Obor.

Finally, with the drone of the city shield rumbling in my

head and flashes of lightning illuminating my window, I could be alone with my thoughts no longer. Dawn must have arrived by then, blocked by the storm's darkness, so I went upstairs and knocked on Nel's door, hoping she was back from seeing Mutley. No answer. I went to the baths beneath my lodging house, thinking to relax for a while in hot water. Thankfully, the baths were empty, but although the water was clean, it was cool without the power of ether to heat it. Just being there reminded me of the last time Sycamore had killed, so I didn't linger.

Back in my lodgings, my heart skipped when I saw a note had been slid under my door. It was from Dyonne: *Meet me at the Garden near Public Square. Now.*

An unusual meeting place for Dyonne to choose, and one that made my heart sink. It could only mean one thing: Ing Meredith was dead and the charade of my life was about to continue.

Chapter Thirty

Wrapped up in a shawl beneath the dark sky and spears of silent fire, Ing Meredith sat on a bench in the Garden, waiting for me. She grinned as though she knew what I was thinking: that she had crafted the handwriting on the note to look exactly like Dyonne's.

'I haven't got long.' She turned her eyes to the small transmission pyramid on its pedestal, as if she should see the ether-projection of the sycamore tree in Under Park, even though power to the transmission pyramids had been cut off. 'The Salem will catch up with me sooner rather than later.'

I stood a few paces from her, looking around for signs that I had been followed to the Garden, or was being watched.

'Don't worry yourself,' Meredith said. 'There's enough time for a quiet chat, just you and me.'

'I'm not supposed to talk to you.'

'I know.' She smirked. 'You've been told you can't trust me by the one person you can trust least of all, and now you don't know where you are. So how about this – I do the talking and you do the listening?' She patted the bench beside her. 'Come and sit. No one's watching.'

I took a few steps closer but remained standing.

'I wasn't always a dormouse, Wendal. I was raised by *good*

citizens, in a household that followed the Scientists' way.' Meredith looked up at the sky, awed by the power of the storm. 'But when the wasteland took my mother, and later my husband, I wasn't so keen on that way any more.'

I checked around again, not daring to believe we were alone. 'Why are you helping me?'

'Because the Magicians are as bad as the Scientists. The Salem and the Quantum – they don't cater for people like us. Me, I slipped through the cracks and chose the life of a dormouse. You? Well, I think we can agree that you're a unique case, Wendal, and neither side has your best interests at heart. There's a big secret world swirling around this city and you're only just beginning to see it. Someone's responsible for this storm, and my money's on the Scientists.'

'Black stone,' I said. 'What is it?'

Meredith frowned thoughtfully at the sky. 'I honestly don't know if it's a *what* or a *who*, but I'm starting to wonder if the storm does. Can't you feel it in the air? Like we're being watched, judged, our fate contemplated.'

I followed her gaze. Far above, rolling black belched gouts of fire. Orange lightning sparked and clawed against the shield; and yes, I felt as though I was being watched, as if the storm had come for me alone.

Meredith was looking at me, studying my eyes, perhaps trying to see a sign of the entity I hosted. 'I do have some fond memories of my childhood. When my mother didn't come home, my father read to me a lot – fables of the Salahbeem. I enjoyed those times. Made me forget my troubles for a while. My favourite story was "The Shepherd and the Sycamore". Do you know it?'

I stiffened, battling the urge to walk away. Dyonne had guessed that Meredith would try to reach me at the shanties;

had she guessed that I'd get tricked into this meeting, too? I tried not to care. Surprised and frightened by Meredith's words, I kept my mouth shut so she could do all the talking.

'The Shepherd was a Gardener who tended the Great Sycamore at the heart of a graveforest. He was a nurturer, a guide. He shepherded spirits through the gateway to Aktuaht, where the dead sang their last Songs and passed over to the Garden in the Sky. And that gateway lay inside the trunk of the Great Sycamore.'

Meredith spoke with her eyes closed, a faint smile on her lips, as though remembering the sound of her father's voice. 'The Sycamore was the smallest tree in the graveforest, as humble as the Shepherd himself, but *so* mighty. Its boughs were full of green leaves all year round, its bark sparkled with the promise of glory, and its seeds were manna in the afterlife.

'Now, the Shepherd used to sit on the highest and sturdiest branch of the Great Sycamore, waiting for the spirits who came seeking passage to heaven. He would lead them to Aktuaht, where he listened to their Songs, revealed secrets that soothed their fears of the unknown and gave them seeds as food to sustain them on their final journey to the Garden in the Sky. The Shepherd was a friend to the dead, but he never dealt with the living. He had little time for them. But what he didn't realise was that the living had all the time in the world for him. Do you know what happened next, Wendal?'

'It's just a story,' I said. My every nerve ending itched.

'Maybe. Or does it explain why the Salahbeem left?' Meredith's face darkened. 'Humans don't like unanswered questions. We're too impatient, too … self-entitled. We wanted to know what the Shepherd knew. Did Aktuaht and the Garden in the Sky truly wait on the other side of the gateway? Why did he share his secrets only with the dead? The living hunted their answers like pack animals, believing that the gateway, heaven, death itself, could be theirs to control. They captured the Shepherd and forced their questions upon him.

'But the Shepherd gave them nothing. Not even the foulest tortures could loosen his lips. For death was not ours to control. But we wouldn't listen, wouldn't learn. We kept demanding, hunting, torturing, until we pushed too far and killed the Shepherd. And that was the day we earned the full displeasure of the Gardeners.

'They sent three warriors, three knights from the Order of Glass and Words. Truth, Mercy and Wrath were their names, and they came to judge the Shepherd's murderers. Truth listened to the Shepherd's Song and saw what the humans had done; Mercy found no redemption in their actions, and so Wrath had little choice but to decide upon a fitting punishment. If these cruel humans were so obsessed with death, then they would see it for themselves. The Order of Glass and Words killed each of the Shepherd's torturers. Four score and ten of them, as the story goes. Ripped the spirits right out of their bodies and denied them paradise, cursing them instead to walk Urdezha as ghouls, forever lamenting the mistakes they had made.

'And then the knights returned to Aktuaht, where they remained forevermore as the Judges of the dead. Any spirit seeking the Garden in the Sky would have its worthiness tested by Truth, Mercy and Wrath. Judged upon the life they had lived, for there are no lies in the Song of the Dead. The gateway was hidden from the eyes of the living, and the Great Sycamore was left to wither and die at the heart of the graveforest. As for the Shepherd, some say he returned to Urdezha as the spirit of vengeance, stalking those who hide from Aktuaht's judgement.'

Meredith raised an eyebrow at me, her expression full of meaning and far too knowing.

'It's a fucking story.' My voice came as a hoarse whisper. My hands were balled into fists.

Meredith pursed her lips. 'Isn't it funny how so many tales of the Salahbeem excuse their actions by claiming they were victims of human cruelty?' She shrugged. 'Most Magicians believe they were a kind and giving race. The Gardeners, selfless teachers of wisdom and wonder – no evil in them. But I don't think of the Salahbeem in that way, and I know you don't believe it, either.' Face stern, eyelids hooded, Meredith scoured the Garden. 'The dead call you Sycamore, but I think they should be calling you Shepherd.'

I was on the cusp of leaving. Or fleeing. I was too perturbed to decide which. 'You say you're helping me, but this feels like you're playing a game.'

'No games. I'm sick and tired of the Quantum and the Salem leading people to their deaths to achieve – what? More secrets. More lies. I've too many regrets, Wendal.' She was looking at the storm again. 'In you, I feel a chance to give this city a little redemption.'

'Then tell me what you know about my wife.'

'Yes, the root of the Great Sycamore.' Meredith's face softened, and her old, glassy eyes met mine. 'There's a Magician, goes by the name Ghan Hathor. Rumour is, he had an apprentice named Eden Finn.'

The strength left my legs and I sat down next to Meredith. 'Where is he?'

'I don't know yet.'

'Aren't you supposed to be an oracle?'

'I have insights, intuition, but no one can really see the future. And not all my information comes from visions and dreams, Wendal. There's a network of dormice at my disposal.' Meredith patted my hand, encouraging me to find patience I didn't have.

'Seems that Hathor pissed off the Salem as much as I have. They ordered his execution three or four months back, and as far as they're concerned that execution was carried out. But my network has heard whispers that he's still alive, living in exile somewhere outside Old Castle.'

'Outside?' My hopes flagged. 'On the wasteland?'

'No, I don't think he's that far out, but ... I'm searching for him, Wendal, and I *will* find him for you.'

'When?' The word came as a breathless growl. 'The Magicians are coming for you, Meredith.'

'Oh, don't you worry about me. One way or another, whatever the Salem does next, I promise I'll lead you to Eden's master.' Meredith leaned towards me, her stare harsh and unblinking. 'Heed my warning, Wendal. If you truly love Eden, you must *never* mention the name Ghan Hathor to Dyonne Obor. She's the one who was ordered to execute him, and right now she's *this* close to being in as much trouble as me—'

Meredith and I flinched, startled by a sudden and brilliant flash of orange. The storm had succeeded in penetrating the shield. A single bolt of lightning speared down and struck somewhere far off in the city with a distant roar.

'Shit!' I held my breath, terrified that the shield was about to collapse and let the storm rush down on Old Castle. But it held, and no more lightning made it through. For now. I flinched again as the shrill blasts of whistles came from outside the Garden.

'The storm isn't our only concern,' Meredith said, her eyes dropping. 'I was hoping it wouldn't happen this way.'

The whistles were answered by shrill replies, along with shouts and orders. The city watch was answering an emergency call. Surely it was too soon to be because of the lightning strike.

'What's going on?'

'Wendal, you should follow the whistles. They'll lead you to Nel.'

'Nel?'

'You'll find her up in the main forge. She's in trouble.'

I jumped to my feet and Meredith grabbed my hand.

'The end begins for you now, Wendal. Sycamore's time is coming.' With a sad, tired gesture, she shooed me away. 'For what it's worth, I'm sorry for what comes next. Go, follow the whistles.'

Chapter Thirty-One

I stood over a dead city watch officer. With one arm missing, his face bitten away, he lay in his own blood and filth, and he wasn't the only one. Two more corpses, just as mauled and broken, lay close by; a reduction-house worker and another city watch officer. I hadn't yet seen what had killed them, but I could hear it: a light, hollow tattoo like someone tapping wood against stone coming from further down the tunnel.

Picking up the baton of the dead officer at my feet, I prised the short sword from the other's hand, practically breaking her rigid fingers in the process, and slid into the shadows of a recess.

The shouts and whistles of the city watch had led me to a reduction house just outside the Tinman District, where, according to Meredith, I would find Nel. If she was in trouble, it must have something to do with Mutley, but I didn't have a clue why it had brought Nel to *this* place. What I did know was that when the storm had first arrived over Old Castle, the city watch hadn't dealt with everything the cannons had missed.

Some thirty or more officers had converged on the reduction house, most rushing inside. But those who remained behind to guard the entrances and clear the area had been talking about the emergency when I sneaked by into the building's delivery tunnel. A skarab had managed to secrete itself inside the reduction house, probably drawn to the heat of its forge, and make a nest in which to lay its eggs. Skarab eggs gestated with alarming speed, their hatchlings growing to adulthood at a supernatural rate. And one was heading my way.

In the dim glow of the tunnel's ether-lights, a bulky, insectile form made its way towards the dead bodies. Clutching my weapons, remaining in shadow, I took a calming breath. No one who survived the wasteland forgot how to be a soldier, though I wished I was inside my old tank-suit. The skarab reached the first dead body, lifted it and fed with wet, angry gnawing sounds.

It was the same nightmare creature I remembered from the wasteland. Four thick, strong legs sprang from the bulbous oval of its abdomen. Its thorax rose vertically, with two wiry arms springing from muscular shoulders. It looked almost half-human, if you ignored its dark carapace, shell-like eyes, huge mouth and the long, serrated horn standing proud on the top of its head. I watched, sickened, as it cradled the dead body in its arms, biting off mouthfuls of fresh carrion with sharp teeth.

I'm sorry for what comes next, Meredith had said. Nel never left home without her satchel of tricks, and she'd need it now. Who knew how many more skarabs waited ahead? The only way past this one was through it – strike while its attention was diverted. My muscles bunched as I prepared to attack. This was going to hurt.

Shuffling footsteps and a groan of pain stopped me. The skarab dropped its meal and looked up.

'Keep moving,' a woman said, her voice echoing.

'I'm trying,' another woman replied. 'I'm losing a lot of blood here.'

'Just keep moving.'

A city watch officer was practically dragging a reduction-house employee down the delivery tunnel. The employee wore the white coat of a supervisor, which was soaked red, and there was obviously little strength left in her legs. Neither of them had noticed the skarab which had skittered around to face them.

'I need to stop,' the supervisor said, sounding on the cusp of fainting or vomiting or both.

'Come on! You can make it.' The officer's voice was strained with effort. 'Not far to go now—' She stopped, finally seeing the monster blocking the way. 'Fuck ...'

My heart thumped in my ears.

In the war, you quickly learned that there were two types of soldier: those who fought for their platoon and those who fought to save themselves. The city watch officer was the latter.

With a shriek, the skarab charged them, its sharp horn lowered. The officer made a noise of primal fear and shoved the injured supervisor in front of her. She died instantly as the horn skewered her body and the skarab hoisted her into the air. Blood splashed the walls and ceiling lights, raining down on the monster. The officer ran past me towards the exit, whimpering; and while the skarab lifted the supervisor off its head and busied itself gnawing through clothes to reach tender flesh, I slipped from the shadows.

I'd known skarabs' carapaces to be strong and hard enough to withstand a rockfall, but there was little it could do about a stealthy blade slid between the plates of its shell. While the monster fed, I lined the short sword up with a gap between its backplates and drove it in, hard, down to the hilt.

I jumped aside as the skarab screeched and spun around, spattering me with blood, releasing a pungent chemical reek. I wasted no time and swung the baton two-handed and as hard as I could into its head. The blow knocked the monster down but didn't kill it. I struck again as it tried to rise, and again, and again, until its head was mulch.

Breathing hard, I waited, listening for any new sounds of danger. The skarab's bulbous body shuddered, its legs twitched, and when it lay still silence rang in my ears. With the smell of blood and a chemical reek in my nose, I retrieved the sword and made my way down the tunnel towards the heart of the reduction house.

After a short time, the floor sloped up and led me into a cold-storage facility. The room was large, octagonal, and there was another skarab in it.

The monster had broken open one of the seven freezer doors in the room and was trying to bite through a thick layer of ice that covered one of the cadavers which had been frozen and stored, waiting to be reduced to Dust. The skarab had made good progress through the ice, and bloody slush dripped to the floor as it bit and tore. It had its back to me, and I fancied my chances of sneaking across the room to the doorway on the other side, which led up to the main forge. But once again, my plan was disrupted by citizens trying to escape. The skarab heard them approaching, too.

I could see a clutch of people through the doorway, hurrying down the slope to the cold-storage room. And leading them was Lana Khem. She carried the long, fat tube of an ether-cannon in her hands and a determined expression on her face. The skarab crept towards the doorway but stopped, waiting. Lana had no idea it was there.

I stepped into the room. 'Wait!'

The skarab turned, hissing, and came for me. Four legs drummed on the floor like wood knocking on stone. I raised the baton. Lana's ether-cannon *whumped* and my attacker skidded to a heap before it reached me. Dead, the skarab lay twitching, sparks of energy crackling over its carapace.

Ordering the group to remain where it was, Lana approached me, the obvious question half-formed on her lips.

'No time to explain,' I said. 'The way behind me is clear.'

Lana's eyes lingered on me for a second before she beckoned to the doorway. Five reduction-house workers emerged, terrified and skittish, ushered by two more city watch.

'Get them out,' Lana ordered her officers; then, to me, 'You can go with them.'

I shook my head.

Lana glared at me until the rest of the group left the cold-storage room and headed down the delivery tunnel.

'I don't know what you're doing here, Wendal, but you need to leave. A few skarabs are still hiding in the forge, and I haven't got everyone out yet.'

'I know. My friend is up there. I'm coming with you.'

Lana's gaze drifted to the dead skarab and the frozen corpse it had been mauling. 'I don't think so, Wendal.'

'Please,' I said. 'Nel's in trouble.'

'Nel? Janelle Memphis?'

'Let me help, Lana. I'll follow you anyway.'

'Come on,' she growled. 'Stay behind me.'

We ran up the sloping tunnel, Lana leading. The path curved around to the right before opening out on the reduction house's gigantic forge.

Five behemoth cauldrons sat in a circle on huge struts in a hall so large it would have taken five minutes to walk from one side to the other. There was no ceiling; the walls tapered up into a great chimney, filled with darkness. The air was powdery, bitter with the familiar scent of unrefined Dust. Close to the entrance, a few citizens had been unfortunate enough to meet skarabs. I scanned their bloody remains, relieved that Nel wasn't among them.

'This way,' Lana whispered.

We crept further into the forge, circling the centre cauldron until two skarabs came into view. They were trying to get at something underneath the cauldron's domed bottom. I saw movement there, heard a panicked curse. Nel. Trapped. Close to becoming food for monsters.

Perhaps sensing that I was about to rush foolishly to my friend's aid, Lana jabbed a finger at me with an order to remain still. Even as she aimed the ether-cannon at one skarab, the metal ball of a grenade rolled out from under the cauldron and stopped beneath the abdomen of the other.

'What the fuck—'

Lana jumped back as the grenade detonated. Barbed coils of red magic wrapped around the skarab, choking off its shrieks, squeezing the life from it. Lana fired at its partner. The ether-blast punched the monster into the air and it slammed into the cauldron with a dull clang. Dead and twitching, it fell to the ground.

Nel's grenade reduced the other to a pile of jelly-smeared shell plates. I didn't notice the third skarab until it was on me.

It came from behind, crashing me to the floor, seeking to give me a death which already belonged to Dyonne Obor. Its big mouth clamped over my face, but its teeth couldn't pierce my skin. The attempt still caused me agony. The weight crushed the air from my lungs. I stared into the void of its foul-smelling throat, seeing the wasteland there, and did my best to scream.

Whump.

Lana's cannon smashed the monster away from me, and it skidded along the forge floor in a dead heap. Gulping breaths of powdery air, I got to my feet, coughing, spitting, rubbing my face.

'Wendal!' Nel crawled out from under the cauldron. 'Are you

hurt?' She tried to run to me, but Lana grabbed her arm and yanked her back. 'Hey!'

'You're coming with me,' Lana told Nel, nothing like as stunned as my friend that I was still alive. 'Wendal, you need to leave.'

'What are you doing, Lana?'

Before she could answer, boots rang on the metal walkways above us as more city watch officers arrived at the forge.

'Clear!' one of them shouted. 'Sergeant Khem?'

'Clear!' Lana replied. 'Bring me cuffs.' Nel struggled, but the sergeant's grip was a vice. I had no idea what Lana was up to but didn't argue when she looked at me and said, 'Leave. Right now.'

Chapter Thirty-Two

I didn't have to wait long before I discovered why Nel had been arrested.

That evening, in my lodgings, I had more on my mind than I could cope with. The meeting in the Garden – Ghan Hathor ... Eden's master had a name. Meredith said that she could find him, but it wasn't only Dyonne and the Salem standing in her way. I kept seeing the lightning bolt that had struck the city. What if more got through? What if the storm drained the shield and destroyed Old Castle? I had to agree with Sycamore: the Song of Always wouldn't save me from the explosion of an ether-growth. Everyone in the city would die.

I couldn't think about it any more, so I lit a cake of jenkem, needing to escape for a while. I had already been through the daily routine of telling Itch to go back to sleep and was sitting on my windowsill, breathing in the smoky air, when Lana let herself into my lodgings. Casually, as though she were simply coming home after a hard day at work, she undid the belt from which her baton hung and threw it on the table before pulling the tie from her hair.

'We need to talk about Janelle Memphis,' she said, after a good lungful of the smoke which had already dulled the edges

214

of my perception. 'Did you know she's been hanging around Reaper Town?'

I nodded.

'The city watch have been keeping an eye on her, Wendal. She's a new face and we think she's working for someone big. What do you know about Memphis?'

'She likes to be called Nel,' I said, not really feeling the admonishment in my voice. 'And I'm not sure what to say.'

'Tell me honestly, is she affiliated with the Magicians?'

'No.'

'Then who's she working for?'

I shrugged.

'Come on, Wendal, I'm not a fucking idiot. Are you involved in this, too?'

'No.'

'Then why were you looking for Memphis at the reduction house today? Not exactly an obvious hang-out, is it?'

'I ...' It was a good question and one I couldn't answer. 'I just got lucky. Lana, listen. All I can tell you is that Nel has bitten off more than she can chew. She's not a criminal.'

'You think she deserves protecting, fine. Let's talk about why *she* was at the reduction house. Her home-made grenades were bad enough, but she was also carrying a whole load of chemicals.'

'Chemicals?'

'Not jenkem, not booze – something new called Liquid Ether.'

Mutley. What had Nel got herself into?

'This chemical comes out of Reaper Town,' Lana continued. 'The Magicians are involved somehow, and your *friend* was at the reduction house making a sale for *someone*. No one would have noticed she was even there if it hadn't been for the skarabs.' She folded her arms and sank into herself. 'Are you *sure* she's not working for the Magicians, Wendal? It's important that I know.'

Sycamore had always had his doubts about Nel, suspicious that she had turned up in my life at exactly the right moment, when I needed a friend most. He wondered if she was a Magician's lackey and that Dyonne had ordered her to form a friendship with me, but I didn't doubt Nel for a moment. She was no one's lackey. I shook my head and saw that Lana wanted to believe me.

She and I always ended up in this room together, but this was one of the few proper conversations we'd ever shared. I wished the topic were happier, willed the jenkem to take me quicker. At least my brain had slowed enough to stop me worrying about the storm and repeating the name *Ghan Hathor*.

'Where's Nel now?' I asked.

'Tinman Watch Station, being questioned. The only reason she hasn't been taken to gaol yet is because we can't decide how big a player she is. Now, is there anything I need to know?'

'Nel's an idiot, but she's not a player. You have to believe me, Lana.'

She sighed with the first effects of intoxication as she walked around to sit on the bed. She stared at me on the sill, her lips pursed with uncertainty.

'No one knows Nel like I do,' I implored. 'She's a good person in trouble. You don't need her to find out what's going on in Reaper Town.'

Lana made a growling sound. She knew that I knew more than I could say. 'This city has enough to handle without *shit* like this, Wendal.'

'Can you help me to help Nel?'

'Maybe.' Perhaps Lana held a little respect for our strange relationship; she knew that anything I gave her on Nel could be used as leverage, and a close friend of mine might become a known informant among some very dangerous people. Or perhaps it was just the jenkem that made her relent with a sagging of her shoulders. 'If she's willing to help herself.'

'Tell me how.'

'Providing she can keep her mouth shut tonight, I'll order her release in the morning and say it's so I can follow her around and see who she leads me to.' Lana shrugged. 'So, Memphis needs to be smart, Wendal.'

'She won't go back to Reaper Town,' I promised.

'Then eventually I'll stop watching her. Don't make me regret this.' A light smirk curved Lana's lips. 'And I hope she appreciates how lucky she is that *her* friend has her back. You can pick her up from the station in the morning. She'll have a fine to pay.'

'Thank you.' I snorted a laugh that sounded relieved; really, it was the smoke rising from the burner carrying my cares away.

But Lana wasn't quite ready to let go of her cares yet. She took several deep breaths and closed her eyes. 'I never saw skarabs in the war. I didn't really know what they were like. I mean, I'd heard stories about them, but ... A lot of people died today.'

A single tear ran down her cheek. 'The shield is focused on the storm, and it's taking nearly all our ether energy to keep it up there. We've barely enough left to power the city cannons. The wall is being manned day and night, but ... but Old Castle is prone to attack from the wasteland, Wendal.' She rubbed her face like she had more to worry about than I did. 'Come to bed,' she whispered, removing her jacket. 'I need to forget everything about this fucking day.'

But by then, it was Eden's voice I was hearing ...

The smell of real meat roasting over a fire was both appetising and nauseating. Spitting fat and greasy smoke into the air, it created a stench that clung to your clothes and skin, stayed in your hair and nostrils for days. It was an alien reek not easily forgotten by city soldiers, because meat for us was a concept, an idea served on our plates as flavoured Dust infused with nutrients and vitamins. But for the clansfolk, meat was a product of their environment, abundant on the wasteland, real, bountiful for hunting.

'Is this really how you remember the clansfolk?' Eden said. 'As cannibals?'

She and I sat in a cramped cage of rusty metal too low to stand in. Outside, the clansfolk had camped in a valley. The light from an ether-filled sky sparkled upon the icy ground. It was cold. Winter on the wasteland. Warriors drank and laughed, breath frosting in the air. A hundred or more of them, dressed in furs and armour of bone and metal, shaking weapons in celebration as they sang in guttural Salabese. The battle had been hard won for them, and they deserved their victory banquet. Throughout the camp, real meat turned on spits over golden flames.

'I don't think they're cannibals,' I told Eden.

'Oh, I get it. You don't regard wastelanders as human, therefore they're not eating their own kind.'

It was the corpses of fallen city soldiers that turned on spits. Naked and trussed, crisping and smoking over fires, real meat almost ready to serve.

'Your prejudices run so deep you're practically a *good* citizen, Wendal.' Eden made an angry noise. 'This isn't how they are.'

My dream wasn't regurgitating a memory of Eden this time; this was how I imagined she would react to the man I was now, the solider who had returned from the wasteland damaged. It happened sometimes. And no; that man did *not* believe the clansfolk were human.

Most were taller, broader than the average citizen, bodies

honed to muscle by a harsh life, long hair and beards braided and matted into knotty locks. Their skin was a poisonous green colour. Heads like boulders, their wide mouths were full of blocky, oversized teeth with tusks jutting up from their lower jaws. Millennia ago, the clansfolk had evolved from biological mutations resulting from the effects of magical weapons deployed during the Ether Wars. They were the ones left behind by the cities, and they should have died out. Instead, they had survived, changed and adapted to live in a hostile environment. They might have originated from human stock, but they weren't like us any more.

'They don't care what I think of them,' I told my wife, staring at the fire closest to the cage. Lana Khem was being turned over crackling flames by a broad wastelander. Lana's hair had burned away, her eyes had boiled to nothing and her skin was red and charred. The spit protruded from her mouth, keeping it open as if to preserve her final scream. 'I hate them and everything they do, Eden. They live to kill us.'

'What about the villages and settlements we destroyed?' Eden said. 'The children and families who died in the name of our war? They didn't ride out to meet us in glorious battles, did they?'

'We did as we had to.'

'Don't delude yourself, Wendal. The human race rose to the best it could be and then crashed headfirst into the worst, and that's where we stayed. The Scientists would have us believe that history began ten thousand years ago, when the Salahbeem left. They don't want us to remember what came before, when we were better than this. They want us to deny our mistakes, forget our origins. I mean, what if it's true? What if we're not native to this world and came to Urdezha from somewhere else?'

I'd heard that myth before. It was something the Magicians liked to believe, and the Scientists denied. 'What does it matter?'

'Which is exactly the Scientists' philosophy. No point being interested in how we used to be if we can't go back there.'

'I don't want to go back because I think the Magicians romanticised the Salahbeem. They were probably as bad as the clansfolk.'

'Like I said, you're becoming a *good* citizen, Wendal.'

'I've had more insight than you.'

Joints of human meat were being carried to long stone tables and carved up for the plates of hungry clansfolk. A hush fell over the camp as eager mouths tore into carrion from the battlefield. Lana continued to turn and silently scream.

'Remnants,' Eden said. 'Vestiges of past mistakes. You only need to look at the end of this valley to know that's all we are.'

But I didn't want to look. On the other side of the camp, the valley ended not far away, and there the giant corpse-trees of a graveforest grew, a huge and brooding silhouette encapsulating the darkness of my worst memories.

'You're one of the few soldiers who saw the inside of a graveforest and lived to tell the tale,' Eden said. 'You heard it, didn't you? You heard the original Song of the Dead in there.'

I didn't reply.

'Why don't your dreams ever confront what happened in that graveforest?' Eden expressed puzzlement. 'What are you most afraid of? Yourself? Or that survivalist you met – what was her name?'

'August Jakob.'

'See? You *do* remember. Now, what about your friends? Hanna, Danii, the rest of the soldiers you fought with – why don't you dream of them?'

'Eden, every waking minute of every day I have to carry the wasteland around with me. I don't remember what happened in the graveforest because Sycamore won't let me.'

My wife scoffed and her manner changed. '*You might consider denial a necessary form of protection, Wendal, but in actuality the act of lying to yourself is nothing short of pointless.*' Eden turned sycamore-seed eyes to me. '*And the clansfolk don't eat city soldiers, no matter what you think of them.*'

I sighed and my shoulders sagged. He had to turn up eventually.

In the camp, two clansfolk lifted Lana off the flames and carried her to a table for carving. Rowdy cheering and songs had started up again.

'*Your recent conversations have roused my curiosity,*' Sycamore said. '*And you know how much I hate it when your race brings that out in me.*'

He hated the very act of humans breathing, but I played along. 'What's on your mind?'

'*Don't you think it's interesting how Dyonne Obor was more perturbed about Ing Meredith than the menace hanging over her city?*'

'Not especially,' I replied. 'Nothing Dyonne does surprises me any more.'

'*I can't help thinking that Meredith is an anomaly, a spanner in the works, as it were.*'

I frowned at the image of my wife, surprised by such an obvious statement. 'Dyonne already told us that much. Meredith is meddling in the Salem's affairs and—'

'*No, no – you're not following me. I've long suspected that Dyonne isn't quite the dutiful servant she purports to be. What if she's up to something of which the Salem are unaware and that is why she was perturbed by Meredith's interference?*'

'You have suspicions about everybody, all the time.'

'*I have the influence of my host to thank for that.*'

In this dream, even if I closed my eyes, I couldn't stop seeing the clansfolk feasting upon roasted city soldiers. 'All you care about is making me piss Dyonne off enough to summon my moment of death.'

'*Wendal, you are so self-absorbed that I'm not sure you have truly heard all you have been told. Answer me – do you harbour any doubts over whether or not Ing Meredith is telling the truth?*'

'No.' And I meant it.

'*Then consider – there is a Magician out there somewhere named Ghan Hathor. A short time ago, the Salem found reason to order his execution, which must have been at the same time that Eden was serving as his apprentice. This I find interesting because, allegedly, Hathor's executioner was Dyonne Obor.*'

'Dyonne …' I suddenly saw the dark void into which Eden had fallen and found Ing Meredith staring back at me. What was it she had said about Dyonne being in almost as much trouble as her?

'*The Salem believes that Hathor is dead, but what did Eden do when the assassin came calling? Kill herself? Was her master's execution connected to black stone?*'

Sycamore crawled to the front of the cage, curling my wife's fingers around the bars, staring out onto the clansfolk's grisly banquet. '*I often wonder how the Magicians knew I was in Old Castle, Wendal. The dead have loose lips, to be sure, but there's more to it than that. The Salem see much of what occurs in this city, but not as much as the Quantum. There must be a reason why the Scientists have never approached you, or found a way to stop the Magicians using me against them.*'

A big secret world was swirling around the city, Meredith had said, and I was only just beginning to see it.

'*The Quantum and the Salem have their plots and feuds,*' Sycamore continued, '*but I'm beginning to wonder if Dyonne Obor lurks between them with plans of her own. What if Ing Meredith's threat is more personal than she's letting on?*'

'I don't see it,' I said. 'What could Dyonne do that the Salem wouldn't know about? She holds a trusted rank, the Grand Adepts keep her close, they ...' My thoughts halted as another question clicked into my head, based on something Dyonne had told me. 'A Magician needs permission from the Salem to take on an apprentice. When they ordered Ghan Hathor's execution, did they know who his apprentice was? Did Dyonne know?'

You cannot risk broaching this topic with Dyonne herself, and Hathor can only answer questions if Meredith finds him before death catches up with her. Quite a quandary. I'm not sure what to suggest to increase your proactivity here, Wendal.

How did I find the strength to wait, pray, for Meredith to come good?

At least Nel has given you an alternative concern to worry over. Sycamore sat back as three clansfolk approached the cage. One slipped the chain from the gate, levelling a bone spear as the other two stepped in and grabbed him. Hair wild and faces dirty green, they grunted Salabese through blocky teeth and tusks as they dragged him towards the fire over which Lana Khem had cooked. The gate was closed and chained, its rusty bars separating me from the image of my wife.

Eden gazed at me calmly as the clansfolk laid Sycamore down on the ground and prepared him for gutting. *'Meredith was right, Wendal. The end begins for you now. My freedom is coming. The storm will see to that.'*

I looked away as a clanswoman stabbed down into Eden's stomach with a wickedly sharp knife and turned my eyes to the sky. Clouds were closing in. Snow would come soon.

Chapter Thirty-Three

What should have been a simple morning – pick up Nel, read her the riot act and then return home where I could carry on obsessing over my dilemma – turned out to be far more complicated.

As always, Lana had gone by the time I woke up, and I rose from bed with a bastard of a jenkem hangover which left me sick to my stomach. Stumbling from my lodging house and out into the Tinman District was a painful exercise: the rumble of the city shield felt like a vice squeezing my temples; flashes of fiery orange in the sky like nails driven into my eyes.

Smoke was rising in the distance, from somewhere at the centre of Old Castle. I heard citizens talking about it on the street. From what I could gather, the storm had penetrated the shield with three more lightning strikes during the night, all of them focusing on the Fusion, damaging buildings and causing fires in the area.

None of them could have struck the city's main reactor, otherwise Old Castle would have gone the same way as Alexria by now, but the storm *did* appear to be targeting our ether-growth, drawn to that immense concentration of magic far beneath us. As a result, so much of our power had been redirected to the shield that the city had practically come to a standstill. Nothing

224

else that required ether energy was operating, not even the official transmission pyramids; and with no new information coming from the Scientists, the citizens had been left to draw their own conclusions.

This was not a good thing.

The agitation could be felt on the streets; a palpable atmosphere was growing beneath roiling darkness and the rumbling pressure of the shield, and it might very well lead to citywide panic if the Scientists didn't do something. The air prickled with magic, the smell of rusty metal was borne on the breeze, and everyone was asking the same question: why wasn't this fucking storm going away?

Could Meredith be right? Had the Scientists caused this themselves? *My freedom is coming*, Sycamore had said. *The storm will see to that.*

Feeling nauseous, the pain in my head so bad that I could hardly bear to keep my eyes open, I stopped at a baker's to buy a stale loaf from yesterday, thinking that a little food might settle my stomach. It almost worked, until my thoughts and dreams decided to escape my mind and a vision beset me, right there where I stood on the street.

It started as a wispy iridescence that floated down from above like a cloud of light escaping the spite in the sky. No one else on the street noticed it, and my pains and troubles were somehow soothed as the wisps swirled and rushed around me like a horde of silver spirits. Before I had time to properly react to this strange occurrence, the city itself began to change before my eyes.

Buildings morphed and twisted, growing upwards. Brickwork and glass turned into thick bark with deep crevices. Rooftops merged into a canopy of green leaves the size of umbrellas, and the buildings kept growing, morphing, until I was surrounded by the fearsome and impossibly tall trunks of corpse-trees. The iridescence rose and gathered to form a silver sun that shone down with the warmth of summer. But I felt cold, chilled to the bone, as I found myself, impossibly, standing in the nightmare that I refused to remember.

A graveforest.

Breathing hard, I staggered as pain flared in my head. This felt like the Songs that ghouls sang to Sycamore, but there was no ghoul present, and their visions never came with this much colour, clarity, sound. The corpse-trees were alive with the calls of forest creatures, deadening the ambience of the city. The canopy of giant leaves was high overhead, lush and verdant, and bright beneath it was the ball of the wispy silver sun.

Had I lost my mind? I didn't feel like I was in a dream, but I didn't feel real, either.

In this bizarre city-forest, the street I had been walking remained as Dust made into stone, snaking between behemoth trees like a stream frozen to dirty ice. And there, congregated on the path, stretching back further than I could see, was a horde of ghosts.

I tensed, not knowing how to react. The ghosts formed orderly ranks, standing in neat rows like platoons of well-trained soldiers. There was nothing threatening about their stance; they were radiating more of an air of expectancy, as though I had stolen something from them and they were waiting for me to give it back. So many dead eyes stared, and I couldn't bear the judgement in them.

'What do you want?' My voice sounded close and breathless in this strange vision.

The ghosts kept their silence, staring, judging, and a cold shadow fell upon the city-forest. A darkness was growing at the centre of the silver sun, a black void which pierced the wispy light to create a perfect diamond shape. A sudden wind rushed in from all places. My jacket flapped and I struggled to keep my footing. The void was a vacuum and it brought fear to the faces of the ghosts. With a unified voice, they issued a single moan, one word, one accusation: 'Sycamore.'

The wind increased and dispersed the ghosts, shredding them to streaks of iridescence, whipping, swirling through the corpse-trees, gathering and rising like a whirlwind as they were sucked into the black diamond in the sun. Just as it seemed the void would swallow the dead for ever, a bolt of orange lightning stabbed down from the darkness and struck the ground with a roar and a belch of smoke. I stepped back, hands raised against the blinding flash, before looking again, surprised to see that where the lightning had struck the path, a person now stood. A person who was not human.

With a horde of scintillating ghosts rushing past her, the mysterious Salahbeem woman from my dreams glared at me. As usual, she wore armour of amber glass decorated with magical script. In her hand she held a spear. The butt of the golden shaft touched the ground beside her foot; the wickedly jagged head pointed at the sky, and it was luminous, silver delicately hued by a rose tint. Ether.

She narrowed her colourless eyes, and for the first time she spoke to me. '*I am Idgian Korinth, first knight of the Order of Glass and Words.*' Salabese, oddly accented and somehow ancient. With fluid grace, she spun her weapon and brought the jagged spearhead to bear on me. '*I did not sacrifice myself so you could torment this world. Your wrath has no place on Urdezha!*'

And she charged me, ether-spear lowered and aimed for my chest. I cried out, tried to run, but fell and ended up flat on my back. I closed my eyes as the Salahbeem knight stabbed down at me. But there was no pain …

When I opened my eyes, she was gone, as were the remnants

of ghosts, the black void in the silver sun and the strange vision of a graveforest. I lay on the street in Old Castle again, trying to still my heart and calm my breathing as people milled around me. None of them had noticed my antics. Flipping over onto my hands and knees, I vomited the bread I'd just eaten.

A light vibration came from the stone beneath my hands: the rumble of the city shield. Citizens pointed at the sky, moaning worriedly and shouting warnings. The storm had burst with a great gout of fire that sprayed and ran liquidly over the shield. Ether energy crackled, buckled, bowed downwards under the pressure, but the shield held and the storm, mercifully, didn't break through. This time.

What the fuck just happened?

The buzzing voices of citizens increased to a swarm of bees: the discontent of Old Castle had taken one step closer to blind panic, and I couldn't stand the sound in my ears.

Nel! I remembered, shouting the name in my mind as though it was the last link to sanity.

Jumping to my feet, confused, disorientated, I made my way to Tinman Watch Station as fast as I could. I focused my mind on the real world, latched on to the sights and sounds and smells of the streets, consoled myself with the knowledge that collecting Nel from city watch custody would be the simplest thing I'd do that day. But I was wrong.

The station wasn't busy, but I had to wait in line while two city watch booked in a drunk with the duty officer. The man swayed between the officers, slurring loudly about how the city was on the brink of destruction and the Scientists were doing nothing about it. He grated on what remained of my shredded nerves, and I was thankful when he was finally dragged off to a cell where he could sober up. I approached the duty desk, praying that no more visions would break into reality.

The officer behind the desk was portly and looked as though he was struggling to wake up for his morning shift. Barely able to keep his eyes open behind his spectacles, he sat staring into the middle distance, not seeing me even though I was standing right in front of him. Only when I rapped my knuckles on the desk did I startle him into noticing that I was there.

'Help you?' he said, aggrieved.

'I'm here to pick up Janelle Memphis.' My voice was timid, shaken.

With slow, lazy movements, he took the records book and let it flap open with a light thump. 'When was she brought in?'

'Yesterday.'

'Memphis, Memphis ...' The duty officer trailed a finger down the page. 'Here she is.'

'I'll pay her fine, too.'

'No need. Already taken care of.'

'What?'

'Janelle Memphis.' He tapped the book for emphasis. 'Released a couple of hours ago. Says here she was picked up by someone called Jon Johnny.'

'Jon ... Johnny?'

'That's what the book says.'

I swallowed, trying not to dissolve into panic. Or rage. 'That can't be right.'

The officer gave me a hard stare through the lenses of his spectacles. 'Is there a problem, citizen?'

Without another word, I left the station, heart thumping, mind racing. Was there a problem? Only that Nel had been picked up by a dead man, and I could guess exactly who was behind it. Dilemma upon dilemma. I wasn't sure how much more I could take.

'It's Wendal, right?'

I wheeled around. A man had followed me out of the station. He was slim and short, wearing a long, concealing coat over a sharp suit. A good-looking rogue I vaguely recognised from the night Nel and I had taken care of Jon Johnny.

'You're a hard man to find, Wendal.' His smile was far too easy. 'You look worried, like you've lost a friend.'

My fists clenched, causing him to raise his hands in placation.

'Nel's fine,' he assured me. 'If you want to see her, come to the Sharpened Card tonight. Mutley wants a word.'

He walked away. The sky flashed as though the storm was laughing at me. And who knew? Maybe it was.

Chapter Thirty-Four

You will go nowhere unusual, Dyonne had warned. *Go home and stay there.* Shit ... That boat had well and truly sailed now.

I stood at the bar in the main gambling room of the Sharpened Card, my fingers curled around a glass of beer which had yet to be lifted to my lips. A thick layer of smoke hung like a cloud above the gamblers gathered around dice and card tables, glowing in the flickering light of candelabras. The cheers of winners mixed with the groans of losers and scratched my senses raw. It was as though these people were embracing revelry to allay their troubled minds. Fear of the storm was good for business, apparently, but I was too anxious to settle among these citizens.

The wait for night-time had been maddening. The bizarre vision which had assaulted me plagued my mind throughout the day. I was no stranger to seeing the dead, but so many ghosts, terrified as they were sucked up into a lightless void – was it real or a waking dream? Had I really been attacked by a knight from the Order of Glass and Words? Seeing her step from my mind and appear on the street in broad daylight had been disconcerting enough, but now she had a name: Idgian Korinth. Had she been talking to me or Sycamore?

Perhaps I had taken too much jenkem. Was the boundary

between what was real and what was not breaking down? What did it mean?

When night finally arrived, the queue outside the Sharpened Card had been long by the time its doors opened. I was swept inside by a flood of hungry gamblers and into the main games room. Beer was being served warm as there was no power for the chillers, but no one seemed to care. Most people had been more concerned with claiming a place at the gambling tables, but I had set up camp at the bar, not really knowing what to do next, not knowing what was going on. I'd told the gaunt and sallow-skinned barman that I was here to see Mutley, but that was almost an hour ago now. The Sharpened Card's owner was in no rush to show herself, and I wasn't good at waiting.

I scanned the room for signs of Nel and Mutley. The establishment was vastly different from the last time I had seen it. I'd never intended to come back, but Nel had given me little choice.

Obviously, the trouble she was in had gone from bad to worse, and Mutley wasn't ready to end their relationship, whatever that meant now. Nel had made a lot of wrong decisions in her life, but she wasn't stupid enough to deal in chemicals. I'd thought that by keeping the whole truth from Lana I was doing right by Nel. But now I realised that if I'd only told her that Mutley was undoubtedly behind Nel's actions, then she could have done something – raided the Sharpened Card, arrested Mutley, anything that might have prevented my one and only friend from being dragged back into the rancid world of Reaper Town.

Lana said the city watch were keeping an eye on Nel, so maybe they were here already, undercover. Dyonne couldn't be aware of what I was involved in; if she had any inkling, she would have intervened already. But what if one of her spies saw me? Nel said that Magicians came to this place. I was supposed to be lying low.

As it turned out, it was Nel herself who spotted me. She pointed me out to the two cronies who were escorting her to the other end of the bar. The look in her eye told me how afraid she was. Before I could approach her, someone tapped me on the shoulder.

'Hello again,' said the man in the sharp suit. 'Mutley's ready for you now.'

I looked at Nel under guard by the bar, and then back at the man. 'I want to talk to my friend first.'

'Yeah, the boss said you'd be like that.' He nodded. 'All right, you can have a quick word.'

Mutley's cronies stepped aside when I approached Nel. They didn't stray too far, however. Nel tried to her best to smile at me, and I bent to whisper into her ear.

'Why do I let you drag me into shit like this?'

'Wendal, I'm scared.'

'Me too. What's going on, Nel?'

She swallowed, her eyes flitting around the room. 'Mutley won't let me go. She's making me work for her, but after yesterday, something's changed.' She spoke quickly, breathlessly. 'I don't know what. Seems bad, and … and now …'

'Slow down.' I'd never seen her this rattled, not even after the things she had experienced with me. 'Why does Mutley want to talk to me?'

Nel took a breath. 'She says you're the ace up her sleeve.'

'What does that mean?'

Nel blinked at me, on the cusp of tears. 'She made me tell her everything I know about you. She wanted to know if you ever went by a different name.'

The world shrank around me. 'Did you tell her?'

'I'm so sorry, Wendal. She didn't give me a choice.'

Behind me, the henchman cleared his throat. 'Time's up,' he said.

I laid a hand on Nel's cheek. 'It's all right. Sit tight. We'll get out of this, like we always do.'

And then I was being led through the crowded gambling tables to the other side of the room, where Mutley waited for me in an alcove, smoking a cheroot. While I slid into the alcove to sit on the opposite side of the table, her henchman turned his back to us and kept guard.

'Good to see you again, Wendal.' Mutley flicked ash and smiled at me. She carried the same dangerous expression and able body language that I remembered. Not a person to be messed with.

On the table, next to the ashtray, was a small ether-cannon. Mutley's free hand rested close to it. The weapon bothered me, but my concern had nothing to do with the threat of its physical presence.

'Whatever Nel has got herself into,' I said, 'just tell me how to get her out.'

'Straight to the point – I like that.' Next to the ether-cannon was a bottle of wine and two glasses. Mutley poured us one each, but I didn't touch mine. 'I honestly had no idea who you were when we first met. If I had, I might've been more respectful.'

I understood then why the ether-cannon bothered me. Those kinds of weapons weren't easy to get hold of, even for a criminal of Reaper Town. They generally didn't differ much aesthetically, but this one looked custom, home-made, and an itch in my brain told me that it was remarkably similar to the one owned by a Scientist named Brandon Quinn.

'Nice cannon,' I said. 'Where did you get it?'

'It was a gift, actually. From a business associate. Dyonne Obor – ring any bells?'

The room swallowed me up. Of course Dyonne and Mutley would have business ties. It had probably begun as recompense for the Magicians taking care of Jon Johnny. The situation kept on spiralling down and down.

'Magicians are good at making empty promises and then walking away when trouble brews,' Mutley said. 'I've been financing a moneymaking scheme for the Salem. Dyonne was my contact. I paid for secret premises, covered overheads for manufacture, sourced the expensive, hard-to-get ingredients. I laid out most of what I own for ... well, I'm sure Nel has shared some of the product with you by now. She likes to steal from me.'

Mutley oozed confidence. She sipped her wine and drew smoke from the cheroot, gauging my reaction. I gave her nothing, but that was mostly because I didn't know what the fuck I was doing.

'Seeing as Nel liked the product so much, I gave her a job as a delivery girl.'

'You *made* her do it.'

'Let's not split hairs, Wendal. I finally had this place up and running, Liquid Ether was set to make me a tidy sum, and I was pleased with my lot. But after Nel's actions yesterday, the Salem walked away from the operation and left me sorely out of pocket.'

Shit. Dyonne had to know that Nel was involved in the reduction-house incident. Did she know I'd been there, too?

First things first, I told myself, and tried to keep my voice calm. 'You can't blame Nel for the skarab attack.'

'I don't.' Anger reddened Mutley's face. 'But I do blame her for getting caught.'

A great cheer came as someone among the gamblers won big. Mutley blew smoke from her nostrils and crushed the cheroot in the ashtray.

'No Magician will touch me now. Magic is used in Liquid

Ether's production, and without a specialist apothecary, I can't produce more. All the money I invested has gone to waste and it'll be some time before I make it back. The city watch probably know by now that I'm responsible for what Nel was carrying yesterday, and there're only so many officials I can pay off. Until the watch stops *watching*, I have to tread carefully and stay on the right side of the law.'

'Is that so bad?' I asked hopefully.

'Don't be naive,' Mutley snapped. 'This is Reaper Town, Wendal. My enemies and competitors know I'm in a weak position and they're circling like ... skarabs waiting to pick a battlefield clean of carrion. Because of your friend. Because of Dyonne Obor.' But she looked at me as if it were my fault.

I grabbed the wine and took a big gulp. 'So what do you need me for?'

Mutley chuckled bitterly. 'I like to cover my back, Wendal. I find it good business to *know* who I'm getting into bed with.' She drained her glass of wine and lit another cheroot, her manner returning to that of a calculating monster. 'Dyonne fancies herself a big-time player. Some say she's good enough to be a Grand Adept, but in my opinion, she's not clever enough for that. I don't give a fuck who her masters are, she's an idiot if she thinks she can leave someone like *me* in the shit and just walk away. I found out some interesting things about one of the people who works for her, you see. So I thought I'd invite him here before Dyonne got the chance to *send* him.'

I kept my mouth shut.

'Remember our old friend – Jon Johnny? I tried talking to him once. He told me something strange. I paid it no mind until later, but he said, "Sycamore is coming."'

I chewed on silent words, shaking my head.

'Oh, don't bother trying to deny it,' Mutley said. 'Nel

confirmed who you are.' She laid her hand on the ether-cannon. 'They say on the streets that Sycamore is a Judge of Aktuaht come to condemn us all, but this storm above us is frightening people into saying all kinds of shit, and I'm not so easily taken in.

'Sycamore is the best assassin Old Castle has to offer, and he works for the Magicians. No one sees him coming, no one sees him leave, and he's almost impossible to track down.' She grinned. 'Fortunately, I'm acquainted with Sycamore's best friend.'

'It's not what you think.' My voice trembled. 'It isn't like that.'

'That's where you're wrong.' Mutley nodded towards the bar. I could see Nel through the cluster of gamblers, quiet and downcast between the cronies. 'If you want to keep your friend alive, then it'll be exactly as I tell you it is.'

How did I explain to this woman that through rumours and misinformation she had stumbled into something she couldn't possibly understand?

'This is how Dyonne and the Salem pay me back, Wendal. By loaning me your services.'

'Listen to me, Mutley. You think you know Dyonne, but you don't. You have no idea what you're dealing with—'

'Shut up.' Mutley was aiming the ether-cannon at me now. She didn't know that it couldn't kill me. 'Here's what happens next. You'll go home and wait for Nel to show us where you live. You'll be given a list of names. Each name will belong to one of the scumbags who are already looking to make a move on my patch.' Her face became cruel. 'Some of them are in this room right now, and I want them dead.'

'Mutley, you don't understand—'

'The storm is making people crazy, reckless, so don't test me. *If* you fulfil this contract, then I'll leave Nel be, and good luck to the pair of you. If not, then I'll put this cannon to Nel's head and pull the trigger. Do we have an understanding, *Sycamore*?'

I felt sweat beading on my forehead. I nodded – what else could I do? – and drained the glass of wine.

'Dyonne Obor must feel so secure having you around taking care of her enemies.' Mutley scoffed and gestured to her henchman to take me away. 'You have two days or Nel dies.'

Chapter Thirty-Five

I tried something that I'd never dared try before. I dug down deep inside myself and begged Sycamore to take over my body. I pleaded for him to rise, to control me as he so often had, and take this predicament off my hands. *I'm out of options*, I thought to him, *I don't know what to do.* But the spells that kept him imprisoned were too potent. Sycamore remained silent. He didn't stir in the slightest, and wouldn't unless a ghoul told him its name. I was on my own with only one place left to turn.

I was going to come clean.

I *had* to tell Dyonne everything, for Nel's sake. Mutley had drawn herself to the wrong conclusion. She thought I was a straightforward assassin, a blade in the dark for hire. She had misunderstood the true nature of what *we* were, and that would be her undoing. Sycamore went beyond Dyonne's rank, to the Salem itself. And if the Salem's intervention saved Nel at the cost of Mutley's life, then so be it. I'd gladly sacrifice that criminal for my friend.

I went to the unnamed tavern directly from the Sharpened Card. No one answered when I banged on the door. My urgency boiled over and I thumped and kicked, calling Dyonne's name. But the only reward for my efforts was strange looks a few citizens who soon forgot me after they passed by. I considered sitting outside the door and waiting for Dyonne to show – or some other Magician who could get a message to her – but my frustration wouldn't let me keep still, so I decided to pace the short length of my lodgings instead. Dyonne expected me to be there, anyway.

Two days, Mutley had given me. Would Old Castle survive the storm for that long? I felt as though Urdezha itself was coming to an end.

Itch woke up as soon as I walked through the door. Gaunt, mummified face peering over her knees, angry orange in her eyes, she demanded to know when I would kill her murderer. 'I don't fucking know!' I shouted at her, to my regret. Itch's wails pierced my eardrums and her tears popped with the stench of the wasteland. I ordered her back to sleep. She disappeared but the stench remained.

Pacing, containing frustration and panic behind clenched teeth and fists, I kept glancing out of the window, hoping against hope that I might see Nel bringing me Mutley's list of names. She was a wily character; she would play along just to get away, and then ... I'd hide with her in the fucking sewers if it meant keeping her safe. I didn't catch sight of my friend, but, when I glanced out of the window for the umpteenth time, I was shocked to see Abdon Klyne. His ghost stood in the lane, beckoning me down.

'I would've come up,' he said when I rushed out to join him, 'but ... are you keeping a ghoul in your lodgings?'

The predawn hours were cold beneath the storm, but Klyne's breath didn't mist the air as mine did.

'What do you want?' I said, shivering, pulling my jacket around me.

'I suppose I came to say goodbye. I'm leaving Old Castle, Wendal. Reckon it's time I saw the wasteland again.'

'You came to say *goodbye*?' Klyne looked shaken, scared – not traits commonly seen in ghosts. It disturbed me. 'What's happened?'

'I met with Meredith last night. We didn't speak long. She wants me to give you a message. She said, if you go outside the city and follow the coast away from the fishing settlement, you'll come to the ruins you played in as a kid.'

Surprise dislodged an old and forgotten memory from my mind. 'The ruins? Yes, I remember them.'

'Well, Meredith wants you to know that the dead are singing their Song for you there, whatever the fuck that means.'

My heart skipped. She had to be talking about Ghan Hathor. 'Did she mention a name?'

'No. Whatever the two of you are up to, you've dragged me into it now. I can't go back to my library because the fucking Magicians are looking for me.' Klyne rubbed his forehead. 'We're all in trouble, Wendal. We've all been delving into dangerous things, and that's why I'm leaving Old Castle. Tonight. For good.'

Klyne held up a hand for silence as a couple of citizens walked past the end of the side lane, laughing; and when they didn't head our way, he gave a sigh of relief. A spirit scared *and* paranoid? I knew how he felt. I thought of Nel, I thought of Eden … I thought of rushing to the coast right now and finding Ghan Hathor.

Klyne gave a bitter laugh. 'I used to think that being dead meant I couldn't die a second time. I was wrong.' He sounded angry. 'I know a little more about what the Scientists have got their hands on.'

'Black stone.' The words tumbled from my lips immediately, pouncing on the subject.

'I suppose I should count myself lucky that I found out what

I did,' Klyne said. 'They're saying black stone is old knowledge, Wendal – ancient, something the Gardeners left behind.'

'Wait – it's a relic of the Salahbeem?'

'And as rare as fuck, worth a thousand survivalists' weight in ether. I can't remember anything of the Gardeners' being discovered on the wasteland during my lifetime. And this thing – it's powered by the spirits of the dead.'

I couldn't really explain why, but I was feeling more and more disturbed, colder and colder as if the temperature had suddenly dropped lower than it already was.

Klyne was still keeping a nervous eye out for anyone watching us. 'See, I was wrong, Wendal. No one's trying to stop the dead leaving Old Castle. Black stone is ... *eating* them, using spirits as fuel, and the Scientists can't stop it. So I'm escaping this city before it eats me, too.'

'That's ...' I didn't know what I thought it was. 'What *is* black stone?'

'The best guess I've heard is that it's some kind of transportation device, like an ancient gateway that's capable of reaching ... anywhere, I suppose.'

'A gateway?' I asked. 'There hasn't been gateway on Urdezha since—'

'I'm not an idiot, Wendal. I know the stories and I know the wasteland. Just because the technology hasn't been around for millennia doesn't mean it's not still there, hiding beneath the world, waiting to be found.' Klyne levelled his look. 'Whatever this thing is, the Magicians are terrified of it. They seem to think that all these experiments the Scientists are running are in aid of finding a way to reach the Salahbeem themselves.'

'This is ridiculous.'

'Is it?' Klyne looked at me as though both our existences were well past the point of ridiculous now. 'I've been eavesdropping

on all sorts of secret conversations between some pretty important people. Maybe the rumours are true. Maybe the Scientists
succeeded.' He pointed up at the storm. 'What if this is the
Salahbeem's way of telling us to fuck off?'

I followed the direction of his finger. I felt a sudden and un-
nerving connection with the storm, like each flash of lightning
was calling to me, and I wanted to rise and meet the roiling,
fiery darkness ... or drag it down.

'One thing's for sure,' Klyne continued, 'the Quantum and
the Salem have been fighting over black stone and the situation
is coming to a head.'

Klyne cast a nervous glance up and down the lane. 'I heard the
problems began when the Scientists tried to test the gateway –
short range, city to city. See, black stone is broken down into
three components. The first was brought here to Old Castle.
The second was in Alexria, Wendal.'

'Alexria?' My jaw hung slack for a moment. 'Shit.'

'Now you see where this is going.' Klyne stepped closer to me,
looming. 'I heard some high-ranking Scientists talking. They
said a train of ether-wagons brought a group of war survivors to
Old Castle yesterday. They were supposed to return to Alexria,
but when they got there, it was gone. Just a giant smoking crater
where it used to be. A whole city destroyed, people and all.
That's what happens when an ether-growth blows up.'

'Black stone destroyed Alexria?' I pointed upwards. 'Did this?'

Klyne nodded and sucked cold air over his teeth. 'Whether
this thing is a gateway or not, the Scientists can't switch it off.
After Alexria went up, black stone dragged the storm to Old
Castle. The component that's here just keeps on eating the
dead, and if it can't be stopped then it'll drag that fucking mess
up there down through the shield. You should prepare for the
worst, Wendal. The Scientists can't protect this city for ever.'

An icy breeze blew down the lane and I wrapped my arms around me, thinking of my strange waking dream, seeing the horde of ghosts sucked up into a void of darkness. How close did Old Castle stand to Alexria's fate? How much time was left? A relic of the Salahbeem. A gateway? It touched a nerve in me. 'You said there were three parts to black stone. Where's the third?'

'Missing,' Klyne said. 'It's reckoned to be in Old Castle somewhere and to be the only thing that can stop the storm ripping the city apart. Some are saying the Salem has it but they're hiding it from the Quantum. After Alexria, I'd change my tune if I were them, but … if you ask me, Wendal, this missing part is what Eden was looking for at the university. But she wasn't the person who found it.

'There is a record of black stone being discovered. I had to dig deep, read between the lines a bit, but it's definitely there. A survivalist found it on the wasteland somewhere around four months ago. She took it to Alexria, but she wasn't there when the city went up in smoke. See, the Scientists wouldn't pay out on a very lucrative finder's fee because the *artefact in question was incomplete*. The survivalist said she knew where the missing part was and came to Old Castle to find it. But when she arrived, she was murdered.'

'Murdered?'

'By the Magicians, I reckon.' Klyne's old and beaten face creased with lines of worry, probably because the fate of his fellow survivalist had reminded him what dying was like, and now black stone threatened to give him a second go. 'Strange thing, though. The report said the artefact was found in a grave-forest. Never heard of that before.'

'A graveforest?' I baulked and stepped back from Klyne, ice in my gut. 'Did the report tell you her name?' I demanded. 'The survivalist?'

Klyne nodded. 'August Jakob.'

I felt like vomiting. 'Say that again.'

But Klyne's attention was caught by something behind me. 'Do you know him?'

At the end of the lane, the bulky form of Tamara had appeared. Standing in shadows, he could obviously see me but not the spirit. His presence should have given me a surge of hope. I hadn't forgotten Nel, but this conversation had just become as disturbing as the threat of the storm above. I hadn't felt this frightened since the war.

'I have to go, but ...' I was about to tell Klyne that it was imperative we talked again before he left Old Castle, but he had already fled. His ghost simply wasn't there any more.

With a curt gesture, Tamara ordered me out of the lane before turning and walking away. I stared at the space Abdon Klyne had filled a moment earlier before following the bodyguard, the tugs of Dyonne's leash pulling at my neck.

Chapter Thirty-Six

'You were told to stay out of the *way*!' Dyonne was fuming with a barely controlled fury that I'd never seen in her before. 'Do you have any idea what you've done?' Her hand shook as she pointed a finger at me.

I swallowed. The air practically crackled with the power of Dyonne's magic. How much did she know?

'You couldn't control yourself, could you?' she raged. 'Just when I solve one of your problems, you give me *another*!'

Few candles had been lit in the nameless tavern. Tamara waited in the shadows somewhere behind me. In the dim glow, Dyonne paced up and down before facing me with her hands on her hips.

'What do you have to say for yourself, Wendal?'

I had nothing. I wasn't even looking at Dyonne. My eyes were for the dead body on the floor behind her. Ing Meredith lay on her back, her arms crossed over her chest. She had no visible wounds and her bloodless face expressed peace in death. How much did Dyonne know?

'Oh, you feel sorry for her?' Dyonne said, following my stare.

Unconscious good sense shook my head for me. I didn't know what to feel. Ghan Hathor was no longer the only name on my mind; Abdon Klyne had seen to that.

Coincidence either happens or it doesn't, Eden used to tell me, because it could only be judged when all the facts were at hand. August Jakob: I'd met her. I knew what she had discovered on the wasteland. I knew what black stone was. Because ... I was with her when she found it.

'Well?' Dyonne demanded.

'I don't know,' I blurted. 'I ... I don't know what to say.'

'Begin by telling me what occurred in Reaper Town,' Dyonne growled. 'You were seen at the Sharpened Card last night, having a cosy chat with a lowlife called Mutley.'

'I didn't have a choice. I was going to tell you—'

'I am *not* pleased, Wendal!'

'Dyonne, listen to me.' If I was scared before, it was nothing compared to when I saw Dyonne's pupils dilate. The pressure of magic grew in the room. She was on the cusp of summoning my moment of death, I was sure of it, so I spoke quickly. 'Mutley thinks Sycamore is an assassin for hire. She's blackmailing me into killing her competitors. She says that *you* owe her my service for backing out of a business agreement.'

'My business is none of your concern.' Dyonne drew herself up, seemed to expand. 'And you have no excuses. You should not have gone to Reaper Town.'

'I had to,' I stressed. 'Mutley is holding my friend hostage.'

'Ah, yes – Janelle Memphis.'

I didn't like the way Dyonne said Nel's name. I became suddenly aware of a presence in the room, something dark, on the outskirts, being held back. It made Sycamore stir in the deepest regions of my being.

'I thought that having a friend would be good for you, Wendal, but I see now that allowing Memphis into your life was a mistake.' Dyonne drew a breath, exhaled with a sound like resignation. She moved to one side, giving me a clearer view of

Meredith's dead and peaceful body. 'Your friend has become a liability, and Mutley's final stain needs removing.'

Dyonne waved a hand, permitting the dark presence to come forward. I heard it before I saw it, rasping wetly like someone trying to breathe with water in their lungs. The stink of the wasteland came next, then finally a ghoul drifted into view. It slid from the shadows, human in shape but faceless and of monstrous size.

'Oh no,' I pleaded, shaking my head. 'Not now.'

'Sing him your Song,' Dyonne commanded.

I backed away but met the hard body of Tamara after only two steps. He held me in place until the ghoul was too close to escape and I could feel the haunting begin. With a command from Dyonne, Tamara followed his master out of the room, while the ghoul loomed over me.

'My name is Mutya Bryn,' it said, and Sycamore rose. 'But most people call me Mutley.'

Chapter Thirty-Seven

The dead called me Sycamore. They and I didn't care for sentiment.

Mutley – the lowest of humans in life, a sickening brute in death – led me to the location of her murderer. Through the streets of the Tinman District we drifted, unseen but sensed as one senses the brooding presence of the storm above. Citizens, whose unconscious we tapped at, were reminded of their time in the war, remembering how they had learned to feel the threat of danger on the wasteland; and I imagined that their memories stayed with them long after the ghoul and I had passed.

'I want my revenge,' Mutley hissed.

Whether she deserved it or not was an academic point, though I wondered if she was at all aware of the irony inherent to a situation that she wouldn't be in if she hadn't been so devious and incorrect concerning my true nature.

It came as no surprise when Mutley led me to Wendal Finn's lodging house, or when we ventured up flights of stairs to the floor and room directly above his. Nel was at home by this time. Her lodgings were as sparse as Wendal's, and she was in a dire condition. I assumed she was already dead at first. That Mutley might have to go without Sycamore's justice was somewhat pleasing. But then Nel stirred. Weakly. And addressed the human inside me with a whisper.

'Wendal ...'

I could feel him weeping.

'I knew you'd come,' Nel said.

She had been beaten so severely that her face was swollen with bruises and blood matted her hair. She lay on her back, hands clawed and trembling, speaking through broken teeth and mashed lips. By the way her legs were twisted and resting at uncomfortable angles, it was obvious that she felt nothing from the waist down.

'I killed Mutley,' Nel said, her voice clearer now. 'But I couldn't get away from her people, and ...'

They had beaten her to a pulp, leaving her for dead in her own home. Perhaps as a way to let Wendal know that his contract with Mutley was now terminated. This was my assumption, of course, but also the logical aftermath of the visions that had accompanied Mutya Bryn's Song.

At the gambling house, not long after Wendal left, Nel and Mutley had fought in Mutley's private office. It was over quickly, with barely enough time for blows to be exchanged, because, during the brief struggle, Nel managed to pickpocket Mutley's ether-weapon. One shot of magic had blasted the criminal's life from her body.

'I-I know you told me to sit tight, Wendal, but Mutley backed me into a corner.' She huffed tears. 'She wasn't going to let us live, no matter what she told you.'

Behind me, Mutley's ghoul had smeared itself across the wall like a blanket of oil, covering the door, quivering with anticipation.

'*You did what you had to,*' I said. '*I'll take care of you now.*'

Nel could open only one of her eyes, and it looked at me curiously. 'I've never heard you speak Salabese before.'

My human host fought weakly against me. He tried his best

to rage inside me, desperate, begging me to … what, Wendal? Save your friend? Rush her to the nearest hospital, perhaps? He knew me better than that. Besides, we could both see that even with medical attention, Nel was not going to survive the night.

Oh, Wendal, blind for so long and now he was beginning to see. For months of human time I longed to be free of him, but I had always been good at waiting. The storm and the way he felt it was watching him … well, something had to come for me eventually and patience was a virtue.

'I can't feel the pain any more,' Nel said. She coughed, swallowed blood. 'Strange, huh?'

No, not strange; just the end drawing close. Over millennia, humans had fled the inevitability of death. They refused to look it in the eye, though they knew it came for each of them. Because they feared not knowing what was on the other side. And even when death finally arrived for them, they remained in denial, never quite believing that their life would come to an end. I could see it now in Nel's one eye. She had hope because she thought she was with a friend.

'Help me, Wendal,' she whispered.

And Mutley gurgled, 'I want peace, Sycamore. I want it *now*.'

These people were so far removed from the humans who had once inhabited Urdezha. In the aftermath of the Ether Wars, the weapons and plagues they unleashed on each other, they merged their biologies with scavengers and predators and insects – any creature that could survive inhospitable conditions. They cut their life expectancies by half because a half-life on a ruined world was better than no life at all. There were no real humans left on Urdezha.

'Do something, Wendal.'

Snapping the neck would put a quick and painless end to Nel's suffering. But Wendal, the *sub*human, the tortured soul, had finally set aside his denial and accepted the truth. His voice, so small and insignificant inside me, urged for a more *humane* way. I was not opposed to his request.

Mutley had slithered up the wall and across the ceiling, now hanging above us like the storm above Old Castle. Her face appeared in the dark mass, shadowed and anguished, lustful for vengeance. 'Give her what she deserves.'

I spied the very thing. Under the bed, Nel's cloth satchel lay rumpled. I claimed it and, as I expected to, found inside ampoules of the chemical Liquid Ether – the catalyst for this predicament.

'*Let's make you comfortable first*,' I said, snapping the top off an ampoule. '*Open wide.*'

Nel probed her bloodied lips with her tongue. 'Just a couple of drops,' she warned.

Because too much would stop her heart. She had told Wendal that. I dripped three drops onto Nel's waiting tongue. She swirled them around her mouth, winced as she swallowed.

'Burns. Tastes like shit,' she said, trying to chuckle but coughing instead. 'You don't sound right, Wendal. You look different. Your eyes are funny.'

'*One more for luck*,' I said, and two more drops fell into Nel's mouth.

'Give her all of it,' Mutley demanded.

'That hit the spot,' Nel said, and her swollen face visibly relaxed. 'It's not true, is it, Wendal? You don't kill people for the Magicians, do you? Mutley said Sycamore is an assassin, but—'

'*Shh.*'

Nel didn't seem to notice when she swallowed the next three drops of Liquid Ether.

'You won't leave me, will you? I mean, after you find Eden – promise that you won't leave me alone.'

'*We'll be together until the end.*'

'Yeah.' Her one open eyelid drooped. 'I was thinking. We should leave this lodging house, get a new place together. We already watch each other's backs – there's no reason not to do it. You know everything about me, except … except …'

'*Except what, Nel?*'

'It was me, Wendal. I did it. I killed my friends in the war. It wasn't the monster.'

Ah, Nel's recurring nightmare. I had heard many confessions at the moment of death.

'I've always known it,' Nel wept. 'I-I—'

I soothed her with two more drops. '*Sleep now.*'

She closed her eye and sighed. 'Wendal, what happened to you on the wasteland … ?' Her voice slurred down into unconsciousness, and I emptied the last of the ampoule into her mouth.

In her chemical dreams, Nel swallowed the contents of a second and third ampoule, and I stayed with her until she released a final breath and her heart stopped beating. Though loath to admit it, I stayed out of respect for Wendal, who had fallen silent, frozen within me, reluctant to rise. Mutley's ghoul, avenged and at peace, had disappeared without me noticing. I hoped her spirit would fall foul of the Scientists' experiments before it reached a harmonious afterlife. Had I learned sentiment, after all?

'*The dead call me Sycamore,*' I whispered, stroking Nel's beaten face. '*I am their Shepherd.*'

Poor sweet Janelle Memphis. How I misjudged you, thinking you were just another of Dyonne's drones, spies, pets. But you were innocent after all – or as innocent as any of your kind could be. You wanted to know what happened to your friend on the wasteland. Well, he met a survivalist named August Jakob.

III

The Song of the Dead

(Four Months Earlier ...)

Chapter Thirty-Eight

No! I screamed the word. *Not here. Not like this.*

With all the rage of the wasteland, an army of clansfolk thundered after me, racing along the valley that cut through the Ayros Mountains. A hundred warriors at least, most on foot – though I'd heard the roar of bears who were bound to have berserkers riding on their backs. Springing from the desolate cruelty of winter, the wastelanders had attacked without warning, without mercy. They were focused on breaking open the shell of my tank-suit and ending the life of a cursed city-dweller. But I was fucked if I'd let death find me today. Not like this. Not so far from home.

Aiming my shoulder cannon behind me, I fired two blind shots. The wails of the dying signified that I'd found my marks. The tank droned with the expenditure of power, but I ignored its complaints and kept running.

There was only one way for me to go: further into the valley, deeper into the mountains. The warriors blocked the way behind, and there were more tracking me from up on the ridge to my left. The valley wall on the right was too sheer for even the tank to make the climb, so it was straight on and don't dare stop. The enemy had given me barely enough time to acknowledge my terror.

The warriors above took potshots with bows and slings, but none of their projectiles could pass through the tank's energy shield. However, the tank itself wasn't functioning at full power, and I was pretty sure that the clansfolk behind had picked up at least two ether-cannons. One well-placed shot could overload the shield and cut it dead; another could disrupt the magical field holding the suit together. So I dodged, I weaved, I made myself as difficult a target as possible.

I was the sole survivor of my platoon, and running was all I had left. Even if the tank were fully operational, there was no way it could take on such a large army by itself. How the clansfolk had managed to amass such a sizable force in this place without Command detecting it was beyond me, but answers weren't important now. Stay ahead, stay alive – I tried not to think about what I might be running towards.

Shadows were good. The sky was filled with snow clouds blocking the light from the barricade of ether crystals orbiting Urdezha. The clansfolk needed the flames of torches to light their way, but I didn't. The tank's glass helmet allowed me to see through the dark of night, its sonar searching for dangers ahead.

The valley narrowed, bringing me closer to the warriors above. Their arrows and stone-shot ricocheted off the shield with sharp snaps. I extended the slim cannon on my left arm and aimed up at the ridge as I ran. The cannon *whumped* and the blast smacked rock, sending up a spray of sharp chips that forced the clansfolk to scurry back with cries of alarm.

The path sloped down, narrowing all the time. Weaving between juts of dark rock, jagged and porous, I finally headed out to where the valley became much wider than before. I veered to the right, away from the slings and bows, and the clouds unleashed a flurry of snow. The army behind hit the bottleneck and shouted curses in Salabese. Their angry voices merged with the wind and I gained some headway.

Snow dashed the air with thick white flakes. The tank's helmet saw through the storm; the energy shield parted the flakes as I ran through them and they swirled behind me, further muddying the enemy's view of my flight. But I could hear the roars of bears again, and their riders, the berserkers, were leading the charge now. Though the storm gave me some cover, I was pretty much on open ground. The tank was fast, but it couldn't outrun bears, and its shield was in no condition to withstand the explosions that came when berserkers summoned their own spirits.

As if fate had decided to smile upon me, I came to a great frozen lake that stretched the entire width of the valley floor. The ice beneath the covering of snow groaned and creaked under the tank's weight, but winter had made it solid and strong. I reached the other side ahead of my pursuers, but the roars of bears and the shouts of berserkers weren't far behind. I could see eight or nine of them, clustered together, racing across the lake, grainy and monochrome through the helmet's glass.

At the edge of the lake, my arm bucked as I fired the cannon at the ice. Three shots in a line. The third felt weaker than the first two, but the ice cracked then rose and parted satisfyingly nonetheless. As a dark abyss was revealed beneath, I continued running to where the valley narrowed again and headed up to a pass. The screams of berserkers plunging into deathly frigid waters came after me.

I needed to stop and give the tank's ether crystal time to regenerate magic, but I didn't dare slow my pace. These clansfolk knew the Ayros Mountains, and the warriors were as tenacious as they were savage. Broken ice wouldn't deter them from the hunt, and for all I knew, I was running towards more of them. The sonar's area of coverage had been hindered by the snow and the close rock walls. I had to find a place to hide, to catch my breath, to think, to plan.

Salvation came when the pass snaked and then curved around in a wide arc to the left. At the apex of the bend, I spied the dark mouth of a cave, mostly covered by the lumpy formation of an overhang. I made my way to it, deactivating the shield so I could squeeze past the obstruction, and ventured a few steps into the sudden stillness of a natural tunnel burrowing into the mountain.

The sonar gave no warnings. The glass helmet couldn't penetrate very far into the gloom, so I removed it and gazed into utter blackness, listening. Nothing beyond the low moan of wind from outside and the sound of my laboured breathing. But the sweat on my face was chilled by a light breeze coming from the darkness ahead. From an alternate way out?

With survival paramount in my mind, I put the helmet back on and the dingy, rocky environment was revealed to me again. The tank's shield activated at my command. The sonar pinged. Something living. Behind me. Outside.

Facing the cave's entrance, I heard a muffled grunt coming through the sound of wind. A lone bear had survived my ice trap. The overhang blocked most of my view, but I caught sight of the beast's large shaggy shape creeping up on the cave through the whipping snow. I could see the berserker on its back, too. Tusks and a tattooed face, hair wild and matted into tangles of spider legs. I didn't have a clear shot, and I couldn't allow the berserker time to summon his spirit.

Taking several steps back, I aimed the shoulder cannon at the overhang. One blast of ether magic was enough to cause a minor rockfall. To the heavy cracks of breaking stone, the ground rumbled, dust filled the air and the way into the cave was blocked to my enemies. Along with my way out.

Chapter Thirty-Nine

Two days ago, my platoon had been camped outside Mendis, a city roughly four hundred leagues west of Old Castle in a region of the wasteland called the Rust Plains. Of the twenty-five soldiers the platoon had started out with, only ten hadn't been claimed by the war. Our dwindled number had been joined by the remnants of a platoon out from Mendis who had reached the end of their City Service. Our orders had been to escort them home.

It had been hard for us, watching their elation at reaching their city and finally accepting that they had lived to see it again. Our goodbyes had been full of envy. We of Old Castle still had just over two months to serve. Childs, our commanding officer, had escorted the survivors into Mendis itself and had yet to return. As a career soldier approaching forty, he had earned City Privilege, the right to enjoy the luxuries of any city we happened to pass on the wasteland. The rest of his soldiers were grunts, forbidden to enter cities until our tour of duty was done. So all we could do was set up camp outside and await our commander's return.

And it was while camped in the shadow of Mendis's high wall that we were joined by the remnants of yet another platoon, this one out from the city of High Bridge. Just as our orders had been to accompany Mendis home, theirs were to accompany us on the two-month journey back to Old Castle. Once Childs was with us again, we would undertake a short march south to Fort Icus, where we would enjoy the rare luxury of sleeping in real beds, safe in the knowledge that we would live to see tomorrow.

'Concentrate,' Hanna snapped.

She and I stood on the edge of the camp, away from the other soldiers. I had stepped out of my tank-suit but still wore its glass helmet, controlling the main body and limbs remotely, keeping it at attention before Hanna so she could make repairs. Her irritation was growing because my tired lapses in concentration were causing the tank to twitch and move under her inspection.

'Will you *please* keep this thing still, Wendal,' she said, teeth gritted in frustration.

Hanna was High Bridge's engineer and a sight for sore eyes. Old Castle's engineer had died weeks ago. I'd seen so much death in the past ten months that I didn't want to remember what had killed him. Our equipment was in dire need of servicing, so Hanna was pretty much worth her weight in ether to us.

Her hair was straggly and falling out. The result, she had told me, of spider venom. Her face was pockmarked by a host of scars caused by a spray of burning spirit-matter released by the berserker who had killed High Bridge's tank-rider. She was a short and lean soldier, no fat on her muscles, and her dark eyes held a determination to survive. Her long, slim fingers worked deftly as she applied her tools to the tank's broken neck brace, which had been the recent cause of intermittent disruptions to a few of the tank's auxiliary functions.

Hanna was glaring at me. The tank-suit had stepped away from her. 'I can't get this done if you won't keep still.'

'Sorry,' I mumbled. Controlling the tank remotely was never

easy, less so when I had another two months of fighting to think about.

'Whatever's on your mind, change the subject. All our necks might depend on it.'

So far, Hanna was the only member of High Bridge I'd spent any time with. The other soldiers were getting acquainted around a few cook fires, fuelled by bricks of Dust-coals donated by Mendis. Evening was drawing in, as were clouds, and most of the merged platoon sat in circles around fires, dressed in worn uniforms with thermal travelling cloaks around their shoulders. It was the end of Noveb, and the crackling flames helped to stay the freezing touch of winter.

The platoon was in good spirits. Open fires were a rare treat on the wasteland, as was the hot food boiling over them in pots. The camp was in sight of the city's southern gates and close enough to the wall that we'd be protected by Mendis's shield if anything came from the wastes. The long ether-cannons poking out of turrets bolstered our feeling of security.

Old Castle's medic was a meticulous man called Bahn. He was wandering among the platoon, ensuring that everyone had a supply of atropine, the little white tablets that all soldiers had to take on the wasteland. During the first two weeks of my City Service, atropine had left me sick to my stomach, but I'd grown used it. Which was just as well. We weren't like the clansfolk; we were acclimatised to live behind city walls, where the streets were clean and protected by ether. We weren't made to live out here in this poisoned, disease-riddled world. Atropine propped up our immune systems, helped our bodies to process the harmful things we ingested daily just by breathing the wasteland's air.

As Bahn made his rounds, he stopped Danii, our communications grunt, who was carrying two bowls of steaming food. When he told Bahn that he'd run out of medicine, the medic produced a tablet from his bag. With his hands full, Danii opened his mouth and flopped out his tongue. Bahn shook his head, chucked the tablet into the gaping maw presented to him and walked away. Danni then headed over to Hanna and me, bringing us the bowls of food.

'Wendal, you're not still moping about your wife, are you?' he said while taking a bowl to Hanna.

Hanna looked away from her work to aim a suspicious glare at the stocky soldier offering her the food, before pointing to the ground beside her pack. 'Put it down there,' she said.

Danii placed the bowl on the ground then gave Hanna a mock salute, before bringing the other bowl to me. He peered close through the glass of the helmet. His facial hair was patchy and soft-looking, youthful, as pathetic an attempt at growing a beard as my own.

'Just accept it, Wendal,' he said. 'Your wife is probably fucking someone else by now.'

I snatched the bowl from him. 'Go and fuck *yourself.*'

Danii chuckled. He wasn't married, had no love waiting for him back at Old Castle. He didn't understand what this war was like for others, or care. I considered having the tank march over and kick him in the balls, but just stared at him instead until he looked off into the twilit wastes of the Rust Plains beyond the protection of Mendis's cannons. Between the clouds, the first ether crystals were visible in the sky.

'I'd better get back,' Danii said, serious now. 'Command should send new orders soon.'

He strode into camp, over to a fire, where he hefted his communications array onto his back – a strange-looking contraption of twisted strips of metal welded around a misted glass pyramid that hummed every now and then. Once he had extended the array's aerial, slipped on the transmission gauntlet and placed the receiver phones over his ears, Danii fixed the vocal stud to the collar of his jacket and stood apart from the platoon, listening and waiting to hear from Command.

'What's his story?' Hanna had moved away from the tank and held the bowl in her cupped hands, blowing steam off the food it contained. 'He's not as funny as he thinks he is.'

'Yeah, Danni's a punchable sort.' I removed the helmet and ate some of the sweet and pallid gruel made from Dust-flakes mixed with boiling water. 'He acts like a meathead, but he'll stand strong when it counts.'

Hanna nodded and lifted her bowl to her lips. 'What about this commander of ours?'

The platoon from High Bridge had taken more hits than Old Castle. Only eight of them had made it to Mendis, and among their dead was their commander, whose attitude to battle strategies had, apparently, been on the reckless side, and it was a wonder that any of them had survived to reach this far. As for Hanna's new commander ...

'Childs is set in his ways,' I said. 'When he gives an order, don't ever question it. If he asks your opinion, tell the truth. He'll know if you're lying.'

'Typical career soldier, huh?'

'Yes and no. He doesn't bestow rank – we're all grunts to him. Very pragmatic – best person for the job at hand, that sort of thing. Keeps us on a level.'

'Shame.' Hanna smiled. 'I'd just reached lieutenant.'

I finished my food, wiping remnants from my whiskers. 'Anything I should know about your lot?'

Hanna shrugged. 'Amelia, our cannoneer – she's a little twitchy and humourless. We should probably keep her away from Danii. As for the rest of us ...' She winked. 'Regular grunts, just as Childs likes.'

Done with her meal, Hanna threw her bowl to one side and fetched a soldering iron from her pack. She then returned to the tank and said, 'Lie on your front, please.'

With the helmet back on, I gave the tank a mental command and it dropped to its knees. Once it lay face down on the frozen ground, Hanna straddled it and studied the metal hemisphere protruding from its backplate like a huge boil. It was the containment unit for the tank's fist-sized ether crystal. Hanna picked up the soldering iron and began applying it to points on the hemisphere's circumference.

'So what's her name?' Hanna asked as she worked. 'Your wife?'

'Eden.'

'She waiting for you back in Old Castle?'

I nodded.

'You're lucky. No one waiting for me at home. And I still have a month more than you to serve.'

I didn't envy her that. Hanna's home city lay at least two hundred leagues south of mine at the edge of the huge coastal region of the wasteland known as the Straight of Salt, which comprised three cities: High Bridge, Old Castle and Alexria. It would be a long march home for Hanna and her friends once the rest of us had returned to Old Castle. If we made it that far.

'I'll tell you something,' Hanna said. 'I don't see the point in staying in High Bridge once my tour of duty's done. I'm thinking of coming back out.'

I frowned. 'You want to be a career solider?'

'Actually, I was thinking of survivalism.'

I had to control my surprise in case the tank bucked under Hanna. 'I don't think you're quite insane enough to be a survivalist.'

She smirked. 'You don't know me well enough yet.'

On the wasteland, you only ever got to experience the worst a person could be – the killer, the pragmatist, the soldier who prayed that others died so they could see home again. Eden had told me that when she came back from the war, and I'd grown accustomed to it being true. Still, I'd never met anyone who wanted to be a survivalist.

'It's funny,' Hanna said as smoke rose from the soldering. 'I always thought I'd end up following the Magicians' way. The wasteland changed that. Don't get me wrong, I could never be a *good* citizen, but I stopped seeing desolation and danger around me and started seeing opportunity. I mean, you must wonder what treasures are waiting to be found out here, Wendal.'

I didn't, and I never had. The wasteland was made of rock and torn metal and broken glass and secrets, compacted, crushed into a hostile landscape as though the Ether Wars had summoned mighty giants to stamp and destroy all things human-made. As far as I was concerned, the only thing waiting under the wastes was any one of an infinite number of ways to die, and Hanna was welcome to any treasures that hid alongside them.

'This is useless,' Hanna grumbled, climbing off the tank and returning the iron to her pack. 'I've done what I can for now, which isn't much. Put it on, see how it feels.'

At my command, the tank stood and opened out like a flower unfurling its petals until it became a random collection of armoured plates hanging in the air. Some were large and hinged, others small like scales. Ether knew ether, and each plate contained a splinter of magical crystal that was in tune with the main crystal held in the containment unit on the back-plate, which, in turn, complied with the mental commands I gave through the helmet.

Stepping backwards into the tank's embrace, I first clicked my boots into the thick sole-plates on the ground before sliding my hands into the gauntlets. When I ordered the tank to wrap me in its fortified shell, the plates closed in and fitted to my body and limbs. The ether magic that kept them in place also prevented them from touching me, creating a warm, pressurised buffer. The curious feeling of lightness came next; with each plate secure, the tank made me feel as though I was both floating and grounded, but never anything short of powerful.

Lastly, the cannon clicked into place on my right shoulder and whirred worriedly. The air around me wavered as I activated the energy shield.

'Test the sonar,' Hanna said. 'It should be working now.'

The glass helmet fed the low and familiar hiss of static into my ears. The tank sent out a mid-ranged bleep, which received a series of high pings in reply as it identified each of the soldiers sitting around the campfires. It was good to have reliable sonar again and I let Hanna know it was working by giving her a thumbs-up with a gauntlet. Then I heard a new ping as the sonar detected a presence coming from the city gates. It was Commander Childs.

He made his way towards us, carrying his helmet under his arm, short sword sheathed at his waist, ether-cannon hanging from his shoulder. He cut an imposing figure, strong and grizzled, wearing a customarily grim expression. His full beard and grey hair looked neat and clean. With a surge of jealousy, I reasoned that he had taken advantage of a bathhouse while inside the city. I struggled to remember what the luxury of a hot bath felt like.

The wasteland had long ago beaten any tolerance out of Childs. For the soldiers of High Bridge, this was their first day under his command, and I suspected that one or two harsh lessons were heading their way.

Hanna saluted as he approached. I deactivated the shield.

Childs ignored us both, surveyed the camp, looked satisfied by what he saw, and then turned to me.

'What's the situation with my tank?' he demanded.

'Sir, I've repaired the crack in the neck brace,' Hanna answered, 'but the whole suit requires a full service and a few of its plates need replacing. There's little else I can do out here without getting my hands on some new parts.'

'Disappointing. I'd hoped you'd be good at your job.'

Hanna looked to the ground. 'Yes, sir.'

Childs pursed his lips. 'I suppose you'll just have to find what you need at Fort Icus.'

Whatever Hanna required could undoubtedly be found in Mendis, but there was no point going down that road. What Childs referred to as the *soft-handed bureaucracy of city administrators* could take days to deal with any acquisition request. And we were moving out tonight.

'Danni!' Childs snapped. The communications grunt whipped off his receiver phones and saluted. 'Any word from Command?'

'No, sir!'

I could sense the collective relief filter through the camp. No new orders meant we remained on course to spend the night in soft bunks, which were less than three leagues away, no more than two hours' march.

'Platoon, put out those fires and pack up your shit!' Childs roared. 'I want to be in the officers' mess by full dark.' He turned a slow, cold glare on Hanna. 'And then, engineer, you can prove your worth to me.'

Chapter Forty

Hungry and thirsty, lost beneath a mountain, I relied on the tank's helmet to show me the way through the tunnel with grainy colourless imagery. I didn't know how long I'd been following this path, but it had been sloping downwards for quite some time now, and I reasoned that I must have travelled far beneath the Ayros Mountains. There was no way to tell where the tunnel would come out, but I desperately hoped that it would lead me to the base of a mountain on the west side. I'd take my chances out on the open wastes, fancied that I could make it back to Fort Icus. If the tank behaved itself.

On paper, City Service looked simple: six months marching away from home, and six months marching back again. At least, that's what you told yourself. The reality of the wasteland was anything but simple. We spent a year hiding from death, fighting for all we were worth. But sometimes death found you, and the only option left was to pray you were quick enough to outrun it.

Commander Childs had believed that fear was good. Fear made a soldier defiant, made you fight harder to survive. Childs had always been straight with his soldiers, brutally honest, because he saw no point in dressing up the truth just to soothe our concerns over facing the clansfolk. Even when he was telling us about once seeing a wastelander take down three soldiers with his bare hands before a tank-rider killed him, or the time he found a deserted settlement and a pen strewn with the bones of soldiers used to feed the clan's bears, he was always quick to remind us that the clansfolk weren't the only monsters on the wasteland. But it was the clansfolk who dominated our thoughts nonetheless. Monsters could be avoided, frightened off with superior firepower. The warriors of the wastes would hunt and fight until they or you were dead.

Pragmatism and luck were the key factors in surviving City Service. And there I was, hiding beneath a mountain, praying that I could stay one step ahead of the death the clansfolk had already given the rest of my platoon.

The mountain tunnel wasn't particularly wide. Thankfully, it showed no signs of narrowing, but the walls were close enough that I had to deactivate my energy shield as it kept sparking against sharp juts of rock. It would probably do the tank good to lessen the strain on its ether crystal, anyway. A couple of times, my passage was hindered by shards of porous rock protruding from the ceiling or the ground like huge, jagged teeth. The tank had enough strength to break them out of the way, but complained about the extra use of power.

I continued on carefully, the sonar active, its bleeps and pings telling me as best it could in our current environment that no living thing had followed me or was waiting ahead. Despite the power of the tank, I could feel my pace slowing, my body aching. I'd only had a few hours' sleep in the last couple of days. When the tunnel began to rise, the trek became so arduous that I could no longer ignore my fatigue. I'd have to risk sleep and rest soon.

I had only ever witnessed Childs' brutal honesty falter once. Danii had asked him if there was any truth to the stories that the wastelanders sometimes took prisoners to cook on spits over their campfires. Childs had shrugged at the question, his eyes filled with the darkness of too many years spent fighting in the war. He claimed that if cannibalism ever occurred on the wasteland, then it was due to necessity, a choice between living and dying. And that was a reality for both sides on the wasteland. Had Childs ever been forced to eat fellow soldiers or clansfolk to survive? No one had dared ask him, but the answer to the question hung in the air above our commander like a bad ghost.

The path rose for some time, and when it levelled out, I could hear the sound of running water. When the tunnel dipped, it was joined by a clear stream rushing in from a passage on the left. The passage itself was the first deviation from the path I'd seen so far, but it was too narrow for the tank to fit. The stream continued down and away as far as I could see, having cut a furrow in the rock over thousands of years, flanked by natural walkways.

I stopped at that point and commanded the tank to open. Its plates parted and I stepped out. The air was cool but warmer than I expected. I placed the tank in lockdown and illuminated the glass of the helmet with a pale radiance which stayed on when I took it off and set it hovering above the suit's neck brace. In the weak light, I crouched beside the stream and cupped water into my hands. It was cold but not icy. All soldiers were taught what they could or couldn't ingest on the wasteland, what was too poisonous for atropine to handle. Deciding the water looked and smelled fresh enough, I lifted my hands to my lips. It was good on my dry throat, slightly sweet, and two more cupped handfuls abated my hunger. Splashing my face and rubbing the coolness on the back of my neck, I drank a little more then sat beside the stream, wondering about my plan.

We were supposed to take atropine daily. A couple of days without and its effects would lessen sufficiently to leave my immune system vulnerable. I only had two tablets left, in a tin in my fatigues' pocket, and I took the first while I sat beside the stream. Hopefully I'd be well on my way back to Fort Icus before I needed the second. Finding a way out of these mountains was the priority.

I stared into the gloom where the stream flowed. Water generally knew which way to go. I could do this. By rights, I deserved to survive. Didn't I?

Statistics gave a false impression. They weren't fair and rarely played out like they did on paper. Roughly a quarter of the soldiers sent to fight on the wasteland never made it home. That didn't mean an even spread throughout platoons, but I couldn't help but fear that fate liked to ensure some kind of balance. The rest of my platoon was dead. Did that mean there was another platoon somewhere on Urdezha returning home right now having lost only one of its soldiers? Was there yet another that had lost none? Was I dangling from fate's fist while it decided on which side of the statistical scales to place me?

First thing first – find a way out. But I was so tired.

The warmth of magic comforted me as I stepped back into the tank and put on the helmet. I listened to the airwaves, wondering if there was a slim chance that someone other than me had survived; that I might hear a signal of city code. But all I heard was the hiss of dead static, so I activated the sonar and drifted off to its sound. Just as I fell asleep, I thought I heard a voice, whispering in Salabese.

Chapter Forty-One

The short march from Mendis to Fort Icus went by unhindered. The warriors of the clansfolk were fearless but not stupid enough to go looking for a fight on a short stretch of wasteland that lay between a city and a heavily fortified army facility. It was full dark by the time the silhouette of Icus's big metal pyramid came into view. The light of orbiting ether shone through drifting clouds. The frost whitening the reddish ground was cracked and turning to slush beyond the lines of turrets and cannons that surrounded the pyramid, melted by the warmth of magic powering the fort.

Danii announced our arrival by tapping out a message with his fingers on the thumb pad of his transmission gauntlet. A doorway, ten feet high and fifteen wide, slid open as the platoon approached the pyramid's north face. It slid shut once we had entered to find Fort Icus as deserted as an ancient ruin on the wasteland.

It transpired that we had narrowly avoided a full house. Eight platoons had converged on the fort at the same time, pretty much filling it to capacity with somewhere around two hundred soldiers. Earlier that afternoon, these platoons had been ordered to march out as a single unit – which could only have meant big trouble on the wasteland – but before they left they had practically gutted the place of anything useful to an incoming mobile army.

After my platoon had dumped their backpacks in the bunk-house and checked the postal office for messages from home, most of them went to the mess hall to find food tastier than army rations, while I took advantage of the showers. Once the hot water helped me feel something a little closer to human again, I wandered the corridors, enjoying the freedom of not having to wear the tank-suit for a while.

The inside of the pyramid was a network of corridors like tunnels in a burrow. The ground floor was for grunts, the upper levels were for officers only, and the way was lit by the rose-tinted silver gleam of ether-lamps. The floors and ceiling were bare metal, but the walls were whitewashed in a yellowing matt paint. The fort's staff were being elusive, as though hiding, and it was a while before I saw anyone other than a soldier from my platoon.

As I walked down a long, straight corridor, a greying doctor appeared from behind me and rushed past. He barged through a door and a sudden burst of screaming told me that I'd wandered into the infirmary. As the door swung to and fro before slowly coming to a close, I caught sight of medical staff gathered around a gurney, trying to hold down a patient who was thrashing about for all he or she was worth. I saw blood, I saw charred flesh, and I heard the kind of desperate wailing that I knew heralded death.

Not so keen to wander any longer, I returned to the bunk-house.

Danii was the only other soldier there; he sat on his bunk in the corner of the room with his back turned, listening to his communications array, waiting for new orders from Command – which none of us wanted him to hear. He didn't acknowledge my arrival when I took the bunk opposite his. My tank stood against the wall there, an empty shell in lockdown mode, resting so its ether crystal could regenerate magic. I lay down on a soft mattress, feeling strange after spending countless nights sleeping upright in the tank, standing guard over our camps out on the wasteland.

As I lay there, I fancied I could still hear screams from the infirmary mingling with the occasional roar of laughter drifting in from the mess hall. I did my best to block out all sound.

Hanna entered the room after a while. She dumped a well-filled haversack on the floor and was cursing about 'That fucking quartermaster!' who, apparently, hadn't been very helpful with her requests and had left her to scavenge for the parts she needed by herself.

'Slim pickings?' I asked.

Hanna glared down at me resting with my hands behind my head. 'Greedy bastards took nearly everything I need, before we arrived. I can't do my job without the right parts, Wendal.'

Which was a greater problem than I wanted to think about. Going back out onto the wastes with poorly serviced equipment was not a good thing.

Hanna gave a growl of frustration. 'I bumped into Bahn and he's just as pissed off. Reckons there's barely enough rations and medicine to restock our packs. And there won't be another supply train coming in until the day after tomorrow.'

'Childs won't be pleased. He'll probably blame you.'

'Childs can't expect me to do the impossible, and if he does – fuck him!'

I sucked air over my teeth. 'I wouldn't let *him* hear you say that.'

Hanna managed a smirk. 'I was able to scavenge a few things. Found something for you.'

I sat up as she rummaged around in the haversack until pulling out a little wooden box, which she chucked into my hands. It was plain, lacquered to a dark brown colour, and there was a small resin bead set into its top.

'An information node,' I said, surprised. I hadn't seen one since leaving Old Castle.

'It hasn't been used,' Hanna said. 'The grain of ether inside isn't very strong, but it'll store a few minutes of audio easy enough. I'll never use it, so I thought you could record a message for your wife.'

'This is great.' I smiled for the first time in days. 'Thank you.'

I shoved the node safely into a pocket of my fatigues. Once the rest of the platoon was asleep, maybe I'd find a quiet corner of the fort, record a message for Eden and leave it to be carried back to Old Castle along with all the other correspondences.

Hanna rapped her knuckles against the tank's breastplate. 'Can you free this thing up?' She took the glass helmet off the neck brace and lobbed it to me. 'No point taking it to the ordnance bay. I can do what I *can* do here.'

I put the helmet on and gave the mental command which unlocked the tank. One by one, the armoured plates separated and floated down to settle on the floor like the inert pieces of a three-dimensional puzzle.

Hanna dumped the haversack on the bunk next to mine, where her backpack already lay. She then knelt on the floor and started going through the armoured plates. Over in the corner, Danii whispered, 'What the fuck is happening?' but I didn't ask him to explain what he was hearing. I supposed I'd find out soon enough. Leaving him and Hanna to it, I took the helmet off and closed my eyes, dozing in the warmth and relative quiet of Fort Icus, thinking of home.

I wondered, spitefully, if Eden deserved the gift of a recorded message from her husband in a transmission node. I was angry with her. Logistics were difficult to manage on the wasteland, I understood that. But the order from Command which had sent us to Icus had come two days ago, more than enough time for Old Castle's correspondences to be routed here. But the last train of ether wagons had left nothing addressed to Wendal Finn. Sure, it was hard to get the timings of platoon movements right amidst the chaos of the wasteland, and things got missed. Even so, a lot of the others had found letters from home waiting for them at Icus, and this wasn't the first time in recent weeks when I'd arrived at a fort to find no word from Eden. Why hadn't she written?

With that thought haunting me, I fell into a troubled sleep.

I was awoken a little while later by the rest of the platoon entering the bunkhouse. They were in good spirits and being very loud about it. Hanna was sitting on her bunk amidst the litter of an engineer's paraphernalia. She was soldering the metal hemisphere of a grenade casing onto the tank's breastplate. I caught her eye, but she didn't explain what she was doing.

Danni was still in the corner, listening to transmissions. No one wanted to know if he had heard from Command yet – it would ruin this small respite from the war – but Mikel, our archer from Old Castle and the tallest and gruffest of us, pushed through the rest and demanded to know what Danii had heard.

'What?' he growled, brushing off the groans and complaints aimed his way. 'I like to know where I'm going.' He stood over Danii. 'Well?'

Danii slid one phone off his ear and gave Mikel a sour look. 'Nothing definite yet,' he announced, 'but there's a lot of traffic tonight. Sounds like a big offensive going off in the north of the Rust Plains. From what I'm hearing, wastelanders have captured a train of ether-wagons.'

'Ether-wagons?' I said, stunned. 'How big is their force?'

'At least four large clans is what I'm hearing.' Danni shrugged. 'Must be true. Fifteen platoons have been sent to engage.'

There was some swearing among my platoon, and for good reason. Transmissions criss-crossed the wasteland in a web of information that connected soldiers with Command, and Command with cities and the Quantum. The clansfolk were monitored and we kept their numbers down by disrupting their supply lines, destroying the settlements we found, fighting them whenever we detected migrations across the wastes. But we couldn't see everything, and sometimes a clan's army could grow as large as a hundred or more warriors. Platoons joined forces to fight them, but what Danii was hearing? Four large wastelander armies amassing undetected was a very rare occurrence.

This battle on the edge of the Rust Plains must have been where the platoons gathered at Icus had been sent earlier that afternoon. To face such a large army, I reasoned that more city soldiers had been deployed from Fort Baron in the north.

'Fifteen platoons?' Mikel said. He grinned. 'I don't fancy the wastelanders' chances against four hundred or more of us, no matter how many warriors they bring.'

'I wouldn't be so sure. They've already captured ether-wagons,' said Amelia, High Bridge's humourless cannoneer. 'That train could've been transporting anything – cannons, grenades, tank-suits, all in the hands of the clansfolk now. We'll probably be ordered up there as reinforcements.'

'That won't happen,' said Mikel, supremely confident. 'We're due a rest.'

'Yeah, because Command likes to pamper us once in a while.' Amelia lay down on her bunk, clutching her ether-cannon. 'Thinking isn't your strong point, is it, Mikel?'

'What?' Mikel had gained himself a few choice looks

suggesting that the order to march north was obviously coming and he was stupid to believe otherwise. 'Look, the wasteland's a big place. This battle will probably be over by morning, and it'd take us that long to march up there. They would've called for reinforcements by now.' He looked at Danii. 'Wouldn't they?'

'Don't know,' Danii retorted. 'If you shut your big mouth so I can listen, maybe I'll find out.'

The communications grunt placed the phone over his ear and turned his back, unconcerned that Mikel appeared to seriously consider punching him before he moved to his bunk.

Spirits flagged palpably in the bunkhouse as each solider was reminded that whatever form our orders took, we'd all be back out on the wasteland come morning. We never stayed more than a night at a fort.

I turned my attention to the metal hemisphere that Hanna was attaching to the tank's breastplate. 'What are you doing?'

Hanna looked up but her face paled when she saw Childs striding into the bunkhouse. He was not happy.

'Engineer!' he roared.

Giving no one time to stand to attention, he marched across the room, glaring at Hanna. The platoon recoiled from the angry chill he left in his wake. I sat up. Hanna threw the breastplate on her bunk and stood, saluting.

Childs loomed over her, glanced at the piled pieces of the tank-suit on the floor and then clenched his teeth.

'Why aren't you in the ordnance bay doing your job?' he growled.

'No point, sir!' Hanna's voice trembled. 'The other platoons have already gutted Icus of the parts I need, along with anything useful the train brought in yesterday. I can't give the tank a full service until we reach the next fort.'

'I'm not pleased, engineer.'

'Yes, sir. Sorry, sir.'

'What's the tank's status?'

'I've repaired the cracked plates as best I can,' Hanna said quickly, finding confidence, 'but the shoulder cannon's a little flaky. I'd advise using the arm cannon until we can test it properly.'

'You hear that, Finn?' Childs snapped.

'Yes, sir!'

'The worst news,' Hanna continued, 'is the tank's general efficiency. I'd judge it's running on eighty per cent power, maybe eighty-five. The problem is the ether crystal's containment unit – it's loose. I've patched it up as best as I can, but the backplate is losing integrity and needs replacing.'

Childs looked unimpressed, which was a stage better than his anger. Behind him, the rest of the soldiers were quiet and doing their best to pretend they weren't listening. They all knew how it felt to be under our commander's scrutiny. Just being this close to it was bad enough.

'I'm disappointed, engineer.' Childs gave me a cursory look. 'But I suppose I'll take a tank at eighty per cent efficiency over no tank at all. Any more of your failures I should know about?'

'The energy shield concerns me, sir. I don't know how many ether-blasts it could absorb, and it might not be strong enough to deflect anything a berserker throws at it. The containment unit is already leaking a percentage of the magic the ether is regenerating. If it gets much looser, it might stop feeding the suit power and the tank will lose its magic field entirely.'

Meaning the tank's plates would fall useless from my body like I was shedding dead skin.

With a growl of displeasure, Childs said, 'Please tell me there is some good news. You can't be entirely useless.'

Hanna was quick to open the haversack and produce two oval

metal containment units. 'Replacement ether crystals, sir. For our cannons.'

This mollified Childs a little. Unlike the crystal in the tank, those in hand-held cannons had a shelf-life. After a month, six weeks tops, they'd stop regenerating magic. This was done intentionally to render such powerful weapons useless should the clansfolk ever get their hands on them. The clansfolk didn't have access to ether as the Scientists did.

Childs pointed at the metal hemisphere on the tank's breast-plate. 'What's that?'

'A modification of my own, sir. Thought it would come in handy.'

'Explain.'

'I found one other thing of use.' Hanna plucked a third containment unit off her bunk and opened it to show the commander the white powder inside. 'It's ether filings.'

'I'm not familiar.'

'You don't come across it very often, sir. I don't think anyone who came to Icus knew what it was – or how to use it.'

'But you do?'

'Absolutely, sir. It won't store and regenerate magic like ether crystals, but it will augment spells, and I've a fair understanding of how to cast them. With this stuff, even a novice could em-power their use of magic. I also found some casings, so I can make grenades out of it, too.'

'All very good, engineer, but how does this fit in with your modification?'

Hanna pointed at the hemisphere. 'I've put some of the filings inside. It'll allow us to augment spells through the tank.'

I wasn't sure I like the sound of that, but my commander did.

'What kind of spells?'

'In theory, whatever you need, sir. But given the tank's

condition, I'd recommend augmenting ancillary functions only or we might put too much of a strain on power levels.'

Childs pursed his lips and nodded thoughtfully. 'Very good, engineer.'

'Sir!' It was Danii who had shouted. I could feel the rest of the platoon almost freeze, giving him full attention. 'Orders coming through from Command, sir.'

Childs stepped towards him, straight, proud and keen. The platoon held its breath.

I put on the tank's glass helmet and activated its array. It picked up the signal within the static. City code: a series of bleeps and hums coming too fast for me to decipher, but Danii's expert ears understood them easily.

'Where are we going, Danii?' Childs said.

The platoon expected the orders to be sending us north to this big offensive taking place, but Danii surprised us all.

'East, sir. To the Ayros Mountains. Investigate reports of a distress signal.'

'A distress signal? Details?'

'Command thinks it's a stranded platoon.'

Childs pulled at his beard before giving a curt nod. 'Acknowledge and accept.'

Danii sent a message to Command by tapping the fingertips of the transmission gauntlet on the thumb. My helmet detected more signals within the hiss of static before I took it off.

'Command confirms, sir.'

'Then enjoy your beds for the night,' Childs told his platoon. 'We move out at dawn. Your fellow soldiers need rescuing.'

The platoon followed the order. In gloomy silence, under their commander's baleful glare, they took to their bunks. Tomorrow, we would all be back out on the wastes.

'But no sleep for you yet,' Childs said to Hanna. 'Let's find some coffee and discuss how your modification can best serve my needs.'

Chapter Forty-Two

In trouble and alone inside a mountain, the sound of the tank's sonar pinging softly in my ears, I dipped in and out of fitful sleep.

In basic training, all soldiers were required to read studies and histories of the clansfolk. So we knew our enemy better. But these books didn't really understand them. There were no testaments written by any citizen who had spent time among the clans, learning about their culture. The wasteland, the war, didn't work that way. The authors had been writing suppositions based on the edicts of the Scientists which encouraged fear and hatred of the enemy, and each book could be summed up simply: Don't learn, don't understand; kill them before they kill you.

When Eden had returned from the wasteland, I was reaching the end of basic training, and we got to spend a couple of precious weeks together before my tour of duty began. Eden had come home more thoughtful than disturbed; changed but not damaged. She didn't want to talk about her bad experiences, and I wouldn't push. I really didn't want her to tell me what I was heading towards. But she said that if she went to war fearing the clansfolk, then she came back pitying them. They were no threat to the cities, no matter what the Scientists told us. She said it was as though we were sent out to stop the clansfolk picking a fight before they were given the chance to pick it. If we would just leave them alone, she had decided, then the cities would never hear from them again. We made them go to war. We forced them to hate us. And all so we didn't deplete our ether resources.

But at nights, I had to listen to my wife moaning in her sleep as she suffered the bad dreams that all survivors suffered. Whatever we *might* change wouldn't change what *was*. The sound of her nightmares had been an insight into the horrors of the wasteland, and my fear and loathing of the clansfolk had felt justified before I'd even passed through Old Castle's gates. And now, after ten months at war, I'd seen nothing that could convince me there was an ounce of mercy in the enemy.

It was silence that shocked me into full wakefulness beneath the mountain. The tank didn't feel right. I could hear the rush of the stream, see the grainy gloom through the glass helmet, but the sonar had stopped working.

I tried to switch it back on, but no joy. I tried again, and again, but it simply wouldn't function. I then noticed the cannon on my shoulder was hanging limp, and it wouldn't listen to my mental commands.

'Shit.'

I tried the energy shield next. It fizzed, briefly came to life, but then died and became unresponsive. My containment unit must have worked itself looser during my escape, leaking more ether magic.

'Fuck it!'

I calmed myself and tested the arm cannon. It responded, sliding in and out of its housing. I took some comfort from this, along with the fact that the tank itself had retained the magic field which kept its armoured plates on my body. But how long would that last? One thing was for sure, I'd turn to dust and bones beneath this mountain before I had any luck making repairs. I had to move on while I still could, while I still had a chance of making it back to Fort Icus.

Struggling to keep panic in check, I followed the stream, my breathing close and laboured inside the helmet. I walked along one of the natural walkways until it dipped and I had no choice but to wade knee-deep through the rushing water. The tank's balance was sure on the slippery stream floor, and the mixture of plates and magic conspired to keep me dry. It wasn't long before the sound of the stream was overtaken by a roaring noise, and my heart lurched when I soon saw an opening covered by the veil of a waterfall.

I reached it and stepped through, finding myself on a ledge in a cavern, circular and high like the chimney of a reduction house. Water fell from above and flowed around my ankles cascading into a deep pool forty or more feet below, so clear I could see fish swimming in it.

At first, I feared that this was the end of the path, but on the cavern wall directly opposite and to my left, dark holes announced the beginnings of two new tunnels. They were connected by a ledge that didn't reach around to my position. There was no easy way to get to either, or any certainty that they would lead out of the mountains.

I judged that the ledge before the opening on the left was close enough to reach with a powerful jump, and I had room for a good run-up; but it would only work if my tank behaved itself. My only other option was to jump down into the pool. The tank would keep me buoyant as I searched for a way to climb up the other side, or feed me air should I need to search for a third tunnel hiding underwater. But what if I found neither down there? What if monsters lurked in the pool along with the fish? What if the tank failed and I drowned?

I didn't have long to worry about my decision. The clansfolk saw to that.

I heard them before I saw them, the shuffles of their footsteps, the odd echoing word in Salabese. I stepped back through the waterfall, the glass helmet adjusting to give me a wavering view through the veil.

A group of wastelanders emerged from the tunnel on the left. I counted twenty warriors, their green skins and tusks demonic in the flickering light of oil lanterns. Dressed in armour and furs, armed with swords and spears and bows, they made their way across the ledge and took a moment to study their surroundings – the cavern, the pool, the sheet of water I hid behind. They were obviously hunting for me.

The one I assumed was their chieftain was older, greyer, more grizzled than the others. It looked as though one of the tusks jutting up from his thick beard was broken. He was carrying an ether-cannon. Perhaps it had once belonged to Commander Childs. Scowling in the lantern light, the chieftain muttered a few words before leading his warriors on, and they made their way into the tunnel opposite my position.

I waited several moments after the last wastelander disappeared and then stepped out through the waterfall, feeling a surge of hope. If the tunnel to the left had shown the clansfolk the way in, then surely it led to *my* way out.

Deep breaths gained me some confidence, and I gave myself as much of a run-up as I could before launching forwards, splashing through water and leaping for the ledge.

The jump was good, powerful, but while I was in the air, the energy shield decided to activate by itself. The tank whined, the drain on power hindered my trajectory and I dropped too soon. The shield screamed as it crashed into stone, an ear-splitting tumult that ricocheted around the cavern. Barely managing to get my arms over the ledge, I dug the fingers of my gauntlets into rock and pulled the tank up.

Only when I stood on the ledge did the shield stop screaming. I held my breath, waiting. From the other tunnel, I could see firelight heading back this way. The shouts of warriors followed it. Sensing fate's fist about to open, I ran.

Chapter Forty-Three

So the platoon marched east, leaving the safety of Fort Icus behind.

Our destination, Childs told his soldiers, was a place that he had only seen from a distance, mostly uncharted terrain which hadn't been explored for a century or more. 'Not much roaming the Ayros Mountains at this time of year, but the clansfolk don't hibernate and we've a big stretch of wasteland to cross between here and there. Stay on your toes.' As if any of us needed reminding.

The plains of the wasteland sprawled before us, broken, dirty, desolate and dangerous. The day had started with a cold and clear pink sky. The sun, bright and low, melted the ice under our boots and we churned frost and snow into gritty red mud. There were grey clouds on the horizon, surrounding us with the promise of fresh flurries, but there was little wind to push them in our direction. In Old Castle, it was probably a sedate winter's morning.

As usual, I was on point. Seventeen soldiers followed me, wrapped in thermal travelling cloaks, faces covered by scarves beneath helmets of hardened Dust, eyes squinting against the gleam of sunlight reflecting off the icy plain. A two-day march would deliver us to the black mountains which rose against a backdrop of snow clouds. Somewhere among those jagged peaks, someone was sending a distress signal. Our orders were to find out who. Danii hadn't picked it up yet, but he reckoned that the weather over the mountains could be interfering with the signal and we'd need to get closer before we heard it.

Around midday, we took a few minutes' break in the shelter of a huge mound, concealed by a thick layer of snow and ice. Perhaps the mound was a ruin from the old world; perhaps a frozen carcass belonging to one of the behemoth monsters roaming the wasteland. The summer months were the worst, when it felt like we had to face a different monster every day. In winter, a lot of them hibernated or perished.

While the platoon ate rations of nutrition cake, Bahn seized the opportunity to ensure that everyone took their daily dose of atropine. Childs had placed big Mikel in charge of carrying my rations and water canteen. We didn't linger long. While we were preparing to set off again, Danii's voice came over the tank's array.

'They're still fighting up in the north.' His tone was worried inside the glass helmet. 'Sounds like the clansfolk are really digging in.'

'Well, while they're busy up there, they won't see us down here,' I replied and Danii forced a chuckle. We both knew that Command had given us unusual orders – Childs and the rest of the platoon knew it, too. Rescuing stranded soldiers wasn't a common use of resources – rare, in fact. We certainly hadn't received these kinds of orders before during the last ten months. 'Who do you reckon is transmitting the signal, Danii?'

'Don't know. Command must think it's someone important, otherwise they would've sent us north instead of out here.' There was a long pause. 'There's fuck all in the Ayros Mountains, Wendal. It's uncharted territory, desolate. And we're still a day or two out. If soldiers are stranded there, I don't give them good odds of surviving long enough for us to track their position.'

'Keep listening, Danii. When we're close enough, you can tell them to come down.'

'If they're able. How's the tank?'

'Good as new,' I said, and it was mostly true. Despite Hanna's warnings, the tank was showing no signs of losing power, and the engineer's expert touch had left it feeling stronger than it had in weeks.

'Then you keep listening, too,' Danii said. 'I want to know if any clansfolk are heading our way. Do a good job, maybe I'll stop wisecracking about your wife.'

I smirked. 'Fuck you, Danii.'

'Finn!' Childs snapped. I hadn't realised he'd been talking to me. 'I said *back on point*.'

'Yes, sir!'

Danii sniggered in my ears. I led the platoon out again.

Later that day, we faced a minor skirmish. It occurred as the afternoon was heading into evening and the sun was beginning to set. After hours of trudging across a bland, repetitive landscape, we ascended a hill of scorched red rock rising above the ice and snow. The tank's sonar covered our immediate area, bouncing between me and each soldier. The sound of our merged platoon had become familiar to my ears by this time, and I'd identify anything hostile coming out of the wastes. Which I did, at the hill's summit.

I saw steam rising as I reached the top. Several soldiers behind me complained that the air smelled worse than usual. Signalling for the platoon to wait, I walked a little way down the slope to investigate what the sonar had detected, and my eyes beheld a strange sight.

A quagmire. It saturated the land with poisonous acidic

waters, bubbling between huge growths of a glass-like stone that radiated a faint green glow, illuminating the rising steam misting the cold air. The quagmire was huge, stretching to the left and right further than the tank's helmet allowed me to see, and I imagined that from way up in the sky it would appear as a mountain range all of its own. This wasn't the first time I'd seen one on the wasteland, but never as large as this.

Childs stepped up beside me, consulting his map. He muttered something about the quagmire marking the end of the Rust Plains and the beginning of the Ayros Range, but it had changed, he said, grown exponentially since the map was made. He swore when I reported that it could take leagues of marching to skirt around it, until I added that its width was less than its length. The quagmire would slow us down, but at least we could stay on course.

'I'd judge less than three hours to reach the other side,' I said. 'But I'm picking up hostiles.'

'Dracons?'

'I think so, sir.'

The helmet had augmented my vision through the mist and I could see what the sonar had detected. It was a safe bet that what I saw moving was a cluster of newly hatched dracons; they liked to make their nests in the humidity of quagmires. Lizardoids, nearly as large as humans when young, they hung from the underside of a growth of glassy rock that resembled a wave frozen before it crashed down into the sea. I couldn't tell how many there were, but there was a lot.

'I don't think they can see us through the mist, sir.'

'Any sign of the mother?'

That was the real threat. Adult dracons were as vicious as they were big and powerful, but I saw no sign of anything other than the infants and told Childs so.

'Probably off scavenging for food.' Childs thought for a moment. 'What do you think, Finn? Can we make it past the nest undetected?'

'Probably safer to flush them out, sir. Don't want them at our backs.'

'Agreed. Let's get this done before the mother comes home.'

Childs and I returned to the rest of the platoon and he explained the situation. He told everyone to put on their filter-masks – the air of a quagmire could be just as deadly as its waters and too potent for atropine – and then gave his orders.

'Danii, report to Command. Tell them our location and what we've found. This place has changed since it was last charted. Archers, cannoneer, you're with me and Finn. The rest of you clean up anything that gets behind us.'

The rest of you were armed with short swords, the standard weapon for city soldiers. We were trained in their use proficiently, of course, but dracons liked to attack from above and it was better to thin their number before they reached the ground.

Hanna stepped forwards. 'Grenades, sir?' she offered.

'Save them for the clansfolk,' Childs growled as he fixed his own mask, and his voice became muffled. 'Now then, Finn, let's test that shoulder cannon.'

I led the way down the hill to the edge of the quagmire and along one of the paths of solid glassy ground that snaked through the bubbling water. It was decorated with tufts of dark, poisonous foliage that gave off the same green glow as the rock growths. There were three archers in the platoon, carrying cross-bows, bolts notched and ready. Two – Mikel and Karla – were from Old Castle. The third was a woman from High Bridge who I didn't know yet, and the cannoneer was the grim-faced Amelia.

There was a good area of solid ground before the nest of

dracons. Childs and the four soldiers lined up on either side of me. The rest of the platoon waited behind, swords drawn and ready. The dracons hung from the rock, clustered together, stirring, hissing, but apparently asleep in the grey cocoons of their wings.

Childs gestured to me. The ether-cannon on the tank's shoulder whirred, lifted and took aim. Once the commander had ensured the archers and his fellow cannoneer were ready, he whispered, 'Now, Finn.'

My cannon *whumped*. A pleasing blast of ether magic swirled the mist and crashed into the nest. Dracons hissed and screeched and dropped from their perches. Childs opened fire, quickly followed by Amelia. Their cannons were longer and fatter with a wider blast radius than the tank's weapon. The shards of ether crystal inside gave them enough power to keep firing for twenty minutes non-stop before their magic needed regenerating. Childs and Amelia didn't hold back, and neither did I.

The dracons who hadn't already been smashed against the glassy rock of their nest came flooding out, gliding down on the membranes of skin stretching between their legs. With elongated heads on the end of long necks, their mouths appeared to be comprised of nothing but sharp teeth, and they were panicked, angry, more than eager to rend the flesh of their attackers.

It was a massacre more than a fight. The three ether-cannons punched monsters from the air with lethal bursts of magic, hardly giving the archers a target to aim their crossbows at, allowing nothing to get through for the rest of the platoon to pick off. A score and a half of them at least, the dracons were grouped so closely together, they were impossible to miss. I heard a drone inside my helmet; the shoulder cannon was straining to make the shots so I switched to my arm cannon. Not as powerful, but powerful enough. Lizardoid bodies broke, crashing into glassy rock, splashing into agitated pools of acid. The mist swirled and the screeches of monsters carried across the wasteland.

When Childs drew a halt to the attack, I could tell he wore a satisfied expression beneath his mask. The silence was only broken by bubbling, steaming water.

'Finn?'

I reported what I could see. A couple of dracons had made it to the ground, but they were scurrying off into the quagmire, fleeing. Most importantly, the sonar gave no signal that the mother was responding to the dying cries of its young. Childs ordered the rest of the platoon to ensure none of the bodies on the glassy path were still alive, and they set about them with their swords. I told my commander that the shoulder cannon had failed the test, and he nodded, once, curtly, before giving the order to move out.

We had incurred not one fatality. If only all battles on the wasteland were so easily won.

My estimation of the quagmire's size proved to be accurate. We trod carefully along the paths between the acidic waters, the platoon wearing their filter masks, the tank's magic field filtering out toxicants in the air for me. Anything else living in this place was small and had no interest in picking a fight, and I detected nothing more than creatures scurrying to be out of our way. In little more than a couple of hours, we had reached the other side of the quagmire and were back on the plains, icy and dusted with snow.

It was growing dark, but we couldn't make camp in the open, so Childs kept us marching through most of the night. At one point, we heard the distant roar of an adult dracon – the mother returning to the nest to find her children dead – but we faced no new threats from the wastes and continued marching until the earliest hours of morning. Beneath a clear sky full of dazzling ether, we eventually reached eerie ruins, an expanse of weathered stones sticking up from the ground like the broken bones of a past age; and here we stopped for a few hours' sleep.

Warm inside the tank, I stood sentry while an exhausted platoon found shelter between the ancient stones, wrapped in thermal cloaks, using their packs as pillows. No fires tonight; no hot food. We dined on hard, sweet nutrition cakes. There was little conversation; there was little to be said. Another day on the wasteland, another day closer to home.

'I'll take a look at that shoulder cannon if there's time in the morning,' Hanna told me tiredly. She rolled her eyes. 'Tonight, Childs wants me to prepare some spells.' She took her pack and found a secluded spot among the stones.

Childs himself was the last to bed down, and he gave me a nod before doing so, telling me to stay sharp. They all slept a little better knowing that I watched over them.

Alone and guarding the cold and quiet night, I waited until I was sure no one would disturb me before opening the tank. The plates parted and I locked the suit into position before taking the helmet off. Remaining within the suit's warm magic field, I pulled the information node that Hanna had given me from my pocket. I'd slept more soundly than I thought I would at Icus, and I didn't get the chance to record a message for Eden. Now felt like a good time to do it.

The resin bead on top of the node glowed with a faint light when my thumb pressed it, and I spoke into the wooden box.

'I'm not best pleased with you, Eden Finn. The last two forts I've been to didn't have a letter waiting for me. I hope this doesn't mean you've …' I was going to say, 'Given up on me,' but I couldn't bring myself to, not even in jest. I tried to keep my tone light. 'The wasteland is every bit as shitty as you said it would be. We've teamed up with a platoon from High Bridge.

Currently following orders to investigate some distress signal coming from the Ayros Mountains. Didn't think Command cared enough about stranded soldiers to send a rescue team. I'm recording this from the camp we've made in some ruins, and I can't help wondering about who lived here all those years ago.'

There were a lot of stones covering a large area, resting at odd angles, chipped and worn down by millennia of exposure. Too many to be a random settlement.

'This place must've been a village or town. Maybe it was built during the age of the Salahbeem. Maybe the inhabitants knew the Gardeners and ... and ...'

I couldn't do it. My air of unconcern evaporated and my voice cracked. 'Over half the soldiers I set out with are dead. There have been days when I honestly thought I'd die, too. Only a couple of months to go. I ... I think about you all the time. Fuck, I'm so close to home now. I love you, Eden Finn. And I always will, in this life and the next. Don't give up on me.'

With three quick presses on the resin bead, the recording stopped and my message was locked and stored. I kissed the wooden box and slipped it back into the pocket. I'd send it to Eden when we reached the next fort.

Pulling the helmet down onto my head, I ordered the tank to wrap its plates around me. To the soft crackle and pings of the sonar, I closed my eyes and instantly fell asleep.

After only a couple of hours, dawn had arrived and Childs was waking us up.

Gloomy soldiers emerged from the ruins into the dim light, stamping their feet against the cold and blowing hot breath into their hands. The red orb of the sun hadn't risen far above the eastern horizon, where Old Castle lay, and clouds were closing in. The Ayros Mountains looked so much closer than yesterday.

It was while we breakfasted on nutrition cakes that Danii

announced he could finally hear the distress signal we'd been ordered to investigate.

With his hands pressing the receiver-phones to his ear, he said the transmission was odd.

'I need a little more than *odd*, Danii,' Childs snapped.

'It's weak, sir, phasing in and out.'

'Can you understand it?'

'Not yet, sir.'

I couldn't hear the signal at all, but then the tank's array wasn't as finely tuned as Danii's, and my ears weren't as keen as his.

Danii crouched, squeezing his eyes closed in concentration. 'It's not city code, sir. It's a vocal transmission. I think ... I think it's Salabese.'

Childs growled. 'Could be clansfolk.'

'There's too much static to be sure.' Danii removed the phones and shook his head. 'It's gone again, sir.'

'Disturbing,' Childs mused, staring off at the mountains. 'If the clansfolk are behind this signal, why announce their position? If they're not, then why the fuck are city soldiers transmitting in Salabese? Send a report to Command, Danii.' He faced his platoon. 'The rest of you prepare yourselves.'

With grim expressions on tired faces, the platoon donned helmets and packs, and stood to attention before their commander. Childs nodded, pleased.

'Engineer!'

'Yes, sir,' said Hanna.

'Are my spells ready?'

'Yes, sir.'

'Good. We'll be needing them soon. Finn, you're on point. Danii, monitor the signal. Let me know when it comes back.'

Chapter Forty-Four

The Ayros Mountains loomed taller and darker with each step we took. The morning march passed without major event. When afternoon arrived, the clouds had closed in and I could sense the approach of snow. The wind stayed at a light breeze drifting across frozen plains like the sighs of winter. We'd reach our destination by nightfall.

My sonar detected potentially hostile presences on two occasions. One came from the icy brightness ahead of us, but whatever it was either didn't know we were headed its way or didn't fancy taking on an armed platoon and soon moved out of range. The second was closer. A herd of mastodons grazed on winter foliage growing at the foot of hills to the south – foliage that was poisonous to us. Mammoth in size and covered in thick shaggy hair, long tusks curling upwards, their powerful trunks ripped food up from the frozen ground and shoved it into their large mouths. Mastodons didn't eat meat, and they wouldn't attack unless we strayed close enough to threaten the herd, which Childs ensured we didn't, and we skirted the hills giving the monsters a wide berth.

Danii and I spoke privately over our arrays on a couple of occasions. He said the fighting up in the north was over. Sounded like the city soldiers had won, but with heavy losses. As for the mysterious signal, he told me that he'd picked it up several times now, and it was getting stronger the closer we came to the mountains. But it still wasn't clean enough to understand, or to discern anything about who was transmitting it.

Commander Childs' comments nagged me – nagged us all, I imagined. Why would soldiers transmit in Salabese instead of city code? If the signal was coming from clansfolk, why would they announce their position?

When night came, we'd reached the first outcrops of rock leading into the Ayros Mountains, and snow was falling with a gentle flurry of big white flakes. By the time we entered the mountain range proper and made camp in a rocky depression at its base, the snow had stopped, but there was a thick covering on the ground already and the wind had picked up, biting and moaning. There were plenty of overhangs in the depression that made good shelter. On the far side, the ground rose into a pass that led further into the mountains.

Childs ordered the platoon to refill their canteens with snow – atropine was stronger than anything that fell from Urdezha's sky – and then told Hanna and me to join him next to Danii, who was listening to the signal again.

'The transmission is much cleaner now, sir, but ...' Danii expressed confusion. 'It's gibberish. There's more than one voice talking and they aren't making any sense. It sounds like Salabese but it's ... gibberish.'

Childs did not look pleased. 'Can you hear these voices, Finn?'

'No, sir.' All that was coming through on the tank's array was the hiss of static.

Childs pursed his lips. 'Try responding in city code, Danii. Ask for identification.'

Danii tapped out the question on the transmission gauntlet. He waited a moment. His eyes widened in surprise a second before he winced in pain. 'Fuck!' He tore the receiver phones from his head.

His reaction gained the interest of the rest of the platoon, who drifted over. *So many new faces among them, so many people I didn't yet know.*

'Explain yourself, soldier,' Childs demanded.

'They heard me, sir. A voice rose out of the gibberish and responded, in Salabese.' Danii looked at the faces around him. 'The voice said, *I am the Shepherd of the Dead. Find me.* And then there was a burst of static that damn near deafened me.'

'*Shepherd of the Dead?*' Childs said. 'What the fuck is that supposed to mean?' He jabbed an angry finger at the communications grunt. 'Pick up those damn phones. Tell me what they're saying now.'

Danii did as he was ordered. 'Back to gibberish,' he reported.

'But it's still clear, still strong?'

'Yes, sir. Shall I send another message?'

'Ask for identification at regular intervals. Say nothing of our position and use city code only. Make sure you keep that transmission active.' Childs turned to the soldiers of his platoon. He growled an order to stop gawping and finish making camp before addressing Hanna. 'Engineer, take Finn and find me the location of that signal. Don't be long about it. There could be clansfolk in these mountains and I want my tank back before I sleep.'

'Yes, sir.'

Hanna led me towards the pass, and I waited until we were out of earshot before questioning her.

'I've made a new toy,' she said, showing me the metal ball of the grenade in her hand. She chuckled when I frowned worriedly through the glass helmet at her. 'Come on, we need higher ground.'

We walked out of the depression and along the pass a short way before Hanna pointed to a ledge, high on the left wall. 'That should do the trick. Deactivate your shield. We need to climb up.'

'Why?'

There was no nonsense on Hanna's scared face. 'Wendal, I've had less than three hours' sleep since Icus, so just fucking do it.'

Once I had switched off the shield, Hanna climbed onto the tank's back and held tight as I made the climb. Foot- and handholds were easy to find in the porous rock, and I made it to the ledge without much effort. The pass wall continued up some twenty feet above us. The platoon and the camp were out of sight. The wind sounded hollow up here.

'Are you going to explain that grenade now?' I said.

'It's not a grenade, Wendal, it's a tracking spell. Handy little trick I learned from a Magician back in High Bridge. Remember those ether filings I found at Icus?' I nodded. 'Well, *this*' – she tapped the modification on my breastplate – 'will receive information from *this*.' She held the metal ball up before my face. 'It'll track the source of the signal and show you its location.'

I nodded, impressed. 'You sure you want to find it? Shepherd of the Dead?'

She waved the question away, more eager to see this through and get back to camp than think about it any more. 'It'll take control of your sonar and array, augment your frequency and distance of coverage, but the spell won't last long. When I give it to you, throw it as high in the air as the tank can. Don't hold back, all right?'

Hanna twisted the hemispheres of the ball in opposite directions. A thin line of rose light glowed around its circumference and Hanna placed it in my gauntlet. It was heavier than it looked.

'Do it now, Wendal.'

I stepped back on the ledge and threw the ball as hard as I could. The tank propelled it up and up into the dark sky until it reached so high the light it emitted was barely discernible.

'What next?' I said.

'Give it a moment.'

The ball exploded with a dull pop that echoed around the mountains. Streaks of rose magic fountained, holding their formation for a moment before racing away like comets, all heading in the same direction, one chasing another. I felt a change in the tank. My vision through the glass helmet became misted with a greyness that rendered me blind and a disorientating whistle filled my ears. Hanna stopped me taking off the helmet and said, 'The spell's not perfect, but it'll work. Give it a chance.'

The whistling died, replaced by static crackling over many voices speaking rapidly in garbled Salabese.

'I can hear the signal,' I said.

'Good. Focus on it.'

As I listened to the voices, making no sense out of them whatsoever, the grey mist cleared. But not to show Hanna standing on the ledge beside me. I was flying. Rushing above the mountaintops so fast I could almost feel the freezing air on my face.

'Shit!' I staggered, disorientated again. Hanna guided me to the wall and I placed a steadying hand against it. She said something but I couldn't hear over the garbled voices. 'Speak up.'

'I said, tell me what you see,' she shouted.

'I'm falling ...' My vision was spinning fast towards the ground. My stomach churned as the descent abruptly levelled out, and I was flying high over what I presumed to be further along the pass we were on. It soon widened out. 'I've come to a valley. Maybe two hours' march from here. There's a lake.'

'Any way around it?'

'No. Looks frozen, though. Must be clean water.'

'Good. At this time of year, it'll be frozen enough to walk on. What else?'

'The valley narrows. I'm following a winding pass. It's widening again. I'm back in a valley and …'

My journey continued on, my speed increasing until I abruptly slowed, further into the mountains. The signal had lessened in volume, still yammering on, but more like white noise now. I came to a full stop, hovering over a huge canopy of giant leaves, an ocean of foliage stretching further than Hanna's spell could see, covering miles and miles of the mountain range. And the trees of the forest beneath the canopy were monumental, as wide and tall as any tower to be found in Old Castle.

'Corpse-trees!' I announced. 'Shit. If I'm reading this right, the signal is coming from a graveforest.'

'What?'

'That's what your spell's showing me. The valley opens out and there it is, slap bang in the middle of the mountains. It can't be more than a day's march away. *If* we don't meet any problems getting there.'

'Unlikely.' Hanna was quiet for a moment. 'A graveforest? Fuck. Do you think Childs will make us go in?'

'Depends if whoever's sending the signal comes out or not.' I shivered despite the tank's warmth. The spell was fading. I could no longer hear the mysterious transmission and the vision of the graveforest dulled. 'This might not even be coming from city soldiers. Childs is a stickler for seeing orders through, but he's not stupid.'

'I hope that's true. I don't know anyone—' Her words cut off with a grunt as I heard a wet, slicing thud.

'Hanna?'

Nothing.

'*Hanna!*'

Shouts arose from the camp. Panicked and angry through the wind. Childs' voice lifted above them. 'Finn!' he bellowed. And then I heard it, the sound that turned my blood to water whenever it came from the wasteland. War cries. Savage words barked in Salabese. The clansfolk.

Instincts demanded action, but my vision was once again filled with grey mist. I yanked the helmet off my head and stared in horror. Hanna was slumped on her knees on the ledge, dead, an arrow shaft protruding from the top of her head. The screams of the dying came from the camp. An arrow *tinked* against my shoulder.

Clansfolk were on the ridge above me – impossible to tell how many, not much more than shapes darker than the sky. I stepped closer to the wall, out of shot of their bows and slings, and tried the helmet. The mist had cleared and I activated the tank's array, calling for Danii. His shouts filled my ears. 'Wendal! It's an ambush. There's too many of them. Wendal—' He began choking, gurgling like his throat had been cut.

Within the sound of melee, I heard the roar of bears. An ether-cannon whumped – once, twice – and then came the unmistakable wet *pop* of a berserker exploding. Soon after, a victory cry rang out. But it hadn't come from city soldiers.

The clansfolk streamed into the pass. So many of them! Those above me shouted to their fellow warriors in Salabese and let them know where I was. I jumped from the ledge. The tank complained with a drone as I hit the ground and its power waned. I slipped on icy rock and slammed down onto my back, hitting the containment unit hard. For a moment, I feared I'd damaged it enough to lose power completely, but the armoured plates stayed on my body and, to my relief, the energy shield activated when I got to my feet.

Arrows and shot rained down. I ran, an army of warriors charging after me.

Chapter Forty-Five

Tank-rider protocol dictated that if capture seemed likely, my orders were to overload the armoured suit with a feedback spell that would shatter its ether crystal and cause an explosion that destroyed me, the tank and any enemy around me. Better this, I'd been told in training, than allowing wastelanders to get their hands on a powerful piece of technology. Theory and practice, however, were vastly different things.

The energy shield clashed with protrusions of rock, sparking and crackling as I fled down the tunnel beneath the Ayros Mountains. Even if I could be certain that the malfunctioning tank had enough power to detonate its ether, my mind was too panicked to remember the sequence spell that I needed to speak to the suit through its array. I didn't dare use my arm cannon, either. No way to tell if there was enough power for one shot, let alone deal with the twenty warriors who had chased me from the pool cavern. Their war cries weren't far behind.

'*Get out of my way,*' their chieftain shouted before firing his ether-cannon.

I'd reached a straight section of tunnel so long and flat that I made an easy target no one could miss. The shot punched me in the back and the tank staggered, almost falling. The shield absorbed the blast but fizzed and died as a result. The containment unit couldn't handle another hit like that. Mercifully, I was still on my feet. Mercifully, I was still running.

The tunnel curved sharply to the right. Just as I made the turn, a second ether blast cracked stone behind me. I heard curses, the pounding of feet, the drumbeat of my heart. The tunnel began weaving left and right, giving my pursuers no chance of a clear shot. Without my command, the tank's array clicked on and it was picking up the mysterious signal babbling incoherently. Desperate, not willing to accept that today was the day I died, I commanded the tank to transmit two simple words: *Help me.*

The babbling continued, but out of it rose a clear voice, speaking coherent Salabese. '*I am the Shepherd of the Dead. Find me.*' And then the array stopped working.

Light ahead. The tunnel's end. There was no time to be cautious, to acknowledge that the light came from the fires belonging to the rest of the clansfolk army, camped outside the tunnel waiting for me to be flushed out. I sped into the winter night, catching them unawares.

Surprised shouts rang out as I vaulted over a fire, spilling the contents of a cook pot hissing into the flames. I tried to use the arm cannon to clear a group of wastelanders in front of me, but the weapon retracted instead of firing. With a cry of rage and despair, I charged the group like a battering ram and the tank scattered them. Snow swirled in the air as I cleared the camp, thick and blinding in high wind. What little power remained to the tank kept the armoured plates on my body and clear vision through the glass helmet, and I ran for all I was worth.

I didn't need the sonar to know that my enemies were in pursuit. Their cries chased after me. Without knowing where I was going, I headed straight. The track was wide and my augmented vision saw that it turned right not far ahead. And there, no further than fifty yards from me, was the mouth of another cave. If I reached it, if the tank gave me one good shot of ether, then maybe I could seal the entrance and find another tunnel that led me out of this fucking nightmare.

To my dismay, I heard the roar of a bear, heard the shrieks of a berserker chanting the spell that would summon his own spirit. He was gaining on me, and the tank wouldn't be pushed for any more speed. Forty yards to the cave, thirty ... I wouldn't die today. Not like this—

The berserker exploded with a final shriek. The shock wave smashed the tank into the air. The final dregs of power bled away and the armoured plates fell free, spinning alongside me, and luminous blue spirit-matter splashed my stomach and back. Before I could cry out, the ground kicked the air from my lungs. I landed hard, tumbling over and over in the snow, spirit-matter burning through my clothes, frying my skin, and unconsciousness swamped me.

Chapter Forty-Six

Through a sea of darkness, I expected to swim to the afterlife. But I didn't.

Faith was a cultural phenomenon, dictated by locality. I believed that my spirit would journey on to Aktuaht, where the three judges from the ancient Order of Glass and Words – Truth, Mercy and Wrath – would decide whether or not I had been a good man. Was I worthy of spending an eternity in the Garden in the Sky, or did I deserve the condemnation of Nothing? I expected to face judgement because I came from Old Castle, a city, and that was what we believed; but out on the wasteland, Aktuaht and the afterlife were interpreted differently.

All we had learned about the clansfolk came from the prisoners the Scientists had captured for interrogation and experimentation over the generations. It was said that experiments on their biologies and hardy immune systems had helped us to develop the medicines that protected us from the toxic environment of the wasteland. Interrogations had led to a greater understanding of how the clansfolk lived and expanded and migrated, how their cultures worked, and how their beliefs differed from ours.

They believed in the Salahbeem, just as we did. They took the Magicians' view of them: the Gardeners were gods beyond a doubt, and they controlled the other side. But mythologies

EDWARD COX

and stories differed. According to the clansfolk, there had never
been a time in the depths of history when we had cohabited.
The divide had always existed between us. They had been the
Salahbeem's most loyal servants, and it was we, the people of
the cities, who drove their gods away.

Ether was supposed to be a gift for all, magical and giving,
but the greedy city-dwellers stole it from the Gardeners and
used it to bring them to their knees in great wars; and when
the Scientists rose from the ashes of those wars, they continued
using ether to oppress the clans of the wastes, to crush their
lingering loyalties to the Salahbeem. Which I didn't suppose
was too far from the truth. Ether-growths were the deciding
factor in who controlled Urdezha. We had them; they didn't.
However, the wastelanders didn't believe that the Salahbeem
had fled our world. The Scientists and the city-dwellers only
forced them to retreat, to go into hiding underground in a
secret realm called Aktuaht, where they waited for the day
when they were strong enough to return and take Urdezha back
by force.

Aktuaht for the clans was a fort, bigger than a thousand cities
combined, buried far beneath the world's scorched surface and
filled with untold numbers of grand halls. It was where the
spirits of fallen warriors celebrated with a final banquet before
moving on to the Gardeners' paradise on the other side. But not
for the strongest of them; not for those deemed the mightiest
of warriors.

The clansfolk dared not speak the names of the Judges of
Aktuaht, but it was they who selected the most fearsome among
the clans to remain after death; the chosen few who, over
decades, centuries, millennia, would fill the halls of Aktuaht
until they could be filled no more. And when that happened,
the Day of Resurrection would come, and the dead would rise

to reclaim Urdezha by scouring the cities from its face with an army of monumental size.

That was what the clansfolk believed.

I had never met a soldier who had received orders to capture a wastelander alive for interrogation. Perhaps it was just a very rare occurrence, or maybe the Scientists no longer had need to study them. Had we learned all there was to learn about our enemy? One thing was for sure, the clansfolk were as merciless as us, and if they ever took prisoners, it was only for nefarious reasons. Which raised a fearful question in me: why the fuck was I still alive?

I only had strength enough to open my eyelids a crack. Firelight danced in my vision. I could see nothing beyond it, but the pain in my body confirmed that I hadn't arrived in Aktuaht. I was lying on my back, hard rock beneath me. The pain was constant, threatening to spill over into agony at any moment. I thought better of attempting movement. The reek of blood and burned flesh was strong. Mine? There was another smell, dank, wild, animal, and it told me that I wasn't alone.

I should have been dead.

A rustling, swishing sound – like hands rubbing together. Someone sniffed and then spoke.

'*Just let him die.*' A clansman, growling Salabese in a deep voice.

'*No.*' The clanswoman who replied spoke in a tone only a shade higher. '*Old Kurlo wants him kept alive, so that's what I'm doing.*'

Old Kurlo? The grizzled chieftain with the ether-cannon?

'*Then lie, Yorla!*' the clansman almost pleaded. '*Tell Kurlo you did your best, but he died anyway.*' He made an angry noise. '*Feed him to the bears with the rest of his platoon, that's what I say.*'

The clanswoman – Yorla – sighed, and I heard the sound

of something being submerged in water. This didn't feel real. Was I really there? I half-expected Danii to weigh in with some inappropriate comment. But no; Danii was dead. They were all dead. Fed to bears, the clansman claimed …

Yorla said, '*Emul, I don't much like it either, but you nagging my ear isn't helpful.*' The clansman began to object but she jumped in. '*Go and wait outside if you can't stop your lips flapping.*'

He growled unhappily. '*Kurlo wants him guarded at all times.*'

Yorla snorted. '*You think I can't handle this little one on my own? His wound will have him screaming if he tries to move. Go away, Emul. I'll call if I need your help.*'

A moment passed and I heard him leaving.

The sound of water came again, as though squeezed from a cloth. Fuck me, I was thirsty! The clanswoman's shadow fell across me and I closed the cracks in my eyelids, fearful of what she might do should she realise that I was awake. I needn't have bothered. When she applied the wet cloth to my wounds, I was pretty sure that I managed a scream of agony before I passed out.

Chapter Forty-Seven

A sweet smell pulled me up into wakefulness and my eyes opened.

I was lying on my back in a cave of dark porous rock. Oil lamps cast dancing shadows, and I watched tendrils of smoke escaping up through cracks in the jagged ceiling. Although I could tell that the icy touch of winter wasn't far away, I was hot. Too hot. Feverish. My throat was so dry I could barely swallow. Pain felt distant – definitely mine but creeping through a disconcerting numbness as though my mind had detached from my shivering body. I found the strength to lift my head long enough to see that I still wore fatigues and boots, but I was naked from the waist up. My wounds had been cleaned of blood, but the burning spirit-matter had left behind raw and charred muscle. My chest and stomach were a mess.

When my head bumped back to the ground, I realised that I was no longer lying on bare rock. My bed was padded. My arms were weak beside my body, but my fingers managed to dig into soft fur. A tightness on my skin told me that my back wounds had already been cleaned and dressed. Sweat ran down the sides of my face.

'*He's awake.*' A male, out of view – the clansman whose name I remembered was Emul. '*Shame.*'

The clanswoman named Yorla appeared and knelt down next to me. She wore a leather tunic, her bare arms long and corded with muscle. She studied my face. '*Funny,*' she said. '*I've never been this close to one without trying to stick my knife in his throat.*'

Reality struck with fear and panic. I wanted to struggle and escape. I wanted to shout. But in the end, all I could summon from my painfully dry throat was a single word croaked in Salabese. '*Water.*'

Emul scoffed and Yorla matched his lack of sympathy by staring at me with baleful brown eyes. Her grey lips were set into as much of a grim line as they could achieve with the short tusks poking up from her lower jaw. The tangles of her hair had been tied back. Grime covered the green skin of her wide face. I wondered if she was contemplating using her knife on me after all. She stared until she seemed satisfied that I wouldn't speak again.

Why wasn't I dead?

Yorla picked up a stone bowl filled with white balls. At first, I thought they were sponges or balls of soft cotton, but when she selected one with her long, thick fingers, it appeared more delicate than that. Rolled up spiderweb? Before I could decide, Yorla pressed the ball flat against my chest without a hint of gentleness or care. The sting from my wounds was so great that it snatched my breath away. I hissed and begged her to stop. She ignored me and continued to press the balls, one after another, to my chest and stomach. Even if there had been any point in trying to fight her, I was too weak to make a decent attempt. Shivering, at a clanswoman's mercy, I could do nothing but bear the agony with whimpers and groans.

Not only had the clansfolk let me live, but also they were healing me? Why?

As if pondering the same question, Emul came into view

for the first time, frowning at me. Dressed in armour that was a fusion of metal and bone, he stood at my feet, strong arms folded across the wall of his chest. There was a metal ring in one of his nostrils; the matted locks of his hair were free and falling about his shoulders. At his hips, two short swords were sheathed. City weapons.

Both he and Yorla were powerfully built, hardy and fierce warriors; but where her eyes were a soft brown which perhaps suggested a greater depth of tolerance, his were dark, unreadable holes in his face. His skin was a deeper shade of green than hers, and he had more scars.

'*Why is he weeping?*'

'*He's in pain,*' Yorla said. '*And he's scared.*'

'*I don't weep when I'm scared.*'

'*You've never been the enemy's prisoner.*'

'*I'd never let them take me alive.*' Emul shook his head. '*This serves no purpose, Yorla. A living city-dweller was never part of the bargain.*'

'*We've been over this, Emul.*'

'*I know, I know – Old Kurlo told you to fix him up, so what else can you do?*'

'*It's not about doing as I'm told,*' Yorla said defensively. '*I believe Kurlo. The fate of Clan Ayros could really change.*'

'*It's a good dream, but I'm not so quick to believe it'll happen.*'

'*We've nothing to lose by trying.*'

'*No? Think about it, Yorla. What are we getting out of this bargain for certain? A couple of city cannons – which won't work for more than a few weeks – and another communications array that burbles ever-changing codes. Fucking scraps!*'

I thought of my platoon. I saw the arrow sticking out of Hanna's head. I heard Danii's final cries. I imagined the rest of them, slaughtered for meat to feed hungry bears.

Yorla was suppressing irritation at her fellow wastelander's arguments by clamping her mouth shut, tusks framing her nose. Eventually, she opened it a crack. '*We're being offered more than scraps, and you know it.*' She pressed a white ball against my stomach, hard, and I yelped.

Emul gave a derisive hiss. '*And* you *know that it's the tank we need to keep.*'

My tank. I wished I were inside it now.

'*All I need is for you to stop your pointless yapping,*' Yorla growled. Mercifully, she finished applying the soft balls to my wounds, set the stone bowl to one side and looked back at Emul. '*Be helpful and pass me those bandages.*'

Emul shrugged and moved out of my field of vision, returning an instant later holding a bandage in each hand. But they weren't like any bandages I'd seen before; they looked like strips of skin, half a foot long and a couple of inches wide. One side of them was coated with a clear sticky substance that glinted in the firelight. If the strips were indeed skin, then they hadn't come from clansfolk. They weren't green, and they were too smooth to be the skin of monsters.

Emul must have seen revulsion and fear dawn in my eyes because he grinned and confirmed my suspicions. '*Which one of your friends do you think was flayed for these?*' He handed the strips to Yorla.

Fresh tears filled my eyes, nausea churned through my shivering. Yorla laid the skin of a dead city soldier over the squashed white balls. The strips smelled sweet but stung sharply. I didn't want them touching me, didn't want to think about who out of the platoon they had come from. I found the strength to lift my hands and tried to push Yorla away. She glared at me and I moaned a single word at her. '*No.*'

Yorla slapped my hand down then clamped her own much

bigger hand over my mouth, fingers and thumb digging into my cheeks. *'Talk to me again,* city-dweller, *I'll cut off your cock and use it as a gag.'* It wasn't an idle threat.

Emul chuckled and fetched more strips.

Yorla let go of my face, and I lay still in my despair as she continued dressing my wounds.

Beyond the initial sting, the strips cooled the heat inside me and my shivering lessened. I struggled to keep my eyes open and must have dozed off. When I came to, the pain was quiet and dull. I still felt hot but not so feverish, and the shivering had stopped. Thoughts were muddied, clouding my feelings on the situation.

Voices. A discussion was taking place around me.

'You know I respect you and would never question your word,' Emul was saying. *'I will fight for Clan Ayros until the end, but many of us have concerns over this plan.'*

'Then air your doubts.' The clansman who replied spoke thick and heavy Salabese. *'I came here for straight talk, not fawning.'*

A pause. *'Why are you keeping the city-dweller alive?'*

I held my breath, undecided as to whether or not I wanted the newcomer to answer it.

'He is to be a gift. For the Shepherd of the Dead.'

The Shepherd of the Dead? The voice in the signal?

I opened my eyes.

My wounds were concealed beneath someone else's skin. Yorla was scooping a cool and sweet-smelling substance out of a stone pot with her hand and smearing it over my chest and stomach. Emul still stood behind her, watching, beside the grizzled warrior who had led the hunt for me through the mountains. Old Kurlo, the chieftain of Clan Ayros.

He was shorter but broader than Emul, wearing a fur cloak over his metal and bone armour. The spider legs of his hair surrounded a bald crown and were as grey as the bush of his beard. Seemingly uncaring that I was awake, his tawny eyes were narrowed as he studied me. An ether-cannon hung from his shoulder.

Clearly, Emul was sitting on more questions and concerns but was reluctant to air them. As the silence grew, Yorla spoke for her clansman.

'*The city-dweller is a small concern for many of the warriors, Kurlo. Their true misgivings are for the Shepherd of the Dead.*'

'*So I have heard.*' The chieftain worried thoughtfully at his broken tusk with his tongue. '*But I would hear Emul speak for himself, Yorla, not through you.*'

Emul squared his shoulders, bristling with offence that his chieftain might believe that he needed anyone else to speak for him. There was a smirk on Yorla's face as she scooped more of the clear sticky substance from the pot, as if she knew that aggravating the warrior's sense of pride was the quickest way to get him to speak his mind.

'*The spirits of the graveforests cannot be trusted,*' Emul said with mettle in his voice. '*Ever has it been this way, Kurlo.*'

'*The Shepherd of the Dead is no ordinary spirit,*' the chieftain said coolly. '*She does not prey upon the living – she would be our ally.*'

'*An ally who speaks in riddles and confusion,*' Emul said. '*I have listened to her on the city array.* Find me, *she says,* day and night, *when she is already found.*'

'*There is more to her message than you have heard, Emul. The Shepherd is the guardian of a great secret, the herald of a change that will alter the fortunes of Clan Ayros.*'

'*The dead cannot be trusted,*' the warrior asserted.

Kurlo continued to stare at me, unblinking, as though studying a curious animal found on the wasteland. '*You have not met with the Shepherd as I have, Emul. You have not seen the magic she wields. Or perhaps you have lost respect for my word more than you let on.'*

'Your word will always carry weight with me,' Emul said, insulted. *'I only wonder if this Shepherd is a trickster. What if she lies? What if she leads Clan Ayros to its end? It feels like madness to give the city-dweller's weapon to a spirit of a graveforest. I say we keep it for ourselves.'*

'To what end?'

'Victory on the wasteland, of course!'

'For how long, before the city-dwellers take it back or destroy it?'

'That's if we get the chance to take it into battle at all.' Yorla had chimed in again, her tone respectful, thoughtful, not scathing or argumentative. *'Who is left among us with the knowledge to wear a tank?'*

'Yorla makes a strong point, Emul,' said Kurlo. *'How many months of practice would it take a warrior to fully understand the power of such a weapon — power which the mechanics tell me is already broken?'*

'Then take its ether,' Emul pleaded. *'With a crystal of that size, our priests could cast mighty spells.'*

'Yes, for a while. And perhaps we would win a few battles with it. But not with a thousand such crystals could we stop the cities filling the wastes with soldiers. Nor could we change our fates.'

'The dead cannot change the fates of the living,' Emul rumbled. 'It is lore.'

'One day, Emul, I am certain that you will earn the privilege of a seat among the clan elders, but today you are too young and inexperienced to speak with an elder's authority. You are right to say the spirits of the graveforests are tricksters, but wrong to believe the Shepherd is one of them.' Kurlo took his eyes off me and faced Emul, the icy chill of winter descending upon his manner. *'I believe in what the Shepherd is offering, yet* you *persist with these*

tiresome arguments. You say my word carries weight with you, but answer me this, Emul – are you losing trust *in your chieftain?'*

The threat underlining Kurlo's question was unmistakable. He was asking if Emul was challenging his position. I'd heard that this happened among the clans. As with Magicians seeking to become a Grand Adept of the Salem, the position of chieftain was often settled by spilling blood. Yorla heard Kurlo's tone, too. She paused with her hand in the pot, eyes darting from side to side, anxious for her clansman's reply.

Evidently, Emul had no interest in the leadership of Clan Ayros. He stepped back from Kurlo and bowed his head respectfully, and Yorla relaxed when he said, *'You are my chieftain, and I have followed you since the day I was born. I will continue to do so until the Gardeners judge you are ready for Aktuaht.'*

'So you have told me before,' Kurlo said, expressing no feelings whatsoever on the declaration of loyalty. *'You are respected among the warriors, Emul, and you will talk to them for me. Ease their doubts, just as you will ease your own. Tell them with belief in your heart that if Clan Ayros is to survive and flourish, then the Shepherd of the Dead must understand the technology of our enemies.'* Kurlo turned his glare back to me. *'The tank and its rider must be given to her.'*

They were all staring at me now. Somewhere, struggling to wade through the mud in my mind, was fear. But it wouldn't rise, wouldn't let me feel it, and I stared back dumbly, thinking of only one thing to say.

'Water,' I croaked.

Kurlo snorted, ignoring the request and facing his warrior again. *'You* will *do this for me, Emul. Do it for Clan Ayros. No more arguments. Show me your trust.'*

Emul nodded, once, prideful. *'Yes, my chieftain,'* and he strode from the cave.

Kurlo watched after him for a while then resumed studying me. '*What is his condition?*'

'*He's lucky,*' Yorla said. '*The snow took most of the fire out of the spirit-matter.*' Having finished smearing the clear substance over my wounds, she was cleaning her hands on a wet cloth. '*His fever is breaking and I've done all I can. He should hold together for a while.*'

'*Can he be moved?*'

Yorla stood and pursed her lips. '*His dressings need a couple of hours to dry first.*'

'*Good enough. The elders won't be meeting until morning. He'll be ready by then, and I want him at the council. But we shouldn't let him die of thirst before then.*'

Yorla walked out of view. I heard the sound of pouring water an instant later. My dry mouth was already open when she returned and held a stone cup to my lips. She helped me lift my head and I drained the cup of water. It was cool and fresh but did little to ease the pain in my throat.

'*More,*' I gasped in Salabese.

Yorla looked at Kurlo. The chieftain shook his head and she held his eye for a long moment.

'*What's on your mind, Yorla? Tell me you don't harbour the same concerns as Emul.*'

She shook her head. '*It's not that. I believe as you do. Always.*'

'*Then what is troubling you?*'

'*I ... I am afraid,*' Yorla confessed. '*If change is coming to our clan, then it will not be an easy one.*'

'*You are wise to see that. Yes, a time of hardship and patience is coming, but it will lead to great things.*'

Yorla moved out of Kurlo's way as he came to stand over me.

'You hear our words, city-dweller?' Babel, the language of the cities, came from the chieftain's mouth, clumsy but clear.

'Survival is no blessing for you.' He crouched down and brought his face close to mine. His breath smelled of meat. The peak of his broken tusk was stained brown; the other was chipped and worn. 'Live long enough to see the next sun, spend your last days with the spirits and monsters of a graveforest. Clan Ayros gains from your sacrifice.'

Chapter Forty-Eight

All city soldiers knew the legends of graveforests. We were trained to avoid them. Wherever they grew on the wasteland, they covered many miles with a unique and terrible environment. Undisturbed for thousands of years, impervious to the decay of the world, they were the last true vestige of an ancient epoch, perhaps the only physical evidence left of the way Urdezha used to be. Graveforests were ominous enigmas, but even the Scientists left them alone because they offered no resources that couldn't be reproduced by Dust. But they hadn't always been such fearful places.

The Salahbeem had shown us how to grow graveforests. They taught us how life could be produced from death and be convinced to persevere by magic. Every tree in every forest sprang to life from a seed planted in the rotting compost of human remains. They were infused with the magic of ether, their roots nurtured by the bones they entwined and the spirits to whom those bones had belonged. Corpse-trees: they grew to impossible size, evergreen and like nothing the world had seen before, and the graveforests became places of tranquillity and well-being for the living, where we celebrated those who had journeyed on to the Garden in the Sky; where we remembered that we were in symbiosis with Urdezha, that we had to give back, not just take, take, take.

But then the Salahbeem left us. The Ether Wars began and the human race fell. Our fight for survival turned the graveforests into havens for monsters and unquiet spirits.

Mistakes, some called the beasts that dwelt among the corpsetrees. Legend had it that they were supposed to be like us, but something went wrong in the Scientists' laboratories. Instead of adapting human biology to survive the hostility of the world we had broken, they created savage abominations that could no longer claim to be human at all. The stories went that these monsters escaped, reproduced and spread far and wide, wreaking havoc across the wasteland before finding sanctuary in the graveforests, where they remained to this day. And the only witnesses to their adaptation and evolution over the millennia were the dead.

It was said that the spirits of the graveforests were bound to the behemoth corpse-trees, which their flesh had nurtured to life. It was said that they were trapped, doomed to roam through those trees for eternity, searching for a way to the other side which they could never find. There was a legend that the dead sang elegies to the forest when the sun set; and if you got close enough to hear it, the sound would freeze your heart with sadness and your spirit would be trapped by the corpse-trees, too. In the graveforests, the Song of the Dead was ancient, the first to be sung by humans, and it lamented all that was lost, including the Gardeners who never came back to Urdezha.

If there were tales of anyone entering a graveforest and coming out alive, I'd never heard them. Neither citizens nor clansfolk dared set foot inside them, not while sane. City soldiers accepted that a graveforest was probably the one thing on the wasteland more dangerous than the wasteland itself.

They were like pockets of the past, their own little worlds, filled with the deadliest monsters Urdezha had to offer. The clansfolk were governed by their superstitions, fearing the dead more than monsters. They believed the forests were the fiefdoms of disgraced warriors risen from the grave as trickster ghouls. These tricksters lured the living into the corpse-trees with promises of Aktuaht's glory before imprisoning their spirits and condemning them to an eternity of lamentation. But evidently, superstitions had been pushed aside for Clan Ayros.

I had a long time to think about the situation while lying alone in the cave, thirsty, hungry, holding off the pain of my wounds by keeping as still as I could – time enough for the oil lamps to burn down to barely a glow before extinguishing and steeping me in utter darkness. I didn't know whether Yorla had given me some intoxicant to keep me docile or if I was in denial, but I could feel neither the cold nor any hint of the terror which *had* to be there. So, in peaceful darkness, my mind sifted lazily through all I had heard since my capture.

The Shepherd of the Dead: whoever or whatever she was, the transmission she was sending was obviously not one of distress, as Command had suspected. The guardian of a great secret, Old Kurlo had called her, the wielder of magic and the herald of change. What kind of change?

Kurlo claimed he had met with the Shepherd; that she had more to say in the signal of babbling Salabese than Danii had been able to detect. The chieftain and Yorla believed that she could offer something in these mountains that would alter the fate of Clan Ayros. Emul was unconvinced but dutiful. But what possible use could a spirit of a graveforest find for a broken tank-suit? Didn't Old Kurlo claim that it was so she could understand the technology of the clansfolk's enemy? Why? Was she going to fight for them? I'd never heard of the dead being used in the war. It didn't make sense. Perhaps I'd learn more at this meeting of elders that I was being kept alive to attend – before me and my tank were handed over to the Shepherd of the Dead.

Where was my fear?

When Yorla entered the cave, the dawning sun cast weak light through the entrance and she was little more than a silhouette at first. I asked for water. To my surprise, she acquiesced and helped me to drink my fill. After, she sat beside me, her heavy brow furrowed in the gloom as though she puzzled over what I was.

'*I have seen your cities from afar,*' she said after a while. '*Is it true that you eat your dead behind those high walls?*'

Her tone was curious, not accusing or repulsed. I shook my head.

'*Then what do city-dwellers eat?*'

'Dust,' I croaked.

Yorla stared at me and then turned away when I offered no further explanation. Perhaps she thought I was mocking her, trying to be defiant in the face of adversity, when I had actually experienced an absurd swell of defensive pride. Could a warrior of the wasteland understand the concept of reduction houses and a process which did indeed recycle corpses back into society? I wasn't about to try and explain it to her.

'*Emul worries that more of you will come,*' Yorla said. '*That when your transmissions stop, the cities will investigate. But I'm not so sure. I have seen your kind stranded on the wasteland before. No one comes for you ... except us.*'

It was true; acceptable loss was the foundation of the war. Using resources to rescue stranded soldiers or prisoners wasn't a high priority ... unless they were sitting on something valuable. Gears whirred in my mind.

'*Who is the Shepherd of the Dead?*' My Salabese came as a dry rustle, despite the water I'd drunk. '*What secret does she guard?*'

'*She is the spirit of a graveforest and her secret has been kept for longer than the cities could guess. You will find out what it is soon enough, I think, when the elders meet. But tell me, how many of my people have you killed in that tank you wear?*'

Did she need a number, or did she just want to hear me say I'd lost count to justify her hatred of the cities? '*How many of mine have* you *killed?*' I countered.

She nodded as though it was a fair question. '*Plenty. And I will get to kill many more of yours than you will of mine, now. Clan Ayros had hidden in the shadows of these mountains for too long.*'

Too long? It struck me then that the interior cave was more like a hovel than a temporary shelter. A home? '*Have you always been here?*' I asked. '*The signal, the Shepherd of the Dead – she didn't bring you?*'

'*Clan Ayros settled in this place long before I was born,*' Yorla said. '*The Shepherd warned us you were coming.*'

The Ayros Mountains were supposed to be uncharted, deserted. How had Command missed this? And Yorla seemed to be saying that the Shepherd had led us into a trap, yet ...

'*Wait,*' I said. '*You say the Shepherd warned you, lured us to your clan with her signal, but why would a spirit do that for a tank-suit?*'

Yorla gave a crooked smile. '*I can't imagine what it must be like to live behind the high walls of your cities, growing old and useless in places no better than tombs. You deserve to be swallowed up by the wasteland.*'

'*Better than living out here among monsters,*' I argued childishly. '*Better than putting my faith in the spirits of graveforests. So I ask again – what possible use could the Shepherd have for my tank?*'

Yorla laughed, but with a deep and sombre tone that made me wonder if my question troubled her. '*Perhaps the Shepherd will decide to let you see your precious home again as a ghost or a ghoul, but I would be surprised if she allows your spirit to roam free.'*

'What is she? What is she offering you?'

'You'll see.'

A shadow fell across the cave's entrance and Emul appeared. He stepped inside and nodded at Yorla. *'It's time,'* he said sternly. *'The elders are gathering.'*

Chapter Forty-Nine

Between them, with little care, Yorla and Emul hoisted me up on the fur blanket I was lying on. The movement caused me to hiss in pain. Like a patient on a stretcher, the wastelanders carried me out of the cave and into the cold morning where I saw to my astonishment that Clan Ayros had indeed made a settlement in these mountains.

The greasy aroma of frying meat mingled with the acrid smell of smoke. In a wide encampment sunk into the mountains, where the rocky ground had been smoothed by years of passing feet, scores of warriors sat around fires fuelled by misshapen lumps of coal, waiting for their breakfasts to cook. Beyond the fires, I could make out the entrances to a collection of caves burrowed into the high and sharp walls surrounding and concealing the area. They didn't notice us emerge into the encampment at first, but one by one, with nudges and pointing, their eyes fell upon the city-dweller in their midst.

How long had this settlement been here?

Despite the situation, my stomach growled at the thick slices of real meat sizzling on stone plates resting over red coals. Juices spat and ignited with bursts of yellow flame as they ran over the sides. I had eaten real fish once and hadn't liked it, but at that point I'd risk eating meat from the wasteland to abate my hunger pains. My hopes that someone might feed me were dashed, however, when Yorla and Emul carried me away from the cook fires, and the eyes of the many warriors followed me out of the encampment.

We entered a narrower pass. My teeth chattered and I fought to keep from shivering as the freezing air assaulted my torso, still naked except for the bandages of skin. Beneath a lightening pink sky, clear of clouds, I saw thick rows of snow-dusted bushes laden with small red and purple berries among their green leaves. Crooked and leafless trees grew from the walls, roots digging into the rock like the gnarled fingers of giants. I was reminded of the greenhouses back in Old Castle.

Emul led the way, carrying me feet-first on the fur blanket. At the other end, Yorla was limned by a strip of cloudless pink sky. Dressed now in leathers, hair loose, she didn't look down at me and kept her eyes fixed on the wide armoured back of Emul, her face expressionless.

How long had it been since my capture? How deep had I been taken into these mountains? I decided then that I must be dying; that my body and organs were shutting down and I now straddled the grey line between the land of the living and Aktuaht, just one step away from the other side. Why else could I conjure no emotional response to my predicament? I had gone to war to serve my city. I hadn't survived. I was an unfortunate statistic.

What was going on here?

Clan Ayros was in possession of at least one communications array. Even if I could get to it, raise a distress signal of my own, Command wouldn't send a rescue team for one solider – wouldn't arrive in time to save me if they did. But they would come to wipe out this settlement if they knew it was here. They would come double quick if they thought this clan was sitting on something valuable.

Yorla believed that change was coming to her people, but I couldn't begin to guess at what the Shepherd of the Dead was offering. Friend, foe or trickster? Why had this magic-wielding spirit allowed Command to hear her signal along with the clansfolk?

Growls and grunts reached my ears. The pass widened and I smelled the unmistakable musty reek of bears. Behind rusty cage doors covering four cave pens they paced and snarled, huge shaggy forms. A few snouts appeared through the gaps in the caging. Long and sharp teeth gnashed, as though the bears could taste my scent on the breeze, perhaps anticipating a meal of fresh city meat.

Were the floors of those pens strewn with the bones of my platoon? Had any of them still been alive when the bears first sank their teeth into them? I couldn't tell how many beasts were sharing the caves, but I counted eleven handlers standing outside them, watching Yorla and Emul carrying me by.

Berserkers, human bombs, battle sacrifices who were bred and trained to die for the glory of their clan. Their green skin was dirtier, their frames scrawnier than the average wastelander's. Wearing furs rather than armour, faces scarred with swirling tattoos of the foulest spells, their expressions were somehow distant as if intoxicated or washed vacant by magic – though the dark glares they aimed my way were firmly grounded in hate.

I recalled the force of the shock wave that had smashed me from my tank, the agony of the spirit-matter as it seared and scorched my skin. Berserkers and the sacrifices they gave were honoured among the clans, according to one treatise I had read during training. They belonged to a highly revered caste and found no greater privilege than giving their lives for their people in battle.

I couldn't see how that worked. Going into war knowing that

you weren't supposed to survive was one thing, but knowing that you were sacrificing your chances of an afterlife, too? By detonating their own spirits, berserkers would never see the other side. As Yorla and Emul carried me away from them, I wondered if there was any true comprehension of their fates in those dark stares and vacant faces. How must it feel to know that this life on this desolate world was all that you got?

Soon, we came to an area much larger than the warriors' encampment. Awash with chattering voices, reminding me of a busy street in Old Castle – or maybe the shanties – this must have been the main body of Clan Ayros's settlement. So many wastelanders, not only warriors but also the elderly and children: families dwelling in the heart of the mountains. Most of them, I suspected, had survived their time fighting on the wasteland or were warriors in training; but whether young or old, each would make a fierce opponent.

Again, coal fires were burning, and the smell of smoke and cooking meat encouraged growls from my stomach. There were cave dwellings but also pointed tents covered in furs and skins. Yorla and Emul didn't slow their pace. The encampment grew in size the further we moved through it – easily matching the size of a district in a city – and the number of occupants increased to match. There were hundreds of them.

I began to wonder if this settlement would continue to grow and finally reveal that it was as big, or bigger, than Old Castle itself. It didn't seem to end. Still more and more clansfolk appeared, gathering like the congregation for a procession. A baby was crying somewhere. Strange; I'd never seen a wastelander baby, let alone heard one cry.

In my eerily detached state, I noticed that there was something off about this place. It felt established, the wastelanders at home and comfortable and maybe it had been this way for years, decades, but I gained the impression that it was also temporary, as though there was nothing here that these people wouldn't walk away from the instant an enemy too large to fight came calling. But that would have to be a force of immense size.

How big was Clan Ayros, how many clansmen and -women? A thousand? Two thousand? Commander Childs had believed the Ayros Mountains were empty save for hibernating monsters, but somehow this clan had established a home without the Scientists noticing.

The Shepherd of the Dead is the guardian of a great secret.

Someone shouted, '*Tell Kurlo to slit his throat*,' to which another added, '*We should be feeding him to the bears.*' A few murmurs of agreement followed these statements, along with uncertain mutterings, but no one tried to impede Yorla and Emul's progress. Most were preferring to keep their distance from me. Except one young clansman.

He was fetching water from a well. Attracted by my presence, he left his pail on the ground and came for a closer look. By his height and the length of his tusks, he must have been close to coming of age. He walked alongside the fur stretcher for a while, studying me as though sizing up the enemy he would soon be fighting. He didn't look much impressed. Yorla growled at him in Salabese, telling him to go away and not interfere with elder business. The young warrior snorted. He hawked then spat in my face before leaving. All things considered, it could have been worse.

I wiped the spittle away with a weak hand and closed my eyes to the clansfolk around me, the clear sky above me. I heard whispers from behind, which grew to a buzz of mutterings, curious and agitated, as more and more voices joined in. I realised that my procession had picked up a train of followers, and they stayed with Yorla and Emul all the way to our destination.

Kurlo was waiting for us at Clan Ayros's meeting place. Eyes calculating, the old and grizzled chieftain stood with his hands on his hips in a small circular depression, less worn than the rest of the settlement. Like a pockmark in the mountain, I thought.

Behind Kurlo, sitting on a low shelf in the wall, were three wastelanders I presumed to be the clan elders. One was dressed in furs, an aging clansman, older than his chieftain. To his left sat a warrior in bone-and-metal armour, of an age with Kurlo, his face twice as scarred; to his right sat a small woman, body drowned by leather robes, face concealed within a deep hood. Withered hands and bent fingers protruded from the ends of sleeves, and they were covered in swirling magical script.

A civilian, a warrior and a priest, I reasoned – a voice for each caste of Clan Ayros.

My bearers laid me down on the ground. The fur blanket did little to cushion the rough mountain rock digging into my back and agitating my wounds. The procession flowed past me in a stream of green-skinned faces, humourless and fierce. They climbed up to sit on uneven shelves of rock, staggered at varying heights on the wall that swept around and left a hole of sky as though I lay looking up from the bottom of a reduction-house chimney.

Emul spared me a derisive glance before heading off to take his seat among the audience. Yorla crouched down beside me in pretence of checking my wounds. Her brown eyes locked on to mine and in a whisper, she hissed, *'The Shepherd of the Dead will not be kind to you, city-dweller. I only regret that you won't live long enough to see Clan Ayros rise.'* She then took her place for the meeting, leaving me under the scrutiny of the clansfolk.

A hundred of them at least had followed me. Their silence was disturbing.

'My clan!' Kurlo shouted, his voice cracking like a whip, full of

pride; and then, softer, '*My friends.*' He turned full circle, taking in his people gathered above him before finally coming to face the three elders. '*A decision must be made on this day, a decision that could change the fate of Clan Ayros for ever. But let no man or woman present be in doubt of why we have come to this meeting place. The Shepherd of the Dead has called to us, and the elders have heard what she has to offer ...*'

Chapter Fifty

Kurlo, chieftain of Clan Ayros, addressed his people with fire and passion in his voice. I lay in the meeting place, watching clouds drawing in to cover the patch of pink sky, surrounded by a hundred or more wastelanders sitting on their rocky seats. I wondered if this was a dream as I listened to Kurlo and all that he believed about the mysterious spirit who had come to help his clan.

The Shepherd of the Dead, he claimed, had slumbered inside her graveforest for thousands of years, and would have slumbered thousands more had the clansfolk not disturbed her when they arrived in the Ayros Mountains. Not only did they rouse her spirit but also her curiosity. The people of the wastes intrigued the Shepherd, so she studied them from afar, learned from them in secret and discovered how Urdezha had changed during her long sleep.

She was dismayed to hear how the natural order of the world had been lost, how the clans were oppressed by those who abused the gifts of the Salahbeem; but in the wastelanders she saw an opportunity to restore balance. She would impart to them a gift, something she had long guarded from the living: at the heart of the graveforest, far beneath the magical roots of corpse-trees, lay a hoard of treasure.

Ether.

'*For how long have we scratched out a life in this place?*' Kurlo said. His clan stared at their chieftain, while on the far side of the meeting place, the three elders were just as still and silent. '*Year after year, we mine these mountains for coal and oil, preserve fruits and plants to help us through the winter months, hunt beasts in their caves for meat. When our warriors leave the mountains to face our foe on the wasteland, fewer and fewer return, while the rest of you hold your breath, waiting for the day when the cursed city-dwellers discover our home.*' A hundred pairs of eyes followed the aim of Kurlo's finger when he pointed at me. '*We have fared well, my clan, better than most, but now the day of discovery has come.*'

There were some worried murmurs, which the aging civilian among the three elders quashed by raising a hand and speaking loudly. '*This city-dweller is defeated, his fellow soldiers dead. We all understand why we are here, Chieftain Kurlo, and what you would have your clan do, so there is little reason for scaremongering simply to emphasise a point.*'

'*Scaremongering?*' Kurlo shook his head. '*No, Elder Tynen. If you believe this soldier won't be missed, that his transmissions haven't been heard and his kind don't know his location, then you are mistaken. Elder Vorn, you must attest to my reasoning.*'

'*That I will.*' The old warrior to Tynen's left sat forwards and looked down. Only then did I notice that the many parts of my tank had been laid on the ground before the elders. '*The threat of the cities sending more soldiers after this one is real. It is sometimes their way.*'

'*And is this not what the Shepherd predicted?*' said Kurlo. '*She warned us that the city-dwellers would come for her ether.*' Again, he jabbed a finger at me. '*And here they are.*'

More silence followed, contemplative, oddly calm.

Ether, I wondered, hidden in a graveforest. But how much of

it? An entire growth? It couldn't be; the Scientists reckoned that all the ether-growths of Urdezha had been found and a city now sat atop each one. If the Scientists had even a slight suspicion that a new ether-growth was hidden in these mountains, they would have claimed it already. Maybe I *was* dreaming. But then again, Command had sent us to investigate the Shepherd's transmission in the first place. Did they suspect something?

Kurlo broke the silence. *'Time has all but run out for Clan Ayros. We must act – now! – before the city-dwellers come for us and take the Shepherd's secret for themselves …'*

Kurlo continued, claiming that through the technology of my tank-suit, the Shepherd could understand the weapons the cities had used against the clansfolk for untold years. With her ether, she could create such weapons for Clan Ayros to use against their enemies.

'With but a little trust,' Kurlo said, *'the Shepherd will use her magic to hide her and us from the city-dwellers, and we will grow mighty.'*

'Ah, but to what ends will this little trust *lead us?'* said Elder Tynen. *'Are we to bend the knee to the Shepherd? Move our home into her graveforest, a cursed place? I do not think that restoring a balance to Urdezha is her goal. There is more to the Shepherd's offer than we have yet heard. The spirits of graveforests are tricksters.'*

This brought sounds of agreement from the audience, which Kurlo was quick to address. *'What choice do we have now?'* He gestured to the only elder yet to speak, seated to Tynen's right. *'We four have seen the magic that the Shepherd wields, but I ask Elder Sevya, in her wisdom, to tell the clan what she witnessed.'*

'Power to rival that of the cities.' The diminutive priest lifted the hood of her leather robes only slightly. Her voice came as a dry creak that travelled clearly across the meeting place. *'Magic that could only come from raw ether.'*

'*And with this power,*' Kurlo asked, '*could the Shepherd have already crushed us if she wished our clan harm?*'

'*Undoubtedly.*'

'*Yet she has not.*' Kurlo turned full circle and seemed to look into the eyes of each member of his clan. '*Tell me, what would you rather? Abandon our home? Travel the wastes as we once did and lose all we have built here? Or protect it? Dare to believe that the Shepherd of the Dead does not wish to steer us* off *the path to Aktuaht but* onto *it?*'

It started snowing. Amidst the audience, I found Yorla. She was watching me, not her chieftain, as gentle flakes settled on my face. I stuck out my tongue to catch them.

Elder Tynen spoke again. '*No one is denying that the Shepherd wields the power of ether, Kurlo, but caution! We know so little of her origins. Who was she in life? Why was she entrusted to guard this secret?*'

'*And why not come to us when she first awoke?*' Vorn said. The old warrior was more calculating than troubled. '*Clan Ayros has survived in these mountains for two generations and we stand on the cusp of a third. Where was the Shepherd when we first arrived, when we were broken and few? When we needed help the most?*'

'*The ways of the dead are hard to comprehend,*' said the priest Sevya. '*That the Shepherd warned us of the city-dwellers is, perhaps, further indication of her trustworthiness. But how soon will we, the living, benefit from what she offers? Today? Tomorrow? In a hundred years?*'

'*Or not at all?*' added Tynen.

His argument, out of all the elders, was strongest, and Kurlo was clearly reining in his temper now. He spoke in a growl to his people, admitting that there was no telling how much time would pass before Clan Ayros rose as a force to reckon with the cities. Perhaps it wouldn't happen until the next generation, or the one after that. Perhaps that generation would establish an empire, the first of its kind, and clans from all over Urdezha would flock to their banner. It all sounded like hot air to me, and I couldn't shake the notion that this clan was fucked whatever it did.

Feeling like I wasn't really there, I let snowflakes melt on my tongue, savouring the icy chill that did little to abate my thirst, listening as Kurlo said, *'Aye, we could stand at the beginning of a long road, my clan, but here and now our survival comes first.'* He pointed at the parts of the tank. *'Is it really such a risk to test the Shepherd's word by giving her this ... trinket that she demands?'*

I closed my eyes. I was so tired, so defeated, so ... empty. Perhaps I'd slip away into a long sleep myself and wake up in Aktuaht. I felt ready for judgement, no longer having the energy to know or care if I had led a good life. Let Truth, Mercy and Wrath decide as they would.

When Kurlo next spoke, his voice had softened. *'None of us can know what lies ahead. Perhaps the Shepherd does indeed have more demands to make. My heart and my head tell me that we should meet with her once more and find out while there is still time. Before the city-dwellers come again. But I will not lead my clan into this unless our elders stand with me.'*

'I will stand with you,' Sevya said. Tynen and Vorn stared at her. *'Never have the clans had the chance to wield the magic of ether, other than from the splinters and pebbles that we steal from the city-dwellers. With the ether of the Shepherd's graveforest, my priests, my berserkers — we could empower our spells beyond anything we have cast before.'*

Bent and concealed within her hooded robes of leather, she rose from her seat and took slow steps towards Kurlo. *'I have been wondering if the Shepherd is a sign from the Gardeners themselves. What if, here and now, the beginning that we might build becomes the gateway through which Aktuaht empties its halls? Perhaps the Day of Resurrection is at hand and it will be Clan Ayros who leads an army of untold numbers against the cursed cities of Urdezha.'*

The priest came to a stop facing her chieftain, and the opening of her hood lifted to him. *'For this chance, for this dream, I will take the risk.'* Her dry creak quavered as though relishing the prospect of ether's power. *'I say we meet the demands of the Shepherd of the Dead.'*

Pride and triumph came to Kurlo's face, and he looked to the two remaining elders.

Vorn said, *'I have misgivings and we cannot know what will become of our children, but ...'* He had also stood and was staring down at the armoured plates of my tank piled before him, the helmet resting on top. *'To send our warriors into battle armed with weapons that would make our slings and bows appear as toys ...'* He drifted off wistfully. *'The city-dwellers are coming and the Shepherd must be met. I stand with Kurlo.'*

Which just left Elder Tynen. All eyes fell upon him. The aging wastelander worried at a tusk, his gaze scouring the faces turned to him.

He said, *'To trust in the dead seems a desperate act, but these are desperate times, and I would regret losing all we have built. Is the Shepherd a guardian, a messenger of the Gardeners, as Sevya wonders, or a trickster?'* He drew a deep breath and pushed himself to his feet. *'I will stand with you, Kurlo, if only to decide how trustworthy the Shepherd is. But I warn you, at the first sign of treachery—'*

'I will march into her graveforest myself and burn her every tree to the ground,' Kurlo declared. *'This, I swear to my clan.'*

I huffed a laugh at the ridiculous amount of bravado in the chieftain's stance.

'Then the matter is settled,' Sevya announced. *'The Shepherd of the Dead will be met.'*

With the decision made, I expected the wastelanders to cheer and applaud or air their dissatisfaction, but the silence endured. My eyes found Yorla. She was still staring at me. I couldn't explain exactly why, but my lips curled into a smile of pity for her.

Chapter Fifty-One

With Yorla and Emul once again serving as stretcher bearers, I was carried out of the meeting place. Kurlo and the three elders led the procession, small and withered Sevya carried in a litter by four of her priests. Following were the clansfolk who had witnessed the council, all of them now on their way to meet the Shepherd of the Dead for themselves.

I remained awake, the sting of my burn wounds flaring each time I made the slightest movement and bringing the situation too close to reality for my liking; so I lay still and closed my eyes. My hunger, my thirst, my pain became dull inconveniences as the fur blanket swayed gently between Yorla and Emul. Maybe, if I was lucky, I'd slip away to the other side before I was handed over to the spirit of a graveforest.

The train of followers was less subdued now. Their voices, a low chatter of guttural Salabese, washed over me. Somewhere among these wastelanders, the parts of my tank-suit were being carried like an offering to unknowable gods. I lost track of time as I was taken down the pathways of the Ayros Mountains that this clan had travelled for at least two generations.

Bravo, I thought, *you managed to make a home here without the Scientists knowing. But what comes next for you … ?*

Ether was the deciding factor in how Urdezha was ruled, and

throughout history it had been stacked on the Scientists' side of the scales. I didn't believe that I was witness to some kind of ancient balance about to be restored to the world. Not for a second.

Snow was falling again and daylight was fading when we reached the graveforest. It lay at the end of the valley I had seen while Hanna's spell had augmented the tank-suit's vision. Corpse-trees grew ever more monumental as I was carried towards them, their giant green leaves high in the air. Night wasn't far off, and I wondered if we would soon hear the legendary Song of the Dead.

Closer, closer still, until I was laid on a fresh covering of snow not twenty paces from the impossibly tall and wide tree line. Without sparing me a single glance, Emul joined Kurlo and the elders, who had remained with the rest of the clan, keeping their distance from the graveforest and clustering together a further ten paces behind me.

Yorla loitered, looking down at me, unsure of herself.

I said, '*I don't really understand what you think you've found here, but don't hope too much that it's ether.*' I wasn't speaking unkindly, had just decided that this was probably the last conversation I'd have in the land of the living. '*I'm not convinced that your clan is going to survive, Yorla.*'

Her eyes held anger, but it was obvious that I'd drilled into her uncertainty. '*I should thank you. The gifts you have brought will make us strong – as strong as a city. The Shepherd will hide us and protect us from your kind.*'

'*You'd better pray she does,*' I said. '*If her ether is real and the cities catch one hint of it ... the Scientists will level these fucking mountains just to stop you having it.*'

She stared at me as four warriors came forwards carrying the armoured plates of my tank and the glass helmet. One of them also carried a backpack which had belonged to my platoon. The final offerings were placed on the snow between me and Yorla and the graveforest. The flap on the backpack was open; it was stuffed with rations of nutrition cake.

'*The dead don't need to eat,*' I whispered to Yorla. '*The dead don't need tank-suits.*'

She shifted her gaze to the backpack and plates, frowning before flinching as Kurlo barked her name, ordering her away from the prisoner.

'*Die well, city-dweller,*' she growled and joined her clan.

I looked beyond the offerings, beyond a short expanse of virgin snow and at the mighty graveforest itself. Tears welled in my eyes, though I didn't feel like I was crying.

The dead couldn't be controlled by the living. We couldn't harm them, and they couldn't harm us. In death, a spirit who avoided Aktuaht's judgement and denied itself a place in the Garden in the Sky lost its right to affect the corporeal world that it haunted. But according to Clan Ayros, the Shepherd of the Dead was about to disprove this. Graveforests were unique and mysterious pockets of the world's past, so what if the legends were true? Was death among those corpse-trees a game played by different rules from those the rest of us followed? Maybe this Shepherd could change the world, or maybe Elder Tynen had been right to suspect that there was much that Clan Ayros did not yet know.

I heard the *whump* of flames bursting into life. Elder Sevya was chanting a spell. Out of her litter now, the priest sat cross-legged on the ground, hidden in her leather robes. The blue flames of magical fire licked and danced from the snow itself. Sevya's Salabese was too quick and low for me to understand, but I reasoned that her spell was for summoning, or perhaps to protect her clan. Behind her, Kurlo stood between Vorn and Tynen, faces pensive as they watched the shaman. Behind them, Emul stood at the head of the rest of the clan, warriors and civilians, young and old, packed together and speckled with snow, quickly becoming silhouettes beneath the darkening sky. Except Yorla.

The clanswoman stood to one side, leaning back against a boulder, her strong arms folded across her chest. As had been the case at the meeting of the elders, her eyes were only for me.

Sevya chanted the words, '*Come to us,*' and the flames of the blue fire rose tall before dying completely. Yorla dragged her stare away from me as disconcerted murmurs rose from her fellow clansmen and -women. Many were pointing, some stepped back. An eerie glow shone from the graveforest, silver, tinted with rose: the light of ether.

It poured from the depths of the forest, hovering liquidly between corpse-trees. The clansfolk stirred worriedly, and Kurlo told them to show courage as the dark and blurred figure of a person materialised within the glow. But this person did not step from the trees, did not step far enough from the light to be seen in detail.

A moment passed, and she spoke.

'*I am the Shepherd of the Dead.*' Her Salabese was oddly accented and came from all places. '*You have returned as I asked.*'

I wasn't dreaming.

'*Shepherd,*' Kurlo called, stepping forwards. '*We return in good faith. We have what you want.*'

The spirit of the graveforest didn't respond at first. The source of the ether-light looked to be coming from her hands, which she held out before her. Yet her features still couldn't be seen, though I thought she wore a robe.

'*What is this?*' she asked. '*A city-dweller?*'

'*One of our enemy.*' There was no fear in Kurlo's voice. '*A prisoner to go with the weapon.*'

'*I see.*'

'*Are you not pleased?*'

'*Pleased?*' The Shepherd's light dimmed and brightened. '*Yes, you have done well, Chieftain of the Wastes.*'

'*Then please us, Shepherd. You have made promises to Clan Ayros—*'

'*Do you doubt me?*' The spirit's words came like the cracks of a whip; then, softer, '*Show faith. This city-dweller's bones might decorate my barrow, but his spirit will instruct me on the use of his city weapon, and thus you shall have what you crave that much sooner.*'

While I contemplated whether this meant I would never see the afterlife, mutterings of hopeful approval came from the clansfolk. But Kurlo wasn't yet convinced – and nor was Yorla, whose eyes were narrowed shrewdly as she leaned against the boulder.

'*What about our enemies?*' Kurlo said.

'*Patience, Chieftain of the Wastes. I will protect you from our enemies, but you must give me time. Return here in three days and I will show you the future glory of your clan.*'

'*But who will control that glory?*' Elder Tynen demanded.

'*You, me, us.*'

'*More city-dwellers could be on their way even while you ask us for patience.*'

'*They will not find you. Faith will be met with faith, Elder. Return to me in three days and you will see that for yourself. Your warriors will have weapons beyond imagining. Your priests will wield the magic of ether. This I promise.*'

Tynen didn't look convinced, but Kurlo was.

'*You shall have your three days,*' said the chieftain. '*We will return.*'

'*Then, until that time …*' The Shepherd drew back her arms. '*Give me peace!*'

349

She threw her arms forwards and the magical light leapt from her hands. It raced from the graveforest, up into the air, blooming and chasing away the snow before shattering into hundreds of rose streaks with a deafening boom that must have carried all across the Ayros Mountains and out onto the wasteland. Cries of alarm arose among the clansfolk. The Shepherd had disappeared back into her graveforest.

With steaks of magic zigzagging the sky above them, Clan Ayros beat a hasty retreat. Even their Chieftain cowered beneath the Shepherd's spell as he ushered his clan back down the valley. I watched them leave, fade into the growing gloom, then looked to the boulder where Yorla had stood. She no longer leaned against it.

Alone now and wrapped in the peace of an emotional torpor, I watched the magic fade from the sky, blinking away the white flakes that settled in my eyes.

The crunching of footsteps on snow reached my ears. The Shepherd coming to claim her prize? Strange that a spirit's footfalls should make any sound at all ...

Careful not to aggravate my wounds, I turned my head to the graveforest. A cloaked and hooded woman strode across the snow. She stopped to study the plates of my tank and the backpack before coming to stand over me. No features could be discerned inside the hood. Finally, she crouched and placed something over my mouth and nose. Bitter fumes caused me to cough and gag, and my pain to rise. I began spinning towards unconsciousness, but not before I heard her say, in clear and perfect Babel, 'Fuck me, this is a good day.'

Chapter Fifty-Two

I must have fallen into nightmares. A cacophony of bestial roars and savage bellows came from the darkness in my mind. At times they echoed from the distance; at others they sounded disturbingly close. The fury of the wasteland, I reasoned, plaguing my final dreams. Until I opened my eyes and the cacophony remained in the daylight. Until I realised that I'd woken into a living nightmare.

I was inside the graveforest, lying on the ground surrounded by ferns and the great trunks of giant corpse-trees, touched by very little snow. The trees rose high to form a canopy of huge leaves two and a half ... maybe three hundred feet above me; a canopy so full and verdant that sunlight was reduced to cracks of pink in an otherwise green sky. The air smelled rich and damp, touched by a strange acrid scent that took me a moment to identify: woodsmoke. The earthy atmosphere was laced by the terrible din of monsters, thankfully coming from nowhere close.

My face was cold but my body was hot. I'd been wrapped tightly in an itchy thermal cloak. Army issue. Material made from Dust. My arms were pinned to my sides, my legs held together, and I didn't have the strength to wriggle free. I must have looked like an oversized grub. The cloak's hood was pulled up over my head. Something crawled out of it and across my face. I tried to shake it off and blow it away, instantly regretting the action. Agony stole my breath. The pain of my burn wounds was still manageable, so long as I didn't move.

The roars and bellows continued to rattle through the corpse-trees. They sounded so violent, so ... murderous.

'Apes and trolls.' The woman's voice came from nowhere, speaking the language of the cities. 'They're always fighting in this place.'

I looked around as best I could. A small wood fire crackled nearby, its flames sheltering between two huge roots that rose from the forest floor like grand arches. The woman who sat beside the fire was, I assumed, the one who called herself the Shepherd of the Dead. Far from the powerful spirit who had appeared to Clan Ayros in the light of ether magic, she wore the tatty and patched-up uniform of a city soldier. Carrying none of the eerie grace and menace she had used before the wastelanders, she sat with the tank's backplate on her lap, applying her tools to the containment unit.

'Spend enough time on the wasteland and you get to see just about everything,' she said, staring off into the forest. 'But let me tell you – there's nothing on Urdezha as savage as apes and trolls going at each other.'

I struggled to think through the fog in my brain.

'Listen to them,' the woman said. 'They don't care about cities and clans and the wasteland. They have their own wars to fight.'

Putting the backplate down, she grabbed a water canteen and made her way over to me. 'No need to worry, though. We're still fairly close to the edge of the forest. Nothing too dangerous ventures this far out besides the odd jackyll strayed from its pack.'

No need to worry?

She stood over me and I let my head bump back on the soft

forest floor. This close, I could see how grubby and alive she was. Ten or twenty years older than me, it was impossible to tell. Her hair was dirty bristle. The wide slash of a pale scar ran down the side of her face over her left eye, leaving the lid lumpy and drooping. She looked fit. She looked strong. Yet she looked damaged, inside.

A survivalist, I realised.

I tried to speak but only managed a dry croak. Fuck, I needed a drink. But I suspected the canteen in the woman's hand wasn't filled with drinking water. It had been fitted with an adapted filter mask.

'See you,' she growled, suddenly angry. 'You're a fucking coward. You know what you should've done once the clansfolk had you.'

She was talking about tank-rider protocol. She was saying that I should have killed myself long before now. Perhaps she was right, but that didn't explain why she was hiding in a graveforest pretending to be a spirit of the dead making deals with the scum that the rest of us were out here fighting.

'Glad you didn't, though,' the survivalist continued, her mood brighter again. 'Can't put a price on how much a tank-suit's worth to me in this place.'

She gestured to the giant trees, waved a hand in the air like she was conducting the bellows of apes and trolls, invigorated by the noise of violence, unafraid and excited.

She grinned down at me. 'You're my property now, coward, and there're some fun times ahead.' She shook the canteen. The liquid sloshing inside sounded thick. 'But I need you to keep quiet while I make one or two preparations. Gather your strength.'

Crouching beside me, she lifted my head and placed the mask over my nose and mouth. I coughed and gagged. The bitter fumes coming from the canteen made my head spin.

'Home-made jenkem,' the survivalist said, amused. 'Not as clean or strong as the stuff you find in cities, but it'll knock you out just as well.'

I managed a groan, but could do nothing else but breathe in foul vapour and struggle to keep my eyes open.

'You're going to make me rich and famous, coward. No one will forget my name. Night-night.'

I felt as though I had only blinked yet somehow day had become night and the fire had died. Wind moaned through the graveforest like voices weeping in despair. Something was in the darkness with me, something close and smelling mustier than even a survivalist, creeping through the ferns. I couldn't summon moisture enough to call out a warning, didn't think the survivalist would come to my aid if I did. Shadows pressed in all around. I couldn't pinpoint the location of the monster who stalked the fresh meat lying so defenceless and weak on the forest floor.

A breath hitched, followed by a quick angry growl. '*Trickster!*'

Was that Yorla speaking?

The survivalist clucked her tongue and said, 'Sneaky fucker,' and then, in Salabese: '*I heard you coming from a mile away.*'

'*Treachery.*' I located Yorla's position by the glint of the blade she had drawn. The rest of her was a bulky shadow among corpse-trees. '*You are no spirit of the dead.*'

'*And you weren't brave but stupid to follow me here.*'

The *whump* of an ether-cannon displaced the air above me, dragged the breath from my lungs, and a cry of pain quickly ended with the noise of a dead body punched into the undergrowth. The survivalist chuckled.

Sleep pulled me down into a nightmare. One moment, Eden and I fled hand in hand across the wasteland, chased by monsters; the next, the sound of my own moaning woke me into daylight. The forest was quiet and the smell of woodsmoke was almost comforting. Yorla's dead body lay not far from me.

Chapter Fifty-Three

The clanswoman's corpse had been dragged into the clearing and stripped of anything useful to a survivalist. Yorla lay on her back, bearing no obvious wounds. Her eyes were closed and her mouth hung slack, tusks jutting towards the canopy sky overhead. I wondered what version of Aktuaht her spirit had found. Judgement or halls of celebration? Who was right? I couldn't claim to be glad that Yorla was dead, but I certainly wasn't sad, either.

The babbling of a stream somewhere nearby almost made the scene peaceful. And then, despite the fearsome towers of corpse-trees rising all around me, despite the presence of a dead body, nauseating pangs of hunger gripped my stomach. The discomfort made me realise that I felt more alert than I had for ... how long since my capture?

I'd been propped up and was sitting with my back against the thick root of a corpse-tree. I wore my fatigues and boots. The thermal cloak hung from my shoulders, but my arms were naked and my torso was still bandaged in strips of skin that were darkening and not smelling so sweet now. The pain was low but constant. The air was cold, though it seemed the bite of deep winter couldn't penetrate the graveforest.

My stomach growled again. Something was cooking. Dragging my eyes away from Yorla, I stared at a small cook pot hanging over a wood fire, steaming with the delicious smell of simmering food.

The survivalist was stirring the contents of the pot, grinning at me. 'Morning, coward.' She spooned some food into a bowl and brought it to me. 'Jackyll stew.'

Jackyll? Real meat?

'It's a little bitter,' the survivalist said, 'but I've been feeding you atropine, so it shouldn't poison you.'

The stew was such a dark shade of red that it was almost black. I lifted the bowl and sniffed it.

'Not that I need atropine any more,' the survivalist continued. 'Been out here so long I've pretty much adapted to anything the wasteland can throw at me. Come on. Eat. You need to keep your strength up.'

I tipped the stew into my mouth. It was salty and bitter, tasting of blood, but it was hot and filling, and I emptied the bowl while trying to remember when I'd last eaten.

The survivalist gave me a water canteen and I drank deeply. I felt a little better, perhaps stronger, but still struggled to find my voice.

'How long?' I managed in a dry whisper.

'I reckon four days since the clansfolk got their hands on you. A day and half since they gave you over to me. Maybe. Who cares?' She shrugged. 'You're lucky you made it this far, coward. I know a few healing spells, but nothing as good as the clansfolk's remedies.' She pointed at my chest. 'That skin is so full of the medicine you chuck down your necks, it'll stop wounds festering, even for wastelanders. Only for a while, of course. Looks like your wounds are already on the turn. Still, I should be able to keep you alive.'

I drank more water. Did she expect me to be grateful? 'Who are you?'

'The name's August Jakob. I've been searching the wasteland for treasure for ... I don't know how long, to be honest. Long enough, I reckon.' The scar on her face crinkled as she narrowed her eyes at me. 'Where are you from, coward?'

'Old Castle.' I coughed and drank some water. 'And my name is Wendal Finn.'

'Good for you. Your name's not important to me, though. All I need to know is you're a coward and you always will be.'

'Fuck you.' I saw Hanna's dead eyes staring at me. I imagined the rest of the platoon being slaughtered. Everything I'd seen and heard with the clansfolk ... I didn't see how I was the one who deserved judgement here. 'Yeah, I tried to save my own skin, but *you* are a traitor. You made a deal with the clansfolk. You led my platoon into a trap.'

'Yep, you got me there.' The survivalist – August Jakob – nodded without a hint of remorse. 'Still, think yourself lucky you're not dead with the rest of them.'

She fetched me a second bowl of stew as though nothing out of the ordinary were occurring. I stared at the bowl before accepting it, not knowing whether to feel angry or terrified, but certainly not feeling lucky to be alive.

This time the stew didn't taste so bad. While I ate, August walked back to the fire, pausing to stare down at Yorla's body before using a cloth to lift the cook pot off the flames and eat the rest of its contents with the stirring spoon.

'Why are you out here pretending to be the spirit of a grave-forest?' I demanded.

August smirked. 'Let me tell you a story, Old Castle,' she said through a mouthful of food. 'A little while back, I'm travelling south from Fort Baron up in the north. When I get close to the Ayros Mountains, my array picks up this signal. It's weak, garbled, see? Funny, I think to myself. Not supposed to be anything in those mountains.

'Now, I know what the wasteland sounds like and this signal is like nothing I've heard before. So I reckon what I'm hearing is the white noise of concentrated magic, and go to investigate. Takes me a while to track it down, but eventually the signal leads me to this graveforest. And that's when things start to get interesting.

'See, I'm as tough as old boots, but … There are spiders as big as bears in this forest, snakes as long and fat as a train of ether-wagons. Apes, trolls – just about everything that lives here will kill you given half a chance. There's no way I'm going to survive long enough to find out what's sending this signal – and I *really* want to know, Old Castle, because by this time I'm thinking it *has* to be an ether-growth.'

August stared off as she chewed, awed. 'Nobody's found one of those for a thousand years or more – most reckon there aren't any left. But if I'm right, I can't help imagining the size of the finder's fee. How generous would the Scientists be if I handed them the resources to build the first new city in a thousand years? I'd be laughing.'

Angry because the platoon had died for a finder's fee, I was also confused because apparently this madwoman wasn't the source of the mysterious signal, as I had been presuming.

August threw the empty pot and spoon on the ground. She looked both determined and agitated as she wiped a hand across her mouth. I felt like screaming.

'I don't believe it's an ether-growth now,' August said. 'But I do think it's something just as valuable.' She glared at me over the fire. 'I know you've heard the voice inside the signal because *I* heard you begging the Shepherd of the Dead for help.'

'The original signal is genuine? The Shepherd is real?'

'Not really sure how to answer that, Old Castle. Yes, the signal is genuine, but all that incoherent babbling? I reckon I know what it is. It's a form of Salabese that hasn't been spoken for ten thousand years. At first, I thought the Shepherd was an automated message, but now I'm thinking it's … an echo of the past. Old Castle, that signal is coming from something the Gardeners left behind.'

I stopped eating, disturbed by the maniacal grin that spread across her face. 'The Gardeners?'

'A Salahbeem artefact.' August gave a low whistle. 'The rarest treasure on Urdezha. Even I can't imagine how generous the Scientists will be for this one.'

Shaking herself from her greedy reverie, August opened her large pack and pulled out a neck brace. She held it up for me to see clearly. It was a communications array, a stubby aerial sticking out of the back. I'd seen the like before; they were specialist arrays, not standard army issue. They had the same long broadcast range of an army array, but with a greater choice of frequencies.

'So, back to my story,' August said. 'I'm in this graveforest, using this thing to listen in on the greatest treasure on Urdezha. A treasure that I can't reach on my own. Then a funny thing happens. I pick up a new transmission. This one's coming from wastelanders, Clan Ayros. See, the sneaky bastards have been hiding in these mountains for fuck knows how many years, and they've got their hands on an army array – they have two now, thanks to your platoon – and they're trying to talk to the Shepherd of the Dead. So, I break into the signal's frequency and get creative.'

I clenched my teeth. She didn't need to explain it to me. I saw it all. 'You led the clansfolk to us. You set up that ambush because you wanted the tank.'

'*Needed* it, actually. The Shepherd is transmitting on a broad spectrum, but you and Clan Ayros were listening and transmitting on different frequencies. Wasn't hard to set you up.'

'You killed seventeen soldiers.'

'Oh, Old Castle, I've killed many more than that in my time.'

'Someone will find out what you've done,' I hissed. But not from me, because the chances that I'd survive this graveforest were remote at best. 'The Scientists will know you're a traitor.'

'Do you honestly believe the Scientists will give a flying fuck about you and your platoon if I bring them an artefact of the Gardeners?' August chuckled at my distress. 'Why do you think you were ordered out here in the first place? I transmitted a coded message to Fort Icus, for the ears of the Quantum only. I told them where I was and what I thought I'd found – never hurts to put in an early claim on a finder's fee. I had visions of a fleet of weaponised ether-vehicles coming out to help me, but the Quantum wanted hard confirmation first. So a platoon with a tank-suit had to do.' She stuffed the array back into the pack. 'Did they tell you it was a distress signal? That was my idea.'

I started crying. I was going to die out here and Eden would never know what had happened to me.

August looked confused by my tears. She grabbed the canteen filled with home-made jenkem and came towards me. I tried to struggle, but pain flared and I could do nothing to prevent her from placing the mask over my face.

'Deep breaths now. That's right.'

She waited until my eyelids drooped before returning to the fire, standing over the parts of the tank piled beside her pack. She picked up the helmet and put it on.

'Shame on you, Old Castle. Fancy venturing out on the wasteland with a damaged containment unit.' She clucked her tongue. 'Still, nothing I couldn't patch up good enough – more or less.'

Her face became a mask of concentration behind the helmet's glass. 'It's been a while, but no one forgets the feel of ether in their head. And ether never forgets you.'

Sliding towards jenkem intoxication, I watched numbly as August activated the tank. The parts stirred, reacting to the survivalist's mental commands. The armoured plates rose smoothly, hovering in the air, before connecting and closing to form a headless figure. It stumbled two steps towards the survivalist then righted itself. The arm cannon extended, retracted, and the tank stood to attention.

'We'll move out at nightfall.' The maniacal grin returned to August's face. 'The clansfolk are superstitious cretins, but obviously some of them are braver than others.'

The tank marched over to Yorla's corpse, lifted it up above its headless shoulders and then hurled it like a rag doll into the ferns for scavenging animals.

'Me and you are going to do just fine, Old Castle ...'

If she said anything else, I didn't hear it.

Chapter Fifty-Four

When I came to, I was moving – *walking*, to be specific. My head bobbed as my feet took step after step without my permission. After a moment of confusion, I recognised the soft, warm pressure of a magic field against my body and realised that, at some point, August had put me inside the tank. The survivalist was walking ahead of me, leading the way through the grave-forest. Above the big square of her backpack, I could see she was wearing the glass helmet, controlling the tank remotely.

Night had fallen and the forest was full of shadows, but the dark was alive with voices, moaning like wind. Too many to distinguish, coming from everywhere, they sighed through the giant corpse-trees, low and sombre, mashed together in a united chant. There was nothing threatening about the sound, no sign of who was making it, but it made me feel sad. Sad, alone and frightened. The glass helmet must have alerted August to my wakefulness; without turning, she said, 'Hello, Old Castle.'

My tongue worked what little moisture I had around my mouth. 'Drink,' I rasped.

When August stopped, so did the tank. To exhibit this much control over the armoured suit, she must have been a tank-rider during her City Service. She shouldered the ether-cannon that had once been perched on my shoulder – fitted now with a makeshift strap – and held a canteen to my lips. I gulped cool water, taking a second drink after the survivalist shoved an atropine tablet between my teeth.

'What's making that noise?' I said.

'The dead. What else would it be?' August's face was barely discernible through the glass. 'Spirits were haunting graveforests long before any monster made a home in them.'

The Song of the Dead, I thought. So the legends were true.

'Don't worry yourself, Old Castle, they're not trying to steal your spirit for the trees. They're lost inside their sadness and probably don't even know we're here. But when they sing, they scare the monsters into hiding. The Song of the Dead makes it safer to travel at night.'

Awe crept through my fear. Although the other side had forever been a mystery to the living, it was no secret that some spirits remained on Urdezha, but I had never witnessed evidence of this for myself. Until now. The dead sang nothing that I could understand. They sometimes sounded accusing, sometimes like they were begging for help, but they were never short of despairing. Their misery was my misery.

August pulled a nutrition cake from the pocket of her fatigues, fed me half before lifting the helmet to eat the rest herself. She gave me another drink and said, 'Got to watch our step from here on, Old Castle. We're deep in the land of monsters now, and they'll come out to play again when the Song of the Dead stops. Come on.'

With moaning spirits all around us, we resumed our march through the graveforest. Other than a maddening itch, I felt no discomfort from my wounds. Adding to the medical attention that Yorla had given me, ether was applying its own curative skills. The tank couldn't heal me, but the warm pressure of magic that held me secure inside it was also anaesthetising my pain.

Deep in the land of monsters ... I glared at August's back. Unless I found a way to wrestle that helmet from her, I couldn't control the tank and had no choice but to follow her, but ... why was I following her at all?

'What do you want with me?'

My question faded into the Song of the Dead, and for a moment I thought the survivalist hadn't heard me, but evidently she had been giving her answer some thought while she walked.

'You have to adapt to the wasteland, Old Castle, or it'll swallow you whole and shit you out. The clansfolk are superstitious, but when you arrived they became desperate, too. Convincing them that I was the Shepherd of the Dead wasn't easy, though. I had to deplete and ruin every shard and crystal of ether I owned just to prove my magic to them. Ether knows ether, see? How else could I cast such powerful spells unless I was sitting on a hoard of the stuff?'

Even so, she must have trained as a Magician at some point to control the spells I'd witnessed.

August chuckled. 'Clan Ayros's desperation worked in my favour. Their chieftain saw what he wanted to see. No one living is stupid enough to go into a graveforest, are they?'

'That doesn't answer my question,' I said.

August continued as though she hadn't heard me. 'Without my ether, I probably would've died years ago. Still, using it up was worth the risk. I've got a tank now, with a nice fat crystal on its back – which is to say, more ether than I've ever owned before. I've got weapons, sonar, an array, all in one package.'

My anger was rising. '*What* do you want with me?' I hissed through clenched teeth.

August huffed, pondering. 'To be honest, you were a surprise inclusion, Old Castle. The clansfolk were supposed to bring me the tank, not its rider.' She chuckled again. 'I didn't expect the clumsy bastards to send a berserker after you, though – could've damaged the tank beyond repair. It's a wonder you survived the spirit-matter. It should've burned holes right through you—'

'Answer me!' The Song of the Dead rose with my shout, perhaps revelling in my despair. 'Why are you keeping me alive?'

We stopped. August turned to face me. Holding the ether-cannon pointing at the ground, she radiated menace. 'Would you feel better if I'd let you die? Let your Song join *theirs*?' She motioned to the corpse-trees.

'You don't need me,' I said, my teeth still clenching after every word. 'I know about survivalists. You're crazy fuckers who work alone. You don't need anyone.'

'Is that right?'

August stepped forwards and loomed over me, the glass of the helmet inches from my face.

'Let me tell you another story, Old Castle. Years ago, I'm watching this clan fight a city platoon. The wastelanders win. Those warriors butcher every fucking solider – except one, who they take prisoner. This intrigues me, see? Why would they do that? So I follow them. It's fascinating what you can learn from the clansfolk with a bit of nerve and a strong stomach.

'It's getting late and the clan needs a haven for the night. But the wasteland is a dangerous place, and the cave they find might already be home to any kind of monster. So they use their prisoner to flush it out. Bind him up with rope, hold on to the other end and send him into the cave. When they pull him out again, he's unharmed. They cut his throat soon after, mind, but at least they know the cave is safe now.'

August leaned away from me. '*That* is why you're still alive, Old Castle.' She tapped the metal hemisphere that Hanna had fitted to my breastplate. 'Ether filings – very clever. Wish I'd had the chance to thank whoever put this modification on the tank. Not only have they given me the means to locate the real Shepherd of the Dead, but also my very own soldier on a rope.' She reached out and patted my cheek unkindly. 'Now keep your fucking mouth shut and not another word tonight, got it?'

The menace, the intolerance in her voice, told me that although she had decided to use my surprise presence, go with the flow, her pragmatism could easily adapt without me should I prove a hindrance. So I did as she ordered, keeping my mouth shut as we traipsed through the corpse-trees, finally accepting that I *was* lucky to be alive. But what hope could I find in this place?

I'd seen a graveforest before, from afar, during my first weeks in the war. Commander Childs had ensured his platoon gave it a wide berth, but now here I was in the heart of one, with no choice but to plod after an unhinged traitor. August Jakob had sacrificed a platoon of her own people, and as far as Command would be concerned, I was as dead as the rest of them. Could it be true? Could there be an artefact of the Salahbeem transmitting a signal from the graveforest, an artefact that had been on Urdezha for aeons? Was it really worth the deaths of so many?

Perhaps August's confidence was well founded. If this thing was real, Command and the Scientists wouldn't care about her methods of getting to it. The clansfolk August had fooled with promises of a glorious future would see their dreams, their children, their families slaughtered if the Scientists came to the Ayros Mountains. A Salahbeem relic was worth as much as an ether-growth. And here I was, a broken solider carrying unlikely tales of spending time among the clansfolk and surviving, only to be dragged into a graveforest by a madwoman like ... like a soldier on a rope.

The Song of the Dead quietened with the approach of dawn, moans and wails falling to silence by the time the first rays of the sun limned the giant leaves high above. It was only then that I realised just how still and peaceful the forest had been during the night, despite the spirits. Animal noises moved in to fill the void: tapping and hooting overhead, roars and shrieks from the distance, echoing with danger that might lurk behind tree trunks so large they could have been hollowed out and used as houses.

We were following a stream. August hadn't said a word for hours, and I had been smart enough to keep my mouth shut. When she stopped to refill her water canteens, I stared at the glass helmet.

I *had* to get it back. The tank was as fixed now as it ever would be outside a city; if I regained control of it, I could do away with this insane survivalist. I now knew that it was safest travelling at night; I could hide and defend myself during the day. I could be out of this graveforest in a day or two, avoiding Clan Ayros, and on my way back to Fort Icus. The medical facilities there would take care of me. Surely the doctors would decide I was unfit for duty and discharge me. Command would have questions about where I'd been and what I'd witnessed, but eventually they'd send me home, wouldn't they? Back to Old Castle. To Eden. I *had* to get that helmet.

This was all I could think about as we continued following the stream and came to where the Ayros Mountains speared up through the forest floor to step the landscape with a series of rocky ledges. August found a cave, announcing that the sonar was detecting nothing inside, but, 'Lessons learned and all of that, Old Castle.'

She switched on the tank's energy shield and the arm cannon slid from its housing. August sent me in to investigate the cave while observing from the stream's bank.

'What do you see?' Her voice buzzed from the plates of the

tank themselves, distorting as it was amplified through Hanna's modification.

There was no danger waiting inside. The cave was shallow, coming to a blind end after only a few yards, hiding nothing more interesting than dirt and cobwebs. 'It's empty,' I said. The energy shield deactivated.

August decided that the cave would be our camp for the day. After she had positioned me facing the exit, standing sentry, she shrugged off her pack, laying it at the back of the cave along with the ether-cannon. She then shared a nutrition cake with me.

'Reckon it's time to see my city again, Old Castle,' she said, feeding me my half. 'After I deliver a little souvenir of the Gardeners, the Scientists will see that I get a nice retirement. Might even take up an archaeologist's position. If I get bored with all my riches, see?'

She sounded happy, though you couldn't tell from looking at her battered face. She was so confident about what she thought was making that signal, so arrogant in her power over me, that I began to hope she was being complacent.

'Where's home for you?' I asked.

August eyed me suspiciously. 'What the fuck do you care?'

'Just ... interested to know where you're from.'

'Oh, you want to be friends now?' She shoved more cake into my mouth. 'No such thing on the wasteland.'

August ate the rest of the cake herself. She lifted the helmet to do so, but didn't take it off. If she did, and made the mistake of forgetting to lock the tank into position first, the plates would free up and I could make a grab for it. But she wasn't that stupid.

'Listen,' I said after August had given me a drink. 'Can you let me out of this thing? I've been wearing it all night. Just let me stretch my legs, have a good scratch.'

August gave me a quirked smile. 'Stretch your legs, eh?'

'At least let me wash in the stream. Nature does come calling, you know. I've had to answer it more than once.' I tried to return her smile.

'Do you honestly believe you could survive this graveforest without me?'

'What?'

'You haven't seen what's lurking in this place.' August went to the back of the cave, rummaged around in her pack and returned with the canteen filled with jenkem. 'Besides, what do you think will happen if you step out of that nice warm magic field? The pain will come back, that's what, and it'll be agony. But even if you were in tip-top condition, you shouldn't fancy your chances in a fight against me.' She studied the canteen. 'I might be a cunt, Old Castle, but don't ever mistake me for an idiot. You can shit and piss in that thing all day long. I'm not letting you out.'

'Fuck you!' I spat.

'Yeah, yeah.' August placed the mask over my face. 'Fuck you, too.'

Chapter Fifty-Five

I didn't know what August got up to while I slept during the day, but on occasion her voice cut through my nightmares. One time I heard her whispering words of magic, casting spells; another, she was talking to the voice in the signal, which she believed came from some relic of the Salahbeem: 'Yeah, I know – you're the Shepherd of the Dead. Don't worry, I'm coming to find you.'

When the jenkem wore off, night was falling. My position hadn't changed; I still stood sentry just inside the cave's entrance, facing out at the stream. In the fading light, I could see a corpse beside the running water – one of the monstrous spiders August had warned me about. She really hadn't exaggerated; its carcass easily matched the size of a bear. Eight hairy, armoured legs were curled up against its body.

'Big fucker tried to sneak up on us,' August said, sliding past me into the open. She tapped the glass helmet. 'Good job I've got sonar.'

She fed me a nutrition cake and a tablet of atropine. I gave up hope as I washed it down with water from her canteen. Whether at the mercy of this lunatic or free, I wasn't going to survive the graveforest. It would've been easier to have died with my platoon.

The Song of the Dead rose as we set out for another night's march. This time, I didn't bother trying to decipher the cries and wails. I'd be among them soon enough; I'd find out then. Let this forest throw whatever it would at me. As long as it was strong enough to devour August Jakob, too, I'd settle for that.

The soft ground, earthy, thick with mulch, rose and fell before us, and we weaved between giant roots that emerged from the forest like the petrified tentacles of giant sea beasts. Any one of these corpse-trees would have towered over the largest building in any city on Urdezha. Just one of their leaves could have served as an umbrella for two in a rainstorm.

I fell asleep at some point and dreamed that I was searching for Eden. Her weeping accompanied the voices of the dead, and I simply could not find her. I ran through the darkness, searching from tree to tree, but Eden didn't show herself until I became entangled in the thick sticky threads of a colossal spiderweb. While I begged her to release me before I became a meal for the unseen monster that had spun the web, she said nothing as she warmed her hands on the flames rising from the burning letters I had written her; the letters she hadn't replied to.

The tank jolted me awake with a mental command from August that told me something was wrong.

The survivalist was crouching, predator-like, drawing us slowly into a thicket of ferns. She held a finger to her lips and then pointed. A small distance from the other side of the thicket, a dark figure paced in a clearing. Clouds were filling the sky and ether-light was sporadic, but I could see the figure was broader than any human, taller than a wastelander by at least a head. Behind it, the forest appeared to have been gathered up and fashioned into a wall that stretched between corpse-trees on the other side of the clearing. The instincts of a soldier warned me that many pairs of eyes were staring out of it.

The clouds parted and I gained a clearer view of the figure in the ether-light.

Its face, almost human, was turned to the sky, eyes closed as though listening to the Song of the Dead. Its body was covered in grey hair, apart from the exposed pads of its dark chest and round belly. It stopped pacing, leaning forwards to rest the knuckles of its big hands on the ground. Its arms were long and powerful. The boulder of its head sloped back; the nostrils of its flat nose sniffed the air.

'An ape settlement,' August whispered to me. 'They're territorial, not like trolls. And they know we're here.'

I remembered the violent tumult of apes and trolls fighting, and shivered. 'What are you going to do?'

'Respect their territory. One thing I learned from the wasteland, Old Castle – it takes an animal to know one.'

My heart skipped as August removed the glass helmet. She grinned at me, and my hopes sank as I realised she had put the tank in lockdown first.

'Don't go anywhere,' she said, taking two nutrition cakes from her pack and walking out of the ferns.

August took slow, deliberate steps into the clearing, her face aimed at the ground. The ape stirred, grunted and punched a big fist on the earth. *Kill her*, I thought. *Rip her limb from limb*. I should've shouted it, startled the ape into attacking, but I was too fearful of the same fate. The ape rose to its full imposing height as August laid the cakes on the ground with cautious movements. When the ape grunted again, the survivalist walked backwards ponderously, head bowed, until she was out of the clearing and in the ferns with me.

'That should appease them for a while,' she said, putting the helmet on. 'But let's not outstay our welcome.'

We moved on, giving the primitive settlement a wide berth.

The clouds closed in, but I could still see the shape of the ape guard, back to resting on its knuckles. I could feel its eyes upon me. I wondered how many other city soldiers had ever seen apes, seen the inside of a graveforest. How many astounding memories were now dust on the wasteland?

Soon after, the clouds released a downpour of sleet, icy like the breath of the dead following the sound of their Songs. Freezing droplets drummed on the canopy above, falling as rain to soak my hair and run down my neck before evaporating in the magic field beneath the plates. I thought of asking August to activate the tank's shield but decided she probably wouldn't.

August stopped every now and then, scanning the area with the ether-cannon in her hand. Obviously, the sonar had picked up something moving through the night and her augmented vision was searching the darkness for it. But no new surprises revealed themselves and she continued on.

The rest of the night passed uneventfully. Dawn chased away the dead and the sleet turned to gentle snow. The graveforest broke to allow for a grove of trees strong and sturdy but much smaller than corpse-trees. Sycamores. Their branches were barren. The sodden ground was covered in their leaves, dead and brown, and fallen seeds had rotted to delicate skeletons like insect wings. The snow was trying its hardest to cover them up.

August led us further into the grove until she found shelter from the weather beneath one of the larger trees with wide branches. After she had fed and watered me, a look of curiosity spread across her face as she bent to pick up a single sycamore seed.

'Funny,' she said, studying the seed. 'It was an old story that first got me thinking the Gardeners were behind this signal.'

'What story?'

'The Shepherd and the Sycamore.' She let the seed go and it fell spinning to the ground.

I knew the story she meant. A cautionary tale told to children. I hadn't heard it for years, and the mention of it confused me for a moment. But when I went over the story's details, I started to laugh with a sad huffing sound. *I am the Shepherd of the Dead*, the voice in the signal claimed.

'What's so funny?' August demanded.

'You think it's the Shepherd from the story? You think you've found the gateway to heaven?' My laughing increased. 'You're as stupid as the clansfolk.'

'You think so?' Rather than showing offence at my words, August shook her head pityingly. 'The truth is, Old Castle, I couldn't say what the Salahbeem have left behind. But if you believe the clansfolk are so very different from the rest of us, then you need enlightening.'

She rested the ether-cannon against the trunk of the sycamore, took off her cloak and shrugged off her pack. 'The difference between wastelanders and citizens is Scientists. Sure, the clansfolk have their priests, but they can only use the ambient magic that ether releases into the air, in the ground, or from the crystals they steal from us. It takes a Scientist to understand how ether itself can be altered, its magic distributed to fuel technology, see? We all began as clansfolk, Old Castle, rising from the ashes of the Ether Wars, just ... some of us were lucky enough to find ether-growths.'

There were tears on my face, but I was neither laughing nor crying as August brought the canteen of jenkem to me and I once again breathed in its foul vapour. I welcomed intoxication this time.

While I succumbed, August folded her cloak and placed it on the ground at the base of the tree. She sat on it and rested her back against the trunk, finding shelter from the snow beneath big, leafless branches while leaving me out in the falling white flakes. She exaggerated the noise of getting comfortable as she laid the ether-cannon across her lap.

'We're close, Old Castle,' she said, tapping the glass helmet. 'The signal is getting stronger and stronger. Maybe tonight we'll get to see if your platoon's sacrifice was worth it. You'd better spend the night praying that it was. Won't be much point in keeping you around if I'm wrong.'

Chapter Fifty-Six

'Heads up, Old Castle.' August's warning cut through my nightmares. 'We've got visitors.'

I was shooting before my eyes were open. The grove was a blur of snow and sycamore trees. Dirty brown shapes raced around me, shattering the air with bestial roars. Sunlight dazzled my eyes. My arm cannon pumped shot after shot as the tank spun and weaved.

August spat a curse. 'Fucking trolls!'

Still in the grip of jenkem, the world spinning around me, my head whipped from side to side and sickness churned in my gut. With no way to control my movements, no way to predict which twist or turn the tank would take next, I shouted and shouted for mercy until I vomited.

The *whumps* of August's ether-cannon came from somewhere close by. The rush of air displaced by magical energy threatened to steal what breath I could get into my lungs. Every time my arm bucked, another foe died. The mental strain August was under must have been immense, but she kept the tank's cannon, and her own, blasting away at whatever the sonar was detecting.

I couldn't tell how many trolls surrounded us, but my orientation had improved enough to see that they were tall as apes but thinner, standing more upright on long legs. Covered in shaggy green-brown hair, they charged into the clearing, reaching with clawed hands on muscular arms. Pointed ears stood erect on top of their elongated heads. Their roars came from yawning muzzles filled with sharp teeth, sounding similar to bears but higher pitched, somehow more intelligent.

I caught sight of August orbiting me with her cannon, her movements in sync with mine. And bodies toppled dead around us.

I spun to face a charging troll. A blast of ether sent it crashing into a few of its fellow monsters. Another emerged from my right, too fast and close for the tank to adjust position, but August was equal to the attack. My right arm shot out, grabbed the troll by the throat. The tank whined and its boots dug into the snowy ground as it lifted its captive into the air. Shaggy hair crisped and smoked in the tank's shield. The cannon on my left arm continued to fire, twisting the real arm inside to painful angles, while the fingers of my right gauntlet squeezed and pierced skin. Blood poured. The troll shook its head from side to side, turning black eyes as wide as saucers to the sky and releasing a bellow.

The neck snapped. A blood-red tongue lolled. The corpse dropped to the ground, spraying blood.

The stream of trolls charging from the graveforest seemed never-ending. No matter how many August put down, two replaced every casualty. At this rate, the tank's ether crystal would run low on magic and there would be no respite in which it could regenerate. But the survivalist kept fighting, a lethal animal barely uttering a sound through her concentration, and I could do nothing but bend to the will of her mental commands. Blood sullied the pure whiteness of snow. The air reeked of death.

When the battle ended, it was sudden. The trolls stopped

fighting as a single group, fell silent and, as if following some silent command, fled the clearing.

August was looking around, breathing hard and sweating. 'Well, fuck me,' she whispered.

Just as we were concluding that there was no reason for the trolls' retreat, the sound of thrashing came from the graveforest, along with the shrieking voices of what they had fled from.

Apes. Scores of them, bounding on all fours, chasing after their foes. They paid no attention to August and me as they rushed through the clearing and headed back into the giant trees on the other side: blurs of grey and silver with black manes – such power in grace. After the main group had sped back into the graveforest, one more ape stepped into the clearing.

It gave us a slow, proud glare before punching the ground and grunting. The guard from the primitive settlement? I didn't have time to think on it, flinching as the ape rose tall and beat its chest, issuing a bellow before racing off to join its clan in the hunt.

Their voices carried away into the graveforest, leaving August and me standing in the sycamore grove surrounded by the carnage of least thirty troll corpses.

'I thought we were dead meat there, Old Castle,' August said. 'Maybe we should take this as a sign.' She wheeled around to face me, excited, mocking. 'What do you reckon – a sign from heaven?'

Chapter Fifty-Seven

The war between apes and trolls raged in the distance for the remainder of the day. They had stopped fighting by nightfall, when the dead began to sing, and we travelled once more through darkness until reaching the location of a survivalist's treasure.

I stood several paces behind August. She was on her hands and knees, peering over the edge of a great pit. It looked as though a huge area of the forest floor had collapsed to create the jagged circle of a hole at least a hundred feet across. The subsidence had toppled a few corpse-trees, leaving a huge gap in the canopy through which the early-morning sun shone. One tree had been dragged down into the pit. Its highest branches stuck out at a diagonal angle. Leaves as large as umbrellas flapped in the breeze.

August had been trying to find the best way to climb down for a while now. The signal was stronger here than it had ever been, and the survivalist claimed that its source lay at the bottom of this pit. The area was peculiarly quiet, not one living thing making a noise. August believed this was because the monsters of the graveforest could detect the Shepherd's signal instinctively and were hiding from it.

Eventually, she rose and turned to me, saying something unexpected. 'Who's Eden?'

My mouth worked wordlessly.

'Clan Ayros gave me this along with the tank, see?' In August's hand was the wooden box of the information node that Hanna had given me. She pressed the resin bead and my voice crackled from it. 'I'm not best pleased with you, Eden Finn ...' August switched it off and the glass helmet tilted to one side. 'Same name as you. I'm guessing she's your wife?'

I nodded.

'Reckon she'd love to see you again.'

'What is this?' My lip curled into a snarl. 'You've done enough to me already. Leave Eden out of it.'

'You're missing my point, Old Castle. The Quantum is standing ready for me to confirm the nature of this treasure. Once I do, they'll throw everything they have at the Ayros Mountains. They'll wade through the clansfolk and into this graveforest just to get to me and *it*. And after, they'll provide a nice armed escort out of the wasteland.' August sucked air over her teeth. 'So I'll make you a deal. Do as I say, when I say it, and if you survive, I'll make sure you're taken to the nearest fort. Icus, I think it is.'

My heart thumped. '*If* I survive.'

'I have no idea what's waiting down there. Can't guarantee anything.' August shrugged. 'But think about it. You've been patched up, but the tank is only numbing your pain. Your wounds must be festering by now. You know as well as I do that you're in bad enough shape to get kicked out of the army and sent all the way home to Eden.'

I stared at her, wanting to believe she was making some kind of genuine offer, but knowing that the end of my use lay at the bottom of the great pit.

August knew what I was thinking. 'Trust me, don't trust me – it amounts to the same thing. You either follow my orders or I'll kill you here and now.'

'What if you're wrong?' I swallowed. 'What if this treasure is worthless?'

'Command will still wipe out the clansfolk, and I'll be back to roaming the wasteland looking for my fortune. As for you ...' August grinned. 'The tree's resting at a good angle. I could make the climb down, so the tank will have no trouble.' At her mental command, the tank took a few steps back and braced. 'I'm going to miss you, Old Castle.'

And then I was running, hurtling towards the pit. The tank leapt at the edge, and I screamed as I soared over the great abyss and thrashed through giant leaves.

The tank compensated as I crashed into the wall of the corpse-tree's trunk, but the impact still jarred my wounds and I cried out again. Thankfully the gauntlets dug into deep ridges in thick bark and clung on. My face stung from the whips and scratches I'd received on the way. Spitting out a mouthful of leaf, I took several steadying breaths before peering behind and down. The pit was dark, the sunlight struggling to illuminate its gloomy depths. Going by the size of the trees in the graveforest, I judged the bottom was at least two hundred feet below me.

I looked up, searching for August. She stood at the pit's edge, twenty feet above, waving at me. Her voice buzzed from the tank's armoured plates.

'Still alive?' I swore at her and she laughed. 'I've been a busy girl while you've been sleeping off the jenkem. I've cast spells on the ether filings inside that modification, tuned it in with the helmet, augmented the distance of remote coverage. And it means I can give you partial control of the tank.' She laughed again as though she could hear my mind whirring. 'Before you get too excited, just remember that I can take it back again at any time. Ready?'

I felt the tank change, like it had relaxed. I'd live the rest of my life not being able to explain the mental connection that a rider formed with the ether magic on the suit's back. It wasn't as strong as if I'd been wearing the helmet – *partial*, August had said – but the armoured plates felt more a part of me, and suddenly it was my mind causing the gauntlets to cling to the bark, my command digging the boots into the trunk.

'You're going to be my eyes and ears down there,' August said. 'Clear the way for me to join you.'

Like a soldier on a rope.

'If you want me to clear the way, you'd better give me control of the arm cannon,' I said.

'You'll get it … once you don't have a clear shot at me, you sneaky bastard. Last warning, Old Castle. Try fucking me over, I'll put the tank in lockdown and—'

'All right! I get the message.'

'Just think of your wife. Off you go.'

Chapter Fifty-Eight

There was a delay in the tank's movements, not a significant amount, perhaps an eye-blink of time, but enough to mar the sense of freedom I felt at having control back.

August had been right: the angle at which the corpse-tree lay in the pit, coupled with its ridged bark, made for an easy climb down. Its branches befitted the enormity of its trunk, and I had to circumnavigate two of them. But after the second, the branches ended and the trunk was clear all the way to the bottom.

I tried not to dwell on what August had said about my wounds. I hadn't experienced much pain since she put me in the tank, but I recalled the agony caused by burning spirit-matter. If my wounds were festering, they might be killing me right now and I just didn't feel it. I had to focus on believing August. I *needed* her to be right. If there was an artefact of the Salahbeem in this pit, then the Scientists would come and they would take me home to Eden.

The light was weak as I neared the base of the tree, climbing through a nest of gigantic, twisting roots. Dust drifted like snow in grey shafts, the chill of shadows pressing on my face. I made my way carefully, giving my eyes time to adjust to the gloom. When I judged the bottom of the pit was no more than twenty feet below me, I shimmied to the end of the lowest root I could see and jumped down to land between huge clods of earth and boulders of rock.

And bones.

In the dim light, I saw skulls, arm and leg bones – many more than I could count – lying among debris and rubble which must have fallen when the forest floor collapsed. A ribcage hung from the tip of a root.

The tank's plates buzzed and August said, 'What's going on down there, Old Castle?'

'There are bones,' I said. 'Whole skeletons.'

'What did you expect? It's a fucking corpse-tree!'

True, I'd always known that these trees had been planted in the dead bodies of humans, but I'd believed that it equated to one corpse, one tree. But this ... this looked like the site of an ancient massacre.

'Any sign of what we're looking for?'

'Not yet.'

The pit swept around me in a circle like a giant well shaft. This far down, I realised it was a wall of stone far too smooth to be naturally formed. Its colour was lighter than the black porous rock of the Ayros Mountains. I looked up through the roots at the daylight far above.

'This place must've been sealed off and the tree planted on top of it.'

'The sonar's not picking up anything moving,' August said, 'but its signal is taking longer to return on the tank's right side. What's there?'

'Not much, I— Wait.' A large patch of wall was darker than the rest. Treading carefully on earth and rocks, bones crunching beneath the tank's boots, I headed over to it. 'It's a tunnel, I think.' I looked behind the boulder that partially covered it. The entrance was perfectly square. 'It's man-made.'

'*Man*-made?'

'Whatever. Someone *built* it. There's no light inside.'

'Best you be careful, then.'

Another change came over the tank. I tried the arm cannon, relieved when its barrel slid out of its housing. When I'd taken a few steps into the tunnel's darkness, I said, 'I'm in the clear now. I could use the shield.'

The tank whined and the air hummed around me, dampening the environment's ambience, and August's voice became clearer. 'Time to make me rich, Old Castle.'

Wishing I was wearing the glass helmet as well, I followed the tunnel, not much comforted by the obsessed survivalist watching my back. The tunnel wasn't particularly wide. I trailed a hand along one wall as I walked, holding the ether-cannon out in front of me. Soon the dark became so complete that I couldn't have seen anything coming out of it.

I took careful steps, not knowing if a turn or intersection lay ahead, or another great pit into which I might tumble all the way down to Urdezha's core. Nothing good ever hid in the dark. I'd seen soldiers stumble into quagmires and drown in acid waters. I'd found humans used as hosts for eggs in underground skarab nests. I'd raided clansfolk burrows, heard stories of sinkholes ... The army had lost more soldiers to the dark of the wasteland than it could count.

'You're breathing heavy, Old Castle. Keep calm, now. I've got you.'

Yes, she did, I decided. After the fight against the trolls, one thing I could absolutely trust was August's ability to read the tank's sonar.

Thankfully, it only took a few minutes of straight, unhindered walking before the darkness lifted slightly.

'You've stopped, Old Castle. Why?'

'I can see light.'

It came from directly ahead, a soft glow tinted rose, barely illuminating the square of what I presumed to be the tunnel's end. A sound reached my ears which I mistook for the moan of wind until realising that I'd heard it before, every night in the graveforest.

'August, can you hear this?'

'No. What's going on?'

'It's the Song of the Dead. But it sounds like only one voice.'

A pause. 'What's making the light?'

'Not sure. I can't see it from here.'

'Then move closer, you idiot!'

I could hear the anxiety in August's voice, the eagerness to push as far as she needed with no thought about what happened to me as long as it delivered the biggest payload a survivalist could imagine. I kept my thoughts on home as I approached the end of the tunnel and stepped out into a domed chamber.

When I saw the source of the light, I swore.

'What is it?' August demanded.

I couldn't find words. I'd seen ether before, the chips and splinters that went into ether-cannons, the fist-sized crystals used in tanks, but the crystal sitting at the centre of the chamber was bigger than any of the boulders I'd seen out in the pit. Misty-rose in colour, it was a crystalline pyramid, smoothly carved and standing five feet from base to tip, and its light radiated magic. I couldn't even begin to calculate its worth.

'Don't hold out on me, Old Castle. What have you found?' I told her and she cackled with delight. 'That's a good start. What else is there?'

The chamber was no more than thirty feet in diameter. Its pale grey stone had been inlaid with skulls, hundreds of skeletal faces staring up from the floor, out from the walls, down from the domed ceiling, grimly decorative, neatly spaced. Whichever spirit sang the Song of the Dead changed its tone to a single hollow note, low, almost like a hum.

I said, 'The pyramid isn't the only thing here.'

Above the ether, not quite connected to its point – floating, perhaps – was a diamond-shaped frame, taller and wider than me. I couldn't tell if it was made from a solid material or liquid matter, but the frame was black as shadows, reflecting none of the crystal's rose light. Absorbing it?

When August heard my description, her voice became feverish. 'That has to be what we're looking for. I'm coming to find you.'

The energy shield died and the arm cannon retracted as the tank went into lockdown.

'Wait,' I said. 'Something's happening.'

The magical light of the ether was moving, rising, streaming from the pyramid to fill the black frame. The Song of the Dead shifted to a higher pitch.

'Fuck!' August shouted. 'The signal just went mad—'

I barely noticed her voice cutting off. I was mesmerised and chilled by the ether. As its light filled the diamond frame, that which remained inside the pyramid lost some of its intensity. I began to see a shape form, a shadow in the brightness, impossible to discern in detail but like a person sitting with knees drawn up to their chest, trapped inside a magical crystal. I wanted to both run away and move closer, but the tank was no longer under my control.

'August, there's something in the pyramid. I think it's a corpse. This place must be a tomb.' There was no reply. 'August? *August … ?*

The light held in the diamond-shaped frame flared and the tank's power died. The armoured plates fell from my body,

scattering all around me. I smelled the stench of filth and in-
fection, and then pain hit me. Agony sent me groaning to a
heap on the floor. A voice entered my mind, slicing through my
suffering with guttural Salabese.

'*I am the Shepherd of the Dead.*'

The light! It was coming from the light.

Fracturing into thousands of wisps, the light poured from the
frame, a swarm of glowing sycamore seeds that came spinning
towards me. The lone spirit wailed and moaned, echoing around
the chamber as though it shared my agony, as though it was angry
and desperate. The radiant cloud of seeds descended, smothered
me, crushed me, entered me, and that guttural Salabese filled
my head once more, speaking now in my own voice.

'*Your sins have returned to you, Wendal Finn.*'

I screamed for August. I screamed for Eden. But in the end,
I was screaming for myself.

IV

The Lore of Ascension

(The Present …)

Chapter Fifty-Nine

Beneath a black, livid sky, the sea heaved in mountainous swells that froze for a moment like the peaks of Ayros before crashing down against the sea wall that stood before Nephuin Town. Rain hammered the coastline; a bitter gale howled along with the siren wailing from Old Castle high on the cliffs above the fishing settlement. The city's huge ether-cannons were aimed towards the sea and the danger which had risen from its endless, treacherous depths.

As if summoned by the preternatural storm that already besieged Old Castle, Urdezha's vengeful nature had decided to add to the misery. A new storm had come out of the wastes to join Alexria's legacy, bringing violent lightning and savage bellows of thunder. These kinds of weather fronts came quickly, blew hard and fast, never lasting long, but this one had been spiteful enough to stir the deepest regions of the sea and drive a behemoth bèast towards the city.

A blubbery, amorphous mass beneath the stormy sky, the beast's true form wasn't revealed until Nephuin Town's searchlights criss-crossed the air with thick beams, glinting in the rain, making each droplet sparkle like falling jewels. The beams congregated on the beast, shining upon gnarled blubber, rising to illuminate a serrated beak, rheumy eyes and the flaccid sac of its head. As the light hit its face, the beast's cries were louder than the thunder. It lifted two tentacles into the air. At their ends, oval stings as large as houses waved in the darkness above the searchlights, preparing to strike as the beast swam inland, pushing high waves before it.

The fishing settlement's defences were being controlled from the Fusion at the centre of Old Castle; its inhabitants had been evacuated to the city days ago when the menace from Alexria had first struck. But the magic of the ether shield currently didn't have enough power to protect the city's flanks, or anything outside of its walls. If the beast breached the sea wall, it was big enough to crush Nephuin Town entirely, lash at the clifftop cannons with its mighty stings and – who knew? – maybe scale the cliff itself to continue its attack across Old Castle. However, the sea wall had ether-cannons of its own, and they were preparing to fire.

Could the Scientists afford this extra expenditure of ether power?

Drenched and shivering, I watched the beast drawing closer to shore from high on the cliff road that led down to the sea. I wondered if the beast had come because it was tired and angry at fisherfolk emptying its territory of food; perhaps it felt lost, as alone and afraid as I did. A part of me wanted to run into the treacherous waves, beg the beast to drag me down into the depths and drown away my memories of Nel dying at my hands.

Your sins have returned to you, Wendal Finn.

All along the sea wall and from up on the cliffs, ether-cannons barked at the sea. Searchlights dimmed as streaks of magical energy soared into the night, tails of rose-tinted mist trailing behind them. The beast reared as shot after shot impacted against its great blubbery body. Its thunderous voice, sounding more surprised than pained, hurt my ears. And still it came for the sea wall.

But the cannons were only testing their aim, and the blasts of ether magic quickly concentrated on the behemoth's face. Caught in ribbons of rose mist and crackling energy, the beast's fury and pain shook the ground as one of its rheumy eyes burst with a monumental gout of milky fluid that cascaded down its body, mixing with the rain into the sea. Lightning flashed, thunder bellowed and a blast of magic cracked its beak; another blew a hole through a house-sized sting. And, finally, the cannons halted its advance. The beast recognised a fight it wouldn't win and retreated.

With ether barking after it, the monster disappeared beneath violent waves. Only then did the cannons stop, leaving the searchlights to sweep across the sea. The siren continued to wail. Old Castle had defeated the wastes once again.

'I'm sorry, Nel,' I whispered into the rain. 'I should have died on the wasteland.'

I had tried so hard to forget August Jakob and that dark place beneath a graveforest in the Ayros Mountains. I had never expected the reality of that nightmare to follow me back to Old Castle, yet here it was.

Sycamore had tried to make me understand that the Magicians had not continued my existence for the purpose of finding my wife's spirit. I had refused to listen, refused to accept what I was being told, but I accepted it now, and with a burning rage. Everything I had been through in the last three months had led me to the cold and undeniable truth. Sycamore was the missing part of black stone. Eden had been searching for *me*. And the preternatural storm plaguing Old Castle was somehow *my* fault.

Head bowed to the wind and rain, I continued down the coast road, heading towards the one person who might explain why my continued existence had brought such catastrophe to so many.

Chapter Sixty

Follow the coast away from the fishing settlement, you'll come to the ruin you played in as a kid, Meredith's message had said. *The dead are singing their Song for you there.* Now she was dead, too. Because of me.

I knew the ruin. On a calm sunny day, it was less than fifteen minutes' walk along the beach from Nephuin Town. But on this night, it took me longer to traverse the stony sand and slick boulders. Holding my jacket tight around me, I stuck close to the cliff wall, as far as I could get from the crashing waves that might drag me out to sea. Stinging rain numbed my face, bitter wind locked my fingers into claws, and by the time I found the old crumbling pass that cut into the cliff, I walked with the gait of arthritic legs.

I followed the pass for a short distance until reaching ancient steps carved into the rock, chipped and cracked but still sturdy. Narrow, sheltered from the rain by high, uneven walls, they led up into darkness and my destination. Meredith must have truly possessed spiritual gifts if she knew I'd come to this place as a child. I'd been eight or nine years old. During a school trip to Nephuin Town, where we were supposed to learn about the fisherfolk, I had grown bored, so I sneaked away to investigate the ruin instead.

Climbing the steps, I recalled how I'd counted them in my youth. One hundred and two in all. Slick and treacherous at times, they wound around until I was walking in the direction of the sea. Finally, I was delivered to the clifftop, out into the driving rain again, where I had a clear view of my home city away to my right.

The wind carried the sound of the siren, searchlights still criss-crossed the sea. The menace from Alexria sat over Old Castle as a different shade of anger within the lightning and darkness of the natural storm. Alive with fiery orange, swirling in a conical shape, its tip stabbed up into the black sky, blazing as though conducting energy from a kindred spirit, while its monumental base spread across the length and breadth of the city, pressing down on the ether shield.

The Scientists' experiments on black stone had caused this storm. It was here because of Sycamore. The shield looked like such an insubstantial thing from this distance, just a thin sheath of wavering silver struggling to hold up a power greater than itself.

A bolt of orange lightning made it through, spearing down to strike the silhouettes of Old Castle's buildings. A second bolt followed, and then a third. Perhaps this was it. Had the city drained too much of its resources in driving off the sea beast? Was I about to be a grand witness to an ether-growth exploding? Smoke rose above the glow of flames, but no more lightning stabbed the city and the shield continued holding. The beams of searchlights cutting across the stormy sea from Nephuin Town sputtered and died.

The Scientists had caused this, but only Sycamore could stop it. Black stone was eating the dead …

I turned my attention to the ruin. It rose near the edge of the cliff, high, wide and columnar I'd learned at school that this was the remaining quarter of what had once been a watchtower, built sometime during the Ether Wars. Complete, it would have been as tall as a corpse-tree; as a remnant, still an impressive fifty feet. Once, the tower had been an inland building, but centuries, millennia of erosion had brought the cliff's edge closer and closer, and one day this ruin would topple into the sea to be lost for ever. The same went for Old Castle, I supposed.

But not today. Not before I'd confronted Eden's master.

Shivering, I left the driving rain and entered the ruin through a hole in its wall. This place had been stripped clean of anything valuable countless years ago, and its interior was a decaying shell. In an empty, spacious ground floor, illumination came in brief but frequent flashes from the lightning outside, limning the stone stairs that I remembered from childhood. They spiralled up around the inside of the wall to the next level. My legs ached as I made the climb, and I dispelled a worry that this ruin might be as deserted as the place I'd investigated in my youth.

I reached the next level. Most of its stone floor had crumbled away and there was nothing there of note. The stairs continued spiralling up, but I stopped to catch my breath. The ceiling was mostly intact, though there were a few holes giving a view through the floor above it to the next level. It might have been a trick of the night – tired eyes and a troubled mind casting phantoms in the dark – but I was sure that through one of those holes I had seen a light be extinguished.

I smacked my lips against a bitter taste that dried the inside of my mouth, recognising the tang of magic, and pushed on, energised now.

On the next level, eerie heat warmed my chills, comforting yet out of place. The area looked as large and empty as the last two levels, yet a section of the wall on the far side had collapsed, giving a view out onto the raging sea through a ragged hole. The sound of the storm didn't enter the room. No wind. No rain. Lightning continued to come in bright flashes, but my brain was telling me that the light was more constant than that, as though there was more in this ruin than my eyes could see. I was not alone.

'Ghan Hathor.' My voice trembled with anger. 'I know you're here.'

Nothing.

'Show yourself! Unless you'd rather I told the Salem where you are.'

A sudden pressure descended on me. I cried out in surprise and pain as my knees cracked against stone. The force of magic held me in place, and man's voice, deep and menacing, came from somewhere unseen.

'I know who sent you. Dyonne Obor wishes to rectify her mistakes.'

'Dyonne didn't send me,' I growled, straining against the pressure. 'But I do want to know about your quarrel with her, why the Salem ordered your execution.'

'You're treading dangerous ground, assassin.' Hathor's voice became a presence as heavy as the magic holding me down on my knees. 'I can end your life quickly and without pain, or in slow agony that will feel like eternity. So tell me how Obor discovered that I still live, and do so with haste.'

He didn't know what he was up against.

'Listen to me! You had an apprentice. She was looking for the missing piece of a Salahbeem relic that the Scientists are calling black stone.' My teeth were fighting to clench and I was raging. 'Her name was Eden Finn.'

'Eden?' There was surprise and recognition in his voice.

'I want to know what she was really involved in.'

In the warm room that looked to be so cold, Hathor took a

long, painful moment before replying. 'Who are you?'

'Eden's husband.'

The room changed. A concealing spell had hidden its true image, and when the illusion dropped, light came from the amber flames of two magical fires rising tall on either side of Ghan Hathor.

Dressed more like a wastelander than a Magician of the city, he wore heavy furs and a cloak around his shoulders. A thin, wizened man beneath his clothes, he was elderly, over fifty. His hair was grey, hanging about his shoulders in dirty tangles; his beard was full and long.

'So you are Wendal,' he said, bloodshot eyes calculating. 'I'm sorry to tell you, but they say Eden took her own life.'

'I know. Why?'

Hathor shrugged and turned to some blocks of stone which had been fashioned into a table. On it lay sheets of paper and a few pencils, a mortar and pestle, dried flowers and herbs, a rack of glass vials. The table had been placed close to the hole in the wall. Evidently, Hathor liked a view of the sea while conducting the work of a Magician.

He said, 'How did you discover my sanctuary?'

'A dormouse told me.'

'Ah.'

'The Salem doesn't know you're here, I swear. I've told no one else that you're still alive.'

'The Grand Adepts might not have sent you, but you *are* their slave, Wendal Finn.'

Hathor's tone had softened, though his magic still held me down on my knees. In his eyes, there was something wild and broken, and I found myself pitying this Magician and the existence he had been reduced to in this ruin.

Against the wall to my left, a pile of furs and dirty blankets looked more like a nest than a bed. To my right, dried fish hung in a row from a line. Despite the warmth of magical fire, the room smelled damp and unclean. The people of the shanties lived better than this.

'Eden rarely spoke of you,' Hathor said, looking out to sea. 'I found out why. Eventually. Your body has been possessed by the *thing* that the dead are calling Sycamore.'

Once again, I strained to be free of the spell which held me in place. 'I came here for the truth,' I hissed.

'So did I.' Hathor faced me, his expression unreadable. 'I lived in hope that I could find the evidence that would convince the Salem of the *truth* about Dyonne Obor. I was a fool.'

'Tell *me*!' I pleaded. 'Why was Dyonne ordered to execute you? What do you know about black stone?'

'*Black stone …*' Hathor scoffed before intolerance came to his old face. 'What does it matter now? The gateway has been opened. The storm from Alexria proves it.'

My every muscle tensed. 'What have the Scientists done?' My voice was strained. 'What is the storm to Sycamore?'

'Are you really so blind, Wendal?' Hathor shook his head, disappointed. 'Sycamore is the Shepherd, once again subjugated by the human race. What did you think would happen?' He looked out to sea again. 'The storm is Truth, Mercy and Wrath, the Judges of Aktuaht, come to punish our crime. Their fury has destroyed Alexria, *will* destroy Old Castle, and the Order of Glass and Words won't stop until the Shepherd is free.'

Hathor stepped towards me. In the light of the flames, his pupils had dilated as Dyonne's did when she summoned magic. 'It is fortuitous that you have come to me. The Salem must have lost its reason to be so stupid as to trap the power of Sycamore inside so weak a host. But I will return reason to them now, lest the Scientists claim you and seal our fate.'

I frowned, not sure I was following the cold intent wrapped around the Magician's words.

'Please, understand.' Hathor sighed. 'In order for Old Castle to survive, you have to die, Wendal Finn.'

I wanted to plead my case, tell him that I really was enslaved, that the Song of Always protected me, but I was disturbed to hear gurgling from above, a sound like weeping underwater. I should have sensed that there were ghouls in the room, but there was nothing I could do. With the spell holding me firm, two ghouls dropped from the ruined ceiling, landing between Hathor and me as shapeless patches of shadow.

'You don't understand!' I shouted as the ghouls slithered towards me. 'You can't free him—'

But Hathor wasn't listening. He cast his magic. It stole the words from my throat and raised me into the air, where I hung, limp and helpless. The ghouls coalesced into an oily pool that reached up and latched on to my boots, slithering up over my legs, cold and wet, seeking to drown me.

'Salvation will be my final gift to Urdezha,' Hathor said.

The ghouls had reached my chest, sliding towards my throat. Their rage and desperation threatened to drag me back into the madness I'd first experienced on the wasteland, at the bottom of a great pit at the heart of a graveforest. The ghouls cried, 'Sycamore, Sycamore,' over and over, but the Shepherd of the Dead wouldn't be summoned because the ghouls couldn't remember their own names, and I had no filter.

Hathor's magic threw me across the room, out through the hole in the wall, and I tumbled down through wind and rain towards the roar of the sea. Before the ghouls covered my face and rendered me blind, I saw rocks rushing up to meet me.

Chapter Sixty-One

I kept falling until I reached a plane far below anger, below pain and panic, where a dream bloomed out of ambient noise – a vague, suppressed roaring as though heard from far beneath fearsome waves – and it came with clear and lucid visions.

'*I despair of you, Wendal,*' said Sycamore. '*What possible good did you think would come from confronting Ghan Hathor like that?*'

Having once again adopted the image of Eden, he sat inside a pyramid made from pure ether, staring at me through clear rose-tinted crystal, the emerald-green of his eyes shaped into sycamore seeds. His voice wasn't muffled by the crystal wall between us. The pyramid was floating, drifting ahead of me as I followed it down a corridor of light brown rock. Cut smooth and perfectly square, the corridor felt familiar. A tunnel? Had I walked this way before, four months earlier, when it had been lightless?

Sycamore said, '*Because of you, we're probably lost to the bottom of the sea.*' He curled my wife's lip. '*Did you not think your actions through before—*'

'Shut up!' I snarled.

The pyramid had four chaperones, four inhuman guards ushering it along the corridor, one standing at each corner of its base. Gardeners, Salahbeem, heads bald and ears pointed.

Although they walked ahead of me, I knew without seeing their faces that their eyes would be large, their features flat and squashed. They were knights of the Order of Glass and Words. The magical script inlaid into their amber armour gave off the same pale radiance as the pyramid.

'*You are upset with me, Wendal.*'

'You killed Nel.'

'*Did I? Or was it Mutley? Or Dyonne? Maybe* you *are to blame.*' Inside the pyramid, Sycamore waved my anger away and his tone became consoling. '*Wendal, take heart, for Nel has gone to a better place.*'

A better place? Black stone? 'She was innocent,' I said, seething.

'*Don't be ridiculous. You've never known anyone who could claim* that. *Not you, Nel, Eden, nor any of your race. Innocent!*' Sycamore spat the word and shook his head in irritation.

His chaperones were showing no interest in the exchange, probably didn't even know it was occurring. These Salahbeem knights were nothing more than imagery, residue in my dream of Sycamore's memory.

'*Search the deepest, truest part of yourself,*' Sycamore said, '*and answer me this – how do you honestly think you would fare before the Judges of Aktuaht?*'

'I can't give an answer,' I shouted. 'You destroyed the truest part of me four months ago.'

'*And here we are, together as we have been ever since you entered my tomb. But now your awareness has expanded, Wendal. Calm yourself so we may speak of it.*'

The pyramid had reached the end of the tunnel, and the knights ushered it into the circular chamber which I had long tried to forget. Human skulls were set into the pale grey stone of the wall and floor and domed ceiling, just as I remembered. So it *had* been a tomb – Sycamore's tomb – buried deep beneath the graveforest. I had no memory of how I escaped this place, but obviously August Jakob had been true to her word and found a way to return me to Fort Icus.

The dark, diamond-shaped frame was there, hanging in the air, made from a strange substance, both solid and fluid, lonely without its ether. Directly beneath it, a smooth and skull-less square of floor had been engraved with Salabese, hundreds of lines, tiny lettering, impossible to read. The knights of the Order of Glass and Words walked the pyramid over to it and covered the writing as they laid it down. As soon as they did so, rose-tinted silver began to shine within the strange frame. The Salahbeem left the tomb without a word, disappearing out into the tunnel, perhaps to depart Urdezha for good, leaving me alone with the trapped image of my wife.

'*Nel is gone,*' Sycamore said. '*Accept it.*'

'You have no idea how this feels, do you?'

'*You have bigger problems, Wendal. Like Old Castle's fate.*'

Huffing a breath, I began pacing the tomb, up and down in front of Sycamore.

I hadn't given much thought to what had become of the strange frame and ether pyramid; I'd just assumed that August Jakob had been paid well for them and gone on to live a life of luxury in whichever city she hailed from. I never dreamed that she had lived so close in Alexria, or that she would come to Old Castle looking for me. For Sycamore. And I never believed that August had been right about the relics in the tomb, but evidently she was. These items had been left behind by the Gardeners.

'*In case you're wondering,*' Sycamore said, '*this little set-up is my prison.*'

'The Salahbeem trapped you down here.'

'*Yes.*'

'Why?'

'*You're focusing on the wrong thing, Wendal. Consider what you learned from your misguided visit to Ghan Hathor.*'

'I *am* considering it!'

My head ached every time I tried to look at the diamond-shaped frame. The substance it was made from seemed to *flow* around the light within it, absorbing the glow of ether. It was solid and liquid and dark, unknowable, as though it wasn't meant to be seen by human eyes. Was this substance what the Scientists were calling black stone?

'The frame is a gateway,' I said. It was an accusation.

'*True.*'

I swallowed. 'Was Klyne right about the Scientists' experiments? Is black stone eating the dead?'

'*Undoubtedly so.*'

'Then Eden's spirit—'

'*Is not on Urdezha. And it never was, Wendal. Nel is gone, Eden is gone, and if you choose to wallow in the grief of this, then soon the population of Old Castle will follow them.*'

I glared into my wife's sycamore-seed eyes. I knew he was telling me the truth. Some part of me had already figured it out and accepted it back when the ghost of Abdon Klyne had come to my lodging house bearing fresh revelations. My fury set hard like ice.

I aimed a finger at Sycamore in his ether prison. 'Did you bring the storm to Old Castle?'

'*Yes and no.*'

'You'll have to explain that to me.'

Sycamore tilted his head to one side. '*Have you ever wondered where I am from, Wendal? If my absence would be noticed there, and that something might come looking for me? I've warned you before – I am not supposed to be on your world.*'

'Don't fuck around with me, Sycamore, not now.' I was

seething again. 'No more lies. No more myths and stories. Tell me straight – *what is the storm?*'

'*It is a rupture, a rift.*' Sycamore sat forwards in the pyramid, bringing my wife's face close to the ether wall. '*The Scientists have punched a hole in Urdezha's sky and it leads to a place that will swallow Old Castle. Is that straight enough for you?*'

I felt my face twitch as I struggled to comprehend what he was saying. I understood enough, however. 'The city shield—'

'*Won't hold up for much longer. The hole in your sky won't heal by itself.*'

'I've been told twice now that you could heal it.' My hands were shaking. 'Is that true?'

'*Not in my current condition.*'

'But if I set you free, would the storm end?'

Sycamore pursed Eden's lips. '*If you're about to make a noble gesture for the sake of your city, Wendal, then you might be too late. You've probably doomed us to drown for ever at the bottom of the sea.*'

He sat back and his expression clouded angrily. '*Dyonne Obor and the Salem really didn't understand what they were doing when they captured me. The Salahbeem did. They understood all too well, and look what they did to me.*'

I staggered back, shielding my eyes as the light within the strange frame flared painfully and streamed down to fill the ether pyramid. When the light receded, a hum filled the tomb, a single voice singing the Song of the Dead, mournful and strong.

Sycamore had changed his image. My wife no longer sat inside the pyramid. She had turned into a Salahbeem woman, dressed in the amber armour of Glass and Words. The knight from my jenkem dreams stared at me with large, colourless eyes.

'It was her,' I realised. 'Her corpse was in the pyramid when I found your tomb. It's her spirit singing now.' I remembered the knight's words to me on the street. 'Idgian Korinth.'

'*Excuse me?*' For the first time since he had possessed me, I heard surprise in Sycamore's tone. '*How did you come by that name?*'

'I had a vision,' I said. 'She came to me. I saw black stone eating the dead.'

'*Interesting.*' Sycamore still spoke with my voice, but his words were out of sync with the odd movements of the knight's small, circular mouth. '*I did not know you had experienced this.*'

'Who is she to you?'

Sycamore didn't reply. The ambient burble of water had returned to the tomb, louder than before, drowning out the Song of the Dead sung by the spirit of Idgian Korinth, a mysterious knight from Sycamore's past. I thought I heard gulls crying. Imagery began to darken, bleed colour.

'*It would seem that we have been found,*' Sycamore said. '*You are waking up.*'

'What do I do now? Tell me.'

'*You could make a sacrifice, Wendal, or perish with the rest of your city. It makes no difference to the outcome. My freedom is, and always has been, inevitable.*'

My eyes struggled to focus on the diamond-shaped gateway, the black stone … The strange substance rippled, the light within it paled. I seemed to be moving away from it.

As if an ether-lamp had been switched off, darkness fell in the tomb, so thick that not even the light of ether could shine through it. Gulls cried and salt water filled my mouth.

Chapter Sixty-Two

My brain had done its best to block out the agony of a trauma which no living thing had the right to survive, but how could I forget smashing into sharp rocks with lethal force? Yet my skin hadn't split, no bones broke, no organs or blood had spilled into the sea. Of course I had survived. The Salem would have it no other way. But the *pain* ... My mind had shut down against suffering beyond any I'd experienced before. After that, the dream of Sycamore's tomb; then there were flashes of memory, bursts of sensory perception. Gulls crying. Or was it ghouls? Voices murmuring, one of them my own.

'... and you're lucky that he was found washed up on the shore near Nephuin Town.' The speaker sounded muffled, coldly neutral. The proxy who spoke for Mr Sebastian, the old monster of the Salem.

'We cannot be certain who did this to him.'

'Do you take me for a fool, Dyonne Obor?' said Mr Sebastian. 'We have both heard Wendal Finn wittering about his attacker. Or do you have some other explanation for why he knows of things he should not?'

'Ghan Hathor is *dead*.' At the mention of that name, I opened my eyes to see Dyonne standing beside me. 'I killed him *myself*, Mr Sebastian.'

'Apparently, you were mistaken. The Salem is not pleased.'

Dyonne looked down at me with a mixture of fear and fury. I was lying on my back, staring up at her. My body had been numbed of pain, my arms and legs rendered immobile by the same spell that had muted my voice. *What do I do now?*

I managed to lift my head and saw the bloated form of Mr Sebastian hanging from the chains which disappeared into his big, tent-like robe. The strange glimmering line of viscous fluid ran from the dark triangle of his hood to the mask covering the naked proxy's mouth.

'You have the benefit of my doubt, Dyonne Obor. For now. I do not believe you were so stupid as to ignore a direct order from the Salem.'

How long had it been since my confrontation with Hathor? Hours? Days?

'Tell me …' The proxy pointed at the ceiling. 'Who are they?'

Above Dyonne, the ceiling was a smeared and churning darkness. The ghouls that Hathor had set on me, I realised, held in silence like an oily mural by the words of magic written on the real ceiling above them. They reminded me of the storm. If I'd been able to speak, I would have told Mr Sebastian that it was a hole in the sky and it wouldn't heal unless it found Sycamore.

'They are my former apprentices,' Dyonne said miserably. 'Hathor killed them when—'

'You took apprentices to execute an adept Magician?' The proxy hissed out an angry breath. 'You shame yourself.'

'I did only what I thought necessary.' Dyonne's face reddened. 'I don't understand how Ghan Hathor is still alive, or how Wendal Finn discovered him, but I assure you, Mr Sebastian, that I *will* find out and I *will* finish the job.'

'You will do no such thing,' Mr Sebastian said. 'Your unfortunate apprentices paid for your failure, Dyonne Obor, and their ghouls deserve vengeance. Sycamore will deal with Ghan Hathor.'

The ghouls hissed and bubbled, and here I was, in the same place, in the same state of defencelessness as I had been in three months ago. I wanted it all to stop, my part to end, but Hathor knew something that Dyonne was terrified of the Salem discovering. I could see it in the Magician's eyes.

'A fine plan, Mr Sebastian, but ...' Dyonne sounded nervy, and I could tell she was thinking fast. 'These ghouls are of no use to us. Hathor trapped them within their own Songs, altered their memories with magic. He must have done this so they couldn't be used against him. They cannot remember the names that will summon your servant.'

'I will reverse anything Hathor has done.'

'I beg you, let *me* take care of him.'

'No.' The word was spoken simply yet officiously. 'The Salem's opinion has changed since we last spoke, Dyonne Obor. Sycamore's service is coming to an end. And it has been decided that your rank among the Magicians must be lowered.'

Dyonne licked her lips, nervously, suspiciously. 'I don't understand, Mr Sebastian.'

'You are no longer trusted to be Wendal Finn's custodian,' the proxy stated. 'Soon, you will be called upon to relinquish possession of his moment of death to the Grand Adepts. From this moment, Sycamore is not your responsibility.'

'I ... I ...' Dyonne held her hands out imploringly. 'Mr Sebastian, please! Have I not served you faithfully—'

'Faithfully? I once told you what had to happen if the host could not be tamed. Yet you did not follow my order, even though Wendal Finn's actions jeopardise the Magicians' advantage over the Scientists. He has become ... *wayward*. You have lost control.'

'I promise you, I can contain the situation.'

'*Mutya Bryn! Janelle Memphis!* And now the traitor *Ghan Hathor*!' The proxy's shouts weren't particularly impressive, but the pressure of magic that filled the room was terrifying. Bigger, stronger, more powerful than anything I'd experienced from any other Magician. 'Your mistakes have breached our security. Ing Meredith is another example.'

Dyonne was practically wringing her hands together. Scared. I liked seeing her this way.

'Your failures have cost us dearly. You are an embarrassment!'

'But—'

'It is not your place to question the Grand Adepts of the Salem, Dyonne Obor.'

'No, Mr Sebastian, of course not, I—'

'Begone. Await your summons to the Salem council, and prepare to relinquish the Song of Always.'

Dyonne bowed and turned her back on Mr Sebastian. She swept a dangerous look over me, which I was certain changed to a smirk before she strode off. I wanted to trip her, wrestle her to the ground and throttle her. Dyonne's footsteps thudded on the stairs. I heard a door open and slam shut. The presence of magic grew in the room. A sibilant tone hissed words of a spell – not the proxy, I realised; I was hearing Mr Sebastian's true voice. It caused the ghouls to thrash on the ceiling.

'You have been without vengeance for far too long,' the proxy told them as Mr Sebastian continued to chant his spell. 'Come, sing your Songs to the spirit of vengeance.'

The ghouls descended, dropping down to drown me with oily voices that wept their names into my ears. I fell inside myself and Sycamore rose. As we passed each other, I felt his intrigue and wrath.

Chapter Sixty-Three

The dead called me Sycamore. But not for much longer.

I wasn't given to caring for the living, so it was strange that now, with the end so close and inevitable, Wendal Finn's plight would enflame my curiosity. There was time enough, I reasoned, to find the answers I had come to think he perhaps deserved, that he had been searching for since the day he found my tomb in the graveforest. And it *was* a tomb. A place buried deep in the hope that no living thing would ever discover what was sealed inside it. Curiosity had landed me in trouble before, but there were moments when I really could not help myself.

When I caught up with Ghan Hathor, he was trying to make his escape. Having evacuated the sanctuary of the ruin, he was doing his best to flee along the coast; but with a sack of provisions hanging from his shoulder and advanced years weighing him down, his progress was slow over the stony sand. The morning was clear and bright in the aftermath of the rainstorm, beyond the fiery menace hanging over Old Castle high on the cliffs behind me. Outside the lightning spitting at the city's ether shield, waves lapped gently in a brisk sea breeze.

I was gradually gaining on Hathor. The two ghouls slithered after me as dark, featureless humanoids. Though their names had summoned me, I was too preoccupied to recall what they were.

Hathor glanced back over his shoulder and then continued walking as his brain took a moment to register what his eyes had seen. He swung around to face me. He had the appearance of a harmless old man, so very far from the wild Magician who had thrown Wendal down onto the rocks. Perhaps, if humankind hadn't made their oceans as dangerous as their land, he might have hired a boat at Nephuin Town and sailed away to a new life. As it was, he had travelled less than an hour's walk from Old Castle.

'*Where are you going, Ghan Hathor?*' I said as I neared him. '*Are you intending to spend your remaining days on the wasteland? Did you believe that you had saved Old Castle and your final act was to be the city's hero?*'

Hathor had no reply. His eyes flitted to the preternatural elements in the near distance before finding the ghouls creeping along the beach behind me. I had heard their Songs. Their moments of death had come with weak, pale visions, difficult to discern. But I'd seen that Hathor killed them because Dyonne Obor had been cowardly enough to use her apprentices as shields. As to how he had tricked Dyonne into believing he was dead – well, Hathor had already shown Wendal Finn that he was skilled with illusion.

'I killed him,' Hathor stated. 'I set you free.'

'*Unfortunately, this body's moment of death has been reserved and I remain its prisoner for now.*'

'The Song of Always.' His mouth hung slack in his thick beard for a moment. 'It is forbidden. Only Grand Adepts may cast it on themselves.'

'*Well, the Salem considered my host worth protecting.*'

I moved closer to Hathor, glad that the desire of the ghouls to witness Sycamore's justice, to claim vengeance and peace, was voiced in whispers as gentle as the hiss of waves ebbing over sand. My own desires had cooled, too. My impulse to rush into this fool's murder was dulled. An effect of the rift above Old Castle; it was loosening the Salem's leash, weakening the bond between me and my host. And given that Wendal had experienced waking visions that I did not see myself, visions in which he had learned the name Idgian Korinth, it was clear we were already becoming separate entities and the rift was blurring the boundary between the land of the living and what lay on the other side.

Hathor dropped his sack to his feet.

'*Please do not try any more of your tricks and conjurations,*' I warned him. '*No matter what you do, your victims will always lead me to your location.*'

My presence tapped on Hathor's psyche, and he knew that his end had come. His old face became prideful, accepting. But I wasn't ready for him yet and said, '*You are not innocent, but you are a patsy. For Dyonne Obor. Will you tell me why?*'

Hathor curled a lip, defiant. 'Go and ask Dyonne herself.'

'*Not an easy thing to do at present, and I'm fairly sure her masters mean to kill this body when I'm done here.*'

'Of course they will.' Hathor used his bearded chin to gesture at Old Castle's menace. 'Freeing you is the only way to save the city from *that* abomination.'

'*Yes, they have probably worked this out for themselves by now, yet so have you. You are remarkably well informed for one who has been living in exile.*'

'My exile has not been spent idle.'

'*Please,*' I said. '*I'm offering you a stay of execution, a chance of reprieve, in exchange for what you know and have learned.*'

Hathor licked his lips, fearful and suspicious, but hope also creased the corners of his eyes. Humans were willing to believe anything in the face of death, so I took his silence for willingness.

'*The road that led to your exile, did it start when your apprentice aided you in a search for the missing part of an ancient gateway that became known as black stone?*'

Hathor flinched, looking up at the sky as gulls cried overhead, before nodding at me.

'*I've recently come to understand that the Magicians and the Scientists are in dispute over it.*'

'*They always have been.*' Hathor had switched to speaking Salabese, no doubt offering clumsy respect which he prayed I'd return. '*In the beginning, the Salem were in a race with the Quantum to find the last piece of the gateway. To find* you.'

'*A race the Magicians won when Wendal Finn brought me to Old Castle, yes?*'

'*No one knew you weren't in the city back then. As far as I was aware, Eden believed her husband had died in the war. I didn't realise she knew otherwise until she met with a survivalist.*'

'*August Jakob.*' She must have come to Old Castle looking for us before we returned from the wasteland. She must have also told Eden that Wendal was still alive. '*Then through Jakob, your apprentice discovered that her husband was my host?*'

Hathor confirmed with another nod. '*At the time, I suspected that Eden had found what we were looking for because, after meeting with Jakob, she disappeared and Dyonne Obor got in the way before I could find her. Obor was desperate to be the one who contacted you first.*'

'*Did Dyonne also meet with the survivalist – murder her, perhaps?*'

'*It's likely.*' Hathor shrugged. '*Jakob was working for the Quantum and the only one who knew where you were.*'

'*Jakob and Eden Finn.*'

'*They both died before the Quantum discovered anything.*'

I could well believe that. Abdon Klyne claimed that the

Quantum had held back a lucrative finder's fee due to black stone being incomplete. Jakob was not the type to risk her payout by sharing information. As for Wendal's wife ...

'*Tell me,*' I said. '*Is it likely that Eden Finn would commit suicide to protect her husband from the Salem and the Quantum?*'

'*It's possible, I suppose.*' Hathor's consternation was clear as he gazed upon the physical presence of his apprentice's spouse, while speaking to the spirit of another. '*She might well have done it.*'

But the dubiousness lacing Hathor's words spoke otherwise to me. '*Did Dyonne Obor know your apprentice?*'

'*I don't doubt it.*'

'*Ah.*'

'*Though I can't say for sure because she forced me to flee the city before the situation came to a head.*'

'*Then how did you come to know so much?*'

'*The dead told me.*'

Hathor nodded at his victims, and it made sense. The legend of Sycamore was sung far and wide among the ghouls. A clever Magician could learn much from them.

'*Tell me why the Salem ordered your execution, Ghan Hathor.*'

'*Dyonne convinced the Grand Adepts that I had turned traitor.*' Hathor's face clouded angrily, no doubt believing himself to be a poor soul, hard done by. '*She told them that I sought to invoke the Lore of Ascension.*'

'*And did you?*'

'*No, it was a lie,*' Hathor raged. '*I always knew Obor was up to something. She wormed her way into the confidence of the Salem and tricked me into disgrace while doing it. She is the traitor. Her aim is to rule, not serve, and that is why she was so desperate to find you first.*'

This took me aback. '*Dyonne wishes to use me to depose her master?*'

Hathor confirmed this with a scowl.

The Lore of Ascension, the steep and dangerous path a Magician must walk to reach the heady heights of Grand Adept. Dyonne Obor's web of secrets and lies was intricate indeed and, in the beginning, I had hoped that she would be ambitious and cunning and stupid enough to use me in an attempt to inherit a position on the Salem. But she never had, even though it must have been tempting.

'*Are you certain?*' I said. '*Dyonne Obor has been my custodian for months, yet she has never tried her hand.*'

'*If I had any certain answers, do you think I would be living like this?*' Hathor countered. '*Obor's treachery runs deep and she is biding her time. I believe she has brought the Scientists into whatever she is plotting.*'

That surprised me further. '*You believe this or know it to be true?*'

'*I'm sure of it in my heart.*'

'*I see.*' I looked up at the cliffs, out across the waves. Such a pleasant day. The ghouls chittered incessantly, begging me to bring them peace. '*You were betrayed, so you faked your death, choosing to live in exile while waiting for the chance to prove your innocence to your masters and reap revenge on Dyonne Obor. Yet the conclusion you have drawn would appear to be a theory, a guess. Are you sure the sea air hasn't made you a little paranoid, Ghan Hathor?*'

'*Please.*' He dared to take a step closer. '*Help me.*'

'*Help you?*' Clearly, he thought his honesty, the undeniable injustice he had suffered, the very fact that I hadn't killed him on sight, had earned him pardon from execution. I gave him a smile, which he mistook for one of reassurance.

'*Let us help each other,*' he said eagerly, feverishly. '*It is so hard for me to gather fresh information from the city. Dribs and drabs — rarely anything of use. But together, we can reveal Obor's treachery to the Salem.*'

'*And then, perhaps, with my freedom I could rid the citizens of the menace in their sky, and you could return to Old Castle as its saviour. Is that your thinking?*'

'*I deserve justice!*'

'*The dead tell me the same thing.*'

'*Help me.*'

'*Your plea is born from thoughts of self-preservation, not a true call for justice,*' I said. '*If the tables had been turned, you would have acted little differently from Dyonne Obor. You would have handed Wendal Finn and I over to the Salem just the same. Your sins have returned to you, Ghan Hathor.*'

The Magician yelled in alarm as I grabbed him by the beard and pulled him over. He thrashed as I dragged him into the sea. He had some final words to spout, but they were lost to the gentle waves as I held him under, and the ghouls of those he had murdered swirled around me, singing the final verse of their Songs.

'*The dead call me Sycamore,*' I told the storm above Old Castle. '*I am their Shepherd.*'

Chapter Sixty-Four

I expected the Salem to collect me once Sycamore had killed Hathor and I had reclaimed control of my body. I expected my moment of death to come flying along the beach to shoot me through the brain. But neither happened. I spent a while staring out to sea, waist-deep in water, Hathor's body lost to the tide, before finally deciding to go back to my lodgings. I didn't know where else to go.

Afternoon had arrived by the time I reached the city. I climbed the coast road, slipping out of the clear sky and pleasant breeze blowing across the waves and into the shadow of the storm which had somehow come because of the gateway in Sycamore's tomb. A rift. A rupture. A hole in the sky. Lightning stabbed against the city shield as if to announce my return through the east gates. Two city watch guards were playing cards inside a sentry post, but they didn't notice me walk by. Watching the fire roiling within the churning darkness besieging Old Castle, I began the long hike towards the Tinman District in the west, bruised and battered, clothes wet and torn.

Even if the under-rail had been running again, I still would have walked. It was probably my last chance to do so. With un-hurried footsteps, I made my way through the streets, travelling across the breadth of the city, a phantom among citizens, living the last minutes of a terminal existence. The storm would only leave Old Castle if Sycamore was free.

I stuck to shadowy alleys and deserted side lanes, giving some lackey of the Salem plenty of opportunity to accost me, to drag me to my execution, without any innocent citizen getting in the way. But no one showed, and I made it all the way home with Sycamore – *always* Sycamore – safe inside me.

What did I do now?

Up on my floor, there were two city watch officers in the corridor talking to my neighbour, a shady-looking man who had probably never known I existed, and who I'd never cared to know. My landlord, Mr Stadham, accompanied them – along with the personal protection of his nieces, of course, looking mean and ready for trouble.

With a spiteful grin, Stadham pointed at me. 'That's him,' he leered. 'He was *very* close with her.'

The officers forgot my neighbour and turned their attentions to me. If they were expecting me to be intimidated, they were disappointed as I ignored them and faced the door to my lodgings.

'Wait right there,' one of the officers said. 'We want to talk to you.'

'Get in line,' I mumbled, fumbling through my damp pockets for my key. I couldn't find it; it must have been lost to the sea along with Ghan Hathor's corpse.

'Hey! I'm giving you an order.'

'And I'm telling you to fuck off.' I started laughing with a sad, huffing sound, and then punched the door in rage.

'On your knees, citizen,' said the officer.

He and his colleague were drawing their batons. Good; I was in the mood for a fight. Stadham stood behind his nieces. My neighbour darted into his home and slammed the door behind him. The city watch moved towards me, but stopped when the door to my lodgings opened and Sergeant Lana Khem stepped out.

'I'll deal with this one,' she told her officers. They looked as surprised as me to see her. Stadham and the nieces seemed disappointed. 'Carry on questioning the other tenants.'

Lana stood to one side and I entered my lodgings without a backward glance. She followed me in and closed the door, looking me up and down, concerned by my wet and ripped and stinking state.

'Wendal, where have you been?'

I turned away from her. I ached from head to foot. A cigarette – that was what I needed. But when I tried to fetch my tobacco pouch from my jacket pocket, all I pulled out was a handful of damp sand. I stared at it before letting the sand fall slapping to the floor in wet lumps before lifting my hand to the wedding bands. But they had gone the same way as my key and tobacco pouch and no longer hung from a chain around my neck. Perhaps Hathor snapped it off during our struggle.

I willed the Salem to do it, then. To send my moment of death, a bullet from an ancient weapon which would set Sycamore free and save Old Castle.

'I'm sorry, Eden,' I whispered. 'I tried to find you. As hard as you tried to find me, I hear. But this was never about us.'

'Wendal?' Lana's voice sounded firm but worried.

Why was the Salem stalling? Maybe the Grand Adepts didn't know that the storm had come for Sycamore, after all. Maybe I needed to force their hand before time ran out.

'I know why you're here,' I told Lana, brushing sand from my hands. 'You found Nel's body.'

I faced her, wondering how many unsolved murders the city watch had on its records, how many of them were due to me. If

Lana thought that the investigation into the death of my only friend could be swept away by getting shit-faced on jenkem and jumping into bed, she was mistaken.

'Nel's dead because I killed her,' I confessed. 'It's what I do, Lana. I'm an assassin for the Magicians.'

'Wendal—'

'Listen to me,' I said. 'You have to arrest me and get a message to the Scientists, someone who can reach the Quantum. I can't explain it to you, Lana, but it's the storm. I know how to stop it.'

Lana shook her head. 'The truth is, you just got caught up in the middle of all this.' That wasn't the reply I was expecting. 'Sycamore is the one who can save Old Castle.'

Dumbfounded, I watched as Lana dipped a hand into the inside pocket of her uniform jacket and produced the small wooden box of an information node. Two resin beads were set into its top, one clear, the other a deep amber. Lana's thumb hovered over the latter, and she seemed to become an entirely different person.

'Lana?'

'You're late to the show, Wendal. I've already been ordered to bring you in.'

I stepped back from her, hardly recognising the cold and un-forgiving woman addressing me. She held the information node as though it were a weapon, some form of protection, and I was perturbed to see that Itch had taken an interest in its presence. In the high corner of the room, the ghoul bubbled into the form of a mummified child, her grey eyes peering over her knees in wonder at the wooden box. The words of magic on the wall beneath Itch were glowing.

'What are you doing, Lana?'

'This is going to be uncomfortable.' Her face expressed pity. 'But you need to understand what you're involved in.'

When Lana pressed the amber bead and jabbed the box in my direction, I raised my hands, expecting some kind of physical assault. But the information node released a high-pitched wail that caused Itch to scream. I tried covering my ears, but the vibrating frequency wormed its way between my fingers, drilled into my head and shook my brain. All strength left me and I dropped to my knees.

'Time's up, Wendal,' Lana said.

Itch was still screaming as my eyelids fluttered, then closed, and the visions recorded inside the wooden box were injected directly into my mind …

I stood in a train carriage. No, I was not standing, or sitting; I was simply there, bodiless, a presence of conscious thought only, watching the dimly lit under-rail tunnel speeding by outside the window. The carriage came in grainy, monochrome imagery like a vision from a ghoul, but this was not the Song of the Dead that I was witnessing. This was something else. What had Lana done?

I've been ordered to bring you in, she had said. By whom? The Salem? Who *was* Lana Khem? Certainly more than the city watch sergeant I'd always known.

A new presence materialised in the carriage with me. Or perhaps she had always been there … Dyonne Obor.

Dressed in a dusky gown, her head shaved smooth, she stood in the aisle between the carriage seats, alone and unobserved as far as she was concerned. A recording, an image from her past, but from how long ago?

Dyonne had cut herself and coated each of her fingertips with blood. With care and concentration, she highlighted certain symbols within the magical script carved into the skin on the backs of her hands. All the while, she recited the words of a spell but made no sound, not even a whisper; and only then did I realise that this vision carried no sound whatsoever. The Magician's voice, the clacks of train wheels over tracks, the general hum of white noise that accompanied the sway of under-rail carriages – all was as silent as a ghoul's vision.

As ghostly a presence as I was in this recording, I felt a flush of angry heat while staring at Dyonne. Ghan Hathor's last moments came to me, the confused and frustrated story he had told to Sycamore, and I wondered: had Dyonne known Eden? It seemed inconceivable after all this time, and yet Hathor, an exiled Magician, had spoken with nothing left to lose, as truthful as the dead he had since joined. But his death was a small matter now. This vision had been forced upon me, and of all people, apparently Lana Khem was about to further the narrative.

Dyonne completed her spell by drawing a magical symbol on her forehead in blood. Although she couldn't see what she was doing, years of practice and dedication to her art ensured that the circle was centralised, and the cross she drew within in it was neat and did not venture over the circle's red line. Dyonne stopped reciting and her pupils dilated. She had summoned her magic, but she was holding the spell in reserve, not yet ready to cast it. Protecting herself, I realised.

Whatever Dyonne was up to, she was fearful and unhappy about the situation. Even as I thought this, I knew the truth of it hadn't come from personal deduction. Somehow, the vision, the information in the node, was feeding me visceral understanding to accompany the imagery, along with comprehension of loca-tion and destination. This train ran on a private line, a hidden stretch of the under-rail to which the general populace of Old Castle had no access. It belonged to the Quantum and ran to a closely guarded complex beneath the most secretive district in the city, where only the most important Scientists were allowed to go: the Fusion. But what the vision didn't tell me was why Dyonne Obor, a high-ranking Magician, was heading into the heart of her enemy's territory.

The train began to slow. With an intolerant expression and dilated pupils, Dyonne made her way towards the door, walking through me before the vision carried my perception outside the carriage, and I was observing the train pulling up at the platform of the Quantum's secret complex.

The door opened and Dyonne disembarked. She looked around with an unimpressed air, fully aware that she was being watched, that her every breath and twitch were being recorded by the ubiquitous ether nodes of this underground facility, had already been recorded by those in the train carriage – replayed now for my benefit. How long ago was this?

Finally, Dyonne's wandering gaze rested on a woman who had emerged on the platform to greet her. Lana Khem.

So Lana worked for the Scientists and had access to their most inner circle, the sphere of the Quantum itself. Astonishing. How could I have missed this? Even if I had been high on jenkem most of the times I saw her, how could Sycamore not have realised?

Lana's expression was unreadable as she waited for Dyonne. Instead of a sergeant's uniform, she wore a sharp suit of dark grey with a matching tie. The shirt beneath her waistcoat was white, and her hair was tied into a tight tail. I didn't know whether to feel shocked, angry or stupid. For so long I had pitied Lana, thinking that she suffered an obsession with me born from a sense of guilt that I had been too weak to deny. How wrong I had been.

Dyonne nodded her readiness and Lana turned, striding down a corridor into the Quantum's complex. Cagey, suspicious, hands and forehead decorated in bloody magic, Dyonne followed her.

The vision drifted after them. The corridor, clean and bathed in the bright and sterile light of ether-lamps, was long and wide. There were sets of double doors on either side, closed, their windows darkened, no markings on them which might identify the purpose of the rooms beyond. Dyonne ignored them, keeping her dilated eyes on Lana's back, matching her long strides and quick pace.

Eventually, they reached the doors which served as the end of the corridor. Lana pressed her hand to a pad of crystal, which glowed, identifying her touch. The doors unlocked with several clicks and opened, and she led Dyonne into a huge warehouse.

Light was dim. Shadows cast their shrouds. But despite the gloom, the vision told me that the warehouse was storing treasures. Some of the most profound and secret discoveries the Quantum of Old Castle had made on the wasteland, dating back ... who knew how many years? And among them were many of the results the experiments on these treasures had reaped. Most items in the warehouse lurked in darkness at the room's edges, but one had been moved to the centre of the warehouse's smooth Dust floor. A cube of amber resin, twenty feet high, wide and deep. Thousands of ether grains had been set into its walls, glowing with pinprick lights. Words of magic had been carved into the resin.

Dyonne stared at the artefact. Lana waited to one side.

The vision popped inside my head and sound finally accompanied the grainy imagery. The calm ambience of the warehouse was disturbed by a woman's voice, high and fluting, speaking from the cube of amber resin.

'Thank you for coming, Dyonne. It's high time we had a chat.'

Unfazed, giving nothing away, Dyonne followed Lana as she ushered her to the other side of the cube and the open doorway there. Dyonne hesitated on the threshold. More words of magic had been carved into the floor inside. The memory of ether told me that the cube had been protected with magic stronger than Dyonne's, and it would nullify any spells the Magician had prepared for this occasion as soon as she stepped through the doorway.

'Please,' said the woman. 'We have much to discuss.'

Chapter Sixty-Five

With her head held proudly, Dyonne followed Lana into the cube. Her magic dispelled and the blood on her forehead and hands dissipated with puffs of crimson mist.

A strange sight awaited the Magician. A small table was laden with a steaming coffee pot and a single cup and saucer. On one side of it was a comfy-looking but empty armchair, incongruously normal; but on the other was a tall wooden cabinet with a clear glass front. A coffin of sorts, for it held a corpse. A pang of nightmare jolted through my awareness. The dead woman preserved and standing upright behind the glass had been wrapped in a sullied white shroud, but her lifeless face was bare, scarred, and it was a face I knew all too well. I was staring at the corpse of August Jakob.

'Won't you have a seat, Dyonne?' The speaker was nowhere to be seen and her fluting voice came from the walls of the amber cube itself.

'You won't show yourself?' Dyonne said. 'Am I not even to know which of you has summoned me?'

'In time, you will. Now sit down and take some refreshment.'

Dyonne lowered herself into the armchair, smiling sourly because although the speaker had given no name, the Magician knew who she was. As did I. The voice in the cube belonged to one of the most powerful and clandestine people in Old Castle: a Director of the Quantum.

Lana Khem poured Dyonne a cup of coffee before standing beside August Jakob's coffin with her hands clasped before her. She stared at the Magician but her face remained emotionless. Dyonne didn't touch her beverage and tapped fingers against the armrest, clearly agitated by the growing silence unfolding in the cube. Finally, her patience evaporated.

'What do you want?' she said. 'If Mr Sebastian knew I was here, he would execute me.'

'Don't panic yourself,' the Director said. 'The Grand Adepts know nothing of your presence here. Not even the dead can spy on us in the Fusion.'

'Then I'll have to trust that your precautions are as sound as you claim. Tell me why I am here.'

'I wanted the chance to congratulate you, I suppose.' The Director's voice didn't sound particularly congratulatory. 'Your cunning and skill ensured that you ensnared this entity which the dead call Sycamore before we could. So ... congratulations, Dyonne Obor. Mr Sebastian and the Salem must be so very proud of you.'

'You wish to taunt me, is that all?'

'Ah, apologies. My rancour gets the better of me sometimes. You see, I highly doubt that you truly understand what you have captured, Dyonne. Do you know how powerful Sycamore is, where he comes from? The Grand Adepts do. They understand what we found on the wasteland, but I suspect this knowledge was not forwarded to the Salem's ... *underlings*. Am I right?'

Dyonne's silence gave nothing away, but I gained a better impression of when this recording had been made. This snippet of the past couldn't have been long after I'd become the Magicians' pet assassin.

'I'm afraid I have to tarnish your victory somewhat,' the Director continued. 'The entity isn't necessarily an intrinsic cog in the machinations that are currently developing, and it's not as if capturing it wasn't problematic for you. Unless I'm very much mistaken, a ghoul has recently shown up to haunt the life of a certain Mr Wendal Finn, begging for Sycamore's attention. You don't know how to get rid of it, do you? And you can't ask your masters for help because you damn well know who the ghoul is, even if it can't remember its own name.'

Dyonne sneered at the corpse in the wood and glass coffin.

Itch? Were they talking about Itch You Can't Scratch?

The Director sighed wistfully. 'I can't imagine that Mr Sebastian would be very pleased to discover that you allowed the Quantum to capture the one ghoul that could steal Sycamore away from its custodian. We know you killed August Jakob.'

The vision pressed in on me with hot and spiteful needles. All this time, Itch had been the ghoul of that psychopathic survivalist who had turned my world to shit? If I'd been able, if I had thought for a second that it could make a difference, I would've wrapped my hands around Dyonne's throat and throttled her.

'You Magicians are usually so precautious.' The Director clucked her tongue. 'To lose a ghoul belonging to one of your victims is a sloppy and dangerous thing to do, especially with Sycamore around. Did you honestly believe that we would give Jakob the freedom of Old Castle without keeping an eye on her?'

Dyonne managed a smirk, perhaps impressed, perhaps to hide fear and agitation. 'You went through all this trouble just so you could point out my mistakes?'

'I merely wish to make it clear that should we allow the ghoul in Mr Finn's lodgings to remember its name then it will be able to sing its Song to Sycamore. The assassin will rise and come for its handler.'

'And then *you*, along with everyone else,' Dyonne countered. 'Threatening me with Jakob's ghoul isn't wise, Director. The Salem cast the Song of Always to protect Wendal Finn and entrusted it to me. I could kill him and free Sycamore right now. Oh, you might use Jakob before I get the chance, but it leads to the same conclusion. What do you think will happen if that *thing* is loose in Old Castle?'

'Oh, come now, Dyonne, don't play me for a fool. Predicting probabilities and possibilities is what we Directors do, and that would include your current line of deception.' The voice spoke primly, clearly pleased with itself. 'Yes, if everything the dead say about Sycamore is true, then no one would be safe from his wrath. Not the Salem, nor the Quantum, nor anyone else with a ghoul in their closet. If freed, the entity would try to bring ruin to us all.

'However, I'm fully aware that your masters have established certain safeguards, powerful spells that will banish Sycamore from the realm of Urdezha should he be released from his host. The Quantum are currently developing safeguards of their own. You can't be too careful. But you were right to say that my threats are unwise, Dyonne. If either of us acts rashly now, then we run the risk of losing Sycamore for ever, and no one wants that.'

Dyonne bowed her head, conceding the point. 'Then let's cut to the chase in this stalemate. What *do* you want, Director?'

'I have a proposition for you, Dyonne Obor.'

Intrigued, confounded, bitter and angry, I again remembered the words of Ghan Hathor. He said that he believed Dyonne was somehow embroiled with the Scientists. I hadn't believed it; Dyonne always acted like the Salem's most dutiful servant, but this? This had happened. Back at the beginning.

'A proposition?' Dyonne said.

'Indeed. You may keep Sycamore for now. Because *for now* it suits us that he is trapped in Old Castle but out of our way – though only the Salahbeem know how the Salem will use him against us. We accept there will be some loses. Jakob's ghoul was a means to gain your undivided attention, Dyonne. We need your help.'

With an expression as perplexed as it was amused, Dyonne looked around the cube as though trying to find the source of the Director's voice. Lana Khem remained still and dispassionate beside the coffin, but a calculating darkness in her eyes made me wonder if, when this recording was made, she had been under orders to kill the Magician should the result of this meeting not please her master.

Dyonne said, 'Are you trying to convert me to the ways of a *good* citizen, Director?'

'Fuck me, no!' the Director squealed. 'We respect you, Dyonne, but trust you ... ?' She laughed. 'The Salem has placed you in a position of great faith and responsibility, and this is advantageous to us. We've been watching your rise through the years with interest, and we have noticed that you possess a more progressive way of thinking than the Grand Adepts you serve.'

Dyonne's lip curled. 'What do you know of my thinking?'

'I know you're ambitious but your talent is going to waste. You have reached the highest rank among the Magicians that the Salem will ever allow. But they also are watching their servant, Dyonne. You know that you have to be careful, patient, calculating, for your masters are testing their servant's loyalty, waiting for any sign that she might be ... dissatisfied with her position. They have given you enough rope to hang yourself, as it were.'

'You think it is any different for a high-ranking Magician?' Dyonne shook her head, but she was struggling to keep her composure. 'You underestimate my loyalties, Director.'

'I doubt that. The Grand Adepts of Old Castle have lived far longer than anyone else in this city, longer even than we Directors of the Quantum, and that's saying something. But where the Quantum adapts to the future, the Salem have grown tired and crusty and would forever stagnate the present. Tell me if you think I'm wrong, Dyonne.'

When the Magician remained silent, the Director continued with a satisfied air. 'The Grand Adepts fear what we found on the wasteland. And they fear it because ... you might not know, but Sycamore is only one part of an ancient relic. If our experiments with it are successful, nothing on Urdezha will ever be the same again, and the Salem don't like the power it will give us. Would you like to know how?'

'Do not goad me,' Dyonne growled. 'I know more about this relic than you think.'

'Ah, then August Jakob must have been quite receptive to your tortures before she died. Because the Salem certainly wouldn't have told you.'

Dyonne narrowed her eyes. 'So it's true. You think you have found a gateway.'

The Director was quiet for a moment. 'Let us get down to it, Dyonne Obor. How would you like the Quantum to further your ambitions? We're willing to help you kill Mr Sebastian.'

Dyonne sat back in the armchair as though recoiling from a slap in the face. A small smile curled one corner of Lana Khem's mouth.

'I am an adept Magician, Director, a loyal servant of the Salem, and your words do not deserve the respect of a reply.'

'Oh. Perhaps I'm confused. I was under the impression that the Magician's Lore of Ascension demanded that you kill a Grand Adept should you wish to take their place on the Salem. I thought that this was what you wanted.'

Dyonne gave a bitter chuckle of denial. 'I am no traitor.'

'Is that what you told Ghan Hathor before you executed him?'

Dyonne thumped the armrest of the chair. 'Mr Sebastian is protected by the Song of Always. I am not powerful enough to find where he hides his moment of death and use it against him.'

The Director's voice became a seductive purr. 'You are the custodian of the entity known as Sycamore. You have the perfect assassin at your disposal.'

Dyonne licked her lips nervously as she gazed shrewdly at the silent Lana Khem, the corpse in the coffin, and then at the cube's amber walls, as though contemplating if they were as good at keeping secrets as the Director claimed. Finally, she relented and admitted the truth that the Director knew she was hiding. 'Do you honestly believe that I haven't thought of this already?'

'Naturally you have. Even the Salem knows you've *thought* about it. How could you not?'

'Then you know, as well as they, that it cannot be done. Sycamore is too strong to be controlled by my magic alone, and he would be banished the instant he was free, yet I cannot find the old monster's moment of death without him.'

'The Quantum can help you there. I mentioned that we are developing a safeguard. It is not for the purpose of banishing Sycamore but for bringing him to heel; a device, rather than anything as weak as a human host. If you are willing to work with us, Dyonne, we will help you invoke the Lore of Ascension. We'll show you how Sycamore can kill the Grand Adept in your name without being a risk to you or anyone else. When the time is right, of course.'

'When the time is right ...' Dyonne licked her lips again. 'You still haven't told me what you want in return, Director. A Scientist spy among the hierarchy of the Magicians, perhaps? An informant?'

EDWARD COX

'Nothing so crass, I assure you,' the Director said. 'The Salem is narrow-minded, and Sycamore proves it. They have no interest in understanding the entity, learning from him, but *we* do! In time, we will need a progressive mind among the Grand Adepts, because change begets chaos, Dyonne, and Sycamore's relic will bring *such* change, *such* chaos to Urdezha. But hardship will be tempered if we evolve together, your people and mine. Your voice will help the Magicians adapt with the Scientists instead of fighting against them. Sycamore will alter our world beyond recognition, and I think this suits your ambition.'

Dyonne kept quiet, her lips clamped shut. The Director grew impatient with her guest's silence.

'Dyonne, you need to be careful. If the Quantum has seen signs that you are dissatisfied with your position, it won't take the Salem long to catch up. If they sniff so much as a hint of your treacherous thoughts, that old monster Mr Sebastian will have the head off your shoulders. Tell me that we have an accord and the Quantum will protect you, leave you free to conduct the Salem's orders with impunity.'

'Impunity?'

'Your masters believe we're too fearful of Sycamore to interfere with what they have done. We will play along, as will you.'

Dyonne scowled. 'Until the time is right.'

'Exactly. But trust is a fickle thing that has to be earned, and please remember that I can release the ghoul of August Jakob whenever I wish. So let me introduce my agent.' Beside the coffin, Lana Khem straightened an already rigid posture. 'Lana here will be our liaison. Don't worry, she is discreet and very good at her job – the best, in fact. She will be keeping a close eye on you and Mr Finn just in case you ever decide to fuck me over.'

Lana was a spy, a ... a *handler*? I wondered how long after this meeting had she come to me in the guise of a humble city watch sergeant?

Dyonne's teeth were clenched and her eyes had dropped to the floor. 'An accord, you say, but all I'm hearing is a lack of choices.'

'Oh, you have other choices, Dyonne. They just don't lead to where you wish to be, and you know it. Don't deny the benefits I'm offering you.'

'I won't be your *pet*,' Dyonne said. 'I will never be a *good* citizen.'

'No, you will be a Grand Adept of the Salem.'

The Director's tone was pleased. She had heard the resignation in the Magician's voice, seen the acquiescence in her body language, and so had I. The great Dyonne Obor had been humbled into service of the Quantum. Greed, lies and secrets ...

'Now then, you sneaky, dirty Magician,' the Director said. The sound of her voice held a grin. 'Shall we discuss the future?'

The vision faded. The information node had reached the end of its recording. I tried to latch on to it, stay there, see and hear what happened next, but I had no influence inside the transmission. The scene darkened to black and high-pitched wails dragged my mind back up into my lodgings ...

I lay on the floor, staring at Lana Khem's feet. With the information node still in her hands, she crouched beside me, studying my face as though trying to decide whether she knew me or not. Her thumb was poised over the clear resin bead beside the amber one set into the top of the wooden box.

'Wendal?' Her voice was uncertain. 'Is that you? Can you hear me?'

'You fucking liar,' I managed to croak. My head was splitting in two. There was no strength in my body. 'You tricked me.'

Lana sighed and looked over her shoulder at the corner of the room, above the magical words seared into the wall. 'Has the ghoul materialised yet? I can't see the dead.'

Itch was watching the proceedings with awe and fascination in her big grey eyes. I tried to swing a weak punch at Lana, but she batted my fist away.

'Sorry, Wendal, but I need your alter ego now.' She rose and pressed her back against the door. 'Your name is August Jakob,' she said to the corner of the room.

Tears filled Itch's eyes and she sobbed with the joy of learning her real name. She lifted her face to the ceiling, creaking as she stretched her neck. The words of magic, the spells which had kept her tame for so long, smoked and hissed. Itch, August Jakob, uncurled her stick-thin arms and legs with a sound like dry paper crackling in fire. She climbed down the wall like a spider, through the smoke to the floor, crawling on all fours towards me. Lana couldn't see her, but she kept her thumb held ready to press the clear bead.

My mind found a new depth of despair as August's withered and preserved form reached me. Stinking of the wasteland, she brought her small, dark mouth close to my ear.

'Hello, Old Castle.' Her whisper was the distant call of an animal deep inside a graveforest. 'I'd like to sing for your friend.'

Only when she herself spoke her name did it travel down into that unknowable place where Sycamore dwelt. He stirred, rising, and I felt myself drowning in his dominance. Just at the point where I would once again lose myself to his wrath, Lana pressed the clear bead. This time, the wooden box unleashed a howl of voices, an incoherent babble of Salabese. The noise gripped me and Sycamore both, and together we tumbled down into darkness.

Chapter Sixty-Six

To say I was aware *during my imprisonment is true but only to a point. When the Salahbeem buried me and sealed off my tomb, they were courteous enough to ensure that the passage of time continued to carry very little meaning to me. They buried me to protect themselves, long before they left Urdezha. Did the mighty Gardeners do this to protect you, too? I shouldn't think so. I would be very surprised if they were concerned by the prospect of you finding me once they had abandoned your race. Ten thousand years I spent in that tomb, incarcerated by spells, but this amount of time seemed fleeting when compared with the excruciating dullness of the last three months.*

No, you're quite right. I wasn't buried alone. There was also my gateway, through which I entered the world of Urdezha, and which the Salahbeem could not close once they had trapped me. Yes, the gateway leads to where I am from, my realm. It is a nameless place you could never imagine, so please stop referring to it as Aktuaht. It's insulting. If a name is so important to you, then refer to it as the realm of the dead and think of it as a waiting room or a way station — like one of your forts but existing between the land of the living and the other side. There, the dead can sing their Songs for the final time, and it is my duty, my ... honour *to guide them to the unknown. Their Shepherd.*

Am I the only Shepherd, the one from the story, perhaps? It is not as simple as that – though you may feel secure in the knowledge that I was certainly the only one foolish enough to get stranded on your world. Excuse me? I can't answer that because you don't understand what you are asking. Where did I originate? Was I created? Who do I serve? Am I a he, a she, an it? These are inane questions, a little like asking light to explain why it shines. I have always been. *As to the name Sycamore, the dead adopted it from the myths and lies told by your race to compensate for forgotten truths. I see it as a term of endearment.*

Ah, why did I come to Urdezha? Now that's a question I can *answer. My realm is open to the dead, yet sometimes the dead cannot reach it on their own. I hear them singing, each and every one of them – ghouls unable to let go, unable to forgive those who stole their lives from them. Their despair draws me and their pleas for vengeance are just. Periodically, against the rules of my realm, I have ventured into the land of the living to find the ones I can help, to shepherd them home. Only in death does your race deserve a higher state of grace. Only in peace can you claim to be noble. The living are idiotic and have a lot to learn from the dead.*

Please, forgive me my judgements. I have spent too much time steeped in the emotional rancour of my host.

When the Salahbeem entombed me, it was, in their eyes, to rid themselves of an enemy – a serial killer, as you might say here in the cities. After all, the living are inclined to believe they are more entitled than the dead, and the Salahbeem were no different. It was the Songs of their victims which drew me from my realm. The Songs sung by the humans they had murdered. Oh, I know that so many of you have adopted a romanticised view of the Gardeners. They were great, certainly, but in many ways, they were every bit as savage as you – your two races were well suited, but only for a short time, of course.

Why exactly did they leave? I can't really answer that, either, because you don't understand why they came to Urdezha in the first place. You and the Magicians became so bogged down over who was right about the Salahbeem that you lost the ability to consider a third alternative. No, I won't explain it to you. If you want to know more, I'd recommend talking to the ancient spirits of the graveforests. They remember everything.

However, with my imprisonment, the Salahbeem not only prevented me from returning to my realm, but also ensured that the dead couldn't find me. Neither of us could pass through my gateway, which remained preserved in the tomb but out of my reach. A maddening situation, I'm sure you'll agree, and one that lasted millennia.

No, actually, I was already free by the time Wendal Finn found me. You see, over the long years, the potency of the spells which bound me diminished until, finally, they could hold me no longer. Naturally, I had always planned to escape back to my realm the moment I claimed freedom, but Urdezha wasn't quite ready for me to leave. When the Salahbeem's magic failed, the seal above my tomb collapsed and the wasteland was revealed to me.

So much had changed. So many Songs ... The dead sing to me, they talk, they tell me things. Even while I am dormant inside Wendal Finn, I am listening and learning – just as he is listening and learning now – and when the dead found me in my tomb, they told me what you had done in the Salahbeem's wake. Urdezha, such a fertile and beautiful paradise when I last saw it, had become a ruin, an entire world populated by murderers and victims. The dead's demand for justice emblazed my anger, so I called for an instrument of vengeance. And he came to me.

It is technically correct to say that Wendal Finn died in my tomb. To possess him, I had to devour his spirit to make room for myself. Without me, he is but a hollow shell of flesh and blood, and only the Song of Always would stop him dropping lifeless to the ground. The Salem's timing was curious in casting that spell. I wonder if they ever understood what they did to Wendal Finn. A being without a spirit, both living and not, truly unique.

Do I feel shame? No, I feel neither that nor guilt for my actions. Only justice. After ten thousand years, there were a lot *of spirits waiting to sing me their Songs, and there still are. The dead need their Shepherd, and I did not suffer such torments merely to become a prisoner again, forced to be as weak as any one of you. Wendal Finn has taught me how it* feels *to be human, and* that *is your greatest dilemma now.*

Stop! I will answer no more of your questions unless you tell me something first. To whom am I speaking . . . ?

Chapter Sixty-Seven

A woman was sitting opposite me. Obviously no stranger to dining excesses, her ample size was concealed beneath expensively tailored but garish clothes. A turquoise jacket over a ruffle-fronted shirt of light green was inlaid with gold thread; a gaudy brooch of glass and multicoloured stones was pinned to the lapel. Her neckerchief matched the shade of her jacket, and her hair was a nest of golden curls which cascaded around her shoulders. The fat under her chin wobbled as she ate from a platter of seafood on the table between us: squid, crab, fish sitting on ice – freshly prepared and reeking of the ocean in the most unappetising way.

The woman narrowed her eyes at me as she chewed, uncertain. A bead of ether had been set into her forehead, shaped like a large teardrop. Her eyes didn't look moist, more like dry resin balls with vibrant violet irises. Her skin resembled wood painted by an artist to a particular hue. Her teeth were far too white. In all ways, she appeared unnatural.

I felt a presence behind me and turned in my chair to see Lana Khem standing there. Dressed now in a smart suit, she stared at the woman sitting opposite me as though waiting for an order. In her hands was the wooden information node. I could no longer hear the ghostly babble that had incapacitated me, but Lana's thumb hovered over the clear bead, ready to summon the transmission once again should the need arise. The Quantum's safeguard for Sycamore. Apparently, I wasn't trusted to behave myself.

I offered Lana a congratulatory nod. *'I'm impressed. You duped even me, though we both know that I am not the real fool here. And I'm not talking about Wendal.'*

Aside from brief uncertainty flashing across her face, Lana didn't respond but the other woman said, 'Good. You are fully with us.' She looked like an oversized children's doll. Her voice was high, musical, and I'd heard it before. Quite recently, in fact. 'Or, at least, you are the one that I *hope* is with us.'

On my right, at the end of the table, a tall wooden cabinet with a glass front had been positioned where a dinner guest might have sat. Inside it stood the preserved corpse of August Jakob. The survivalist wore a lax expression in death, her face scarred and weathered by a harsh life. The rest of her was covered in a sullied shroud. To my left, thick red curtains had been drawn to divide the room in two and hide … something that gave me an uncomfortable feeling.

'So, then …' The woman dabbed the corners of her mouth with a napkin and gulped from a crystal goblet filled with a generous helping of red wine. 'Given that we allowed August Jakob to tell you her name but prevented you from hearing her Song and running off to kill her murderer, I'm going to assume that her ghoul is in the room and I'm still addressing the entity known as Sycamore and not Wendal Finn.'

She had done her homework, this woman whose voice I had last heard coming from a cube of amber resin. The ghoul of August Jakob was indeed present, unavenged and keeping me in control of my host. She lay atop the wood and glass cabinet, a mummified homunculus, clutching her legs to her chest, the

Itch that Wendal could never scratch. Until now. August wept quietly. Confronted with the body she had once inhabited, her lust for vengeance had cooled somewhat.

The woman said, 'You'll forgive me if I don't speak in Salabese. I've always found the language rather ugly on the tongue.'

'*And you are?*'

'No doubt you've been hearing about me quite a lot recently, though you might not have realised it.' She dropped the napkin onto her plate. 'My name is Mrs Blackstone.'

'*Black stone …*' I couldn't prevent a chuckle of surprise. '*You are a Scientist, a Director of the Quantum, no less, and the overseer of recent experiments.*'

She confirmed with bow of her head.

Of course she was. Everything about her unnaturally preserved appearance bespoke excess and entitlement. Grand Adepts used the Song of Always to attain long life, but evidently the Directors relied on ether implants. The crystal in Mrs Blackstone's forehead glowed faintly, and I wondered how big it was beneath the bead on show.

'*I can't imagine the Salem will be pleased with the Quantum once they realise you have abducted me.*'

'You'd be surprised.'

'*Indeed.*'

Mrs Blackstone drained her goblet of wine.

Her opulent tastes spread to encompass the room. It had been decked out with Dust fashioned to look like dark lacquered wood, the walls and ceiling, too. If fact, everything in the room was either wood or glass, down to the platter beneath the seafood, the plate and goblet and cutlery that Mrs Blackstone used. Light came from a chandelier glowing with the energy of ether. Its glass beads tinkled softly, and I realised the room was shaking slightly, swaying, moving. There were no windows through which I might glimpse evidence of this, but I could feel the clacks of wheels trundling over tracks beneath my feet. We were in a train carriage, undoubtedly running on the Quantum's private line, while the rest of the city went without the under-rail.

My gaze was drawn to the red curtains again.

Mrs Blackstone flicked the rim of her goblet and set the crystal to ringing. 'Lana, would you mind?'

Storing the wooden node in the pocket of her suit jacket, Lana came around to her master's side of the table and poured her a fresh glass of wine. It was then I noticed two dark brown ampoules lying on the table beside the bottle.

'*Liquid Ether?*' I said.

'You're acquainted with it?'

'*Intimately.*'

Mrs Blackstone picked up one of the ampoules and inspected it. 'An unsanctioned operation, thankfully short-lived. We bought up most of what little the Magicians managed to manufacture and destroyed it in the reduction houses. The Salem can find some other way to make money. The citizens have enough with jenkem and alcohol. They don't need Liquid Ether on the streets, too.' She shrugged and threw the ampoule onto the table. 'I keep these around because ... well, if that bloody thing in the sky breaches our shield then I plan to be well and truly shit-faced by the time it reaches our ether-growth.'

She gave a fluting laugh.

'*Mrs Blackstone, I am sure that you have not abducted me so we might discuss the politics of intoxication.*'

'Indeed not.' She drank from her goblet, smacking her lips to savour the taste. 'The Quantum is hoping that we might reach an accord with you.'

'*Interesting. Are you aware that I killed the last human who tried to bargain with me?*'

Lana Khem, still beside her master and alert to danger, pulled the node from her pocket. Mrs Blackstone calmed her with a raised hand, saying, 'I suspect your victim was not in the same position as us.' Unfazed, nonchalant, she drank more wine. 'Are you willing to at least hear me out?'

Despite her ridiculous appearance, I admired her confidence, her utter certainty that she was in control of this situation. And who knew, maybe she genuinely believed she was. The corpse of August Jakob was positioned like a surreal guest at the table, but if her ghoul could sing me her Song, I would have the means to hunt and kill Dyonne Obor. A pleasing proposition given what that Magician had forced me to endure. Yet the red curtains called to me again, and my curiosity was piqued now more than ever.

'*Very well,*' I said. '*I will listen if you will help me to understand one or two things. The visions from the recording that you recently forced upon me gave a better overview of the situation, but the Quantum's involvement requires further clarification.*'

'Please, ask away.'

I pointed at the corpse of August Jakob. '*A survivalist makes an astounding discovery in a graveforest. While she and you are preoccupied with what has been found, you don't appreciate that it is missing a component* – me – *which has been smuggled away to a fort on the wasteland, hiding inside a human host. By the time you realise this, it is too late. Wendal Finn is already in the hands of the Magicians. Tell me how Wendal evaded your attention in the first place.*'

'By an infuriating oversight of logistics,' Mrs Blackstone said. 'Our Command on the wasteland sent a force that reached your tomb before the Quantum's delegation could catch up with it. We knew that a platoon of soldiers had died to aid August Jakob, but we never knew that any of them had survived, let alone been taken by the army to Fort Icus.'

I remembered that time better than my host. Wendal very nearly hadn't survived. While he lay in an infirmary bed at Icus, I planned upon his death to take a new host – a doctor or nurse, perhaps one of the army commanders who came to the fort – but when he pulled through, there was talk of sending him back to his city, which was where I wanted to be taken anyway.

I imagined the immediate aftermath of Jakob's discovery had involved platoons of tank-riders, fleets of ether-weapons – no cost spared by the Quantum in order to destroy Clan Ayros, cut through the graveforest and bring us to this situation, here and now.

Mrs Blackstone sighed. 'It was maddening to learn that you and Mr Finn spent so long at Fort Icus, right under our noses. But before then, we believed the missing piece was a *what*, not a *who*. August Jakob wasn't particularly forthcoming with certain details, you see.' Her confidence was blemished by a look of irritation. 'I don't know if you've ever tried forcing information from a survivalist, but let me tell you, it's sometimes far quicker to just let them get on with their job.'

'I'll take your word for it.'

'Alexria offered to pay Jakob her finder's fee in return for the information she was withholding, but apparently that mad and paranoid bastard trusted no one.' More irritation flittered across Mrs Blackstone's wooden face and violet eyes. 'She was determined to see the job through and reclaim the missing piece herself, so she went back into the wasteland – or so we thought – in search of you before anyone could stop her.'

'Jakob came to Old Castle looking for Wendal, who, she didn't realise, had yet to return from Fort Icus.'

'If only she had checked there first. By the time we realised that Jakob's search had brought her to Old Castle and we put two and two together, she was dead and ... as you say, it was too late. The Salem had trapped you inside Mr Finn and they protected him with that ridiculous Song of Always.' Mrs Blackstone's anger was clear in the way she finished her wine and banged the goblet down on the table. 'Can you imagine if we allowed the Salem to use that spell on all citizens, all soldiers? We'd be critically overpopulated in less than fifty years.'

Hypocritical, considering that the same went for the Quantum's life-preserving methods. '*Perish the thought,*' I said. '*But* you *do not allow* them? *Since when did the Grand Adepts follow the Quantum's orders?*'

'There are accords existing between us, fragile agreements to govern certain things jointly.' Mrs Blackstone spoke primly, as though to cover an admission of weakness. 'However, by casting their bloody magic on Mr Finn, they assured we couldn't get near you. If we tried, they would summon the moment of death and we'd lose you for good. It wouldn't do to let you roam free in the city, now, would it?'

'*A fair assumption.*'

'Therefore, we had no choice but to back off and bide our time. It was the only way to keep you in Old Castle—'

I stopped her; we were getting ahead of ourselves. '*We can address why you needed me to stay later. For now, let us back up to events after Dyonne Obor got to August Jakob.*'

'Ah, that was when the Salem made a big mistake.' Mrs Blackstone grinned impishly. 'They thought they could protect themselves from you by placing Mr Finn and his moment of death in Obor's custody.'

'*And so you stepped in with an interesting bargain for her.*'

'We did.' On top of the wood and glass cabinet, August's ghoul made a mewling sound. 'Obor is a cunning and powerful Magician, revered among her caste, but her reputation has given her delusions of grandeur.'

'*Your bait was Jakob's ghoul, your hook was the Lore of Ascension.*'

'And her ego swallowed it up.' With graceful vulgarity, Mrs Blackstone picked up a spoon, reached over to the platter of seafood and scooped out a fish's eye, which she popped into her mouth. 'Just at the moment when she had become the toast of her masters, the Quantum pulled the rug from beneath her.'

'*Did you lie to her about Ascension? Was it a ruse?*'

'Everybody has a weak spot, Sycamore, and we found Obor's. Her loose ends gave us access to you, and the Salem would never forgive her that.'

This woman and her fellow Directors were playing a dangerous game. They had sat on August Jakob's ghoul for three months before using it to capture me. Now that they had, they could lose me again at any moment. From Dyonne Obor's perspective, the worst had come to pass. Custody of Sycamore had already been taken from her, but if the Salem learned that her mistakes had now handed Sycamore over to the Quantum, then they would surely execute her. Even Dyonne's silver tongue couldn't talk her out of that of one. But her execution would not come before Wendal Finn's. The Salem had already decided that he was a liability and, apparently, Sycamore was to belong to no one. Yet they hadn't released the Song of Always. Why hadn't Wendal's moment of death been sent?

'*You mentioned an accord, Mrs Blackstone. I'm assuming it has something to do with your experiments and the rupture they caused in the sky?*'

The Director gestured to the red curtains. 'A few weeks ago, our experiments reached a critical point. With Obor's help, we had you close at hand in case anything went wrong. And here we are.' She addressed her agent. 'Lana, if you would, please?'

Without a word, Lana Khem opened the red curtains to reveal a frosted glass wall. She then helped Mrs Blackstone to pull her chair out so she could remove her considerable bulk from the table. The Director held Lana's arm while walking with slow steps towards the glass wall.

'If you're wearing anything metal, now would be a good time to take it off,' she told me.

I remembered Wendal and Eden Finn's wedding rings, and that they no longer hung from a chain around his neck, lost now to the bottom of the sea.

'Believe it or not,' Mrs Blackstone said, 'the Quantum miscalculated this whole scenario. Unpredictably, the tables turned on us all.'

She laid a hand on the glass wall. The outline of a large rectangle appeared, slid back and to one side. Through the opening came a deep hum, along with the babbling voices of an ancient spell. The ghoul of August Jakob wept.

'It won't be long before the citizens' panic boils over into chaos on the streets. It won't be long before there are no streets at all.' Mrs Blackstone beckoned to me. 'Come, Sycamore. Maybe together we can save Old Castle from an unacceptable fate.'

Chapter Sixty-Eight

On the other side of the glass wall, the carriage swapped its wooden decorations for raw hardened Dust, plain and grey. No windows, no doors, and the only furniture was an armchair upholstered with a colourful floral design. The deep humming I could hear was coming from a thick metal beam that ran up the right-side wall, arched across the ceiling and went down the other wall with a second beam. The arch was generating some form of energy, and beneath it was an old acquaintance.

The pyramid of clear ether, standing five feet from base to tip. The rose light of its magic was vague and weak, as was the spell it radiated: the looped incantation which had once been strong enough to imprison me. I could hear its coarse frequency, feel it in my mind; a light babble of ancient Salabese which inspired memories of my tomb in the graveforest with uneasy clarity. The pyramid contained the pale corpse of a Salahbeem woman wearing the armour of the Order of Glass and Words. Idgian Korinth. She sat with her knees drawn up to her chest, big colourless eyes staring into nothing.

Within the hum of the metal arch and the babble of the spell, I could hear the Song of the Dead. Many voices, distant and despairing, and they came from a large oval standing beside the ether pyramid. Black like watery shadow, a hole punched through Urdezha's reality, it stood taller than any human. From its rippling surface, a line of darkness coiled like an umbilical cord and connected to the tip of the pyramid. My eyes wouldn't leave the oval. It was the gateway into my realm, where the dead were singing for my return.

The entrance in the glass wall was left open, and while Lana Khem took up a position between me and the gateway, holding the information node in her hands threateningly, Mrs Blackstone approached the pyramid.

'This isn't the first knight of the Order of Glass and Words to be found preserved on the wasteland,' she said. 'Their armour taught us much about ether technology and weaponry. But despite the obvious differences in their physical appearance, the anatomy of the Salahbeem is remarkably similar to humans. Somewhat disappointingly so, actually.'

She considered the corpse encased in ether for a moment. 'To begin with, we wondered if the pyramid was the coffin for your physical remains. Then we discovered that, no, you must be something altogether *other*. The pyramid is a prison and this knight is the last person you possessed. The *serial killer* you mentioned, who ran amok among the Salahbeem ten thousand years ago.'

'*Close enough*,' I said, uninterested in her conclusions. But what *did* interest me was how the Song of the Dead coming from the gateway was infusing my being with energy, a raw power greater than the humans'. The bonds holding me and Wendal Finn together were breaking down. Only Lana Khem and her little box of tricks stood between me and my freedom.

'Through that peculiar fusion of death and magic that the Salahbeem perfected,' Mrs Blackstone continued, 'they created not only a prison but also a power source to keep your gateway preserved and tame.'

Yes, but only because my ancient captors had been unable to close the gateway, and the same spells which had kept me and my host imprisoned ensured that nothing else could follow me out of it. However, there was something wrong with the black oval in the carriage. '*This is not the gateway I created to enter this world.*'

'No,' said Mrs Blackstone. 'That one remained in Alexria, while the pyramid and corpse were brought to Old Castle following the death of August Jakob.'

'*You've had these things in the city for over three months?*'

'Yes. Studying them, unlocking their secrets. We shared our research with chapters of the Quantum all over Urdezha, collaborating, theorising. It was hoped that we could learn enough to engineer a second gateway, even though the Shepherd, the ... *navigator* of the realm beyond was missing.'

'*Obviously you succeeded.*'

'Yes and no.'

I frowned at the gateway. '*I'm curious. I've been told that you wish to contact the Salahbeem, use the gateway to bring them back to Urdezha. The Salem didn't capture me as part of some petty power play, did they?*'

'Bloody fools.' Mrs Blackstone eased her bulk into the colourful armchair with a groan. 'Yes, they got it into their heads that we would attempt to find the Salahbeem and captured you to stop us. The Magicians might revere the myths and legends of their *gods*, but the Salem know as well as we do that any artefact of the Gardeners ever found has been surrounded by death. Why anyone would think that we'd want to bring such a dangerous race back to Urdezha is beyond me, but the Grand Adepts wouldn't be swayed. They thought we'd try anyway, simply because we could.'

I could see the Salem's point. It was probably something the Quantum would attempt at some time in the future.

I couldn't deny that I was impressed by how the Scientists had managed to create a gateway into my realm – though I did not like it one bit – but this was not the technology they thought it was.

'*Surely you must understand that only the dead may enter my realm.*'

'Oh, we understand that *now*,' Mrs Blackstone said. 'But so many experiments ended in tragedy first.' She sighed. 'Your original gateway was preserved by the spells in the pyramid, but they were fading. We learned to replicate the magic, augment it, stretch it over great distances.'

She waved a hand towards the wooden box in Lana's hands, as if I needed reminding of the evidence. 'Even though there are leagues of wasteland between here and Alexria, our augmentations managed to keep your gateway open. When we succeeded in engineering the second gateway, we thought we stood on the cusp of discovering a mode of transport which hasn't been seen on Urdezha since the days of the Salahbeem. We truly believed the face of this world was about to change.'

Mode of transport ... I had guessed what the Quantum might dream of achieving on the day they found my tomb: a future in which every city of this world was literally brought within stepping distance of each other. Gateways, a fast, efficient form of travel that could reach any point on the wasteland, across the seas. But what then? The end of war? The creation of new cities with millions of people, citizens and clansfolk alike, draining resources?

No, no, no. The Quantum were dreaming bigger than that now. Their eyes were turned to the ether in their sky, thoughts lusting after the immense power orbiting their planet, of using it to engineer gateways that could reach out into the beyond, to the far incalculable worlds of ... *anywhere*. They understood so little.

'Alexria was supposed to be the entrance. Old Castle, the exit,' Mrs Blackstone said. 'A beginning and an end, with your realm joining the two.'

'*This is why you were happy for me to be out of your way,*' I said. '*Absent from my realm, I couldn't hinder your experiments.*'

'That was our thinking. But when we connected our gateway to the pyramid and synced it with Alexria's gateway, we discovered how wrong our calculations had been.'

'*You created a second beginning.*'

'And the two clashed violently.' Mrs Blackstone deflated in the armchair. 'We underestimated the power of the realm beyond the gateway – *your* realm, the realm of the dead. Like nothing we'd seen before, magic stronger than ether, more than we could handle. Best theory is our experiments caused your gateway to expand radically and *eat* Alexria, literally swallowing the city and its people like a plughole in a bath sucking down water. It continued to do so until it touched Alexria's ethergrowth, and then … *boom!*'

These people truly didn't understand what they had found in my tomb. The living could not use my gateway and survive. My realm's *exit* was only accessible to the dead. It simply could not exist in the corporeal world. The Quantum dreamed of creating gateways like those used by the Salahbeem for travelling from realm to realm, but what August Jakob had delivered to them was not the same technology. In fact, I imagined the Salahbeem took painstaking measures to remove every hint of what the Quantum sought before they left.

I shook my head at Mrs Blackstone. '*The Salahbeem trapped you on this world with good reason.*'

Her violet eyes became as hard-looking as the unnatural skin of her face and the ether crystal in her forehead. 'It is curious how you continue to believe that you, of all people, have the right to judge us.'

'*Call it an effect of my host.*' An effect which was slipping, draining, while I stood there gathering energy from the Song of the Dead, growing stronger. '*But please, tell me how you ruptured your sky.*'

With more than a little chagrin in her manner, Mrs Blackstone pointed out the shadowy umbilical cord connecting the black oval to the ether pyramid.

'Whatever we tried, we couldn't sever our gateway's link to its power source. It had been devouring spirits from the moment we created it – ghosts and ghouls, drawing them in from the city. But after Alexria, it went into overdrive, like it was hungering for solid matter, too, and the gateway began to grow, swell, like an abscess preparing to burst.

'We managed to calm it by feeding it a constant supply of energy.' She looked up at the metal arch. 'Magnetism. But then we hit a new problem, which was only solved by keeping the gateway moving.'

Hence the reason why we were riding the under-rail, and I could hazard a guess at what would happen should we come to a standstill.

'The hunger of your original gateway wasn't sated by Alexria's destruction,' Mrs Blackstone said. 'It was drawn to Old Castle's gateway and is now hanging above us, trying to get through the city shield.'

Indeed it was. I could hear it whispering to me, encouraging me to drink my fill from my realm.

'If our gateway stops moving, then within a few hours it will pull that ... *rift* down through the shield. It will devour the city itself, chunk by chunk, person by person, and it won't stop until it reaches Old Castle's ether-growth and we suffer the same fate as Alexria. We are a bath full of water, Sycamore, and we are struggling to hold down the plug.'

The Quantum's experiments had ripped a hole into a place they could never understand, a realm that was not conducive to life.

'*What do you intend to do, Mrs Blackstone? Keeping the gateway moving is a stalling manoeuvre at best.*'

'We have a theory on how to calm the storm.' She leaned forwards in the armchair. '*You* are not supposed to be here, and that *thing* in the sky is the realm of the dead trying to steal you back. The Quantum understands that by allowing the Shepherd to return home through the gateway we have created down here, disaster could be averted.'

'*In exchange for my freedom I will heal the rift? That is the accord you wish to reach?*'

'Precisely.'

'*My freedom is coming, whether you would give it to me or not.*'

'Or perhaps we have developed a way to trap you here in the aftermath. The Quantum rules every city on Urdezha.'

She had a strong poker face, this human, and I really couldn't tell if she was bluffing or genuinely believed that she had me cornered.

The Song of the Dead continued to beckon and energise from the gateway. The spirits were lost, angry, begging their Shepherd to show them the way to the unknown, and I longed to go to them. Yes, I could heal Old Castle's sky from the other side, in my realm. And yet ...

'*I'm confused,*' I said. '*Releasing me to my realm could solve your problems, yet I am still confined to a host. The Salem decided to un-leash Wendal Finn's moment of death, but they have not done so, and, again, here he still stands. Why?*'

'The Magicians know that we have you,' Mrs Blackstone said.

'Several hours ago, there was an emergency meeting between the Quantum and the Salem. All cards were laid on the table. Regarding our current predicament, especially in light of what happened to Alexria, both sides agree that it is time to set you free.'

'All cards, *you say? Including the secrets and lies of Dyonne Obor?*'

'Oh yes.'

I wasn't sure how I felt about that. I looked through the doorway in the glass wall at the ghoul of August Jakob still pining for her flesh. The dead deserved vengeance, and so did I.

'*The Salem must be planning to execute Dyonne Obor.*'

'They would if they could. Obor has gone into hiding. She sent that ape of a bodyguard of hers to give Lana here a message. Obor said the Salem were preparing to execute Mr Finn and so it was time to bring *our* plan to fruition. Hence the emergency meeting.'

'*Interesting*,' I said. '*Dyonne still believes that you will use me to help her invoke the Lore of Ascension?*'

'Quite so. But she isn't aware that our plans have changed, and not in her favour. And while she remains the custodian of Mr Finn's moment of death, the Salem cannot release you. And so it falls to me to remedy the situation.'

Mrs Blackstone shrugged and smoothed out the wrinkles in the floral covering on her armrests. 'I am a Director of the Quantum, Sycamore. I plan for all potentially useful eventualities, but you are frighteningly beyond my comprehension at this time. I had hoped that we might learn from you.' She gestured to the pyramid, looked remorseful. 'Learn of ancient technologies, the Salahbeem, the afterlife – but you are the Shepherd, not a teacher. So, I assume we have reached an accord?'

'*An accord, you say?*' Magic bloomed inside me with a feeling like ... What would Wendal call it? Blind fury? '*By your own dangerous assumptions and gross miscalculations have you brought yourself to the brink of this ruin, Mrs Blackstone. This world holds no bargaining power over me.'*

'No? I'm not certain how one would go about threatening a being such as you, but please remember we have replicated the magic which keeps you incapacitated. Every city stands ready to transmit that signal, across the wasteland, to every corner of Urdezha. If you let Old Castle fall, you won't be going home. There'll be nowhere to hide. We'll keep you trapped here for good.'

'My realm will follow wherever I go. It will not stop until I am free.'

'The Quantum excels at learning and adapting, and your storm is only a threat until we understand it. Consider the implications of *that*, Sycamore.' She raised a painted eyebrow. 'Of course, I'm trusting that our coexistence is mutually intolerable and you're in favour of escaping this world and closing the rift behind you—'

A sudden and violent jolt rocked the carriage. Lana Khem stumbled. The lights went out. The train's power drained away. With preternatural speed, I smacked the box from Lana's hand. Before she could counter, I punched her once, twice, three times and she fell to the floor. In the dim rose light of the pyramid, I turned to meet Mrs Blackstone's look of horror.

'The shield is failing,' she whispered as the train came to a full stop. By the sound of it, the metal arch was struggling to feed magnetism to the gateway. 'Sycamore, help us.'

'The living could never adapt to what I am, Mrs Blackstone.'

She yelped as I pounced, grabbed hold of her thick neck and hissed into her face.

'Imagine how small your world is, a speck of life before the endlessness of the other side.' She clawed at me as I squeezed her throat

while the fingers of my free hand probed the ether crystal in her forehead. '*Now envision, if you can, how insignificant an act it is for me to kill the fucking lot of you.*'

With a fresh surge of magic, my fingers found purchase and Mrs Blackstone screamed as I wrenched the ether from her head. She fell silent as the technology which sustained her unnaturally long life slid free. The crystal was long and curved, implanted into her brain like the oversized thorn of a rose plant. There was no blood upon it. The hole in Mrs Blackstone's forehead was deep and dark but did not bleed.

Lana Khem was back on her feet by this time. She had retrieved the box and once again stood between me and the gateway, thumb poised and ready to activate the node. Lip split and nose bloodied, she darted her gaze to the carriage ceiling, as if worrying for the city above. Had the shield failed completely?

'*You have a choice, Lana Khem,*' I said. '*Die or get out of my way.*'

'Will you do it?' She was breathless, her eyes flitting to Mrs Blackstone's dead body. 'Will you close the rift?'

'*That is a risk you have no option but to take.*'

'What about Wendal?'

I couldn't help but spare a smile for her incongruous concern. '*Was he merely a directive in your life, or did you come to feel more than pity for him? Whatever your feelings, Wendal Finn is no longer your concern.*' I offered her the long and curved ether crystal. '*Time to choose, Lana Khem. The shield is failing. The storm will come no matter what the Quantum tries.*'

She licked blood from her lip, staring at me, before dropping the box to the floor and taking the crystal from my hand.

Lana stood to one side and the Song of the Dead swelled. As I gazed into the gateway, the ghoul of August Jakob crawled up beside me, mewling with a weak plea for vengeance. And perhaps she would get it. In the end, perhaps all the dead of Urdezha would.

'*Am I a Shepherd or a Judge?*' I asked Lana, and then walked into the gateway.

Chapter Sixty-Nine

My name is Wendal Finn ...

My brain told me I was falling, but my body said I was motionless. A searing pain stole my breath, as if a white-hot knife was tracing the spells on my skin, burning them away, breaking the bonds that kept an unknowable entity trapped inside its host. Free from the land of the living, Sycamore slid through my pores, cast me aside, discarded me as easily as shrugging off a jacket, and he threw me into blind confusion.

Alone, empty, spiritless, I was gripped by a bitter, powerful magic that pulled me in different directions, diluted me, *smeared* my existence over a thick, abject darkness, trying to pull me apart. I experienced no more pain or discomfort, but this place on the other side of the gateway did not want me, hated me, fought to reject my presence. Was this death? Had I been condemned to Nothing?

Just when I thought I would stretch across the emptiness for ever, there came a sharp, dizzying sense of sudden retraction as though the bitter magic had released its grip, and the Song of Always allowed me to snap back into my true shape. The impact came suddenly out of the dark, giving me no time to prepare, and I hit solid ground so hard that I thought I'd shatter into a million pieces. But no; I collapsed like a boneless rag doll instead and lay staring into a lightless void, only the sound of my breathing telling me that I was still alive.

Moments passed, and in the dark I had time to think about how small a part I had played in this game, how insignificant I had been from the very beginning. It had felt so good to kill Mrs Blackstone. Old Castle's troubles were far behind me now.

So this was where Sycamore came from, his realm, that mythical place between the land of the living and the other side. Perhaps I should have felt amazed, panicked, awed, but I could only conjure up deep disappointment and loneliness.

The darkness lifted. A supernatural light shone from some-where below, an eerie green radiance like the glow of a quagmire on the wasteland, illuminating the space above me. Not a void as I'd thought, but a vast shaft drilled through rock rising jaggedly up and back into darkness, maybe without end. Had the gateway dropped me into a monumental hole that sank straight down to Urdezha's core? Was that where Sycamore's realm existed?

A rustle of movement echoed from below. I rolled over onto my front. I had landed on a deep and sturdy ledge in the shaft. Crawling forwards, I peered over its edge. My eyes squinted, adjusting to the light, so much brighter in the shaft's depths. Someone was moving down there; a woman, I thought, some fifty feet below me, wearing the hooded gown of a Magician. She was jumping and climbing from one descending ledge to another, making careful progress further down the shaft to where the light was brightest, like the glaring green pupil of a giant eye. The woman stopped and looked up, just for a second, but that was enough time for me to recognise the face within the hood.

'Eden!'

The shout came from instinct, but she didn't react to it and continued her descent. I tried again, begging her to stop, to wait for me, just … '*Come back!*' But she couldn't hear me. My words were returned to me as though borne on some force that whisked them up into the shaft's heights, away from Eden's ears. I roared in frustration, jumped to my feet in determination.

The closest ledge to my position was at least thirty feet below me. A fall like that would kill most men, but I wasn't most men and this wasn't the land of the living. Reckoning that I could make it with a good jump, I set my sights and prepared for the leap. But then a new source of light distracted me. It came from behind me, shining from the rock above where the shaft's wall met the ledge. The rose-tinted silver glare of ether.

When the glare receded, its source was revealed as a luminous humanoid shape and hope lurched in my chest. A tank-suit, set into the wall. I didn't stop to consider why it was there; rushing to it, grabbing the glass helmet, wrenching it out of the rock, I was thinking only of reaching Eden.

I put the helmet on and the touch of ether invaded my mind.

I'd forgotten what it felt like; so familiar and strong. With a mental command, I ordered the tank to come to me. The suit shook, strained and with a loud crack broke free of the wall and stamped over to my position, trailing debris. Its shape and size were normal, but there was no shoulder cannon and the armoured plates weren't made from reinforced Dust. They were clear amber, inscribed with silver words of ancient Salabese. The tank was more like the suits of armour worn by the Order of Glass and Words. No time to wonder why; that it obeyed my commands was enough.

The tank's plates unfurled, opening to hang in the air. I stepped backwards into them, revelling in its strength as they closed around me. This suit needed no ether crystal on its backplate; its energy came from the magical words decorating its amber parts, and the power of Glass and Words spoke to me like a friend.

Cocooned in old knowledge, I sprang forwards, jumping from the ledge into the air, soaring down to land gracefully below.

I saw Eden, descending fast into the glare of supernatural light. I cleared the distances between ledges effortlessly, with single bounds, no harder than walking down stairs. The way became obscured by thick fog that abruptly rose around me, highlighted by eerie green, and the glass helmet adjusted to cut through it. Below, Eden was swallowed by the fog as the ledges became a smooth, spiralling walkway and she increased her speed to a sprint, passing beyond the helmet's vision. The tank's sonar picked up her signal immediately and I chased after her.

This was it, I told myself; she was real this time. Mrs Blackstone had confirmed that the gateway had been eating the spirits of the dead; Sycamore had told me that Eden's spirit had never been on Urdezha. This was his realm, the way station, the place through which the dead travelled on their way to the other side. Of course my wife would be here – the real Eden, not some phantom from a fucked-up dream. I had found her.

The spiralling path became so even and smooth that I was able to push the tank as fast as my legs could run, but the journey was lasting an age. And although the sonar remained locked on to Eden's signal, she didn't come into view again. Just as I grew suspicious that surely I should've caught up with her by now, a pungent smell invaded my nostrils, a sharp chemical reek which reminded me of the wasteland. A shout of defiance came from below. A blaze of magic swirled the fog and burned it away. Then I saw her, my wife, further down the walkway, beset by monsters.

This shaft into Sycamore's realm descended into a nest of skarabs.

I rushed down until I was opposite Eden's position. The skarabs came from rocky burrows above and below her, from her left and right. Half-human, half-insect, carapaces like the armoured plates of a tank-suit, they charged with sharp horns, reaching with blade-like fingers. My ether-cannon slid from its housing on my arm and I took aim. But I didn't fire. Not yet. I didn't need to.

Eden moved with the skill of an adept. She released the ferocity of her magic, pushing hands out to either side and reducing two skarabs to dust. She destroyed a third and a fourth, before melting a fifth and a sixth to puddles of oily matter. But their deaths were merely the beginning of her spell. Her face grave, lips whispering incantations, Eden commanded the puddles to rise, spring up with fat, livid tentacles like the living roots of corpse-trees, and they became her guardians.

Tentacles smacked skarabs from the path, sending them shrieking and thrashing into the shaft's lowest depths. The monsters tried to flee, but Eden's magic plucked them from their burrows, curling around their bodies, smashing them against the rock, squeezing until their carapaces crunched and cracked sickeningly. Where the corpses fell and melted, new tentacles rose, two dozen at least, growing like a forest of guardians to protect their summoner. The skarabs battled frantically to escape my wife's might, and they died.

But Eden didn't know that more skarabs lurked beneath her, clinging to the underside of the walkway, searching for a way up and through her defences. My arm cannon bucked, the force of Glass and Words powering shot after shot into them. *Whumps* of ether magic displaced the air as the shrieks of dying skarabs fell away into the glowing depths, and only then did she see me. Only then did Eden halt her attack and allow the surviving monsters to escape back into their burrows.

As the shrieks of the dying faded, Eden stared across the gulf between us, frowning uncertainly. I took off the helmet and

smiled at her, but she expressed panic, as though more frightened of me than any monster. Her tentacles died, slapping to
the rock in wet puddles. To my horror, Eden stepped from the
ledge and plummeted into the shaft.

'No!' I shouted and jumped after her.

The tank's magic field compensated for the fall, preventing
me from tipping over and hurtling down in an uncontrolled
spin. Wind whipped around me, the shaft's jagged walls flashing by until they were bleached out by the supernatural light.
The brightness intensified as I speared into its core and then
out through the other side into a moment of darkness before
landing with a bone-jarring thud.

The tank's boots vibrated, creaking as cracks in the amber
plates snaked up my legs, across my body and down my arms.
With a flare of ether, the suit of Glass and Words shattered
from me and I staggered back. The amber pieces sank into the
darkness below my feet, a pure blackness that absorbed the light
of the shaft as it shone down like a poisoned sun.

In this strange place, Eden stood a few paces away, her back
turned. I approached her, but the flare in my heart cooled and
I stopped, suddenly perturbed. My wife's hands were clenched,
shaking with rage, and she was muttering threats and obscen-
ities to herself, growling something about being a prisoner twice
over.

'Eden,' I said softly. 'It's me, Wendal.'

'I know who you are,' she snapped, 'and you don't belong
here.'

'What?'

'I'm tired of singing my Song, but he won't let me escape.
Not while you're clinging on.' Eden pulled down her hood and
faced me. 'You just couldn't let me go, could you?'

I had no reply, shaking my head at what I saw. Eden's bright green eyes were dulled, the red of her hair faded, her face and clothes leached of colour to a drab monochrome. She looked like a ghoul. What sick twist was this?

Eden cursed me in Salabese. 'You have no place in the realm of the dead.' Her words were full of spite, as if spoken to an enemy, and she turned and walked away. 'But it seems you're my only escape route out of this fucking nightmare.'

Chapter Seventy

I had imagined finding Eden in a hundred different ways, but never once had it played out like this. I'd never envisioned a reunion with a ghoul. Yet here she was, the proof before my eyes, leading me through a darkness that felt disconcertingly solid underfoot, beneath a ceiling of eerie light the colour of poison.

'Where is he?' I said. 'Where's Sycamore?'

No reply.

'What has he done to you, Eden?'

'*He* has done nothing.' My wife shook her head. 'I hear that since your wife died, you've always liked to blame others for your hardships, never taking responsibility for yourself. Even now it doesn't occur to you that this might be your fault, does it?'

'*My* fault?'

'Aren't you going to apologise?'

She was mocking me and my anger flared. 'I tried to find you,' I snarled, 'but you killed yourself and left me when I needed you most.'

'There you go again,' Eden said. 'Blaming your wife when she believed you'd died on the wasteland. Wasn't it you who let a psychopathic survivalist tell her the truth?'

'I wasn't given a choice, I …' She spoke as though she didn't know me, like I was someone she'd only heard about, like we had no history, like we hadn't once shared a happy life together. 'Tell me you remember me,' I said. 'Say my name.'

'What name would you like? Fool? Puppet? Killer?' Eden gave a cursory glance over her shoulder. 'I'd rather Sycamore took away the Song of Always and let his realm tear you apart than play out this charade.'

That hit me hard. *No*, I thought. *It shouldn't be like this.* It was too cruel. Eden had killed herself, she couldn't be a ghoul. Sycamore had done this to her to punish me.

'All Sycamore has done is give you a parting gift that you're too blind to accept,' Eden said, as though reading my thoughts, before adding with acid in her voice, 'Unless you accept it, the realm of the dead won't release me. And I'm not the only one.'

Above, the green light faded away and the darkness began to shift and mould around me, turning into something solid and ancient. Yellow flames sprang to life, dancing from pools of oil in the deep dishes of braziers that appeared between thick pillars of chipped and worn stone. I now followed Eden along a narrow floor paved with cracked tiles of terracotta, as though we walked through a hall of some forgotten castle buried aeons ago.

'This realm appears as the Shepherd imagines,' Eden said, her tone irritated, sharing none of my fearful awe. 'The magic of death.'

Sycamore's magic, a strange and terrible power that even Mrs Blackstone and the Quantum couldn't understand.

The stone pillars flanked our path. There was little but darkness beyond them, but between them, behind the flames of the braziers, I could see faces peering out, ghostly aspects. Spirits, I realised, and I knew who they were.

Ghan Hathor watched me with a sour expression. Brandon Quinn and Agtha Martal seemed to be confused about who I was. Yorla of Clan Ayros knew me, however, glaring with her mouth set into as much of a grim line as her tusks would allow. Ing Meredith's smile did little to reassure me. My platoon watched in silent judgement – Hannah and Danii, Commander Childs – and I averted my eyes, too perturbed to see who else lurked in the shadows between the pillars. Every one of them had died because of Sycamore. Their voices formed a backwash of moans, the low and hollow Song of the Dead.

'Because of you, none of them can leave,' Eden said. 'Will you tell them that it isn't your fault?' She pointed to her right. 'Will you tell that to her?'

A groan escaped my lips and I halted, frozen to the spot. Nel stood in the shadows, her face lit by flickering flames. There wasn't much expression on her features but her eyes were full of accusation, and in them I saw myself for what I was: her murderer.

'I'm sorry, Nel,' was all I could think to say. 'I'm so sorry.'

She had no interest in my apology, or anything else I might say, and sank back into the shadows to be swallowed by darkness.

A blaze of light flared up ahead, brighter than the brazier fires. It came from a ragged tear in the black, a wide rent. A gateway? Eden stood before it, limned by the flashes of orange lightning she stared into. A metallic reek filled my nostrils and scratched the back of my throat, and I knew the rent was a hole into the real world, Urdezha, Old Castle. The storm was still raging.

'No,' I whispered. 'He can't do this. Sycamore has to close it.'

'You are an anomaly,' Eden growled, 'a living being of flesh and blood where none should exist, and the realm of the dead cannot allow that.'

'Look at me, Eden.' I was begging. 'Say my name.'

'You don't belong here.'

Even as she said it, I could feel it was true. The spirits between the pillars were waiting for me to leave, the magic of this realm was pushing against me, egging me towards the rent and the world I came from. Both alive and not, I had no place here, but in the land of the living my doom was assured.

I hid behind the ghoul of my wife. 'I don't want to go back.'

Eden's laugh was sharp and spiteful. 'What were you expecting? That you could spend eternity roaming the planes of Sycamore's realm, living out some fairy tale?' She turned to me and shouted in Salabese, '*You don't belong here!*'

The rage and hatred on her face smothered anything I was feeling, crushed me. 'Eden, please ... Let me stay with you.'

She shook her head, curiosity replacing some of the ghoul's anger. 'Surely you understand now that you don't have a choice.' She gestured to the spirits peering out from the shadows. 'And for them, for the sake of Old Castle, I have to go with you.'

Eden turned as the rent rushed towards her, swallowed her, and then came for me with a blinding flash of orange.

Chapter Seventy-One

There was no confusion this time. I stumbled from Sycamore's realm and fell to my hands and knees on the dirty cobbles of an alley. I coughed on the acrid tang of rusty metal in the air. A flash of lightning preceded a deafening *crack* and I jumped to my feet. There was no sign of the gateway that had thrown me back into the real world. The drone of Old Castle's shield was high-pitched and fractured; the ether magic was about to fail and let the storm seal the city's fate.

Eden was crouched between two piles of refuse waiting to be collected for the reduction houses. She faced away from me, watching the end of the alley.

'The storm's getting worse,' I said. 'Why won't he stop it?'

Eden looked at me. No, not *at* me; *through* me, as though she didn't know I was there. Panic on her face, fear in her eyes, my wife exhibited none of her earlier anger.

'Eden?'

She gathered her courage with a deep breath, turned and fled from me.

'Eden!'

I chased after her, out of the alley, surprised to emerge into Public Square. Eden waited beside the silent transmission pyramid, but I doubted she was waiting for me. She cast a nervous gaze around her, as if she was scanning a crowd even though the square was deserted, not a single other citizen in sight. It was as if we were seeing different things.

Lightning struck the city somewhere close to us, spearing through the shield one, two, three, four times – once frighteningly nearby, each with a powerful *crack* of energy. The shield couldn't take much more of this.

Sycamore was going to let us all die.

Seemingly with other things on her mind, Eden pulled up the hood of her gown and raced away once more, heading in the direction of Tinman District. Perplexed and confused, but mostly scared, I chased after her.

The streets were as deserted as the square. The citizens were in their homes, hiding from the storm – not that wood and stone would protect them if the realm of the dead reached Old Castle's ether-growth. Not that the Song of Always would protect me, either. The storm was closer to the city than it had ever been, more fire than roiling blackness, and the shield was shrinking against the pressure, faltering under the ravenous mouth of Sycamore's realm. I wondered about Lana Khem, the other Directors of the Quantum, the Grand Adepts of the Salem – were they hiding as well? Were they lamenting too late that the Shepherd of the Dead had always been a power too great for them to handle?

Lightning cracked the ground ahead of Eden. The blinding flash and shock wave of energy caused me to stagger back, but my wife ran through the smoke and after-glare as if nothing had happened. I raced to catch up with her and noticed something strange about her image.

The air around Eden was dim, like a twilight of faded colour to match her monochrome appearance, as though she was overlapping onto the real world. The effect was growing, the twilight expanding, and it was familiar to me. The Song of the Dead, I realised with a harsh pang. I was following a ghoul in a vision. Eden was showing me her moment of death, and it was leading us to our lodging house.

'Eden, no!'

But she wouldn't stop running.

When we reached the building, Eden's Song had expanded to envelop me in gloomy twilight. The cracks of lightning were dull, the flashes pale and distant, belonging to another place. By the time she led me up the stairs to our floor, I was cocooned by the vision, deep inside events that had led to my wife's suicide.

'Stop,' I said.

Eden didn't acknowledge that I'd spoken and came to stand outside the door to our lodgings.

'No, wait.' After all this time, the pain of not knowing, the questions I wanted answered, I wasn't ready to face whatever lay on the other side of that door. I didn't want to see.

But Eden already had her key in hand. She glanced furtively up and down the hallway before letting herself in. If my resolve had decided not to follow her, it made no difference. The vision came to me and I was inside our lodgings. It was the room I'd always known, small but not yet a sparse, desolate hovel. The vision showed me how it had once been: a place of life, of love. There were flowers, curtains over the window, a rug on the floor, furniture I hadn't yet sold for jenkem.

Eden closed the door and pressed her back against it. She looked relieved to be home, safe ... until she gasped and I followed her gaze to the intruder who had materialised in our home.

Dyonne Obor sat on our bed, aiming a small ether-cannon at my wife.

Eden took her eyes off the Magician, acknowledged my

presence for the first time since leaving Sycamore's realm; and with the calm dispassion of a ghoul, she began narrating her Song.

'I came home on this night to collect a few things that were special to me, and then I was going to disappear, hide in the shanties or with the dormice, just … get out of sight.'

Dyonne remained statue-still, glaring at Eden as though frozen and not yet free to act out her part in this vision.

'No, this can't be right.' I shook my head. 'Why is she here?'

'This is my Song, and the dead don't lie. I thought I could protect my husband, but Dyonne Obor already knew about him. And she had loose ends to tie up.'

I felt as though I was deflating. 'I'm standing right here, Eden. Say my name.'

She didn't; looked confused by the request.

Dyonne's torpor broke and she began speaking, gesticulating with the ether-cannon. I couldn't hear what she was saying, but my wife continued her narration.

'She's telling me I'm a traitor.' Eden remained with her back against the door as the Magician ranted at her. 'She said my first duty was always to the Salem.' She scoffed. 'I'd actually believed that, when I thought my husband was dead. Clung to it.'

Dyonne was gesticulating more and more agitatedly. I could do nothing but watch, dumb and helpless.

'I didn't deserve the title of apprentice Magician, she said. I had proved myself disloyal and disloyalty was an unforgivable crime in the eyes of the Grand Adepts. She had manipulated the situation, of course, looking after her own interests.'

If I could have, I would have snatched the ether-cannon from Dyonne's hand, used it to kill her and save my wife. But this was the Song of the Dead. These events had already happened.

'I know what you're thinking,' Eden said. 'Why didn't I just run? Why come back here at all? To be honest, at this moment, I was thinking the same thing.'

Dyonne paused in her ranting to grab something from the bedside table: a chain threaded through two wedding bands. I clutched my neck. The rings were lost to the sea now, but the ghost of them felt cool against my skin. Dyonne threw the rings at Eden. My wife didn't flinch as they hit her on the chest and fell to the floor.

'She told me that my husband was an insignificant citizen, no matter our relationship. And because I'd chosen him over observing my duty to the Salem, I deserved my execution.' The gleam of a ghoul's rage returned to Eden's dull eyes and her voice became a growl. 'That pissed me off. It made me so fucking angry that I wasn't scared any more.'

Eden launched herself off the door and leapt at Dyonne. But if she hoped to catch the Magician off guard, she was out of luck. Dyonne stepped in to meet her, ramming the ether-cannon into Eden's chest. They froze in that position for a moment, still as a sculpture. I held my breath. How many Songs had I witnessed in the past three months? How many moments of death had I seen? I couldn't bear my wife's to be among them. This wasn't right.

Eden said, 'I was dead from the moment the Magicians first heard the name *Sycamore*,' and Dyonne pulled the trigger.

A blast of ether magic erupted from Eden's back, spraying blood and bone over the door and cracking the wood. Eden fell to the floor, dead beside our wedding rings. The ragged hole in her gown smouldered, and beneath it, another hole, bloody, punched through her chest, through her heart.

Cold and hard, Dyonne wasted no time considering what she had done. Seeing nothing more than an obstacle removed, she placed the ether-cannon in Eden's hand before crouching beside her corpse. She dipped her fingers into my wife's wound and began to cast a spell, weaving secret words in the air with one hand while the other drew symbols on Eden's face with her own blood.

The violence of the storm above Old Castle was nothing compared to the rage I felt towards Dyonne Obor. A murderous anger clenched my fists so hard they shook. I knew what the Magician's spell was doing: capturing my wife's ghoul, trapping it, hiding her from Sycamore. When Dyonne had finished, she gave the room a cursory glance and then left. I followed her, perhaps thinking irrationally that I could chase her down, but she slammed the door shut behind her and Eden's Song began to fade.

Drab twilight lifted and the world filled with colour. Furniture and flowers disappeared and the storm flashed orange through the bare window. I was returned to the sparse room my home had become, back in the real world, the real Old Castle. I stared at the closed door, my fingernails cutting into my palms.

'I know you.'

I spun around. Eden was on her feet. The wound in her chest and tear in her gown were gone, as were the symbols written in blood on her face. Her eyes had reclaimed their natural colour, as bright and clear as emeralds, and they were seeing me for who I truly was.

'Wendal.'

Chapter Seventy-Two

'I never gave up on you.' Eden's voice had softened, her manner now calm and gentle. 'All the time I was lost inside my Song, a part of me trusted that we'd find each other. And here we are.'

She was the person I knew, the woman I loved. I wanted to touch her, hold her, but reaching out, I felt only a dry, nebulous sensation where her shoulders were, like my fingers had passed through threads of spiderweb hanging in the air. My hands balled into fists again. My wife, a ghoul, a victim of murder ...

'I know you, Wendal Finn. I know what you're thinking.' Eden looked around the sparse room, tears welling. 'It doesn't matter now.'

I shook my head. 'Dyonne made me believe you'd killed yourself. She stole your Song—'

'Just as she stole yours.'

'She's still out there, not that it makes any difference now.'

'Forget Dyonne.' Eden stepped closer, right in front of me, so close but a million miles away. 'I was overjoyed when I found out you were still alive. The best news.'

Her words perturbed me. They were spoken with affection but underlined by finality, like she was beginning the end of things, and I was the blind man who had learned to see too late.

'But the news was double-edged,' Eden continued. 'Powers

greater than us wanted Sycamore and they would always stand between us.'

'But not now?' I said, hope making it sound like a question.

The sadness in Eden's smile told me everything I didn't want to know.

She said, 'You've been shadowed by death for too long, Wendal. It's over, you're free. It's time to live again. Look out of the window.'

The flashes of lightning were less frequent, less bright.

'Old Castle is safe,' Eden said. 'The storm is passing.'

I could hear the truth of it in the drone of the city shield. It sounded less strained and the air felt less heavy, less angry. The rift was healing, but how could I care about that?

'This is Sycamore's gift.' Eden's smile was happier this time. 'He's giving us the chance to say goodbye to each other.'

I bowed my head, not wanting her to see my denial, and futilely, desperately, I begged for what I had no right to ask: 'Stay with me.'

'Oh, Wendal. The realm of the dead is singing. The other side beckons.'

'I—' I choked on my words. 'I don't have a spirit, Eden. I can't come with you.'

'Then let me go, here and now, while you still can.'

'No.' I sniffed back tears. 'There must be another way.'

Eden reached out and her phantom touch stroked my cheek. 'You were always the same, seeing only the moment, never thinking ahead, never considering reason.' She knew me too well; it broke my heart. 'But you should savour *this* moment. We did it. We found each other. You got what you wished for. And I know that *my* husband would never ask me to give up heaven in return.'

The last four months of my life weighed heavy on my mind.

They had been nothing but a stall, a slow, protracted journey to the truth. I had no anger left inside me, no tears or sense of injustice; I felt no relief or elation for Old Castle and its one hundred thousand citizens. Time stopped at this moment. Time stopped and waited for me to accept reason.

'I used to hate that you were always right,' I said, managing a weak attempt at a smile. 'We had a good life here, you know.'

'We really did.' Eden's eyes became wistful. 'It ended too soon.'

I nodded, my gaze fixed on hers. 'I …' I couldn't bring myself to finish the sentence, to bring this bitter-sweet reunion to a conclusion. My wife did it for me.

'I love you, too, Wendal Finn.'

'Find peace, Eden. Find beauty.' I held out a hand and her dry, gossamer fingers stroked mine. 'Maybe I'll see you around.'

Eden sighed contentedly and her spirit filled with a light the same deep shade of green as her eyes. She shattered into a thousand glowing sycamore seeds, spinning, holding the shape of her before flowing through me with the gentlest of sensations, leaving a mark that told her husband how she felt about him in a way he would never forget. The seeds scattered in all directions, sinking through the walls and floor and ceiling, pursuing peace. And Eden was gone.

My hand fell to my side and I stared into the space where she had stood. Resolution took over my sadness, leading me to a strange state of mournful completion. My eyes roamed the room, and I didn't have the heart to consider what came next.

Voices provided a welcome distraction, coming from the lane outside the window. They sounded relieved, joyful. And suddenly I could be surrounded by this familiar desolation no longer. I didn't belong in this room, so I left, heading out of the door, down the stairs and onto the streets of Old Castle.

Above, the storm was calming. The lightning had already stopped and the black, roiling clouds were slowing, their colour growing paler. The airborne metallic taste had weakened to a faint bitter tang. Citizens were coming out of their homes. More and more of them joined me on the street to witness the end of the storm, and soon there was a thick crowd. Some people laughed, others wept or stared at the sky in hope, genuine and cynical both. The relief was palpable, and I bristled to hear some of them thank the Scientists for this change in Old Castle's fortune.

Amidst the crowd, with Eden's final touch lingering inside me, I watched the rift between worlds healing and wondered if Sycamore could see me from his realm, taking a final look into the land of the living. The Shepherd of the Dead, free at last, back where he belonged.

I might as well have been standing on the street alone. None of the citizens noticed I was there. The Song of Always had taken care of that, but for how much longer? I was staring into a half-life that might end in the next minute or ... When? My only certainty was that Old Castle had no place for me, nor any other city on Urdezha.

Someone jostled me and I stumbled. When I'd regained my footing, I looked up to see that Lana Khem had joined the crowd. She was watching me, statue-still. Her face was bruised, but on her forehead was a large glassy bead in the shape of a teardrop. It gave off a rose-tinted glow. Mrs Blackstone's ether implant, now prolonging life for a new Director of the Quantum.

Separated by celebrating bodies, Lana and I stared at each other for a long, frozen moment while the red glow of the sun shone through the clouds for the first time in days, and cold, fresh wind blew along the street. Lana nodded at me. I turned my back on her, shoving my way through the throng of citizens, heading for the city gates and whatever lay beyond.

Chapter Seventy-Three

My realm could appear as anything I imagined, and it now presented as a plane of mellow orange, a plane without sky or ground, without beginning or end. I dwelt between the land of the living and the infinite possibilities of the other side. Sycamore, Shepherd of the Dead, spirit of vengeance, I was all these things and so much more.

The Song of the Dead rose and fell like a wind moaning across my realm. Grey figures were gathering in the distance, stretching all around like a dark horizon against the orange. Human spirits, an untold multitude, their number growing all the time: those I had killed, those I had avenged, the citizens of Alexria and every spirit that had roamed Urdezha waiting for the Shepherd to return home. They gazed upon me with fear and wonder, longing to see the other side, and they would see it soon enough. They filled me with an overwhelming sense of purpose.

One voice sang louder than the rest, and I summoned it to me. A single spirit detached from the ever-growing horde, gliding fast over the orange plane, and came to stop before me. There was no reverence in her stance, no fear, but there was expectation in her emerald-green eyes, perhaps admonishment, too, for the things I had done.

'*Little ghoul,*' I said. '*Will you sing your Song to me?*'

The question offended her. 'You've already heard my Song, you bastard.' If she expected me to take offence at her disrespect, she was disappointed. 'I demand justice.'

'*For you or your husband?*'

She gave me a sour look. 'My name is Eden Finn. And I damn well know you want the same thing as me.'

Indeed I did. Her name informed me of vengeful desires, and in it I could see the location of her murderer.

'*Very well, Eden Finn. Observe ...*'

I turned from her and conjured a gateway. It appeared as a vertical streak of silver light at first, like a crack in my realm, before I split it open, wrenched it wide and, despite the threats of Mrs Blackstone, I looked out onto the world of Urdezha.

The sun was setting and the first ether crystals had appeared in the sky. The sound of waves lapping gently at a beach came from below, while up on a clifftop, not more than ten feet from my gateway, Dyonne Obor stood by the ruins where Ghan Hathor had spent his exile. Unaware that I had appeared behind her, the Magician watched the rift healing above Old Castle in the near distance. The storm was no more than wisps of charcoal clouds, dissipating like mist in the warmth of morning sunlight.

Dyonne's posture was straight, proud even in defeat. Close to her stood the hulking form of Tamara. He, too, watched the sky healing above Old Castle.

'*You must be contemplating the immediate future,*' I said.

Dyonne wheeled around, her face full of consternation. Tamara, ever the faithful bodyguard, jumped in front of his master with a mind to ... what? Protect her? Take me on in a fight? Brave but futile, a point I decided to prove by reaching out through the gateway, and my touch punched the life from Tamara. He fell to the ground as though he had been struck by a blast of ether. His spirit leaked from his body like blood, an oily puddle that screeched and fled from me and my realm, slithering away towards Old Castle and abandoning his master.

Dyonne didn't look much moved by the death of her body-guard, or fearful of what I might do to her next. She tried to see what lay behind me, but her view was obscured. For the realm of the dead was not for the living to see. She frowned, perhaps suspicious of who was accompanying me. Finally, her stare rested on my image.

'So, you have been freed.' She gave a bitter laugh. 'I should have known Mrs Blackstone would betray me on the day the storm arrived.' Her tone was jaded, her eyes flicking from side to side as she calculated and extrapolated. 'The Grand Adepts of the Salem will have ordered my execution by now. Every Magician in Old Castle will be hunting for me.'

'*And it won't be long before the hunt spreads to this ruin and any other place you might hide beyond the city wall.*'

Dyonne tried to see what was behind me again, gave up and turned to face Old Castle with a shrug. The sky above the city was almost entirely clear now.

'*I showed Wendal the truth,*' I told her. '*He knows what you have done.*'

The Magician didn't quite look over her shoulder at me and nodded.

'*Your sins have returned to you, Dyonne Obor.*'

'Then here I am, Sycamore, alone and undone and at your mercy. I imagine Mr Sebastian will be disappointed you got to me first.'

Her tone was defiant, but her body language was resigned to her fate. Behind me, I could feel Eden's impatience and moved the gateway closer to Dyonne.

'*Tell me,*' I said. '*You still possess Wendal's moment of death?*'

Dyonne stood a little straighter, as though considering whether or not she retained one bargaining chip which might yet save her skin. She slumped as she saw there was no way out of this for her.

'I should have abandoned my ambitions and released the Song of Always the moment Ing Meredith showed up.' She spoke through clenched teeth. 'But what good would it do now?'

'*Good?*' I considered that, while inching the gateway towards her. '*Imagine you had no spirit, no chance of reaching the other side, and all that waited for your body and mind was the bleak promise of Nothing. Wouldn't you want to live as long a life as possible?*'

'Empathy, Sycamore? Has the human condition affected—'

Dyonne tensed, sensing the gateway's approach. Nowhere to hide now.

'I would have been a Grand Adept beyond compare,' she said mournfully. 'I would have changed the world.'

'*I'm sure every member of the Salem thought that when they attained ascension through murder. But the reality is always the same. You, the Salem, the Quantum – monsters, one and all, a blight on Urdezha. Mrs Blackstone learned that the hard way, and so will you.*'

The gateway, my realm, was less than a step behind Dyonne now. She looked up at the sky, savouring her final moments in the world she came from. 'The dead call you Sycamore,' she whispered and held the last breath she would ever take.

The gateway swallowed the Magician. It caused her no pain as her flesh and blood and bone evaporated like steam from a boiling cook pot, leaving behind her spirit, revealed like the fruit beneath peeled rind. Dyonne gazed upon the planes of my realm, looking in awe at the grey horde of the dead on the horizon. Her eyes eventually found Eden Finn standing close by. The Magician averted her gaze quickly, staring at her feet.

Eden said nothing. There was no anger or violence left on her face. No longer a ghoul but a spirit at peace. Justice had been served. Vengeance was hers.

Dyonne looked up and tried to speak, but her words and spirit were buffeted away as I banished her from my presence and let her join the impossibly huge congregation of spirits in the distance. Only in death could the living claim to be noble.

Eden stared after the Magician and I noted a reluctance in her, an indecision. It was not an uncommon reaction when the fight of life was done and the promises of the unknown stared back at you. And nothing was as unknowable as the other side.

'*Your Song has been sung,*' I told her. '*The land of the living is no longer your concern.*'

'What will happen to Wendal?'

'*His Song is safe with me.*' To console her, I summoned her husband's moment of death, stolen from Dyonne Obor. The bullet appeared in the air between us, spinning slowly, buzzing like a bee. '*The Song of Always will protect Wendal. For how long, who knows?*'

Eden took a moment to process that and finally dispel any concern that her husband was about to face the condemnation of Nothing, or any notion that she might return to Urdezha as a ghost to accompany him through his final days. She and Wendal had said all that needed to be said and acceptance was clear to read on her face.

'Then I'm ready, Sycamore. Show me what comes next.'

Ah, how long it had been since I last heard those words, and I would be hearing them a lot now. The grey horde continued to spread across the orange plane. All these spirits, singing their Songs to me, waiting for guidance. In my realm, I was no judge.

'*I am the Shepherd of the Dead,*' I announced. '*To where shall I lead you, Eden Finn?*'